CRY FOR JERUSALEM

BOOK ONE: 63–66 CE

RESISTING TYRANNY

WARD SANFORD

PUBLISHED BY STADIA BOOKS LLC

WWW.CRYFORJERUSALEM.COM

D1453420

CRY FOR JERUSALEM

JERUSALEM

BOOK ONE: 63–66 CE

RESISTING TYRANNY

WARD SANFORD

CRY FOR JERUSALEM

BOOK ONE: 63–66 CE
RESISTING TYRANNY

WARD SANFORD

Copyright © 2019. All rights reserved. No part of this book may be reproduced or transmitted in any form or by any means, electronic or mechanical, including photocopying, recording or by any information storage and retrieval system, without written permission from the author, except for brief quotations as would be used in a review.

PAPERBACK ISBN: 978-1-950645-01-5

PUBLISHED BY STADIA BOOKS LLC
WWW.CRYFORJERUSALEM.COM

Cry For Jerusalem is a work of fiction that has been inspired by eyewitness records of historical events. Some characters, many scenes, and most of the dialog have been fictionalized for dramatic purposes.

Front cover artwork created by Tony Foti.

ACKNOWLEDGMENTS

This book would not have been possible without contributions from a number of people. First, my parents, Richard and Eloise, lived a selfless lifestyle which eventually allowed me to have the resources to undertake this project. Second, my wife, Chris, was supportive of my many hours on the computer over many long months. Finally, the professional writing skill of Dennis Lowery was indispensable in helping to put these characters and their adventures on paper.

CONTENTS

Dramatis Personae

Yosef ben Mathias
A young, upper-class, educated Jew, sent to Rome as an envoy to free imprisoned priests.

Rebecca
Yosef's mother, who has a lineage of Jewish royalty from the Hasmonean dynasty.

Mathias
Yosef's father and a leader in the Sanhedrin, the governing body of the Jews in Judea.

Matthew ben Mathias
Yosef's older brother, an officer in the Jewish Temple guard.

Miriam
Yosef's younger sister, her betrothal broken off.

Leah
Yosef's cousin, mutually attracted to Yosef at age sixteen and afterward.

Yonatan
Leah's husband, a rebel with a dislike of Roman collaborators.

Rachel
Leah's younger sister, Yosef's cousin.

Nicanor
A Roman centurion who befriends Yosef. His father was also a Roman legionary and his mother was Greek.

Cleopatra (Cleo)
A young Roman woman of high social standing who marries a newly appointed Judean procurator Gessius Florus. An admirer of Jewish culture, before their wedding she tours the eastern Roman provinces.

Sayid
A young man from Syria; volunteer Roman army auxiliary whose father was a Roman soldier. He is assigned to Lady Cleo's retinue in her travels.

Gessius Florus
Roman tax collector who marries Cleo and becomes the Judean procurator.

Nero
Despotic Roman emperor, who brought the empire to the verge of bankruptcy. Under his reign Rome was nearly destroyed by a great fire.

POPPAEA
Nero's wife, Cleo's best friend and former sister-in-law.

AGRIPPA II
Rome's loyal client-king of Judea, Jewish by heritage and religion.

BERENICE
Sister of Agrippa II, sympathizes with the plight of the Jewish people.

ZECHARIAH
A craftsman living in the Lower City, virtually blind, befriends Miriam.

ELEASAR BEN ANANIAS
Captain of Jewish Temple guard, a rebel leader, though not an extremist.

YEHUDAH ISH KRIOTH
A respected member of the Sanhedrin, formerly a prisoner in Rome.

YOHANAN BEN ZACCAI
Member of the Sanhedrin, respected by both moderates and rebels.

MENAHEM BEN JUDAH
The leader of the Sicarii (Jewish assassins) who hates all Romans and collaborators.

ELAZAR BEN YAIR
Member of the Sicarii and Menahem's chief lieutenant.

YOHANAN BEN LEVI (OF GISCHALA)
A rebel leader in Galilee, often at odds with leadership in Jerusalem.

SIMON BAR GIORA
Top rebel leader from Judea and a very competent field commander.

CESTIUS GALLUS
The Roman legate (governor) of the eastern Roman provinces including Syria and Judea. Commander of the 12th Legion.

OCTAVIA
Wife of Cestius Gallus, friend of Cleo, sympathizes with provincials.

GALERIUS SENNA
Senior Military Tribune of the 12th Legion.

TYRANNIUS PRISEUS
Camp-prefect of the 12th Legion, made so after the sudden death of his predecessor.

Map 1 – Judean Provinces

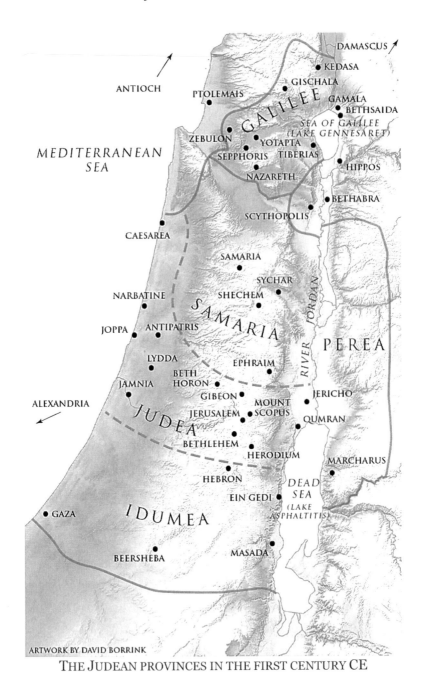

THE JUDEAN PROVINCES IN THE FIRST CENTURY CE

MAP 2 – JERUSALEM

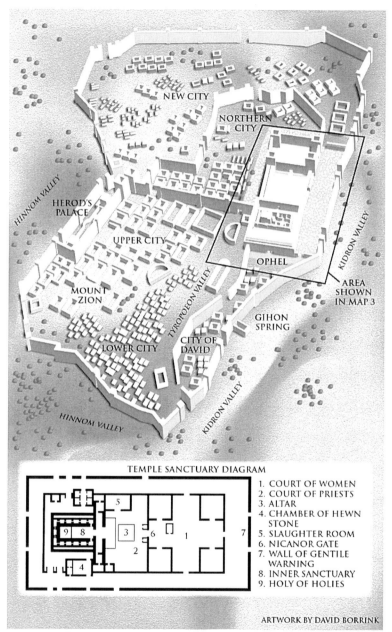

NEW CITY

NORTHERN CITY

HINNOM VALLEY

HEROD'S PALACE

UPPER CITY

OPHEL

KIDRON VALLEY

AREA SHOWN IN MAP 3

MOUNT ZION

TYROPOEON VALLEY

GIHON SPRING

LOWER CITY

CITY OF DAVID

KIDRON VALLEY

HINNOM VALLEY

TEMPLE SANCTUARY DIAGRAM

1. COURT OF WOMEN
2. COURT OF PRIESTS
3. ALTAR
4. CHAMBER OF HEWN STONE
5. SLAUGHTER ROOM
6. NICANOR GATE
7. WALL OF GENTILE WARNING
8. INNER SANCTUARY
9. HOLY OF HOLIES

ARTWORK BY DAVID BORRINK

THE CITY OF JERUSALEM AND THE TEMPLE IN THE FIRST CENTURY CE

MAP 3 – THE TEMPLE COMPLEX

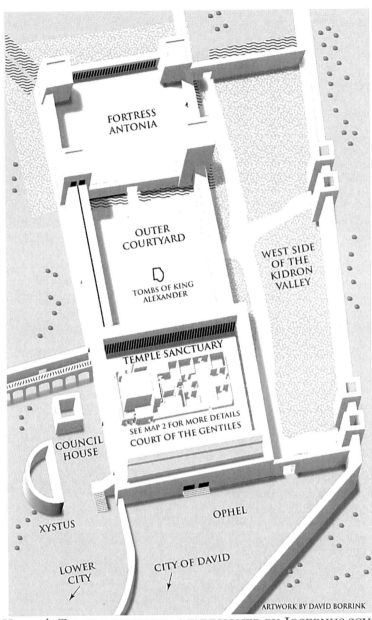

FORTRESS ANTONIA

OUTER COURTYARD

TOMBS OF KING ALEXANDER

WEST SIDE OF THE KIDRON VALLEY

TEMPLE SANCTUARY

SEE MAP 2 FOR MORE DETAILS
COURT OF THE GENTILES

COUNCIL HOUSE

OPHEL

XYSTUS

LOWER CITY

CITY OF DAVID

ARTWORK BY DAVID BORRINK

HEROD'S TEMPLE COMPLEX AS ENVISIONED BY JOSEPHUS SCHOLAR
THOMAS LEWIN

MAP 4 – ROME

THE SEVEN HILLS

I -- Aventine (*Aventinus*)

II -- Palatine (*Palatinus*)

III -- Capitoline (*Capitolinus*)

IV -- Quirinal (*Quirinalis*)

V -- Viminal (*Viminalis*)

VI -- Esquiline (*Esquilinus*)

VII -- Caelian (*Cælius*)

A -- Nero's Palace (*Domus Transitoria / Aurea*)

B -- *Circus Maximus*

C -- Tullianum Prison (*Carcer Tullianum*)

D -- Appian Way entry to Rome (*Porta Appia*)

E -- Temple of Jupiter (*Optimus Maximus*)

───────── City wall in First Century CE (inner dark line)

THE CITY OF ROME IN THE FIRST CENTURY CE

FALLEN, FALLEN IS BABYLON THE GREAT,
THE CITY THAT SITS ON SEVEN HILLS...

FOR SHE WILL BE CONSUMED BY FIRE.

YOHANAN BEN ZAVDI
FIRST CENTURY CE

ACT I

I

JERUSALEM

It was a small thing that Leah had given him nine years ago—a remembrance. Yosef wrapped its cord around his fingers and then twirled it in the opposite direction until it unwound and hung straight down, twinkling in the lantern light. Once its pendulum swing had stopped, he lifted it over his head to settle around his neck and slipped it under his tunic. He had never told his recent wife, Ruth, its true meaning. Then Ruth had died, and that guilt remained.

When he first gave it to Leah that year, they realized they loved each other, he had joked it was a kinyan, but it was just a coin. Then on the eve before he left for Ein Gedi, she had given it back to him—not as a repudiation but as a physical symbol of their love. A kinyan signifies two people are transforming to become one. She told him, "It now holds my heart, and my heart is yours." She left him with a single chaste kiss.

Then he didn't see Leah for the four years he was with the Essenes. At the end of his training, just past his twentieth birthday, he had returned to Jerusalem to find her married to Yonatan, a Zealot. There had been nothing he or she could do. He had to move on.

* * *

Yosef's knees buckled, and he lurched a step to his left to catch his balance. He felt something change in the air. Wind—the sound a half-second ahead—blasted the wall he faced, and the shaking traveled through the floor and up his legs. He stumbled to the window just as a wave of foam-choked water crashed through, slamming him in the chest and driving him back onto the low cot he used as a bed. Sea-green water churned to black, and everything slipped away as he gripped Leah's parting gift.

Yosef jolted awake still gripping the coin on the cord. He was drenched—the water—and disoriented. He tried to sit up. A hand—cool on his brow—was soon accompanied by another on his chest gently pressing him down.

"Rest...." The voice came from a woman's shape, discernible by the light framing it from behind. "Rest, Yosef. It's just the fever."

"Mother?" He thought that the shape shook its head. "A friend?" Again, the headshake. "Leah?!" The shape paused, and hope grew within him. Then it slowly shook its head. It leaned down and light caught its face for a second. She was beautiful. "I know you...." But he knew somehow that was wrong. He had never met a woman that looked like her.

"Rest, Yosef." Her voice was music, a lullaby to soothe him. "It's okay."

He heard water swirling as it rose around him. Bits of wood, spars, and rope collected around the shape—around the woman—who straightened. Then she was swept away.

The vestiges of the dream still fogged Yosef's mind as he came from his room to acknowledge his father's prompting.

"Your brother is here. We'll eat and then go."

Yosef, his heart heavy, sat at the table laden with bowls of figs, pomegranates, and plates of bread and honey.

"You look better, but tired, Yossi."

Yosef looked at his mother, Rebecca, and smiled at hearing the nickname she'd always used for him. "Did you check on me last night?"

She set a cup of goat's milk in front of him. "Just twice... the second time, it seemed your fever had broken." Rebecca turned to her husband, Mathias. "Can't you wait another day or two?"

"No," his father replied. "It's late in the season, winter will be upon us. The Romans invoke their *mare clausum*, and their ships stay in port during that time. They won't sail on to Rome."

"Mother—"

Yosef turned to his brother Matthew at the end of the table. He seemed agitated, which, unfortunately, had become routine when Yosef talked with him.

"—Mother, the longer the elders are held in Rome, the more likely they'll never leave." Matthew shook his head. "They'll die there."

"Why must Yosef go, then?" It was a demand and a question their mother had raised before. As she said it, she looked at Matthew, but it was her husband who—rightfully—replied. She thought if anyone had to go that Matthew should be the one.

"They are House of Shammai," Mathias said, "and I'm Hillel. I'm too moderate, and those men disagree with my belief that we should—could—coexist with the Romans." He looked at his oldest son, his namesake, who was about to say something and so held up his hand. "Yes. We'd remain under their rule. But if they let us

2

practice our religion, then"—his look at Matthew hardened—"no trouble should be stirred up."

"Father," Matthew said, shaking his head, "we should tolerate the Romans, but only until the time is right."

"And when is that? When is the time right to rebel, to fight Rome? They rule a vast empire, but they're not evil. Yes, I know some are. Like us, they have good people and bad ones, both just leaders and politicians and corrupt ones. But not all of them are as you want to believe," he looked at Yosef and then back at Matthew, "or as others want to portray them. That kind of thinking, Matthew," his hand went back up as he leaned forward, "is why those men were taken to Rome. And Yosef knows many of them from his study of law and his time with the Essenes. I think they will listen to him. They have listened before in other matters, and the Romans that hold them will listen to him also if he speaks reasonably, as I know he is capable of doing." He turned to his wife. "That, my dear, is why Yosef must be the one to go. We've talked about this before."

Yosef knew he had no say in the matter, and he did want to see Rome. Few were afforded that opportunity, and he knew the only way to find a means to coexist in a society was to better understand the other side. But it was the sea travel that now made him uneasy.

* * *

It was seventy-five miles to Caesarea on the Roman trade road that ran northwest from Jerusalem and then along the coast. His father had retained a large cart pulled by a donkey for the fifteen to twenty hours it would take to travel there.

"You don't have to go with me, Father," Yosef said as he put his bag with clothes and personal items in the back, underneath the bench behind the animal handler's seat. "Nor you, Matthew."

His father moved the bag over to make room for a basket of fruit and two large jugs of water. "When I took you to the Essenes at Ein Gedi, I knew it would be a long time before I would see you again." He put his hand on Yosef's shoulder. "I escorted you then and want to now. I don't know how long it will be until you return."

Yosef could see the worry and concern on his father's face. He— like his father—knew far more than his mother about how dangerous things were becoming. It was the increasing militancy of people like his brother and the unwillingness of the government to compromise and effect change diplomatically, rather than with force, that caused such concern. He had been observing these things since the death of his wife. Personally, it was made worse because Leah's husband,

3

Yonatan, had been leaning toward physical resistance. It was hard to bear that Yonatan took out on Leah his growing hatred and distrust of any Jew willing to tolerate the Romans. That abuse came also—Yosef believed—because Yonatan knew Leah still had feelings for Yosef.

* * *

"Have you been to Caesarea before?" the innkeeper asked.

"No," Yosef said, shaking his head. "But I have studied its history. It was a Phoenician naval port, wasn't it?" Yosef knew that Herod had built his palace on a nearby promontory jutting out into the sea, with a beautiful pool surrounded by stone porticos known as stoas. Caesarea was the civilian and military capital of the Province of Judea and the official residence of the Roman procurator, Antonius Felix, and his predecessor, the prefect Pontius Pilatus. Thirty-eight years ago, Pilate's order to plant eagle standards on the Temple Mount of Jerusalem had led to a significant protest in Caesarea.

The man had a blank look for a moment. "I don't know about that. But the harbor"—he pointed as if Yosef could see it through the wall—"my grandfather worked on building it. For nearly ten years." The innkeeper waved the hand he had pointed with to encompass the room and building they were in. "King Herod and the Romans rewarded the men who supervised the workers. This"—he waved his arm again—"was his payment. The land and use of surplus materials for constructing this inn."

"Yesterday when I arrived, I walked the length of the harbor," Yosef replied, sitting on a bench near a heavy table of dark wood. "It doesn't seem like a naturally favored location, but the engineering and construction are beyond measure. I've never seen anything like it. The sea will never overcome it."

The breakwaters were made of lime and pozzolana, a type of volcanic ash, set into underwater concrete. Herod had imported more than twenty thousand cubic yards of pozzolana—Roman concrete—from Puteoli to construct the two breakwaters. They were five hundred yards long on the south and almost three hundred yards long on the north. It took more than forty shiploads of four tons each, and twelve thousand cubic yards of kurkar quarried to make rubble, plus the same cubic yards of slaked lime mixed with the pozzolana.

"What ship do you sail on?" The innkeeper brought Yosef a large terracotta mug full of wine and then used the front tail of his tunic to wipe his hands.

"The *Salacia*. She will be carrying grain with the outgoing tide."

4

"A good name, that one." The man turned away.

Yosef sipped his drink and asked, "Why is it good?"

"Why is what...?" —the man half-turned back to look at him— "The name?"

"Yes."

"*Salacia* is the Goddess of Seawater, the wife of Neptune—a well-favored name for a ship. Right?"

Thinking there was no getting away from water on this journey, Yosef agreed—hopefully—with the man. "Yes, for a safe voyage."

II

Caesarea

Yosef had left the inn early to walk the pier. He stopped across from the *Salacia*, which had been pointed out to him. Nearby, an old man sat on a block of sandstone splicing a fishing line. He was occasionally sipping from a wineskin of what looked like cured goat hide.

Studying the ship, Yosef noticed its hull ran up to a bird's-head carving above the bow and a bird's tail at the stern. In its middle was a high mast of cedar wood and near the prow a smaller one for hoisting a small sail. Two large oars were used to steer. On the deck were two cabins, the smaller a wooden hut for the helmsman, which was also used as a temple of worship and contained an idol. The larger cabin was for more affluent or important passengers. All others slept on the deck, open to the elements or shrouded by small tents.

"She's a big one."

Yosef turned to the man who had spoken. "Is it?"

The man squeezed a jet of red liquid into his mouth before answering. "She's a hundred and eight feet long, about forty-five feet wide and extending to just nearly that deep through the hold. And then the height of the mast, with its huge yard... and what a forestay it takes to hold it! She's a beauty, even for a grain hauler."

He started to ask the man why he referred to the ship as "she," but then he took in the lofty stern with its gradual curve and its gilded beak, balanced at the other end by the long, rising sweep of the prow and the figures of her name-goddess on either side. And there were other ornamental details such as the painted wood and the scarlet topsail. If a ship could look like a "she," this one did. He watched as the crew—like a horde of suitors—scurried from the dock to the ship, from stem to stern.

"She'll carry enough grain to feed every soul in Attica for a year."

"Have you ever sailed on a grain ship? Like—like her?" Yosef cast a thumb at the *Salacia*.

"Oh no," the man laughed. "My time—long ago—was, at first, as a remiges, or eretai—an oarsman and rower on triremes and biremes. I was a paid freeman but rower still, until I knew my business and the difference between bow and stern. I was what you call 'peregrinus,' which is not a citizen of Rome but I served its navy for my term—

6

twenty-six years. Now I'm a citizen." He paused for more wine. "I became a proreta, a lookout stationed at the bow, and in the end, a pentacontarchus, a junior officer." He cast an eye at the *Salacia* and then at Yosef, who seemed wary.

"She looks like a fine vessel."

The man glanced down at the bag at Yosef's feet. "She's seaworthy, boy, but"—he looked up at gray clouds building on the horizon—"she needs to put to sea before too long or not at all."

* * *

Aboard the ship, the shipmaster, brusquely acknowledged him, and motioned toward the larger structure. "You'll be housed on deck, and you should find room to get yourself settled next to the cabin. But you'll need to speak with the centurion who commands the lady's escort. She's in the cabin with her companion—a handmaid, I believe." He turned away from Yosef, back to more important matters.

"Excuse me, where can I find the centurion?"

"Nicanor's up at the bow, mustering his squad or something."

"The bow... and his name is Nicanor?"

The captain, with a look of consternation, pointed to his left. "That way until there's no more deck to walk."

Yosef was used to seeing Roman legionaries, but Nicanor, a centurion, was distinctly different from them. His helmet had a transverse horsehair crest on top, and his greaves were metal. He wore his sword on the left (unlike the legionaries) and a more ornate harness of much better quality. He also carried a short vine-wood staff of about three feet in length. He held it in his right hand and tapped it—near its middle—into the palm of his left hand.

"Centurion?"

The man turned to Yosef, and his eyes swept him from his toes to his head: he saw a young Jew, seemingly prosperous, or from an affluent family. Yosef noted that he did not shift his gaze away as other Romans often did around Jews. His look was steady and stern but not unfriendly. "Yes."

"I'm Yosef ben Mathias—I'm traveling to Rome." He waited, but the centurion did not react. "On this ship... with you."

The wood staff slapped into the man's palm with a snap. "And why are you telling me this?"

"The captain," Yosef gestured back toward the stern, "told me I would need to speak to you about arranging myself by the cabin—the one occupied by the lady you're escorting. I'd like to, if I may."

7

"Follow me," the centurion said, taking off without looking back to see if Yosef was behind him. They approached the captain, whose head tracked as they passed him—passed the smaller structure—and walked on to the larger one, where the centurion stopped. He motioned to where his and his men's small tents, bags, and equipment had been staked to the deck. "Back there, I think there's room." He scanned Yosef again, top to bottom, and studied the bag he held in one hand. "Do you have a tent or bedding?"

"No." Yosef shook his head, chagrined that he was so unprepared.

The centurion slapped the staff in his hand. "Find Sayid"—he pointed back toward the stern where the legionaries were grouped. "He'll get you what you need."

* * *

"Uh, the lady's pet?" The burly soldier eyed Yosef up and down before he answered and then cocked the thumb of his right hand over his shoulder. "He's over there."

Yosef followed where the soldier had pointed and saw a scrawny young man, ten paces away, untangling wooden blocks and ropes probably used to handle cargo. Thanking the soldier, who ignored him, Yosef walked toward the other soldier, who was in his teens and distinctly not a Roman. Dark brown and lean, the boy looked up when Yosef stopped in front of him. He guessed he was not a legionary but a Roman auxiliary soldier, probably a volunteer from a nearby province.

"Sayid?"

Dark eyes, under equally dark and heavy brows, blinked up at Yosef. "Yes?"

"The centurion," Yosef gestured back toward the stern where Nicanor had remained speaking with the captain, "told me to see you about a tent and bedding. I'm traveling with you—on this ship to Rome."

The eyes blinked twice. Sayid was young, but he been around enough to know Romans did not always treat Jews so well. For one to go to Rome of his own free will... He shook his head but smiled. "Yes, I can help you." Setting down the blocks of wood he had worked free, he stood and coiled the rope he had straightened and set it neatly next to the three other coils on the deck. "Come with me."

As they headed back the way he had come, Yosef wondered how many times between Caesarea and Rome he would walk the length of this ship. He nodded to the centurion and shipmaster, who were now standing near the mast in the middle of the vessel. The captain did

8

not react, but he thought the centurion had given him the briefest of nods in return.

Sayid was quiet as they walked, his face straight ahead when they passed the soldiers and sailors. Yosef followed him toward the large cabin. Its entry faced toward the bow, and next to it was a tent, somewhat larger than the others that clustered around it to the right in an arc around the structure. "This is the centurion's"—Sayid gestured at the largest as he passed by it, stepping over the smaller tent's lines and stakes that had been driven into the deck of the ship—"And here are ones for the rest of us."

Yosef had counted eleven smaller tents. "A centurion with so few men?" He looked at Sayid, who seemed to have paid no attention to what he had just said.

"Here's mine." Sayid stopped at the tent closest to the gunwale, where the ship's sides rose up higher than the main deck. It was the area most likely to be drenched by spray coming up and over the sides of the ship. "There's a spot for you." Sayid knelt and dragged over a rope-bound bundle from a pile of equipment secured along the back side wall of the cabin and began to untie it. "I'll help you." He started to unroll the bundle into the remaining small, open spot next to his. Once the canvas and hide were unfurled, he squatted back on his heels and studied Yosef. The smile was back on his face. "He's not too happy."

"Who?" Yosef had a wooden stake in his hand but no idea where to peg it into the deck.

Sayid took it from him and pulled a heavy mallet from a loop on the belt at his waist. "The centurion—Nicanor—isn't." With three powerful blows, the stake was driven three-quarters of its length into the planking. "Hand me another." Three more stakes, nine more heavy hits of the mallet, and they were secure. Within a few minutes, Sayid had the lines attached to them and then to the canvas and was erecting the tent. He got it settled, plucking a line to make sure it was taut, then rocked back on his heels again and grinned at Yosef. "There you go."

"Thank you, Sayid. So, you said the centurion is unhappy..."

Yosef saw the youth's dark eyes scan the area behind them. "Because he's a hero—or something like that—he's going to Rome to be rewarded for saving a Roman official from an attack." Sayid's wary look told Yosef it must have been an incident with Jewish Zealots or maybe even the Sicarii, who scared even veteran Roman soldiers.

"It's okay," Yosef responded. "I understand you have to be careful about what you say."

9

Sayid relaxed, but his eyes continued to watch for anyone approaching. "So, the centurion—Nicanor—was ordered to take command of the lady's escort for her return to Rome. I don't think he likes babysitting, and I know he doesn't trust these men assigned to the duty"—Sayid waved a hand at the other tents—"men he doesn't know."

With the tent now standing, Yosef tossed his bag inside with the two rough blankets Sayid handed to him. "I must go now—we're to sail within the hour," Sayid said, rising and looking forward toward the bow.

"Thank you again, Sayid." Yosef looked up at him.

With a wave of his hand to Yosef, Sayid headed to join the group of men gathering by the bow to bring the last of the ship's stores on board for the voyage.

Yosef studied the tent. He had spent three years with Bannus, an ascetic Essene hermit, so sleeping in the elements would not bother him. He stood and stepped to the gunwale and peered over it at the harbor's brown water, placid and peaceful just feet below. He looked up and beyond the concrete breakwaters, where he could see the wind-feathered white caps of open water and wondered what it would be like out there, at sea.

III

AT SEA

That first evening at sea, Yosef had not seen the lady but had seen her maidservant and knew the lady was there in the cabin. He had learned that Sayid acted as an orderly or aide to the centurion to help assist her. It also seemed Sayid had adopted Yosef, too. Yosef watched a sailor hand two baskets of bread and fruit to the red-cloaked young maidservant, who then entered the cabin. Sayid had followed the sailor with another three bowls of food.

Yosef turned to study Nicanor, who had been sitting quietly watching closely as the woman secured the door behind her. Nicanor motioned to Sayid to sit down with the three bowls that he carried and then stood and walked to the door, checking to make sure that it was secured properly from the inside. He called through it, "Just checking, my lady." Yosef couldn't make out the muffled reply.

Nicanor returned, sat cross-legged on the deck and accepted the bowl of sprouted barley gruel from Sayid, who then handed one to Yosef before raising his own.

Yosef had never tasted this staple of the Roman army. Although it was bland, at least it was warm and filling.

Just hours out to sea, the land was still faintly visible on the horizon, and the sunset was a glorious mixture of scarlet, orange, and yellow that darkened to purple and then a blue so deep as to seem almost black. As the colors in the sky became more muted, Yosef overheard the master tell Nicanor, "Good weather and we'll make four or five knots, even this laden. Sixteen days and I'll have you in Puteoli."

The *Salacia* carried a full load of grain and wallowed like a pregnant animal upon the water. Yosef sensed the movement beneath them, the slow sway that all on board were starting to feel. It made the half-bowl of gruel he had eaten shift around—an unpleasant lump—in his stomach. Yosef swallowed saliva mixed with a hint of bile and put the bowl down, one hand holding his stomach.

"Done?" Sayid asked with a smile on his face, "You don't want more?" as he looked at Yosef's bowl.

Yosef handed it to him, "You can have it."

Sayid took it and ate greedily, and soon it was as empty as his own bowl.

Nicanor watched them both as he silently ate his own gruel, impressed with the Jew's fluent Latin with him and how easily he switched to Aramaic with Sayid. Finishing the last morsel, he handed the bowl to Sayid and ordered, "Clean up and stow the cooking gear. I'm going to check the lookouts." He had assigned three of the legionaries to stand lookout watch at the fore, aft, and amidships—not so much because he distrusted the sailors but to give his men a duty to perform.

* * *

That night Yosef tried to settle down, badly needing to sleep, but the snores coming from Sayid's tent, the queasiness—he'd lost his dinner twice already—and his thoughts kept him awake. Back in Jerusalem, when his father and others from the Sanhedrin had approached him about going to Rome, he had balked. Each had presented his reasoning and asked Yosef to serve as an envoy to free the imprisoned priests. He had told each of them no. Not accepting that as his answer, the contingent left, unhappy at his reluctance, and promised to return the next day and discuss it further. But it was after they had gone that his father had finally convinced him.

"You've told me many times that you admire the Romans, what they've accomplished." His father paced the room, not looking at Yosef.

"Father, I admire their organization and how their discipline and will can reach so far. And I think of all the wonders I've heard that they've erected throughout their empire and of the magnificence of Rome and what it would be like to see them. But that doesn't make me best suited as an emissary to Rome."

His father had stopped, stepped closer to Yosef, and gripped his arm, locking eyes with him. "But you know the law, our law. And you know your people. You have a bond to it—and with them—that others may not." They both knew who he meant; those others who collaborated with the Romans even when it hurt the Jewish people and diminished their religion and culture. "Without such a bond they may weaken before the wealth and might of Rome. I know that you will not."

"Father, I—"

"Yosef, since your wife's death, I have seen how you sit in the evenings, alone and thinking thoughts I do not know. Seeing something or someone I cannot see. And longing—yes, I know she longs for you, too. That's why Yonatan treats her so." His father sighed and took his hand from his shoulder. "Leave that part of Jerusalem... that part of your past... behind. Help secure our future. Help bring home those who will surely die otherwise. Because their death, if we cannot prevent it, could easily set Jerusalem ablaze."

His father had left him that night, and the next morning Yosef had agreed to go.

A deeper roll, the ship's timbers creaking, brought him back to the present. He steadied himself with one hand. The rumbling snores coming from Sayid's tent made Yosef wonder at their volume for someone so slight. He rose from sitting cross-legged beside his tent and thought of the fiery sunset earlier that evening. He faced that direction—the blackness beyond the reach of the ship's lanterns—and the wind lifted a whisper from his lips: "I think it already smolders, Father, but I'll do what I can to stop it from growing and spreading."

* * *

Over the next several days, the routine was the same, and Yosef, between bouts of seasickness, came to enjoy the talks with Sayid. Except for seeing a robed, shrouded figure talking with Nicanor in the light of a handheld lantern on the second evening, he had yet to actually see the lady or maidservant up close. Nicanor, at first just at dinner, had begun to talk to him—at least to rather tersely answer his questions. The next morning, he saw him speaking with someone who might have been the lady, but when Yosef mentioned this, he received only a grunt as a return answer. Curious, he persisted.

"Did you know the lady before you were assigned to escort her?"

Nicanor barked a laugh, "I'm a soldier and have never served in Rome. I know men, military men, but little of ladies, like her." He shook his head, and Yosef thought he heard him mutter, "and I pity her."

* * *

Several days into the voyage, they had rounded Cyprus and were off the coastal city of Myra. "Is there no more fruit?" Yosef asked Sayid as he brought him and Nicanor their ubiquitous bowls of gruel.

"No, that's for the..." Sayid cocked a thumb at the cabin and its occupants.

"Nicanor, can't the captain pull into one of the ports and replenish supplies?" Yosef asked.

Nicanor glanced up at the low clouds overhead. "He does not want any delays and claims there's enough, but the lady comes first."

"Is she ill? I've not seen her leave the cabin yet."

"She is sick at times," a sly grin began to play on Nicanor's lips, "as are you." He parodied holding his stomach, as Yosef did before rushing to the side of the ship to heave, which had not helped at all. "But she was already weak from an illness that had delayed her return to Rome." He looked around. The ship's lanterns swayed with each roll, creating shifting shadows across the surrounding deck. "That's why she's here on this grain ship," he waved his mug of wine, "and not on a finer vessel." He looked into his empty bowl then up—not at them—into the night. "As am I." He shook his head and said, "the last ship out of Judea before the stormy season."

Yosef thought of his father, the Zealots and the Sicarii, and what brewed in his homeland. "The other day," he said into the silence. "I heard you say that you pity her."

Nicanor's head snapped up, and for a moment, it was a stern Roman soldier looking at someone lesser than himself, someone not allowed certain thoughts, not allowed to say certain things, and never allowed to see any Roman weakness. But it passed from his face as quickly as it flared. "I do," Nicanor said.

"Why?" Yosef realized he should let the subject go but couldn't. "Isn't she highborn, with a life of status and privilege?"

"Sometimes, being a citizen of Rome—even a noble—can have its own shortcomings, often ones that are just as confining as those without that privilege."

"What do you mean?" Yosef asked.

Nicanor lifted his mug of wine, draining it. "I'll never see you once we leave this ship," he looked at Yosef. "And you'll never be able to speak of it to the lady." He wiped his chin with the back of his hand and gave Yosef a long, hard look. "I pity her because I'm told that when she returns, she is to marry Gessius Florus. And you'll never meet a more despicable and corrupt man."

"I know nothing of him." Yosef searched his memory of all that he had read of Roman leaders.

"I do," Nicanor looked over his shoulder at the structure on the deck behind them. "And once she weds him—though I don't know her, I can still feel pity—she will wear a shackle just as strong and bitter to bear as those worn by any chained rower on a Roman naval vessel."

* * *

She screamed. He couldn't reach her. Splinters of wood flew and bit into his face. The rain lashed him, sheets of it coming down—then slanting—only to change within seconds into horizontal bands that scoured and blasted him sideways. The water, now solid, was a bludgeon that hammered him against the wall and then became a heavier, dead weight dragging him down. He struggled up. Once for no air, only a mouthful of grit-laced water. Twice, he fought to the surface and managed a deep, shuddering intake of rain-laden air that made him cough and choke. That second time he saw her—close, so close, her face staring at him, stark white shining through the swirling gray and black cascades of sea water. It dragged him down. He clawed for anything that would buoy him—flotsam and jetsam, chunks of wood, anything to save him. He grabbed the largest and felt fingernails tear from his hands as the maelstrom spun him away. In a moment, where spray cleared the blood from his eyes, he saw her a final time. She straightened and screamed again into the wind. She staggered, and the storm... the storm took her. And he sank down... down... down.

"Yosef! Yosef!"

Someone was shaking him by the shoulders. He struggled, trying to pry the hands off. He must get to her but couldn't see. He stopped fighting the hands pinning him down and felt for his face and forehead, where sharp slivers of wood had sliced into his flesh. He opened his eyes and looked. His hands came away but with the dampness of sweat, not blood. He turned his eyes from his hands to Sayid, who was holding him on the deck amid the tangle of what had been his tent.

"It's just a dream, Yosef. Just a dream."

"The storm..." Yosef got to his knees and stared at Sayid, then looked down at his hands. Not a mark on them. "She's gone," he muttered under his breath.

Seeing that Yosef had stopped trying to get to the side of the ship, Sayid let go of him. "There is no storm, Yosef. It's just past sunrise and the sky... the weather is clear."

The wracking memory of his dream—his vision—still gripped him. Yosef took in deep lungfuls of the salt-brined air. "She's gone," he cried a last time, softly, then looked up at Sayid. "Something's coming. Sometimes I get these dreams." He looked around him, then out to sea—"Something..."

But nothing was there.

* * *

"I talked to the captain," Nicanor said, looking at Yosef, and though it was evening, many hours past the nightmare of dawn, he was still pale and drawn. "He says the weather will hold, and I have to trust what he says. Though I'm told he's being paid extra—a bonus"—he looked over his shoulder at the cabin—"to get his cargo to Rome as soon as possible."

Yosef shook his head. "I don't know. Maybe it was just a dream."

"Let's hope it doesn't happen again." Nicanor shook his head. He hadn't shared the remainder of what the captain had said. The stern lookouts—a sailor and one of his own men—had heard Yosef. A superstitious lot, wary of the gods and goddesses and their quixotic interjection and interference into the affairs of men, worried that they had brought a cursed man onto their ship—one whose dreams foretold their demise.

IV

AT SEA

"What city are we headed toward?" Yosef asked Nicanor.

"Lasea, I believe. At least that was what our shipmaster told me would be a necessary stop for stores." Nicanor stepped closer to where Yosef stood by the gunwale looking at the coast the *Salacia* was closing in on. The port was becoming visible in the gray dawn. "We'll stop again in a few days at Phoenix before going on to Melita."

"Can we go ashore here?" Yosef waved a hand toward the cluster of light—open fires in huge bronze bowls set on pylons—that marked the port's entrance.

"We'll enter with the tide, but I don't think you should go ashore." Nicanor glanced at the captain, who stood only ten paces away studying his rough-bound sailing notes, comparing a sketch of landmarks in them to what he was looking at. "I told you not to talk to him about your dream."

"I tried asking him in every way I could if the weather should be a concern," Yosef said.

"Yes, your speaking Greek and Latin so well surprised him—me, too, when we first met—but you didn't just tell him you were worried about the weather."

"I know that he has that periploi"—Yosef pointed at the document the captain was referring to—"He said he's aware of storms that come this time of year, and I shouldn't worry, but—"

"—You didn't have to tell him you dreamed we sank"—Nicanor interrupted him as he scanned the deck, noting that a number of the sailors' eyes now cut sideways glances at Yosef. "Now the captain and his crew..." Nicanor laughed but not with humor. He knew the best vessels and men had sailed well within the safe season, and the *Salacia*, no matter its name, was not in that category, nor was its captain and crew. "The sailors look at you in a way that tells me that if you go ashore, you may not get back on board. Or you could return and find the ship has sailed without you."

Nicanor held a hand up to stop what Yosef was about to say, then continued: "These men are a superstitious and greedy lot, which is a bad combination if they feel bad luck jeopardizes their pay, much less their life."

Yosef looked from Nicanor to Sayid, who had been silently standing beside him. "What do you think?"

Sayid nodded toward Nicanor. "I agree. You should stay on board, Yosef."

* * *

The *Salacia* left Lasea on the evening tide with full water barrels, several crates of fruit, and news. At mealtime that evening, Nicanor told Yosef, "The people in the town were surprised we didn't plan to stay in port and wait for the clear season." He quaffed his mug of wine, gesturing at Sayid to pour more for him. "But they also said the weather has been uncommonly good, with not a hint of an early storm. That's a good omen, right?" Nicanor looked at Yosef, who remained quiet with his thoughts. It was the omens it seemed only he could see that made him fearful.

Two days later, having passed Salmone, when the ship pulled into Phoenix, Yosef remained on board again. They brought on more water and news they had heard previously in Lasea—of the periodic ground shakes. It did not seem to alarm the sailors as they exited the harbor.

"From here we enter the Ionian Sea, right, captain?" Yosef saw the look Nicanor shot at him but could not help adding, "and several days crossing it to Melita." It wasn't a question but a statement.

The captain ignored him, looking instead up at the bright sky, then stabbed a glance at Yosef as he walked away. A brisk, steady wind bellied the sails, and the *Salacia* moved at a good pace, even so heavily loaded. That evening, Yosef's sleep was broken by the tendrils of his dream—the face and voice of the woman—teasing him awake, and so it went for three days and nights.

* * *

The wind fell off in the middle of the fourth day crossing the Ionian. No longer steady, the breeze came in sporadic gasps. Then that evening, during the meal, it died completely. The sails slumped, slacking the ropes and lines. Yosef heard the spars and masts relax, almost with a sigh that the strain on them had passed. The *Salacia*, no longer underway with full-breasted sheets and taut lines, now showed her age as she drooped and settled into stillness on the water with only a slow roll.

Yosef looked at Nicanor, who was staring up at the hanging sails. The only sound around them was the creaking of wood beneath their feet. Earlier in the day, he had noticed that the gulls and seabirds that accompany ships along the coast were no longer wheeling in the air above them. Whether this was an affirmation that they were far from land or a portent of change, the loss of their calls and cries had not been as disconcerting as this.

One of the lady's escort soldiers went to the cabin at a request that came hand-carried by Camilla, the maidservant whose name Yosef had learned from Sayid. The lady, too, must have felt the oddness in this new quiet. After a moment, he walked past them again—nearly stepping on the tail of Yosef's cloak—heading to the smaller cabin containing the captain.

An hour later there was still no wind, and they saw oars being taken from their mounts and put in place. The unhappy men performing the job cast long, dark looks toward where Yosef stood.

"I hope the wind returns soon," Yosef said.

Nicanor grunted looking up from finishing a pomegranate. "You should pray, also," he glanced at the sailors who were staring at Yosef, "I think those men blame you."

* * *

Through the night, the meager number of oars on the *Salacia* barely pulled her along. At best, they made half the speed that the wind had given them. The centurion had put his men in the rotation to row, and their angry looks were more menacing than those of the crew. Sayid had completed two extended stints on the oars already, and Yosef was amazed at the wiry strength of the boy. The second time Sayid went to the oars, Yosef had gone with him and attempted to take a turn. The men—soldiers and sailors—had snarled at him and threatened harm if he so much as touched an oar.

"Stay clear of them, Yosef," Nicanor had warned him from where he stood nearby. His hand was on the worn hilt of his pugio, the broad dagger at his belt. Seeing that, the man closest to Yosef had muttered under his breath but backed away with a sneer.

* * *

Nicanor still shook his head at Yosef's gesture to help row. There was much that he liked in the Jew: his intelligence, his skill with languages, his attempt to do his share without complaining. This was more than he could say for the crew and Roman soldiers, including the other centurion. They all continued to complain, moan, and lament. *Damn them*, he thought, *and this lack of wind, too*, as he joined Yosef where he stood in the shade offered by a now-useless sail that had been turned into an awning over the cabin and its surrounding area. He followed Yosef's gaze to where a wake should trail behind the ship.

Yosef turned toward him, legs spread as the ship rolled in low troughs, and Nicanor said, "I asked the captain about that chart he was using—I think you called it a periploi?" Nicanor spread his hands out in an empty palms-up motion.

"That's what the Greeks call the set of papers—the records—that they sail by," Yosef said, smiling at him. "It's their sailing instructions."

"Well, he called it his itinerarium"—Nicanor shook his head—"Anyway, he said there are records of this happening when there's no wind, but it passes in a day."

"If it will pass so soon, why risk making the crew, and the soldiers, mad by forcing them to row?"

Nicanor rubbed his thumb and forefinger together.

Yosef knew what that meant. It made him think of similar instances and situations in Jerusalem when some lined their pockets with Roman gold even at a cost to their own people. He had seen the sour look on Nicanor's face as he made that gesture. It was just that universal feeling of what's decent and what's not—the positive side in some people's nature—that he hoped to find, to build a bridge between their two cultures. He hoped it would help bring the imprisoned priests home to Jerusalem. Maybe that would stabilize the city, stop some of the rumblings, and ease tensions.

Nicanor wiped his hands on the hanging sailcloth. "So, hopefully, we have only another day of this."

V

At Sea

The next evening came but still without wind. At meal's end, Nicanor had left with another centurion to help resolve an issue with the legionaries. Sayid had fallen asleep on his side with an empty bowl in his hand, and Yosef tried to drag him into his tent, but he was heavier than he looked. Covering him where he lay, Yosef stood and stretched, catching sight of Camilla, the lady's maidservant, coming into the arc of light from the lanterns, approaching the cabin. Her russet robe had bright saffron yellow trim that caught the lantern light. He had learned her name, but he had never spoken to her. She nodded her hooded head as she opened the cabin door and slipped inside.

* * *

"Every new beginning comes from some other beginning's end." Those were the words Yosef had read on a scrap of parchment during one of his father's meetings with a Roman administrator, and the words had stuck. It was only some years later that he knew Marcus Annaeus Seneca, the Roman rhetorician, had written them. Why those words came to him now, or what had awakened him, he had no idea. He felt the canvas over him shift. It was dark, he couldn't see, but it seemed his tent had breathed in, lifting on the lines tied to the stakes that pinned it to the deck. He felt it then—the first wisps of a breeze. He scrambled out on his knees and forearms to stand. As if a reed bending toward the wind instead of away, he faced what he thought all aboard surely felt was a blessing. The Roman-named wind gods, the Venti, had returned. Sayid was on the oars so he could not smile with Yosef at the thought of ending their seeming endless time on the water. Maybe that's why the words were on his lips as he woke. They had many miles—days—to go, but at least the *Salacia* would make progress toward Rome.

The wind gusted, stiffened, and then stretched the sails, drawing tight the lines. Their vibrating hum was now back, a sound he had not noticed until it was absent. He came around the cabin to where Nicanor's tent was, to find him standing and grinning in the lantern light. Yosef heard the calls and laughs of sailors and soldiers as they happily pulled the oars from their sockets, shouldered them, and returned them to their brackets. Yosef watched as one of the dark shapes, smaller than the others, came into the arc of light. It was Sayid, with a smile equally broad.

The sound of a feminine laugh made Yosef turn. In the open door of the cabin, framed by lantern light from behind, were two figures: the lady and Camilla. Yosef saw that the taller one, nearly as tall as he, wore a vibrant ruby-colored cloak, with glints of silver and deep gold trim like burnished metal. *The lady,* he thought, and in that instance, her hood came up, throwing her face in shadow even as she stepped back. The smaller figure wearing the brown robe with light yellow trim—Camilla—reached out to close the door.

* * *

Yosef turned and twisted in the dark, something was no longer coming—he knew that now it was upon them. He jerked awake, fearing the dreams had returned. His hands felt the wetness on his face—*another fever? Is that it?* He felt the world tip from beneath him and heard a demon's scream over the wind. Of hate? Of fear? He slowed his breathing to settle down. He drowsed as he sensed the tilt lessen and start in the opposite direction. He knew the ship would right itself—*Salacia* always had. He closed his eyes tighter and held on. But the roll deepened, and he slid into, then onto, the wall of his tent as he came crashing fully awake.

He had gone to sleep feeling the ship moving solidly and quickly through what was left of the night. As he untangled himself from the blanket and the collapsing tent, its pegs pulled free. The canvas, whipped by a screaming wind, snapped at him, catching him on the face, stinging and leaving what he knew must be a hand-sized welt. Thankful it had not taken an eye, he scrambled away from the water coursing over the gunwale.

The wind-driven spray was as stinging as the canvas had been. As he watched, the wind and a wave scoured the deck clear of the tents around him. Men spun away, carried overboard into a churning mass of black water. The ship still heeled over, he clawed along and up the deck to what had been the front of the lady's cabin. To his left were the splintered remnants of the captain's cabin. He hadn't seen Sayid and prayed he had not been washed overboard.

"Yosef!" the scream turned his head. Hanging from what had once been the stout wooden door of the lady's cabin, Nicanor was the only thing keeping the two women from being swept away. They both had two-handed grips on his forearm. In rivulets of blood and seawater, Nicanor's arm showed where their nails had gouged him deeply. The opposite wall of the cabin had been splintered, and each pounding wave tore more of it away. A blast of wind, coming from opposite the sea's fist, grabbed the remnants of *Salacia's* torn sails and pushed her upright. Seawater drained from the deck, pulling more bodies along with its outgoing tide and spilling them into the sea over the gunwale now pockmarked with ripped and missing timbers and planking. He took a deep breath and, still on hands and knees, crab-walked over to Nicanor and the two women.

Nicanor let go of the frame, but the women did not let go of him. With his free hand, he wiped sea-wrack and other detritus from his eyes. "Looks like you were right," he gasped, his chest heaving, "about this bitch of a storm." He looked over Yosef's shoulder. "Bastards!" he shouted and surged toward what he saw, but the women still would not let go. "The sons of whores are leaving us!"

Yosef turned to see the two dinghies that *Salacia* carried being cut free and filled with the remaining sailors and soldiers, abandoning the ship and them.

Yosef had never been so afraid. "What do we do?"

"We live," Nicanor grunted and let out a deep breath. "The storm seems to be letting up." He looked at the women, their soaked cloaks clasped around them and their heads bent under sodden hoods. "We live."

"Have you seen Sayid?" Yosef asked.

"Just as I got the door open to get the women out," Nicanor coughed and spat to one side, "I saw him struck by a piece of the wall. He was bleeding"—Nicanor touched the side of his head—"here, and then another wave lashed us and took him away." He looked at the women still holding his arm, the one in the red cloak weeping as the other in the brown spoke to her in tones so low Yosef could not hear them over the wind. "The boy must be dead, and I hate the gods for that."

The rain had eased, and the wind dropped a little. In the gray dawn, they could see the *Salacia* was settling deeper in the water. "Hull is ruptured somewhere, and the cargo holds are probably taking in water," Nicanor coughed again, "it must have gotten in the grain."

Yosef thought of how the barley gruel set so heavily in his stomach after each meal. The *Salacia* now had a belly full of such a sodden mass that it would drag her down as more water poured in.

"What do we do?" But Yosef knew Nicanor did not have a solution to what they faced.

"We live... and watch for other ships." The *Salacia* groaned beneath them. Nicanor looked between his feet at the deck starting to show standing water pooling around them. He looked up at Yosef. "—At least as long as we have something to stand on to watch from." He grinned, but that faded as he felt the air change around them.

A waking version of his dream gripped Yosef. He saw the woman from the dream—her face flashed in his mind. "Something's coming," he whispered to Nicanor, who had instinctively pulled the two women closer to him, encircling them with his brawny arms.

Then a large rogue wave slammed into the *Salacia*. The ship had no chance—it rode too low in the water. The last thing Yosef saw was a writhing maelstrom tearing Nicanor and the two women from each other, pulling them away.

Then darkness. Nothing but darkness, in which he could not breathe.

VI

AT SEA

Cold, so cold. A light flared nearby. Warmth? Where? He could see a city that spanned seven hills, its size beyond measure based on any single person's perspective. It was teeming with people, most of whom served the few. The eternal city, the mistress—the ruling head and beating heart—of the world. The glow spread in size and breadth across the city, flickering orange-yellow and scarlet that painted the sky. It was not a sunset. It was fire. The city was burning.

The dream faded, and Yosef choked and then vomited seawater that now floated, a sickening miasmic mass, just inches from his face. He raised his head and looked side to side, then over his shoulder. Rising—carefully—to his knees, he discovered underneath him a section of still-joined planks. Whether it was a wall or part of the hull or deck from the *Salacia*, he did not know. But it floated and raised him out of the sea—barely. Water lapped over what had saved him from drowning. He didn't know how he had made it to this small island of safety, and it shifted beneath him as he moved. Steadying himself, he felt a stabbing pain in his right thigh. He reached around behind and felt the long dagger of splintered wood piercing his flesh, the slickness of blood thicker than seawater. Instinctively, he knew better than to just pull it out. It was surely stoppering the blood that would pour out upon its removal.

A bandage—he needed a dressing. He shook his head and felt caked blood on his left temple plastering hair to skin. He had taken a blow to the head as well. Blinking, trying to focus and shaking with cold, he tried to rip a strip of cloth from his tunic. Sodden, it would not tear, or he was too weak. Everything around him grew dark as he sank down onto the wave-washed wood.

* * *

Trying to turn over from his stomach woke him, and the agony from the piece of timber in his right leg brought him fully conscious. He rolled to his left and got that leg bent under him to push up. He swung the right leg out, partially bent, as far as he could and slowly, ever so slowly, increased the bend until he could tuck it under him as well. On his knees, he could now look around.

The sun overhead was bright, without a cloud in the sky. On the water drifting along was a litter of ship fragments, the largest of which was his own. A barrel floated some distance away, maybe thirty or forty feet. He squinted in the sharp sunlight; his eyes were still blurred with the sting of seawater. He rubbed them with the heels of his hands, blinked several times, and they cleared. An arm draped over the barrel came into focus on the side toward him. Trailing the barrel, now bunching around it in some subtle current, was a tail of dark clothing with a lighter trim that caught the sun slanting down. As he watched, the arm slid higher on the curve of the barrel. It slipped, losing its purchase, but the long fingers of what he could see now was a finely formed hand clawed weakly and then lost their grip and slid out of sight.

Yosef breathed deeply and, without thinking, tumbled forward into the water. At his best speed—a slow crawl—he splashed his way to the barrel. It pirouetted away from him as he disturbed it with his motion. There was no sign of a body on its far side. Treading water as stabs of pain from his right thigh coursed through him, Yosef felt his chin and mouth dip, and he spat out seawater. Again, his head dipped in the wash of waves, and he spat.

His head barely above water, he scanned all around him—nothing. No one he could see. Beneath the surface, his left foot brushed something. Scared to think what it might be, he knew he must look. Ducking his head under the surface, he saw, just below his kicking feet, the end of a cloak slowly sinking and settling deeper. Lifting his head from the water and pushing his face higher, he gulped a deep breath and then dove. He stroked and kicked hard, feeling an instant relief as the jagged piece of wood—loosened by water and his frantic kicking—worked its way free from his leg. The saltwater stung ripples of pain to life that ran the length of his leg. Heading down into a darkening world, he dug handfuls of water to pull himself deeper.

He was close. He reached and grabbed, only to miss it. He reached and caught the cloth, hoping to save a life, then pivoted and clawed one-armed for the surface. Where sunlight penetrated the water, he saw the crimson cloud that he was rising through. With each kick, streamers of blood from his wounded leg created its own sanguineous current that threaded around and rose with him. A fist grabbed his chest—he needed to breathe.

Fighting to not open his mouth, he despaired of making it. He felt his grip slipping—either from unconsciously wanting to let go and now save just his own life or from the numbness that had spread from his hand to his arm. Near letting go, near to reflexively opening his mouth and letting the sea fill his lungs, he broke the surface. Gasping and puking water, he pulled the cloak to him by handfuls until he felt the body. The fullness of chest told him it was a woman, but the large hood had fallen forward and shrouded her features.

Yosef was weakening fast and barely made it back to his accidental life raft. Thankfully, it had not drifted further away. He tried to push the woman up onto it, but all he managed was to sink them both. Sputtering, he got his head above water again, and—keeping his grip locked on a fistful of the cloak—he pulled himself onto the wood and then dragged the woman up. The planking was barely wide enough for both and settled even lower in the water. Almost as an afterthought, he wondered if it would break apart beneath them, rendering pointless his rescue. As he slid her along the slick surface of the planking, the brown cloak's yellow trim caught his eye. The hood fell back to reveal the woman's white face.

Sharks can detect one drop of blood in a million drops of water; they can even smell it from a quarter mile away. Unfortunately, many from the *Salacia* had not just drowned, they had died bloodily. And that drew the predators to the tiny raft that held Yosef and the woman.

* * *

Nicanor straddled two pieces of what must have been the *Salacia's* mast he had bound with the lengths of rope entangled with them. Using his dagger, he cut the excess away above the knots. He carefully coiled that remnant and tied it to a loop on the belt at his waist. He wore his leather vest and under it a wool tunic tucked into the balteus—his broad belt, with the sheath for his dagger—and braccae, the breeches Roman soldiers wore in cold weather. Also wrapped around his waist was his focale, the long scarf worn to protect his neck from armor chafing. In the night, when the storm broke, his career soldier's instincts had told him to grab what was needful and nothing more.

He studied the sky. Clouds were building overhead, bunching together as the wind from the east drove them into clusters. The surrounding waves had increased, and feathers of white showed at their crest. Not seasick, but not exactly well, he leaned and spat bile to his left with the wind that carried it away. Ahead in the direction of the gusts and current, he saw more debris from the ship. Hoping to find one of the sealed water casks, he used the planking he had pulled from the water as an oar. That, along with wind and sea, got him to the broad patch of flotsam and jetsam.

Breathing heavily through dry, already blistering, lips—licking the salt from them—he rested the length of board across his lap. He felt something jostle his leg and looked down to a string of wineskins in the water. Pulling them up, he discovered that most were the large traveling skins—not the smaller ones carried by individuals. He wondered at the need of some sailor—and his optimism—to have used two empty bladders inflated to ensure their flotation. He, Nicanor thought, must have expected to survive the storm with his wine to help him.

Checking all the seals and taking one of the smaller ones from the string, Nicanor tied the line with the remainder securely to the timber that he rode. Unstopping the one he held, he wished that it contained water, but the too-sweet liquid washed the taste of brine from his mouth. He wiped his lips with the back of his hand, wincing at how sensitive they had become, then replaced the wineskin's plug and tied it to another loop at his belt. Pushing debris from around him, he paddled to a wadded mass of what seemed sailcloth or canvas and wood. Two dark-skinned legs stuck out and dangled into the sea. He grabbed one ankle and pulled himself closer. Taking the free end of the coiled rope at his belt, he crafted a loop to slip over one foot and cinched it tight around the ankle to anchor himself in place.

Nicanor, hands now free, gripped the edge of the heavy, wet cloth and—it took two tries—flipped it off the body. Pulling and tugging it, he pivoted the mass so that the body was now parallel to him. He bent forward and down and carefully lifted the head of dark, wavy hair. A gash ran through it, ragged and a brownish red where blood had dried and brighter where his jostling had freshened the bleeding. The wound ran from crown to left jaw, narrowly missing the eyeball but bisecting the corner of the socket. Beneath it—under the body—was a pool of what looked like more blood. Nicanor shifted the body and could get it onto its back. It was Sayid. And what he lay upon was the scarlet-and-gold robe of a Roman noblewoman.

"Futuo," he swore as he scanned the area but did not see her alive nor her floating body. To return to Rome without her might mean that his surviving wouldn't last for long. Even though he was blameless, he knew men like Gessius Florus always looked for someone to punish. He started as he saw Sayid's chest rise with shallow breaths. Well, the boy was still alive. He shook his head and thought, *for now, at least.*

* * *

Nicanor had worked his way around the canvas, discovering that the chunks of wood trapped beneath were keeping it afloat. He used his own slab of planking to carefully push them further under the canvas to better secure them. Coming back around to Sayid, he again anchored to his leg. He moistened Sayid's lips with a little wine and poured a small sip between them. In seconds, Sayid choked and coughed as wine, mixed with seawater, bubbled from his mouth. He turned on his side, slid into a canvas trough filled with four inches of water and spat, then touched the wound on his head and groaned. He tried to sit up, and then, supporting himself with one forearm, carefully lay back and watched as Nicanor also drank from the wineskin.

"Glad you're alive, boy," Nicanor rumbled, loosening his first words—other than a curse or two—since finding himself in the water after the height of the storm.

Sayid cautiously shook his head, touching the robe still partially beneath him. "I couldn't save her. I tried, but..." He lowered his head and held it with both hands. "We got off the cloak that had been dragging her down, but then, in the night, she drifted away from me." He looked up and around at the sea, empty but for pieces of what had once been a ship. "She's gone."

The swirling of ocean currents around land masses—their push and pull coupled with the vagaries of wind over water—directed the drift of objects on the sea, some drawn together and others shoved further away.

* * *

The sun had sunk into the sea, and Yosef noted that the woman's shallow breathing had steadied and then changed to a deeper cadence. She still had not responded to his ministrations, and Yosef wished for some fresh water to help revive her. The seawater he had laved her forehead and hands with had dried to a rime of faint flakes on skin that had reddened until Yosef had pulled the dry, salt-stiff hood forward to protect her face. He studied the brown robe with its saffron trim now fainter in the nightfall as he watched the moon rise. His vision adjusted, and he was surprised at how well he could see.

The evening sky was an ebony blanket darted with bright points of light that only faded as they neared a glowing gibbous moon. Yosef lifted the hood, folding it back from a face that gleamed in the light, with long, dusky lashes on the closed eyes, and black brows that had been precisely trimmed to form perfect arcs. He wondered what color

29

the eyes were beneath the pale eyelids. As familiar as the features were from within his dream, he had no idea if the eyes were dark as the night above or bright as the sea had been throughout the day. The woman in his dreams had been Camilla, he knew now. "How could I have seen your face in those dreams?" he murmured, knew that he had asked that question aloud, and realized it felt good to talk. "We don't know each other, but I feel we will. We will become..."

He saw the eyelids flutter, then open wide. Like silver coins, her eyes surprised him as they caught and reflected the moonlight. And, not as he expected, she looked up at him.

Despite the rasp of her too-dry throat, he recognized the voice. "Who are you?" With what seemed a reflex, she attempted to pull the hood from behind her head.

"I'm Yosef, a Jewish scholar—an envoy—traveling to Rome. I was on the *Salacia*... the ship, with you." He dipped his head, not quite a bow but an acknowledgment of an introduction never made. "I know that you are Camilla, the Roman lady's maidservant."

"What?" She looked around and then back. Her eyes clouded then cast down, and it seemed she would shake her head. Then she looked up into Yosef's eyes with a small nod. "Are there others?"

Yosef knew she meant other survivors. Those eyes—like perfect orbs of argentum—had not wavered from his. He swallowed, "No. No one else."

Her eyes closed, and she lay still. A minute passed and then two. A single cloud, a solo rider on the night wind, crossed the moon. She opened her eyes again, and the gleam tugged at him in a way he could not explain. "I'm scared," she said. "Please talk to me."

So he did. Yosef talked about why he was going to Rome, and even when her eyes closed again—perhaps she slept but he thought she still listened—he continued. The moon had crossed the sky and was now dropping toward the horizon when he stopped with a whisper: "I dreamed of you."

Before sleep took him, he turned to face the wind coming from the direction of setting moon. The sharp pain in his leg had dulled to a deep ache as the cold numbed him. He wrapped Camilla's cloak around her and lay beside but not touching her. He had not felt the wad of canvas he had jammed into the wound come free. Dried, clotted blood loosened, and the pooling drops lapped over the edge of the wood to fall into the water below.

VII

AT SEA

Nicanor opened his eyes. The wine had quenched his thirst but had him feeling slightly drunk even as sparing as he had been with drinking it. He had gotten Sayid to swallow some, and the boy was now resting more easily beside him. He sat up and looked around, blinking in the morning sun. Tying himself to the section of mast and canvas he had affixed together had worked well enough. He had slept, albeit sporadically, through the night.

"Futuo!" he swore. In the growing light, he saw the triangular fins cutting through the water in the distance, cruising parallel to them and, thankfully, not closing in. No telling how many bodies from the ship were strewn over miles of ocean. It was feeding time, and they were seeking every source of blood.

"Futuo," Nicanor cursed again, wishing he had never stepped forward and protected that highborn fool who thought visiting the provinces was like walking the streets of Rome surrounded by servants and slaves to kneel at his command. Saving such an ass had resulted in his reward—a position in the Praetorian Guard—that awaited him in that city. That bothered him even more. He had been born in Patras, a Roman port on the northwestern Peloponnesus, to a legionary and a woman of Graecia. He had joined the legion at about Sayid's age and had served all over the southern and easternmost points in the empire, but never in Rome. In those provinces, he had seemed pure Roman, with only the occasional conflict over his half-Greek blood, and usually from some ass of a senior officer serving outside of Rome for the first time. The promotion was a great honor, but he wondered if he should somehow have contrived to avoid it. He laughed at that thought. You cannot ignore any orders from Rome... well, at least not and live.

His mind—and eyes—focused back on the situation at hand. Chances were that he would never live to see Rome, anyway. He squinted, there—near the fins—low in the water, was a large object. Flat and awash, but it contained two shadowed humps that rose above the water, and one of them moved. Cursing more, he knew he must untie himself and paddle over to see what or who it was. It might be other survivors, and he couldn't ignore them.

31

He cast off from the canvas-and-wood raft and carefully paddled toward them. Unfortunately, they were in the same direction of the sharks, whose number seemed to have grown just in the minutes since he had first spotted them. "Damn creatures," he spat into the water. "Neptune's demons." Raised in a coastal city, he knew of sharks from tales told by the fishermen and, more recently, from an armorer, a former legionary in Caesarea. The man had lost a leg to one when his trireme went down off the coast of Melita, a place Nicanor thought might not be that far north of where he and Sayid had ended up.

Nearing the object, he saw it was a piece of decking barely staying above water. The figure that had moved was now raised on one elbow and looking around, stopping once he saw Nicanor. The man got awkwardly to his knees, favoring the right and wincing with pain. Nicanor saw he was bearded, with a head of wiry dark hair stiff with salt and a prominent nose, lean-jawed, with slightly bushy brows.

Nicanor shook his head with surprise; it was the person on the *Salacia* more frightened of water than anyone he had ever met. He had survived—Yosef, the Jew. "Ho," he called to him and, then once near enough, leaned forward to grasp Yosef's outstretched hand and pull himself closer.

"It's good to see you," Yosef croaked.

"Have a swallow of this," Nicanor untied the wineskin from his belt and handed it to him. "Careful, don't expect water." He was surprised that Yosef did not immediately put it to his own lips. Instead, he turned and bent over the figure beside him. Nicanor stretched to see who it was as Yosef gently raised the head with one hand—*A woman!*—and lifted the wineskin to her lips with the other. The hood fell back as the woman's eyes opened to drink the wine greedily. Nicanor's salty and sun-dried lips split and bled with his grin. "It's good to see that you're alive, Lady Cleo."

Yosef turned back, looking over his shoulder, to stare at him. "Who?!"

Nicanor was puzzled at first by Yosef's astonishment, thinking only of how, if they all lived, and if they kept her alive, her return home would be celebrated and fêted. And for those with her, the welcome in Rome could include a more appealing reward—for him, a promotion and maybe a command in Hispania instead of an assignment to the guard. He looked again at Yosef, whose startled look had not lessened, and he couldn't hold his laugh that rang out across the water.

32

* * *

Nicanor checked over his shoulder as he paddled. The line was still secure as he towed Yosef and Cleo on their small section of deck toward where he had left Sayid. He looked ahead and couldn't decide whether what was in front was any better than what was behind. If the waves picked up, both miserable excuses for life rafts would be swamped. But there was not much that could be done—that was all they had.

The sun bore down on them—no escaping it. Nicanor shaded his eyes with a forearm as he scanned the water around them and the horizon. The fins, nearly a dozen, were still no closer. He wondered if they were feeding on bodies just beneath the surface. Sayid didn't move as Nicanor tied more securely the piece of deck and the mast pieces he rode and then tied them both to the canvas Sayid lay upon, all of it kept afloat by the wooden flotsam beneath. Cleo had risen to her knees quickly as they came to rest, shifting about once Nicanor secured the connecting lines.

"Careful, my lady," Nicanor said as he tested the knot and held up the palm of his hand. "Stay low and move slowly."

She crept to the edge of her piece of the raft, closest to where Sayid lay. "Is he alive?"

"He was when I left," Nicanor said. Lifting his legs out of the water—for the first time in over an hour—he balanced precariously on the trunk of the mast. "He has a bad gash along the side of his head." Nicanor was surprised at the flash of concern on Cleo's face. "He fades in and out."

Cleo looked over at Yosef, who had not moved or spoken since learning who she was. "Yosef is injured, too."

Nicanor looked at the scarlet robe spread beneath Sayid and then to the brown that Cleo wore. "Sayid said he managed to pull a woman from the water. He got that robe off her—it was dragging her under—but then he passed out. When he came to his senses, she was gone." He lifted the gold edge of the cloak, "I saw this and assumed that woman was you."

"Camilla and I heard the talk of worry—concern—about a storm," she glanced at Yosef who watched and listened but was still silent, "and became uneasy. We remained clothed as we lay there sleepless but didn't wear our robes. When the storm hit, we were flung from our beds in the dark, and I suppose we each grabbed the other's cloak."

Nicanor had followed her look and couldn't understand the expression on Yosef's face. Seeing the blood in his hair and crusted around one ear, he asked him, "Yosef, how's your head?"

"Fine." Yosef shook it, but his white face belied the pain from his leg. His weight was all on the left knee, and his right hand gripped his right thigh as if to force the pain away. He was trying to straighten his legs so he could sit.

Nicanor said, "My lady, let's see if we can move you over here," he gestured to a spot next to Sayid. "Don't worry. I'll tend to Yosef, and then I'll get this... us," his hands spanned the two rafts, "more secure." He held out both hands to lift and help her get settled next to Sayid. "There you go."

She carefully stretched out on the canvas, distributing her weight evenly, and said to Nicanor, "I'm glad he survived. Sayid has been with me since I got to the provinces." She reached over to touch his arm. "He's a kind boy."

Nicanor grunted in reply. In his experience, the kind ones ended up abused and eventually died. Kindness in the Roman army did not get you far. "Let's look at you," he said to Yosef, sliding carefully toward him, aware of how every time they moved, something shifted beneath them all. Yosef lifted the long tail of his tunic, showing the wound had become more than a puncture—the torn flesh was red, swollen, and still bleeding. Nicanor unwound his armor scarf from around his waist. Unslinging the wineskin from his shoulder, he opened it and squeezed wine onto the middle section of the cloth. "Can you move closer?"

Leaning forward onto his hands and arms to bear his weight, Yosef slid forward and turned slightly, so his right thigh was rotated toward Nicanor, who poured wine over the wound, cupping it to get some inside the puncture. Yosef did not cry out, but his teeth clenched as he held the cloth in place while Nicanor quickly wrapped the scarf around the wound. Pulling it tight forced a moan from Yosef as Nicanor knotted the ends together. "I hope this holds."

Nicanor eased backward and turned to check the lines binding the various pieces of raft together. The work of the waves, moving the bits and pieces their lives depended on, would require that he repeat that task periodically. He scanned their surroundings and the horizon, knowing that, too, would be a never-ending responsibility until he became too weak to continue. He looked at his companions. It was likely that in a matter of days, he would watch them die one by one and then the sea would take him last.

For a moment he recalled his mother, always willing when he begged her to tell "one more story before bed." She had died young, and his story would end as had hers, when she was the age he was now. *Still, we live for the present*, he thought. Out of the corner of his eye, he caught a flash from something—it had to be metal—to his right, near a small mass floating in the water some distance from them. They had nothing to signal other ships if the gods should favor them with one coming close enough. He had to find out if that was metal and retrieve it.

"Lady," he inclined his head toward Yosef, too, "something caught the sun over there. We need something to signal with, so I'm going to see about it."

"Of course, centurion," Cleo glanced at Yosef, "we'll be still while you're gone."

* * *

The sun glancing off the water had become like slivers of metal cast like darts into Nicanor's eyes. The urge to rub them yet again was as hard to resist as that of needing to lift the wineskin to his lips and drink deeply. Nicanor clamped down with what will he could muster and pulled hard with his makeshift oar. He had reached the shape floating in the water. A dead man, one of the legionaries. He had tied himself to a spar, a splintered six-foot length of timber. The rope around his chest had twisted around his throat and strangled him. The torn tips of the man's fingers—white and now bloodless from seawater washing over them—had dug into the flesh of his neck under the rope. Locked there in death, what the man had carried in his tunic had slipped into the crook of one arm. The current had slowly pirouetted the body so that its angle had reflected the sun. Because his own hands were tired and stiff, roughened by sea brine and sun, Nicanor very cautiously lifted the bronze mirror. Its convex disc flashed in the bright sun.

VIII

AT SEA

"May I have some wine?" Yosef asked Cleo, pointing at the wineskins secured to the canvas bunched at Sayid's feet. "Please."

Cleo had been watching Nicanor, who was now quite a distance from them. She had felt Yosef's eyes on her and wondered at his silence. She untied one of the skins and, leaning forward, stretched to hand it to Yosef.

"Thank you." As he bent his fingers to tug on the stopper, he noticed the fine line of fresh blood on his knuckles. The exposed dry skin had tightened and, when flexed, cracked and bled. He drank, and the wine's bitter taste gave only slight relief. Managing two swallows, he handed it back to her.

Cleo held the wineskin in her lap and checked again on Nicanor, who was nearing whatever he had seen. She raised the wine and drank, making a face at its warmth and the taste.

"I know," he said.

She looked at Yosef with the trace of a smile. "I didn't think you would speak to me again."

"I think I've probably spoken to you too much." Yosef shook his head. "I thought you..." He shook his head again and looked away.

"—You thought I was someone you could talk to." She smiled again. "I am, and you can." A low swell passed beneath them, making them fall and rise as their eyes met.

"Why didn't you tell me you were..."

"—The mysterious Roman lady?" Cleo and Camilla had overheard the mealtime talk between Yosef and Sayid. "Why should it matter who I am?" Even as she asked, there was no escaping the proper Roman society answer to that.

Yosef's voice was tinged with regret: "You're highborn, I was told, and so seems true from the way Nicanor treats you. That fact, among other things." His head drooped to his chest.

"What other things trouble you? I wasn't aware I'd become a discussion between—"

"—Non-Romans, provincials..." Yosef cut her off without looking up. He started to shake his head, and the increased dizziness stopped him. He brought a hand to his brow, avoiding the cut but rubbing the bruised area just above his ear. "It was not a discussion, just a passing comment." His eyes lifted to Nicanor, a hazy shape in the distance.

"That you were—are—to wed a Roman official, a Gessius Florus, on your return to Rome."

Cleo had followed his look, then turned back to him. "What exactly did the centurion say?"

Yosef kept his head down.

Her voice sharpened: "What did he say?"

The tone made Yosef squarely meet her eyes. "I shouldn't have told you about me, my mission," he lowered his head again, "of my dreams about the storm and of you."

"What did Nicanor tell you about me, Yosef?" Her voice softened.

"That he knows of your husband."

Cleo studied the mass of dark, wavy hair on the bowed head, just arms' length from her but separated by far more than that scant distance. Her marriage had been arranged by her father, and even her best friend, Poppaea, thought Gessius Florus was a rising star in Rome. A sound match for her with good fortune favoring him. Having met the man and having her own feelings about love and marriage, Cleo found her conclusions were much different. This trip had been intended to put off Gessius Florus a little longer. Yosef had told her the purpose of his own reluctant trip to Rome. Little did he know that she, too, was unhappy about what awaited her there.

Yosef was now lying on his side, his back to her. Sayid stirred beside her, and she helped him sit up with a groan.

"My lady!" Sayid said, rubbing his eyes and leaving one hand raised to lightly trace the line of the wound he had suffered when blown from the *Salacia*. He blinked and looked around. "Where's Nicanor?"

"He'll be back soon—see?" She pointed toward the returning figure on the water.

"Where has he been?" Without waiting for an answer, Sayid looked around and spotted the supine shape on the wooden deck floating next to them, recognizing him by the cut of his tunic. "Yosef!"

"Shhh..." Cleo cautioned, "I think he sleeps."

But Yosef was awake, listening. He didn't want to sleep. He wanted never to dream of her again.

* * *

Cleo checked on Sayid and then crawled to the edge of the canvas to stretch an arm and hand out to touch Yosef's shoulder. Nicanor did not know much about the ways and mores of ladies and their lives in

Rome, but he doubted that most would care for others as this Cleo apparently did. He checked the sky. They were nearing a pitifully short period of relief between the sun's broiling rays and the too-cold night, their second since the *Salacia's* sinking. They had not eaten in three days and had only wine to drink. He thought something he never would have dreamed of three days ago—by the gods, he was tired of wine! As it was, he should be thankful for finding it afloat among the remnants of the shipwreck. But only one large wineskin was left. It would get them through the coming night and the next day. Then no more. Within days, they would all die—weak from hunger, parched from thirst, with only a memory of the taste of sour wine in their mouths.

As the sunset kissed the sea to the west, both Sayid and Yosef raised themselves to face the ocean's evening breath, a brisk wind over the waves that soothed their burning brows. Cleo, who had been kneeling, sat back, extending her legs, with her face turned up to the deepening twilight. She took another mouthful of wine and closed her eyes as she swallowed, trying to focus and to stop or at least slow how it had made her head spin. "Nicanor, how long has it been since you've been to Rome?" She swept salt-stiffened hair from her face, fingers trying to loosen the clumps and knots in the strands.

Nicanor took the wineskin from her, took a long drink and passed it to Yosef. "Never, my lady."

"Never?"

"Not once."

"How can that be?" She looked at Yosef, who drank and passed the wine to Sayid, who took only a small sip and handed the skin back to Cleo.

"I don't understand what you mean, my lady." Nicanor felt uncomfortable at how she stared at him. Yosef, eyes closed, swayed with the gentle undulation of the waves and whisper of wind, so unlike what had torn the *Salacia* apart.

"If you have not been in Rome, how do you know of my coming nuptials and anything of my husband-to-be, Gessius Florus?"

That stern Roman soldier aspect came over his face as he locked on Yosef's now-open eyes. To his credit, Yosef did not shy away from the look. Nicanor turned from him to Cleo. "The *Salacia's* captain told me," he explained, "that an important man in Rome had sent him a message via the cursus publicus, the empire's messenger system, on a fast trireme recently arrived in Alexandria, and then overland to Caesarea. The message was that he, the captain, would be rewarded for fast transit." Nicanor turned the mirror in his hands, looking down as it glinted in the moonlight. "I assumed that he must mean you, my lady. And as he held that message parchment in his hands, I saw that it had come from Gessius Florus."

Nicanor looked up and continued: "The captain told me that an ardent official in Rome wanted his betrothed in his arms soonest." He paused as something less than ardor showed on Cleo's face in the slanting rays of the moon. "And"—he took a deep breath—"a few years ago I knew of a man—an official—with that name when I was stationed in Cilicia, with a legion near Tarsus. Florus was a quaestor, a tax collector, and administrator in charge of local conscription and recruitment for the legions." He took another deep breath. "—And he had a reputation of having a heavy hand." There were other unsavory things he could have said but left it at that. "That's what I know of a man by that name, my lady."

Her hands, still working at the tangled tresses, paused and then lowered to her lap. "Gessius was born in Clazomenae," she said, "and before Rome, he served in Cilicia. His Rome posting was a reward for doing so well there."

Night fell quickly, and the moon rose high to cast its pale light on them in their silence.

"Camilla"—Sayid spoke into the quiet—"told me you enjoyed the provinces, my lady." His head was still fuzzy, and he didn't fully understand their talk of some man in Rome—quickly spoken conversational Latin, so different from the barking of orders—but he sensed how it had made all of them uncomfortable.

The ghost of a smile came to Cleo's lips. "I'm my grandmother's granddaughter. She was born and raised in Hispania, and the pomp and grandeur, the pretensions of those in Rome, never appealed to her." The smile faded as fast as it had appeared. "She cared for me as a child until I was of an age to dedicate my dolls to the goddess Artemis. She helped me weave my recta. That's the tunic worn by Roman girls entering adolescence. Then my father had her sent away. She died not long after."

Nicanor raised an eyebrow at that and saw Yosef straighten and shift his position on the raft.

The sadness was gone from Cleo's voice, replaced by a tinge of regret. "I've always admired the quiet dignity of most men and women I've met from the provinces. There's honesty in their eyes and in their voices."

Nicanor saw her eyes lift to look at Yosef, who matched her gaze. Something in that exchange puzzled him. Even in the moonlight, he saw that Yosef was drenched in sweat. His wound was likely festering, and fever was upon him. But Lady Cleo's brow was dry and her eyes bright in the moon's glow. He shook his head, thinking what had been said was mere words spilled from wine cups, soon forgotten.

"I think we should all try to sleep," Nicanor said, moving to loosen and stretch his cramped legs. He did not want to do what he must do next. "I'll check that all's secure." He swung his legs over the side and slipped into the water. As he made the circuit, he tied in knots and lines as best he could. Back where he began, he lifted himself out of the water. The wind, cold now, had a bite to it, and he shivered. On his knees, he straightened and looked around. Not far away, he saw triangular shadows cut through the phosphorescent tips of waves. Neptune's demons, he muttered. The gods damn them. He checked the others to be sure they were away from the edges. They were far enough toward the center of the raft, and the three were already asleep. He soon joined them.

IX

AT SEA

Yosef awoke to Cleo's crying. The night wind had dropped, and the sound was soft but clear. Chills wracked him as he raised up on one elbow. "Lady Cleo?" He inched over to the edge of his plank closest to where she lay—a few handbreadths of water between them. He felt a jolt beneath him. Then another. He realized that was what had wakened him as he watched something just under the surface of the water rise under the canvas at Cleo's side. A small tent shape snagged, then pulled free, its crease running parallel to her body. Another appeared, and this one touched her, then slammed up and into her as if trying to come through the material. As the shark moved beyond Cleo, in the moon's waning light, he saw chocks and chunks of wooden pieces pushed from under the canvas. The broad nose of the beast shoved them along, its long tail thrashing behind at the edge of the canvas, forcing it under water. Its slow sinking was spreading toward Cleo.

"Nicanor!" Yosef reached for the centurion who had positioned himself to sleep next to Yosef on the splintered deck. Cleo's scream tore through the night, and Yosef scrambled up, not feeling the stab of pain from his leg. Beside him on the slab of decking, Nicanor—alert quickly as only an experienced soldier is capable of—rolled half off the raft, anchored only by Yosef throwing himself across his legs. Nicanor grabbed the edge of the now-rapidly-plummeting canvas, pulling with his arms while simultaneously—somehow—rising to his knees. He surged backward, dragging it with him, as Cleo, water washing over her, tried to clamber toward him. And failed.

Another shark hammered her from below, and the canvas bellying up beneath threw her off to the side and into the water. Yosef, tangled with Nicanor, saw the flash of a monster's maw, the gleam of razor-sharp teeth rushing at her.

"Lady!" Sayid's scream startled Yosef. He watched as the boy, who had been on the other side of Cleo, pulled himself from the drag of collapsing canvas and wood that no longer supported them. As the gray shape, trailing bits of phosphorescence that streamed from its torso, slid by him, Sayid jumped on its back. The boy punched at the massive head; raining blows down on it. That turned the beast from

41

Cleo, who floundered, caught in the clinging weight of her cloak. She spat mouthfuls of water as seawater churned by the tail of the beast lashed her face.

Yosef heard Greek curses as Nicanor pushed him off his legs and plunged into the water, his dagger in hand and white teeth bared in his dark, sunburned face to match the shark's predatory look. Sayid had stayed astride the shark, but as it turned and twisted, one of his legs flung forward and that mouth of knives clamped on it beneath the knee and yanked Sayid under. As the shark rolled on its side, Nicanor was on it. His blade stabbing... stabbing and stabbing, drawing blood with each thrust. The demon let go of Sayid to attack the new threat. In close, its head slammed into Nicanor's head, which snapped back as the dagger dropped from his hand. An ebon eye, seemingly as large as his hand, stared at Yosef. At that moment—frozen in time—he heard Cleo's screams again, and gripping a long, jagged piece of plank in both hands, he leaped onto the shark himself, jabbing the wood as hard as he could into that hungry orb. Without a sound, the shark rolled over and pulled the wood from Yosef's hands. Its body grew still. The only sounds that remained in the dregs of the night were the choking cries from Cleo.

Yosef reached Cleo as she was sinking, and he caught the hood of the cloak and pulled her up. Clasping her to his chest, he kicked backward, hoping that he had kept the direction straight in his head. Moments later, he knew he had, as the back of his head struck the deck section, thankfully still afloat. "Cleo... Cleo..." he shook her, "I need you to hold on long enough for me to get on and pull you up." Her head was tilted up, and her face turned toward him. He saw a burble of water spill from her lips as she spat and then opened her eyes. She raised her arms, and her hands gripped the edges of the splintered wood. Letting go of her, Yosef pulled himself onto the planks and then swung around to drag her up and alongside him. Gasping and coughing up the seawater still rattling in her lungs, she took Yosef's hand. For a moment, he squeezed it in return, and then let it go.

"Where are you going?" Cleo called out as he slipped back into the water.

"I have to find Sayid and Nicanor."

* * *

Dawn was near, its dark purple shading giving way to orange-yellow painted low on the horizon. As the sun climbed, Yosef saw the fins... more sharks.

Not long before, the stalwart last pieces of the *Salacia* had come apart. Nicanor was in the water next to Yosef. On the small remnant of deck, barely large enough for a single person now, was Cleo. She held across her lap an unconscious Sayid who had bled heavily from the gashes between the knee and foot of his left leg.

"More of them," the hatred and fear in her voice were clear, "are coming this way." Cleo pointed to the west, where her slightly higher vantage point allowed her to spot them first.

Kicking hard despite the pain, Yosef rose in the water just long enough to see what she meant. Five or six dark shapes, gray-black fins cutting the water, were racing toward them.

Nicanor had been quiet since Yosef had found him and then they both had searched to find Sayid still alive, too. The stream of curses coming from Nicanor now made Yosef look up at Cleo, who spoke Greek, to see if she understood him. Some of what Nicanor said was vulgarly embarrassing.

"I hate them," Nicanor muttered, waiting for them and then expecting to die, but hoping to take at least one with him.

Yosef looked east into the brightening morning. That group did not seem as swift as the ones from the west. He turned back as Cleo—no longer crying—called out, "No! The shape of their heads seems different."

Moments later, the angle of their fins seemed to change. Then they were on them. Dark, sleek shapes raced by Yosef and Nicanor, then drove straight into the cluster of fins, the giant shadows in the water, coming at them from the east.

"Dolphins!" Nicanor bellowed in Yosef's ear.

"What?" His head now ringing, Yosef knew nothing of sea creatures, and from what he had seen of them, had absolutely no desire to learn.

"Sharks are Neptune's demons, but dolphins are a sailor's protectors!"

Still feverish, Yosef was confused. "But we're not sailors, Nicanor."

Shaking his head and spitting out seawater, he laughed. "No, we're not, Yosef. They'll save us still. It's a sign from the gods. Don't you see?"

Yosef did not see. The raft suddenly shifted, rocking a jutting corner into his head.

"There..."

Yosef blinked, sputtered water and looked up. Cleo was pointing southeast. He still could see nothing.

"What is it, lady?" Nicanor was straining to lift his chest higher out of the water, looking in that direction. "It's not more sharks, is it?" The dolphins had remained, forming a screen around them, but who knew for how long?

"It's a ship!"

"If she can see it, we can signal it." Nicanor took one hand off the bobbing deck section, and his other went underwater to his waist.

Yosef saw Nicanor's hand loosening his belt and going into his breeches. "What are you doing?"

"Thought it would castrate me... but it was worth it." With a grunt of pain, Nicanor pulled the mirror out. "Good thing I saved this, and that it stayed there during the fight with the sharks." He lifted it out of the water. "Lady, take this, but don't drop it!"

"It's a quinquereme," Nicanor said as the ship got closer and then angled directly toward them. Its prow, an enormous spur, was pointed their way. "I sailed on one from Tarsus to Tyre."

The morning sun, now higher in the sky, had lit the ship's side as it approached them tangentially before changing course sharply once Cleo's signaling caught their attention. They saw the sweep of the oars clear—three banks, stacked—once the bow was in view.

"It's even bigger than the *Salacia*." The wonder in Yosef's tone brought a snort from Nicanor.

"There are some bigger, but this type carries three hundred rowers, twenty to thirty sailors, and up to a hundred and twenty auxiliary legionaries.

"More than four hundred men... on a single ship..." Yosef shook his head. Barely staying above water, his face had burned red, and despite his being mostly submerged in cool seawater, runnels of sweat poured from his head. Dazed and weak, he reset his grip on the slick wood. The Roman ship seemed to be racing toward them... looming larger... as if it didn't intend to stop.

Nicanor nodded, understanding Yosef's feeling, but kept his eyes on the ship. A sharp call—the bark of a command—rang over the water and the oars—a bank at a time from bottom to top—lifted. The angle of the broad paddle changed and then reversed direction. The oars dropped and dug in, backing water to slow and then bring the ship to a relative stop just forty feet from them. The press of water, the swell pushed by the vessel's mass, slightly lifted and lowered Yosef, Nicanor, Cleo, and Sayid for a couple of minutes as the sea settled.

The faces of sailors and legionaries adorned with a bulwark of sculpted pseudo-shields—appeared above the railing. Behind them rose three masts. The center—midship—was the tallest and had its sails rolled and tied. Soon a section of that bulwark and railing was removed, pulled back and away, and they saw a boat, maybe twenty feet long, as it slid toward the opening. Lines were affixed to the bow and stern, and no doubt along its length as it was pushed through the opening and lowered to the water. As the lines lifted and tugged, then pulled the boat to settle it upright on the waves, above it a rope ladder unfurled from the ship's deck to drop to just above the boat. Once it was secured, eight men climbed down and took positions. Two sailors and four rowers pulled two long oars from their mounts and socketed them into place, resting them parallel to the boat's sides, while legionaries supervised.

A flash of bright metal in the sun caught Yosef's eye, and he looked up. The horsehair crest and flowing red cloak signified a centurion was joining the men on the boat, climbing down the rope ladder. He got settled in the boat, and the sailors pushed off from the ship. Soon it was beside their tiny bit of wreckage.

Nicanor called to him, "Ho, the ship! I'm Nicanor, a centurion newly assigned to the Praetorian Guard." He turned in the water to include the others, "And we are off the *Salacia*, which sailed from Caesarea, headed to Puteoli," his glance swept the others again, "and then, from there we're on to Rome. Our ship was wrecked and sank in a storm."

"Help them get aboard," the shipboard centurion ordered the two legionaries. They moved to the near side of the vessel, and one sailor threw a line to Nicanor, who tied it to a projecting plank and then pulled to draw their raft closer to the boat.

"Take the boy first," Cleo said as she tried to raise Sayid to them, but her numb arms wouldn't serve. "Careful!" she called out as they roughly dragged him from her and laid Sayid in the boat's bottom. The crude bandage she had made to stop the bleeding of his torn leg had slipped, revealing the bright red of fresh blood. She took the hand of the largest of the legionaries and tried to stand, but her legs failed. "I can't," she said as she slumped down.

With both hands gripping her waist, the legionary lifted and pivoted to place her behind him in the boat. At the same time, the other legionary leaned over and offered a hand to Nicanor. Grasping each other's forearms, Nicanor and the legionary both pulled and swung him up and into the boat. He then spun on his knees to grab Yosef—who had been losing his hold—by the front of his tunic and dragged him aboard. Their eyes met, and each nodded. Yosef then went to Cleo, who was beside Sayid, retying his leg bandage. He glanced back at Nicanor with some emotion that clouded his eyes, and as he blinked it away, Nicanor leaned toward Yosef: "Well, we live."

X

AT SEA

Yosef stood beside Nicanor on the deck of the ship. He had been the last to board, and only Nicanor had called encouragement over his shoulder to climb the rope ladder—then offered him a steady hand as he reached the deck. The centurion from the ship had ordered the largest legionary to carry Sayid up the ladder and then on to somewhere—below deck—where he could be looked at. He had then taken Cleo to a structure at the stern of the ship, calling back to the two rescued men, "Wait here for me."

Yosef lifted his face, savoring how the breeze cooled it even as a chill shook his body. The wind carried a smell from home—a warm, woodsy smell that enchanted a boy raised in a city. He remembered being a young boy and watching a craftsman work with the wood brought from Phoenicia into the port at Jaffa and then over the trade road to Jerusalem. He had encountered that fragrance again at sixteen during his time with the Sadducees because they used the wood to maintain and make repairs to the temple.

"Cedar..." Nicanor, too, was pleased with the scent of the aromatic wood. He looked around them, at the joints and fittings in the deck beneath them. A shout made him look up, and he and Yosef watched as sailors climbed and pulled lines. In minutes, the mainsail bellowed, its clean, unfrayed sheets sharp and crisp against the cerulean sky. Nicanor stamped his right foot on the deck—"She's new construction."

"Yes, it is." The ship's centurion had returned for them. "This is her first true voyage, from the Alexandria shipyards to Ostia Antica." He eyed the bedraggled Yosef from his bare feet to his tangle of hair and then turned to Nicanor. "Follow me, centurion." Shortly after, he ushered them into the aft cabin where they found Cleo standing with a man wearing a blue tunic and baldric. She turned with a smile.

"This is our quinquerarch... the captain of the ship—"

"Of the *Mithras*, my lady," the officer interrupted her proudly.

"The *Mithras*," Cleo repeated, nodding to him, and he bowed his head. "I'm Cleopatra—"

"Lady, I recognize you even after your hardship. I have the good fortune to have met your father in Rome, and he pointed you out to me. Such a fine—"

"Thank you, Captain," Cleo cut him off. She did not care for her father and was unsure about letting Nicanor and Yosef know more about her family and position. Many she met became servile upon discovering it. Though, from what she had learned of their manner through their actions, she believed—hoped—that the bond among Yosef, Sayid, and Nicanor would survive finding out. She would rather not think of family and Rome just yet.

The *Mithras's* captain obliviously moved onto another topic: "It's fortunate that we spotted you... were it not for the man we found, we would not have dropped sails and taken to the oars to better maneuver and watch more diligently."

"A man," Nicanor asked. "From the *Salacia*?"

"Yes," said the centurion. "He's been tended to, and you'll likely see him soon."

"How long will it take to get to Rome?" Cleo asked the question that was on Yosef's lips, but the captain had barely glanced at him.

"Five or six days at sea, my lady—perhaps less if the wind strengthens and holds. Then six days by carriage." His smile broadened. "You must be anxious... your wedding awaits, does it not? And your husband-to-be is such a fine—"

"Thank you," she cut him off again, "but we're tired and would like to bathe and then rest."

"And afterward—this evening—I'll have a special dinner prepared for you."

"For us," she looked at Yosef and Nicanor, "these men and the boy—all three—saved me. Were it not for them...."

The captain bowed to her. "Of course, my lady."

* * *

Nicanor looked around. There was more open space on this ship, and their end of the berthing compartment was unoccupied. The *Mithras* would not have her full complement of auxiliaries, conscripted soldiers from the northern and western provinces until the ship was ported in Ostia. The centurion had led him and Yosef to where Sayid was resting. The boy was awake but waited to speak until the centurion left.

"I dreamed that I found my father." Seeing that Nicanor and Yosef didn't understand, he explained: "I joined the legion as soon as they would take me—I wasn't conscripted—hoping that one day I'd find my father and show him I had become a man, strong, and a good soldier." He sighed and shifted on the rough bedding. "But when I opened my eyes... no father." Sayid raised up on his forearms, and the sadness faded as he looked up at them. "But they told me I was found with two other men and a lady, a Roman noblewoman." He blinked, and his infectious smile spread across his blistered face. "And I was happy because my friends lived, too!"

* * *

Despite the fever, Yosef felt the bath—fresh water from a barrel, large ladles full of it dumped over his head—had revived him. And heeding Nicanor's warning, he had drunk the water slowly and sparingly. Too much, too quickly, would be vomited up as fast as it went down.

"You still don't look well." Nicanor clasped his shoulder.

"Thanks, that really helps." Yosef's sardonic grin did not hold long. He didn't know if the ship's roll caused the dizziness or if the fever brought a renewed sweat to his forehead. Minutes before, two sailors had taken the litter bearing Sayid up to the deck where they would dine with Cleo, the captain, and the centurion. Cleo had held firm despite their private protest about including them, insisting that Sayid be brought to join them.

As they passed where the conscripted rowers were stationed and berthed, Yosef recalled the man he had met before boarding the *Salacia* in Caesarea and wondered how many of them would live through—endure—their experience in the Roman navy. How many would make it to twenty-six years and reap their reward of citizenship?

* * *

"So, you understand Greek?" The captain was surprised with Yosef and Sayid. Cleo had been telling them—in that language—of how much she had enjoyed seeing Antioch, Phoenicia, and Judea.

"And we speak it, as well," Yosef replied in that tongue. Greek was a common language for the educated; Yosef had spoken it since he was a child, and Sayid—much brighter than many in the auxiliaries—had learned it from conscripts from that region. The officers of the *Mithras* clearly did not think much of non-Romans.

The captain had dutifully smiled at Yosef's comment, unsure why this Jew mattered to the lady. But he was glad his only responsibility in the southern provinces had been to oversee the *Mithras* construction and then to sail her to Ostia. Even in Alexandria—through other Romans—he had heard that the Roman procurator in

Judea, Albinus, was having difficulty with Jewish terrorists. The Sicarii grew bolder every day, and hostage-taking of Roman officials and citizens was becoming commonplace. He had heard the rumblings that a heavier hand was needed in Judea and hoped never to return there.

A sailor entered the room and leaned down to whisper in the captain's ear. He nodded to the sailor, who then left them.

Yosef was sitting down but swayed—it wasn't the sea causing it. Cleo watched him with a concerned look in her eyes. During the dinner, Sayid had sipped water—no wine for any of them—and ate some dried fruit, and then had fallen asleep. Nicanor, to one side, was in a deep conversation with the *Mithras*'s centurion. Yosef's vision blurred. He said to Cleo, "I think I'd better go—"

"He asked to see you, Centurion." The captain reached to tap Nicanor on the shoulder and looked up at the sailor who had returned with a man whose skin was as dark as the wooden deck. "This is the other survivor from your ship."

Cleo looked at the man without expression. Nicanor glanced up from his conversation and studied the man, who seemed familiar. Yosef turned to look over his shoulder at the man, but that movement made his head spin and stomach lurch. The man's features doubled, blurred, and then sharpened before going out of focus again.

"Captain! That man," the dark man pointed at Yosef, "he is cursed; he is why my ship sank. He brought the storm!"

Yosef recognized the sailor who had threatened him on the *Salacia*. Then everything turned upside down. The last thing Yosef heard just before he passed out was the man's cry: "He will doom this ship, too!"

* * *

Yosef woke when his hand struck something hard, and he realized that in his turning and twisting in sweat-soaked blankets, his arm had slipped off the low, narrow cot. He raised his hand to his eyes to rub them, blinked and looked up at a dark shape bending down to him, backlit by swaying lantern—a familiar scene—his dream had returned. His head sank back; Yosef was too dizzy to hold it up. The hooded figure leaned further down and extended a delicate hand to rest on his brow. It felt good... comforting.

She spoke softly as he slipped back into a dreamless sleep. "Rest, Yosef. I wish you well." The figure straightened, paused, and then knelt again, leaning closer.

Next to her, Sayid was already frightened that they would be caught attending to this man some onboard considered a harbinger of ill fortune. He swiveled his head, looking for sailors that might have found a reason to leave the deck or their stations, even though they were now entering the harbor at Puteoli. He was surprised when the Lady Cleo lowered her face to Yosef's. Sayid looked around again, the lantern now shaking and not just swaying with the ship's roll, and then back. Her lips had stopped at Yosef's ear, and he heard her whisper, "Thank you." She stood and turned to Sayid. "Let's go on deck, we've arrived."

As much as Cleo knew Rome, and that the man who was to be her husband would change her life dramatically, she was ready to get it over with. Her grandmother had often said, "Sometimes in life you have to make the best of things," and Cleo had always listened to her. She had put her dolls away when in the temple of Artemis. Now foolish thoughts must be put behind her as well—to become a wife to a man she would find a way to love. Glancing one last time at Yosef, she followed Sayid.

XI

At Puteoli, Nicanor watched as Lady Cleo climbed into the four-wheeled carpentum, pulled by two mules, that the *Mithras*'s captain had arranged. The arched roof of the carriage allowed her to stand, and the inside was spacious and comfortable. He had never seen a carpentum before—there were too few nobles riding in them over the streets in provinces he had served. Earlier that morning he had inspected its intriguing arrangement of metal and leather straps that formed a suspension to ease the roughness of its ride on iron-shod wheels. He had been told by the *Mithras* centurion that the road they would take to Rome, though mostly smooth, had rough patches in some areas. The road was also cambered, slightly convex in the middle for water runoff, and had ditches on either side protected by retaining walls. Familiar with such trade roads in the provinces, he was curious to see one here at the center of the empire.

He shifted in the four-pommeled saddle to get a good grip with his thighs. The design left a Roman soldier's hands free to hold an oval shield and use a sword, spear, or short javelin. The centurion had equipped him, replacing what he had lost. The *galea*, the helmet, had seen much service, and the hair of its transverse crest was worn down. His armor included ocreae, greaves, to protect his legs. They usually had engraved decoration, but these were plain, as was the bronze cuirass—chest and stomach plate. His sagulum, the cloak, was frayed in spots, a pallid blue-green with a yellow border, and tied at the front with a simple brooch. He had no spear or shield, declining them when offered, but the gladius hispaniensis, a sword he was most familiar with, was in the silver scabbard that hung over his shoulder and across his chest. He regretted losing his previous dagger—his oldest companion—to the sharks. *Damn those demons.* But having one again, sheathed on the belt at his waist, made him feel better than he had since before the wreck of the *Salacia*. Most of his life had been lived with these weapons at his side. To be without them had made him feel almost naked. He would likely need them on the road if only to dissuade temptation.

They would stop at way stations, mansiones built at regular intervals about fifteen to twenty-five miles apart. There they—and their horses—could drink, eat, and sleep. The centurion had told him prostitutes and thieves looked to steal from travelers frequenting the path. He moved the reins to his left hand and rubbed his rump with the right. By the time they entered Rome in six days, he would remember every reason he disliked riding horseback. At his left, Sayid had a mix of distress and joy on his face—anxiety overcame him and the beast beneath him as it twitched and stamped its feet. "Easy, boy," Nicanor said, leaning forward to pat the neck of his own horse. "You must always show them who their master is."

Sayid nodded and hesitantly did the same to his horse. It exhaled and blew through its lips, turning to look—left-eyed—at Sayid. The horse shook its head and stamped its right hoof again. The tail flicked up and along its side, causing Sayid to flinch as it brushed his wounded leg.

It was because of his injured leg that the Lady Cleo had asked that Sayid be mounted instead of walking. Nicanor thought it was also because she desired him to ride alongside so she could talk to him through the window of the carriage. Nicanor turned to take a last look at the *Mithras*. Yosef would debark later. After he had passed out amid the sailor's accusations, Cleo had given the captain and centurion her personal assurances for Yosef and had insisted that he be cared for. Nicanor had said his goodbyes to Yosef early that morning as he lay in his cot, but he didn't know if his words had been heard. He hoped so. Although he would never see Yosef again, he owed him his life.

* * *

Yosef awoke and for a moment was disoriented. He felt and smelled the cleanness of the blanket he had wrapped himself in and the softness of the bedding beneath him. The cauponae in Rome was far more of an inn than he had expected. As was the two-man carriage, the carruca, drawn by a mule, that had arrived in Puteoli for him seven days before.

There at a taberna near the port, five days after the arrival of the *Mithras*, Yosef had awoken with a clear head. Other than leaving a slight limp and soreness, the wound in his leg had healed well, and the fever was gone. Two days later, he had recovered enough to travel and was prepared to continue his mission. He had been ready to find a donkey cart or join a group of tradesmen traveling to Rome. When he awoke, he had found a bundle of clothes, which included two plain gray woolen tunics, a pair of sandals with openwork uppers and straps that—a little loose—almost fit his feet, and a leather pouch on a lanyard. He found that the money belt he had worn under his tunic had miraculously survived all that had happened since boarding the *Salacia*, although the flesh beneath it had been rubbed bloody and raw since he had been cast into the sea by the storm. From the taberna owner, he had learned that a Roman noblewoman had arranged for a week's lodging and a doctor—a freed Greek—to care for him. His money belt had been taken off by the Greek to treat the wounds, but not a coin was missing from what he had brought with him. Cleo had paid for it all. He had dressed in the new clothing and transferred his old belt's contents into the pouch. Then that same morning a two-man carriage had arrived, its driver calling for him. He had been glad to leave Puteoli. Even after more than a week, he was still not used to the smell of sulfur from the nearby mineral springs.

The six days on the road had left him travel-sore and wondering at both the magnificence of such a road and at the number of beggars—many seemingly Jewish—that they had passed, their number steadily increasing as they got closer to Rome. Late afternoon of the sixth day, with the sun dropping lower in the west, he had seen through the carriage window a great wall ahead. They soon approached a large gate. It was at least thirty feet high and a dozen feet wide, judging by the carts and people passing through it. "Are we in Rome?" he had asked the driver.

"That's the Servian Wall and Porta Capena gate, so yes, we are about to enter Rome." The driver then had leaned back and pulled the reins to slow the mule's pace.

As they slowed to a crawl, Yosef noted the darkening sky and called to the driver, "Is the beast too tired to go on?"

"We must enter the city proper after sundown. Carriages such as this," he leaned to one side to point down at the iron-rimmed wheels that rang on the stone with a metallic echo, "aren't allowed on the streets during the day."

An hour later, with the nightfall, the road was lit more regularly by lanterns and torches along the way, and the carriage had finally stopped at an inn, whose keeper evidently expected him.

XII

The next morning Yosef looked out the window of his room on the second floor to view the length of the wide avenue that ran a far distance to join the Appian Way. Across the street were stalls of vendors, from which the smell of ripe fruit and other foods wafting up to him on the morning breeze made his mouth water. He left his room and went down the stairs, but at the door to the street, the owner of the inn stopped him.

"I have a message for you," the man said. When Yosef had arrived the evening before, he had looked at Yosef's attire and then his face and features, matching the Jew he had been told to expect. The innkeeper studied Yosef as he fingered the small scroll of fine parchment in his hand; its quality was not easily available to common Romans. "He said the sender was a noblewoman."

Cleo! Yosef's heart jumped before he could convince it not to, but he managed to withhold a smile as he held out his hand for the message.

"The arrangements for you are here," the innkeeper tapped the scroll in his hand, "and for this..." he paused, "you must have highborn friends."

Yosef knew how much difference well-placed connections made in many places, not just in Rome. He was not used to using those connections but answered the man with only a nod. "Could you have fresh water and fruit taken to my room, please?"

The Roman's expression changed to less of an assessment and more of an acceptance and even avarice. He handed Yosef the scroll. "Yes, honored guest." He smiled and half-bowed.

The same two-man carriage that had brought him to Rome picked Yosef up that evening. He recognized it by the deep scratch—almost a gouge—that ran an arm's length inside the left-hand doorjamb. On the long journey from Puteoli, he had idly wondered different scenarios for how someone had intentionally scarred the beautiful woodwork. Perhaps out of boredom on such a long ride as the one he was on.

The message he had received that morning—both an invitation and an expectation—said someone would pick him up after sundown and bring him to a small event, a special gathering to welcome him to Rome. He unrolled the parchment, tracing, for the third time, the delicate writing in a woman's hand. He smiled and thought of Cleo, though he knew he should not. He had never thought he would see her again.

The carriage's route passed through the southern part of the city, and soon, in the twilight, he saw a vast stadium to the left nestled between two hills, in the Vallis Murcia. It must be the Circus Maximus—he had heard many stories of the chariot races held there.

The carriage turned away from the stadium, following a broad lane hedged with hundreds of sculpted topiaries that ended before a complex of buildings sprawled over two hills. They—and all he had seen around them—made Jerusalem seem paltry. A portico ran along the front of the two-story Domus Transitoria, on its south-facing side. The driver had barely stopped the carriage before two slaves, who must have been Greek, rushed out. The young boys, dressed in tunics that were far higher quality than Yosef's, opened the carriage and escorted him inside. A young girl, another slave, took the scroll from his hand. "Please wait here for my lady."

He pivoted on his heels, taking it all in. It was a sumptuous and beautifully decorated palace, the central—lower—floor mostly a sunken garden, one wall occupied by a magnificent nymphaeum decorated with polychrome marbles. He might never adequately describe such a scene to those who lacked the context; few had seen buildings of this type and grandeur, and no one in Jerusalem would understand him. Only five minutes later, the girl brought him a white toga of the softest wool and showed him how to drape it over his shoulders and around his body. It was the finest cloth he had ever worn.

"I understand that you are highborn in your country." The words were Latin, and he turned toward the woman's voice. She was beautiful, nobly so, but she was not Cleo. And though he knew Cleo was also a noblewoman, he would have been surprised to see her in such a grand palace as this.

"Yes," Yosef replied. He was confused where he was, who she might be and why he was there. "And thank you, my lady...?"

She approached him with a questioning, curious look. "I'm Poppaea." She gestured and added, "Please come with me."

The name meant nothing to Yosef, but he followed her. They passed through an interior arch to an open area, whose center contained two pavilions with small columns, and between them, garden beds with vertical walls of curved slabs of marble. The wall opposite the nymphaeum was decorated with niches and a flight of marble stairs that ascended to the upper floor. They passed many beautiful paintings. From his Roman and Greek studies, Yosef believed these were likely from the Homeric cycle telling the story of the Trojan War, including the *Cypria*, the *Aethiopis*, the *Ilias Mikra*, the *Iliupersis*, the *Nostoi*, and the *Telegony*—all in frames of blue and gold. The walls were marble at the bottom with their upper parts frescoed in myriad colors. Yosef's eyes followed them to a painted ceiling that covered the building from end to end, as far as he could see, with mythological scenes.

While staring in wonder at such opulence, Yosef cast occasional glances at the woman. A smile now curled Poppaea's lips, and her eyes occasionally darted sideways toward him as well. But she remained silent. They passed down a long hallway that opened into a forest of columns in a massive room with a large fountain in its center, around which were grouped several men and one woman. Poppaea and Yosef's footsteps echoed as they approached.

"I bring you our final guest!" Poppaea called to them.

They turned, and Cleo's face was as shocked as Yosef's. Next to her, looking as if he wanted to scratch an itch under his toga, though wearing it well, was Nicanor. And next to him even more uncomfortable, was Sayid. On the other side of Cleo, but standing off three or four feet from the others, in his own space, was a young man—about the same age as Yosef—that Poppaea introduced him to first.

"This is my husband, Nero Claudius Caesar Augustus Germanicus... Emperor of Rome." She stepped closer to Cleo and took her by the arm, "And I believe you already know my best friend."

At that moment, Yosef thought all that had happened—the trip, the *Salacia*, the storm, being afloat and lost on the sea... the last several days of his life, including this moment—must still be a fevered dream.

***

"He's very handsome," Poppaea commented as she took a goblet of wine from a servant and turned to Cleo. The men had split off, trailing after Nero, who had been drawn away by the sound of a beautifully played lyre. "You didn't tell me that," Poppaea leaned toward Cleo, "when you spoke of him."

"Why did you bring him—them—here?" Cleo's whisper was low and severe. She had been surprised when Nicanor had arrived with Sayid in tow. Then shocked when she had turned to see Yosef. And he *was* handsome. The thick wavy hair had been brushed and was not awry and stiff with dried saltwater, his beard trimmed in Greek fashion. His face was no longer blistered, peeling and stretched tight with pain. He was striking, and the circumstances had never been such for her to observe it—but here and now, she saw he carried himself with quiet dignity and maturity beyond his years. She had never met a man who somehow seemed instantly in tune with her.

"When you talked of... them," Poppaea's sly grin and that pause said more to Cleo than her words, "I knew I must give you an opportunity to properly thank them." She waved a hand at the returning group led by her husband: "And so that Rome could thank them for saving you." She turned to Nero. "Isn't that right, my husband? Rome must thank these brave men."

Nero waved a hand, and two giant slaves came forward with a massive ornate chair they positioned beside the fountain. He sat, and slaves brought six more chairs, and the largest—not as big as Nero's—was placed at his side and slightly behind. The remaining were arrayed before him. "Sit, and let's hear Cleo's saviors tell their tale." He held out a jeweled hand that was immediately filled with a brimming chalice. "Regale me."

XIII

No one spoke, and just before it became more than awkward—Yosef could see the frown forming on Nero's face—he heard Nicanor mutter under his breath and then stand.

"Sire," Nicanor bowed, then straightened, raising his right arm straight out in front of him. At Nero's nod, he lowered it. "There's not much to say. Our ship sank, and we survived."

"I'm told there's more to the story than that. About your bravery." Nero's eyes were dark and caught glints of light from the nearby bronze braziers alight with burning aromatic wood.

"These men," Nicanor gestured at Yosef and Sayid, "were as brave... or braver. Each saved the lady's life at least once."

Those murky eyes shifted to study Yosef and Sayid and then went back to Nicanor. "There's great turmoil in Judea," Nero said. "... a growing faction disloyal to the empire."

A chill—an icy presentiment—passed through Yosef as Nero turned back to study him as if he stood in judgment. But Nicanor's next words warmed him.

"Sire, I've lived and served in the provinces all my life, and I'm no less a Roman than any man here. True, Yosef and Sayid are not Romans, but they are honorable and courageous. As much as any men I've served with. As much as any Roman. Yosef saved my life. If not for him, I would not be here to continue to serve the empire, Sire."

Nero held up his empty cup, and it was replaced with a full one. "I'm also told that you come to Rome for a reward."

"Well, I was given an order to come to Rome, Sire." Nicanor shook his head.

"You are to be rewarded for saving a nobleman—a friend of the throne—who lives to serve me because of you." Nero wiped his lips with two fingers. "I'm told to place you in the Praetorian Guard as thanks from a grateful empire." The fingers now tapped his chin.

The look on Nicanor's face must've held long enough to be noticed. "You do not wish it?" Nero's tone was sharp, unbelieving.

Nicanor took a deep breath. "Sire, if the empire wishes to reward me, then let it be something... somewhere I can be of value."

"And where would that be, centurion?" Nero glanced at Cleo and then back at Nicanor.

"Antioch, Sire. I know the provinces. I know the people in Judea..." He half-turned to squint at Yosef, "If there is unrest, I can best serve Rome in that province."

"I'll think on it, centurion. I have many decisions to make regarding Judea." Nero's eyes lifted to something beyond them. Nicanor followed his gaze, as Cleo, Yosef, and Sayid turned in their seats. The slave girl was escorting another nobleman, attired in a toga, toward them.

Nicanor treated that as his dismissal and sat. The new guest—lifting his robe and shifting the tail to his other arm—seated himself next to Cleo. It seemed to Yosef that she stiffened as he leaned toward her and whispered in her ear.

"Boy."

Yosef and Nicanor turned back to Nero at the same time. He was pointing to Sayid, who was still looking at the man next to Cleo.

"Boy!" Nero repeated, "Stand and tell me what reward to bestow on you for your bravery," as his eyes flicked from Cleo to the man who had joined them and back to Sayid.

"Si... Sire..." Sayid's voice trembled then steadied as he stood to face Nero. "I would like to find my father. I was young when he left my mother and me in Syria... and I want to—"

Nero cut him off. "I—the empire—am not interested in reuniting you with a father who abandoned you."

"He's a legion—"

"Boy!" Nero's face switched from bored to stern. "Your father doesn't concern me, nor the empire. What reward do you wish that we can grant you?"

Sayid bowed to Cleo and then turned back to Nero. "To continue to serve the Lady Cleo... Lady Cleopatra, Sire."

"It's done, then." He noted that the slave with stylus and tablet had made a mark and then waited a moment with his eyes narrowing at Sayid, who was still standing. "I said it's done, boy." Sayid dropped into his chair, and Nero's stare moved on to Yosef. The two fingers tapped his chin harder. "And what of you?"

Yosef stood. "Sire, I am Yosef ben Mathias, a representative of the Sanhedrin in Jerusalem."

An uninterested look was growing on Nero's face. "And you are here in Rome. That is—you are—important... why?"

The chill was back—stronger—and for a second an image of cold flames that ravaged the hills around them twisted and climbed in his mind. Yosef closed his eyes and forced the vision down. "I come to Rome to discuss the imprisoned priests taken from Jerusalem and held here, in Rome."

"By all accounts here, you're a brave man." Nero's gaze swept over Cleo and Nicanor then back to Yosef. "What reward do you wish for saving the Lady Cleopatra?"

It was as if he'd said nothing about the prisoners, and who he was or why he had come from Jerusalem did not matter. Yosef knew he must take an indirect path. "To learn more about Rome... and for Rome to learn more about my people and, I hope, to take my countrymen home with me."

Nero stood, drawing all to their feet. "I think it is important that you," the smile that curled his lips revealed the edges of teeth, "... and your people should learn about Rome... and its might. You shall remain with us for a while." Without looking around, he held out his arm, and Poppaea stepped forward to take it. As they walked away from them, the glance she cast over her shoulder at Cleo was meaningless to Yosef. But Cleo now had a concerned look of her own.

The Roman nobleman who had joined them to sit next to Cleo stepped around her, toward Yosef. The man looked at Nero's receding back and then at Yosef. "So, Rome thanks you for saving Lady Cleopatra." He took Cleo's arm in his, holding it loosely. His eyes went to her and studied her expression. He raised an eyebrow and inclined his head toward Yosef.

Cleo's face was smooth... with no smile, no sign of what she was thinking. "Yosef, this is Gessius Florus. He and I are to wed."

"Soon..." Florus shifted his look from her, and his eyes drilled into Yosef, who felt the sharp edges of the man's ego. "The Lady Cleopatra and I have something in common," the man's smile was even sharper than Nero's, more like that of the sharks they had faced in the sea, "... a great interest in Judea."

Florus's grip tightened on Cleo's forearm, and Yosef could see something—a gleam—behind his hard stare. Yosef had seen that glow—avarice—before, in some leaders in Jerusalem, just not as naked.

XIV

ROME

The next morning, Yosef rose from his tangled bedding. Not from dreams, the sleepless night came from thinking and having—for the first time—doubts of his ability to communicate and get people to listen to him. At fourteen, first the Lesser then the Greater Sanhedrin had recognized him for his understanding of Jewish law and his fluency in articulating and explaining nuances that supported or clarified rulings and debates. He recalled standing before a seated arc of them—seventy-one venerated priest-judges—in the Hall of Hewn Stone. Some of those he had first met that day twelve years ago and two thousand miles from Rome were now imprisoned in this city. This he thought of as he stood looking out on a metropolis grand beyond his imaginings. Those priests were out there somewhere in Rome—and he'd never get anyone to pay attention.

That was only part of what had kept him tossing and turning throughout the night. It seemed some—if not all—of what had transpired last evening contained layers of meaning he couldn't grasp—at least not yet. He had always been observant, with an eye for detail and an ear for the meaning behind words and how they were spoken. There was an undercurrent of tension between the two ladies and Nero. The fact that he had met the Roman emperor still astounded him. And he also met that man, Gessius Florus, Cleo was to wed. What caused that tension, Yosef could not fathom.

He rubbed his eyes and turned from the window. Maybe he had imagined it, perhaps it was that all of it—the sea, the wreck, their survival, the rescue... and now Rome—maybe it was all too much to absorb in such a short time. He glanced toward the corner at his cot, and its pile of twisted blankets called to him. He was tired, but ignored the bed and reached for the baked-clay water jar and basin to wash his face. Finding them empty, he picked up the jar and went downstairs.

The cauponae's well was conveniently dug in the inner courtyard. As Yosef stepped into bright sunlight, he left the chill of the main floor behind him. He had wrestled with sleep—and lost—for longer than he thought. The morning sun had climbed over the building's roofline to slant down full upon the courtyard. He felt the sun's warmth on his shoulders and back as he drew water from the well's depths. He brought the bucket up and used the attached wooden ladle to let a quick drink soothe his dry throat.

"*Ahem...*"

Yosef heard that uncertain sound he now associated with the innkeeper—he used it when speaking to those who were not slaves but not Romans, either. Next to the man was a slim, fair-haired boy wearing a tunic, brilliant white in the sunlight, of the same type he had seen the night before—the kind servants and slaves of highborn Romans wore. In his hands, the boy held a rectangular piece of wood he attempted to shade with his body.

"Yes, innkeeper?" Yosef nodded at him.

The man nudged the boy in his direction. "Another message for you."

The boy stepped closer and raised the object to Yosef.

"Who is it from?" Yosef took from the boy two wooden frames joined on one side. He looked up at the boy, who had not answered him. The boy shook his head and pointed at his mouth.

"The boy's tongue's been taken," the innkeeper scratched his eyebrow and shifted his weight from one foot to the other.

"Taken?" Yosef looked from the boy to the man, who shrugged as if that were a common thing.

"Cut out... either the boy talks—talked—too much or maybe he cried too much as a child." The innkeeper shrugged again.

Yosef looked at the boy, his golden locks forming a curly cap crowning his head. He was a handsome teen whose bright blue eyes now seemed dimmed by clouds. He might not speak, but he could hear.

"He had this..." The innkeeper held a scrap of parchment with Yosef's name on it in Latin and Greek. "He's waiting for a reply from you." The man nodded at the boy.

Yosef opened the two wooden halves to find that the right-hand side had a wax tablet inset. This top half of it was inscribed with a message to him in Greek. "Yosef, if you can join us—just myself, Nicanor and Sayid—this evening after sundown, write 'Yes' below, and I'll send a carriage for you." Underneath it was a large Greek letter Kappa. He knew quickly this was K for the Greek spelling of Kleopatra. He took the stylus that was held within a deep notch in the left-hand frame and noted a YES, signing it below with the letter I, Iota, the initial for his name in Greek. Closing the framed tablet, he handed it to the boy and felt his return gaze for just a moment. Then the boy turned and hurried from the courtyard. Yosef picked up the jar of water he had rested at his feet and straightened up with it.

The innkeeper was scratching again, his chest this time, as he studied Yosef. "Two messages, in your first two days... from two noblewomen... hmmm."

* * *

This two-man carriage was different, but the route was similar until it continued straight where it had turned the night before. Still, not too much further on it angled toward a lower rise, then up a shorter hedge-lined lane to stop at a less imposing domus than Nero's. But Cleo's home was still the grand and massive residence of a prominent Roman. As his carriage came to a stop, only one male servant—an older man with close-cropped gray-bristled hair visible in the light of a lantern he carried chest high—met him.

"Welcome, sir. I'll take you to the lady." The slave carried himself with the ease and self-awareness of someone who had served long and was appreciated and trusted by those whom he served.

Yosef followed him into the vestibulum and through halls and rooms less decorative than Poppaea and Nero's, but still splendid in their simple adornment. The man stopped at a central portico entrance to a large open courtyard, the perimeter of which was tiled with large squares of polished stone. At its center was a large fountain surrounded by a wide circular swath of grass that somehow still bore a trace of color in winter. A square formed by corner chairs separated by small tables was arranged in front of the fountain. Each chair and table combination was warmed by large bronze bowls full of burning wood. Aromatic smoke rose in ribbons that twined up into the starry sky. A woman sat alone in the nearest chair, facing the closest fire bowl with her back to him. He looked at the servant still beside him.

"You may go to her, sir. There is" —he gestured at the laden tables— "a variety of drink and food for your pleasure." He turned and walked back the way they had come.

"Don't you wish to join me?"

Yosef turned to Cleo and smiled without thinking. The robe she wore was a deep blue that flashed its richness as she moved and the flickering flames glinted on its costly threads. The murmur of water spilling from the fountain in the chill night air recalled that night at sea he had spent talking to her. He had thought it would be the last time he would speak with anyone, and he had felt it—what he told her—should be honest, from the heart.

"Lady Cleopatra," Yosef started toward her then stopped, "where are the others?" He was unsure about being alone—he a non-Roman—with a Roman noblewoman, even if in such a private setting and at her request. Or a Jewish man alone with a Gentile woman for that matter.

"They should be here soon." Cleo bent to pour wine from a carafe into two elegant, Argentum goblets that gleamed in the fire's light. Handing one to him, she gestured at the chair next to hers, then looked up. "Aren't the stars beautiful?" Her glance switched from them to Yosef.

He took a sip of wine—his first since at sea—and studied her. Her face was turned up again to the blanket of the night sky, points of light spread across it and created a celestial ceiling fresco unmatched by any artist. Illuminated by the shifting flames, her neck was a finely shaped, rose-tinted pillar that emerged from the dark robe that framed her shoulders and upper chest. At the sound of footsteps on stone, they both turned.

"Your man said to walk right in, Lady Cleo." Nicanor's gruff tone sounded pleased. "On my way in I spotted this boy and thought it best to not let him wander around alone and get into mischief." Behind his broad back, Sayid leaned out to smile at them. Nicanor poured a large portion of wine for himself and a smaller one for Sayid, handed it to him, and then sat down with a grumble. "This," he tugged at his tunic, "is much better than that thing last night... much more comfortable."

* * *

The moon had risen high above them now. Although he was glad to see them, especially Cleo, and although he enjoyed the wine and his freedom, Yosef could not help but think of the men he knew who were locked away staring at seeping stone above them instead of stars. And back in Jerusalem, under a Judean procurator like Luccieus Albinus, the Zealots and Sicarii were becoming emboldened by a tragic combination of rising discontent and threats the procurator could not back up... yet. So, while he stood in a Roman garden on a clear night, storm clouds were building in Judea.

"I didn't realize you were entertaining guests this evening."

Just before turning toward the voice, Yosef saw Cleo's eyes close, and her head dip to her chest before rising again. The man, though wearing a purple-trimmed toga signifying his high rank, was not very impressive. They all stood as he approached.

"Father, these are the men who saved me." Cleo introduced each of them.

Yosef noted how the Roman's response—not exuberant to begin with—dwindled from Nicanor to Sayid... to him. The man did not meet Yosef's eyes, which would have required that he look up. He barely acknowledged him. Even in the fluttering light from torches and fire bowls, he could see in his pained look the disdain he held for Cleo's plebeian friends.

"It's late," her father said, and with the last sweep of a severe look, he left them with the hint.

After a moment's silence, Cleo apologized. "I thought he was away."

"Well," Nicanor said, setting his empty cup on the table, "he's right. It is late, and we should go."

"Lady Cleo," Sayid said, concerned about seeing her father sitting with her, "do you need anything before I go to my quarters?"

"No, thank you, Sayid."

The boy nodded his goodbye and goodnight to Nicanor and Yosef as he walked away.

Cleo looked at Nicanor and Yosef. "I'll have carriages called for both of you." She beckoned to the gray-haired servant who had remained at the entrance to the courtyard.

"Lady, if you don't mind," Nicanor turned to Yosef, "you're south toward the gate at Porta Capena, right?" Yosef nodded, and Nicanor turned back to Cleo. "Then one carriage should do. I'm near where Yosef is staying."

* * *

It was quiet in the carriage except for the clop of the horses' hooves and the ring of iron wheels on stone. Yosef shifted on the bench seat to half-turn toward Nicanor. "Do you think Lady Cleo's father would help me?"

"With what? Your imprisoned priests?" Nicanor shook his head. "Why would you think that?"

Yosef squirmed inside and out. "Well, I helped save his daughter, and Nero wants to reward me." The words tasted sour in his mouth, but he had to do something. He had to find someone to help them get home.

"If you try, expect little." Nicanor snorted and spat out the window. "I'm Roman... but these people," he flipped his hand at the view passing by outside the window, "he—Lady Cleo's father—is a Rome Roman. They're different." He leaned out the window as they came to a stop. "Nice place you're staying at," he raised an eyebrow. "I've been told to rest and relax," he said, leaning back with a grunt. "You should try that... and this," he waved a hand at the entrance to the cauponae, "is a much finer place to do that than where I sleep."

XV

ROME

A week had passed, and Yosef's attempts to connect with any official that could help him had proved fruitless. The season of Roman festivals was upon them, so, he walked the city. With the sunrise the third morning after their meeting at Cleo's, he set out heading north and west. He came upon the Circus Maximus and knew he was approaching the city center and the area of palaces and nobles. As wide lanes narrowed into a market area full of vendors and sellers of almost everything Rome offered from its far-flung empire, he realized he was famished and looked around for a place to eat.

* * *

"Gorgeous, don't you think, Cleo?" Poppaea dangled a string before her. "See how they have an iridescent sheen in the sun."

"They are lovely." Cleo admired the colors that rippled along the pearls' surface, the linea margaritum. "These are from the Red Sea, I believe." But Cleo did not enjoy shopping as much as Poppaea did, and particularly now as everyone clamored for the empress's attention. She much preferred the Poppaea who had started out as her sister-in-law when Poppaea had been married to her brother Marcus and became not just an older sister but a best friend. Then Nero had schemed to take her from Marcus, his friend—forcing him into a divorce so Nero could have Poppaea—and much had changed. Cleo scanned the crowd just beyond Poppaea's escorts, who served as a buffer from the people on the street. A man a head taller than those around him, with dark, thick wavy hair, caught her eye. He turned and the line of his brow, nose, and jaw, the trimmed beard, took her breath. *Yosef!* Perhaps the gods had made it so, but since that night at sea on the raft, just the two of them under the stars, when he had bared his soul, talking to her through the night as an equal—since then she had realized how different a man could be from the Roman men she knew.

"Cleo?"

She moved in front of Poppaea to block her friend's view of the street. Her knowing smile whenever Cleo mentioned Yosef was irritating. Cleo did not want her to see him there so close. And she did not need the complication that Poppaea had suggested to her that morning: "You marry for the position, for status, Cleo," then that smile had bloomed on her face, "... and you take a lover... for other things." But that's not how Cleo felt, not how she could treat her emotions. That wasn't what she wanted from life. She knew of her mother's regrets about her own marriage and her grandmother's claim that regret had sickened her daughter, leading to an early death.

"Cleo!" Poppaea wasn't asking now, "That's your Yosef!" She tapped her centurion escort on the arm—"Bring that man to us." She pointed toward the street, at Yosef.

The centurion barked an order to two men. They went after the wrong man.

"No!" Poppaea corrected them, shaking her head and pointing. "The tall one."

* * *

The legionaries had cleared the tabernae, and now the two women and Yosef were its only customers. Not long before, Yosef had been lost in a maze of streets and wondering at the size and sprawl of Rome that had overwhelmed him as he noted the squalor of tenements amid the grandeur. Now he sat with a plate of food before him, the likes of which he had never seen, much less tasted. He wondered if it were kosher, although he had finally given up trying to keep to that law while in Rome. And more incredibly, he was sitting with the wife of the Roman emperor and her best friend—who, he was sure, he had fallen for before he had even met her. It was madness. He must be mad. Why is it the women he was attracted to were always married—or engaged to be—and this one from the Gentile nobility? There was a strong taboo in his religious circle for Jewish men to get involved with Gentile women. And this was all a distraction from his main mission here.

"What makes you shake your head, Yosef?" Poppaea leaned forward and studied him.

Yosef smiled. She seemed to want to know what he thought and had qualities that made him understand how she and Cleo had become friends. "At all this, your ladyship."

"This tabernae?" Poppaea smiled at Yosef to let him know she knew what he meant and then glanced sideways at Cleo, who was intent on her food, though it looked more pushed around then eaten.

Yosef couldn't help but return her smile. "I don't know how to explain, your ladyship. Where to start." He shrugged.

"Start what?"

The smile dropped from his face, and she did not understand. "With what I told your husband, my lady. How I can get to speak with my imprisoned countrymen and how to open a discussion about freeing them to return to Jerusalem with me. They are not enemies of Rome, your highness." It was the truth, but Yosef could not tell her that their imprisonment, along with the worsening actions of the Roman procurator Albinus, was creating enemies and solidifying his people's hatred for Rome.

Poppaea did not reply. She seemed to be in thought—or perhaps was just uncaring—as Yosef ate some of the strange food. After a while, despite Cleo's outward discomfort, small talk resumed, and soon Yosef dismissed himself, feeling despondent at another day gone with nothing of importance resolved or even said.

* * *

A rough hand shaking his shoulder woke Yosef the next morning. He squinted and saw that a bare sliver of sun was peeking through the window of his room at the cauponae.

"What the... who...?"

"Get up, Yosef. I'm waking you far more gently than I was awakened an hour ago."

Yosef looked up at Nicanor in full dress uniform and armor. "What?"

"Get up now if you want to see them." He handed Yosef the tunic he had found draped over a chair. "Follow me now, or I'll leave. Orders be damned, I'm not a nursemaid or lackey."

Minutes later downstairs, Yosef saw the donkey cart on the street and felt the innkeeper's eyes go from him to the centurion. Nicanor climbed up and took the reins. "It's the only thing I could find at this hour," Nicanor said, offering Yosef a hand up.

"What?" Yosef was still half-asleep.

Nicanor scowled at him. "You say that a lot." He snapped the reins up and down across the back of the ass, which got it moving. "I've been ordered to escort you."

"Where?"

Nicanor turned to him, and the slanting sunlight caught the gray stubble on his slab of unshaven jaw. "What? Where?" He mocked Yosef with only a half-joking tone. "The where... is to the Tullianum. It is the carcer, the prison, where your priest friends are being detained while awaiting trial." He held up a hand. "Don't ask me why

Yosef. I'm just following orders." He let out a deep sigh. "You must've found someone with authority to help you."

"Who?" It came out before Yosef could stop it. He saw Nicanor shake his head and not say anything, but Yosef knew it must be Cleo, or perhaps Poppaea.

* * *

Nicanor had taken a wide loop around the outer wall of Rome to reenter the city in the northeast section near Capitoline Hill. He had referred to a scroll with a map of the city and notes for directions.

"This area is the Comitium"—his hand waved to span a large, open-air amphitheater sun into the ground. "This was the original public meeting space of the Roman Senate," he pointed with a thumb at a nearby structure, "there's their meetinghouse." He turned and faced back toward the northeast, pointing into the distance. "And there on the slope facing us is the prison."

An hour later, they had entered the prison, and Yosef understood the purpose of Nicanor's full regalia. His commanding bearing had brought the administrator of the jail to attend to them. "Read this," Nicanor had said, handing him another scroll with its red blob of a seal intact, the wax recent enough to not have become brittle and flaked off. Stepping closer, Yosef studied it before the official broke the wax to unroll the parchment. He had seen the design before—on the signet ring that he'd seen on her hand just the day before.

"As the Empress Poppaea Augusta Sabina commands—take them to the Jewish prisoners." Two guards came forward.

Minutes later, Yosef had been lowered from the prison's main floor and now waited for Nicanor, who had insisted on joining him.

* * *

The dungeon was dank and dark, lighted intermittently by clay lamps that burned poor-quality oil that sputtered and spat hot drops that caught him unawares. Yosef rubbed the stinging, scorched spots on his neck and cheek that he had received from standing too close.

The prisoners, in a single cell that stank of urine and excrement, were gaunt and pale. They did not show signs of beating or abuse but were weakened by hunger. One—Yosef did not know him—was healthier and more alert than the others. When Yosef announced himself, the man waved him closer, first glancing at Nicanor, who remained impassively standing where he was with brawny arms crossed. As Yosef came to the bars of the cell, the man spoke: "I know of you, Yosef—from your father. You can work with some Romans.

Try to find the ones who can, if handled in the right manner, make arrangements to free us."

Recalling the introduction to Cleo's husband-to-be, Yosef thought that if she were reluctant to speak to her father, perhaps she would arrange a meeting with Gessius Florus. She was marrying him, after all, and maybe he was such a Roman as the imprisoned man spoke of, one who had influence and could grant favors.

* * *

The brisk wind made Yosef draw his cloak tighter around him, but he blinked up into the sun and appreciated the daylight after an hour in a murky, smelly hole without it. As he and Nicanor climbed back on the donkey cart, Yosef felt that at least he now had a direction. He hoped to see Cleo soon... and that she would see him and help.

They rode in silence for quite a while, and then without looking at Yosef, Nicanor spoke, his tone edged with distaste: "Men—unless it's proven they committed crimes to justify such punishment—should not be confined in such a place."

"That must be the Greek half of you," Yosef commented, surprised at Nicanor sharing that thought, but then they had faced death together. "Thank you for taking me to them and for going down in that hole with me."

Nicanor grunted, "I was ordered to." He gave Yosef a brief glance and then went back to studying the road ahead. "And I've been ordered to begin—tomorrow—showing you Rome's military. The Roman part of me is to make sure you realize the power of the empire."

XVI

The next morning Yosef expected him, and he was waiting as Nicanor entered the cauponae.

"Good. You're ready." He spun on his heel to go back through the door he had just entered.

Yosef followed him out to the street to find him about to climb up on one of two horses—they seemed very tall to Yosef, who was used to donkeys. Nicanor handed Yosef the reins to the second, then mounted himself and settled into the saddle. He stared down at Yosef, who still stood there looking from the horse to up at Nicanor.

"Well, what are you waiting for?" Nicanor looked at Yosef. "Up you go—I have a lot to show you today."

Yosef stepped to his horse's side and hesitated. "I've never ridden a horse." He looked at Nicanor and then at the four-pommeled Roman saddle. How was it that Nicanor got his leg up and over that?

"You jest." Nicanor shook his head and shifted his horse a step sideways to give Yosef more room.

"Never. Just a donkey with a blanket across its back, and only a few times at that. We usually walk or ride in a cart." Yosef shrugged.

Nicanor dismounted with a scowl but showed Yosef how to get up on the horse and in the saddle.

"Where are we going?" Yosef let go the breath he had held as he climbed up on the horse.

"First, to the manufactories." Nicanor's horse moved, and Yosef's followed. "The armorers, weapons, and siege engines."

"Do they supply all the empire?"

Nicanor laughed. "No. Most provinces and legions stationed there have their own suppliers if they have raw materials available—though sometimes if quality or quantity is an issue, equipment comes from another province or from here." Nicanor thought of his dagger—the pugio that had belonged to his father—now resting in the carcass of a shark at the bottom of the Ionian. "And many legions and legionaries have equipment and weapons—still good and serviceable—that have been handed down or left by the dead for new recruits to use. So, new equipment is usually for replacements of damaged, destroyed, or lost equipment."

"How many men are in a legion?"

"Between five thousand and six thousand men."

"Do they all ride horses?"

Nicanor grunted. "No, that's heavy infantry. Cavalry—horseback soldiers—come from the auxiliary and conscripts."

"How man legions are there in the Roman army?"

Nicanor blew through his lips, a loud horse-like sound that made Yosef mount's ears twitch. "It usually varies between twenty-five and thirty now. There used to be more under Julius Caesar and Augustus."

* * *

An hour later, coming down the rise of a low hill, Nicanor and Yosef came upon a large open area filled with men. Before them were groups of legionaries with sword, spear, or javelin and bow and arrow, separated according to the equipment they worked with and the drills. Nicanor waved an arm, covering the entire field. "This is a regular morning in the Roman army. Men train every day."

The clang of metal on metal, the grunts, and curses of men, sometimes disjointed and often in concert, rang across the field. To that point, Yosef had let his horse follow Nicanor's and not done much in the way of directing it, but he wanted to look closer. Having seen Nicanor do it, he nudged his horse with both heels and, using the reins, angled it on downward and toward where men were swinging swords.

"Something interest you?" Nicanor followed Yosef and saw his hands tighten on the reins. "Lean back a bit more in the saddle when you're heading downhill—don't pull his head in or back toward you. Trust that your horse will watch his steps."

Yosef nodded and loosened his grip, kept his weight evenly balanced in the saddle and canted his torso backward, which stopped his fear he would spill forward over the horse's head. "My brother, Matthew," he said, "when we would spar, would always get the better of me with our wooden swords." Yosef shook his head and wondered what Matthew and his family were doing. He looked at Nicanor. "I've never been good at that sort of thing."

Nicanor studied Yosef and saw someone he had—unexpectedly—learned to respect. And even though he needed to reflect on it more before he was sure, someone he considered a friend. "Is that something you'd like to change?" he asked.

"How would I?"

Nicanor shrugged. "I think I told you not to expect much by way of action in response to what you hope to accomplish here in Rome. So, it's likely we have more time to pass than either you or I would wish. If you want and are interested"—Nicanor scratched an eyebrow beneath his helmet's brow ridge and settled it more comfortably on his head—"I'll train you each morning." His gaze went from Yosef to the men on the field. "Besides, I'll sit around and get fat and rusty if I don't do something like that." He grinned at Yosef.

* * *

After the first few days of showing him training and Roman manufacturing facilities—the siege engines were impressive—Nicanor worked with Yosef each morning. Two weeks after they had started, Yosef had gotten better—smoother and more confident in his handling of the sword.

Nicanor looked beyond Yosef to where the sun was approaching midday as they sparred. "Who can that be?" He raised a hand, palm out, motioning to Yosef to stop and step back. They watched as a rider that had accompanied the four-wheeled carriage approached them. He must be a servant with some authority since he was on a horse.

"The lady wishes to speak with the two of you," the man said, gesturing back at the carriage.

Nicanor and Yosef followed him, and as they approached and stopped, a woman's hand drew the side curtain away as she leaned forward to look out the window. "Centurion"—a smile curled her lips as her eyes shifted from him—"... you and Yosef—please join us for lunch." Poppaea leaned back, and from his angle, Nicanor could now see that the other woman in the carriage was Cleo, who sat with her arms crossed and was not looking pleased.

With just a glance at Yosef, Nicanor agreed. Just as at their welcoming, one did not refuse an invitation from the emperor's wife. In silence, he and Yosef followed the carriage.

* * *

"Centurion, I see you were teaching our Jewish friend." Poppaea looked from Nicanor to Yosef. "Why?"

"My lady"—Yosef answered before Nicanor could—"he does so because I asked."

"Interesting." Her eyes went from Yosef back to Nicanor, who looked uncomfortable. "But I guess it's good—as my husband mentioned—for Yosef to see the empire's army up close, even including such close attention paid him by one of our centurions."

75

"I'm thankful for the empire's—for your—hospitality and for Nicanor's courtesy, my lady."

Through lunch and the chatting afterward, Cleo—despite it being her domus Poppaea had taken them to—had said little, evading Poppaea's attempts to draw her into the conversation. Ignoring them, she had fed bits of bread to a colorful bird, feathers of green and blue with a splash of red, in a cage of silver with a gold base inlaid with tortoise-shell and ivory.

"And have you reached the point with the sword where you will switch to another weapon... and, say"—her eyes danced to some private thought—"learn the bow and arrow?"

"I don't plan to extend the training that far, my lady," Nicanor answered.

"Are you good with a bow, centurion?" Poppaea asked.

"I'm... adequate, my lady. But I'm more comfortable with the sword."

"Well, perhaps we should have someone who is skilled train our friend." Poppaea leaned forward as if to stand.

"No, don't"—Cleo reached out a hand toward her.

Poppaea stood and left them with Cleo trailing behind her, asking her to stop.

They returned minutes later. Poppaea held a bow and a quiver containing a bundle of green- and blue-feather-fletched arrows in her hand. "If you if you want to learn the bow, Yosef, perhaps Lady Cleopatra can instruct you." Cleo had gone quiet, standing there unhappy with Poppaea. "Come, follow me."

They followed her through Cleo's house, to and through the inner courtyard from their evening meeting, to exit onto a broad landscaped span of lawn. Off to the right was set a target beyond a set of parallel lines that marked off distance. Poppaea stopped at the furthermost line from the target—the one closest to them. "Show them, Cleo, and perhaps if the centurion doesn't mind, you and he can have a little match."

Cleo shook her head in resignation. After a moment of uncomfortable silence—exceptionally so for the men—Nicanor stepped forward and took the bow from Poppaea. "If the lady wishes." He bowed to her and then to Cleo.

Checking the bow, the tautness and fit of the string, Nicanor took an arrow and nocked it. Not using the thumb ring that dangled from the quiver, he pulled the string back and let fly. The arrow struck the target, low center.

"That would surely injure, centurion." Poppaea smiled, then took the bow from him and handed it to Cleo. "Will you try?"

Cleo took the bow and hung it over a forearm as she took a leather wrist guard and the thumb ring from the quiver. Slipping them on, she stepped to the same distance as Nicanor and in one smooth motion nocked an arrow, drew the string, and released. The bolt struck the precise center of the target. Chest, heart high, if it had been a man.

"I told you!" Poppaea clapped her hands and laughed. "I told you she would be a good instructor, Yosef."

XVII

The slave took Gessius Florus through many of the halls and galleries he had passed through on that recent evening when he welcomed home Lady Cleo. The day revealed more of the grandeur of the palace. The fountain in the large public room was much larger in the sunlight streaming through windows set high in the walls and spilling in from the column-framed entrance to a private courtyard off the main hall.

As he stepped into the courtyard, Florus noticed Praetorian Guards were in the far four corners and another one pacing the perimeter, keeping a straight line from point to point. All wore full battle armor and swords and carried pila. Florus had seen legionaries cast the two-meter-long iron-shanked and iron-tipped javelin with such force that it penetrated body armor and shields—a deadly weapon at a distance. The four legionaries also had bows slung, at the ready. The centurion carried a sling, long leather thongs twined in his hand, no doubt with several lead bullets in a fold of his cloak. He had seen a deadly attack from a sling at a distance, too.

At the center of the courtyard was a small fountain, two chairs facing each other with side tables, and an L-shaped divan, its low back lined with cushions for reclining. A nobleman in a purple-trimmed patrician's toga stood facing the fountain, his back to Florus. Next to him was the largest man Florus had ever seen, a slave nearly seven feet tall and twice as wide as an ordinary man, shifting his stance and then standing still to watch Florus approach.

"I've learned about you..." the nobleman said, without turning.

"You sent for me, Your Highness?" Florus stopped ten feet from him, noting that the giant had moved closer to Rome's emperor.

Nero turned, a goblet of wine in his hand. "Yes, Gessius." He took two steps and sat in the larger, more decorative chair and lifted a goblet brimful of wine from the table beside it. "Sit." He flicked a hand at Florus and then at the second chair.

"I'm honored, sire." Florus hesitated as the giant slave positioned himself behind the chair, he had been directed to sit in. The man's pillar-thick legs spread shoulder wide, and he rested his fists, the size of men's heads, on his hips. Florus sat and resisted the urge to look over his shoulder and up... and up... at the impassive craggy face of the slave.

"We'll talk privately." Nero drank and then set the empty cup on the table.

Florus gauged the distance to the guard's positions and the marching centurion. They were too far to hear anything said. He couldn't help it and half-turned his head and up to look at the man who cast such a large shadow over him.

"The brute is deaf and dumb"—Nero's tone was dismissive, then he continued: "A tool, a force to be sure, with the strength of five men—but controlled." Nero gestured above and behind him, and Florus followed where he pointed. A second-floor balcony protruded over the courtyard, and behind its low marble balustrade were a white-haired woman and a young girl wearing rough, gray slave tunics. Behind them stood two legionaries, their short swords drawn and flashing in the sun.

"His mother and his daughter?" Florus asked. "Your Highness?" He dropped his eyes to Nero's.

"Mother and sister... the brute is a eunuch."

Florus nodded. "How can I serve you, Your Highness?"

"You have proven to be one of the most effective quaestors in the empire."

"Thank you—" But Florus stopped at the expression on Nero's face and felt a trickle of sweat form on his brow. He did not move to wipe it away.

Nero continued: "Tax revenue has at least doubled in the provinces you were assigned... that alone drew my attention. But then the Lady Cleo's father also mentioned you." Nero's jeweled left hand rose, and two fingers tapped his lips. "Being that he is a loyal Roman and father of my wife's best friend, I listened to him." His thumb, replacing the fingers, pulled at his lower lip. "He told me you and she had an interest in each other." He studied Florus, who nodded without speaking. "So, bringing you to Rome, and Cleo back home, serves my purpose"—Nero paused and lowered his hand—"and may reward you both."

Florus did not know if he meant the reward was for Cleo, her father, or himself, and watched as Nero's hand flicked and the looming shadow behind him moved. From the corner of his eye, he saw a tree limb of an arm reach for the jar on the table and pour wine into Nero's cup. Another flick from Nero and he filled the second cup. Setting the jar down, he handed Nero's to him and slid the other closer to Florus, who waited for Nero to drink before taking the cup and speaking. "My lord, how can I serve you?"

"I see a much grander Rome, more befitting my rule, with new and better construction, especially to replace the older, poorer quarter of the city."

Florus had risen high in Roman administrative ranks through his shrewdness, and now, sitting before the emperor, he had learned the importance of not speaking too quickly. He stilled the hand that twitched to wipe his face as he waited.

Nero smiled. "What do you think? What would be the cost of such an undertaking?"

Understanding there was more than one answer to that question, he paused a moment to consider his response. "A substantial cost, Your Highness." And that answer, too, had a dual meaning.

"Yes, to be sure." The emperor's fingers were back up to his lips and tapping. "Is there a way to do in Rome what you have done in the provinces?"

Populated predominantly by subjugated people, the provinces had been squeezed hard. Florus also knew that doing the same here, at the empire's center, would be a far different matter. The denizens of Rome, many of whom were actual Roman citizens with long lineages, would not stand for increased taxes for such a purpose. "Sire, the increase in levy would likely raise dissent... of a most unfortunate kind." Florus took a gamble and continued: "And there's much of that already in the provinces."

He paused at Nero's sharp look and then pushed on: "To provoke it here... wouldn't be wise." He took another breath. "Your Highness"—he raised the wine to his dry lips, feeling Nero's studied look that faded and then turned from him. In the silence, Florus heard the rustle of the wind as it carried over the roofline and swirled in the courtyard. Now was the moment to leverage the attention he had hoped would come from interesting Cleo's father in a marriage to his daughter. Florus had found her appealing once he learned of her friendship with Poppaea. But he had also learned the threads of such connections would not bear much weight or strain. Florus had taken care to concoct events that would earn a response that furthered his agenda for self-enrichment.

None of his machinations had been as risky as this, so he tugged lightly on the delicate one in his hands now. "Your Highness, what if"—he let Nero's attention swing back to him—"In a natural disaster is it not true, sire, that Rome—its citizens—would pull together to rebuild?"

"Yes. Doing so for the common good is a burden many shoulders of many Romans would carry. It's a legacy of the republic."

"I think so, too, sire. What if Rome experienced such a calamity?"

"Like the ground shaking some of the empire has experienced, causing damage in provincial cities?"

"Exactly sire, but—"

"—No one knows when that will happen"—Nero cut him off, scoffing, and his eyes shaded toward disinterest. "If it ever will happen, here in Rome. And there's no way to confine or control such a thing." His eyes went flat as he looked away again.

Sensing he was close to being dismissed, delegated to the disregarded, Florus leaned forward quickly, raising his hands to emphasize his words. He ignored the giant as he tensed at the sudden movement toward his ruler and brought his large hands up to either side of Florus's neck. "What if, sire, what if it was a different disaster?"

Nero's head slowly turned back to lock eyes on Florus. "What do you mean?"

"An orchestrated one, Your Highness." Florus could see the gleam of interest rekindle in Nero's eyes.

"Such as?"

Nero's tone strengthened Florus's belief that the timing was right. "The gift, sire, told of by the Greeks... that boon to Man—fire."

The fingers touched royal lips but did not move until Nero spoke behind them. "Could it be controlled?"

"Much—if not all—of what you envision can be accomplished. That area you wish to rebuild will readily burn and can then be cleared easily for reconstruction. Men can be found to guide that fire, keeping it where it is wanted, and other parts of the city," Florus's gaze swept the courtyard seeing beyond it and the walls that bound it, and came back to Nero, "can be protected."

* * *

"Gessius!" Poppaea called out, surprised at seeing him arrive unannounced within the Domus Transitoria. Her eyes went from Florus's back to the servant accompanying him, who had turned to her and then ducked his head from her gaze. When Florus turned, she saw a sudden shift of his eyes and an expression that transformed into a smile that did not reach his eyes.

"Your Highness... Lady Poppaea, so good to see you."

"Yes, you, too, but it seems"—her gaze swung beyond him, to the direction he had been headed, toward the entrance to her husband's private rooms—"it seems I almost didn't."

His smile remained but sharpened, the lines that ran along his aquiline nose tightening. "The emperor sent a message for me to join him, my lady." He half-bowed.

"Why so late in the evening?" She could see his body language signal he had been inclined to turn from her after the exchange of greetings but had stopped. A sign of an odd reluctance to extend the conversation when he always been more than willing to chat before.

"I'm not sure, my lady." He glanced over at the slave who had brought him through the domus, who now stood—face discreetly angled down—near the emperor's room entry. "But perhaps I should go and..."

"Yes, of course. Do not keep my husband waiting." She let them go.

"Thank you, and good evening, my lady." Florus spun on a heel and followed the slave.

"Hmmm..." Poppaea murmured thoughtfully as she turned toward her own private quarters and paused. Scanning around her to be sure no servants were near, she quickly changed direction and walked to a nearby room, then through it to the portico of the tiled stone terrace that ran along Nero's private courtyard to the double doors of Nero's private rooms. Wrapping the robe more tightly around her, she slipped off her sandals and stepped out onto the cold stone. A minute later she was listening through the door she had slightly opened to her ear's width.

"You will not be connected to it, sire..." she heard Florus say. "I understand your concern, and it will appear to be nothing more than an accident." There was a moment of silence, and the sound of footsteps on the stone within grew louder. Poppaea readied to close the door and slip away, but then the steps stopped.

"You mentioned something in our previous meeting," Nero said, "about other sources of gold for the taking and circumstances being right to do so with justification." His voice belied the tension that prompted the need, layered beneath his words, and Poppaea knew how he felt. His spending had drained Rome, and he and she often argued about it.

"Yes, sire." Florus's voice grew louder as he now came toward her; she stiffened and gripped the door. "Gold and silver, in the hands of rebels. Taking it from them—a punitive measure—and crushing them, that could reduce the taxes or certainly lessen any increases borne by Romans."

"You're thinking of my Judean problem?"

"Yes, sire. I have connections through the southern and eastern parts of the empire. The temples of their religion contain much treasure."

The wind picked up, chilling Poppaea even through her thick robe and making it harder for her to hear. A frigid ache had climbed above her now-numb feet, and she shivered at its slow crawl up her legs.

"Poppaea has told me how much Cleo enjoys that region. Perhaps—once you are wed—I'll assign you there. I need a new procurator in Judea. Someone of a like mind, who'll protect my—and his own—interests. But only after what's done here, something near at hand. We have to act just as you have convinced me. Yes?"

"Yes, sire."

"And you are certain there will be no way it will be traced to us."

"Yes, sire. If the need arises, I have an idea who can be blamed and bear the consequences. There is a cult that refuses to acknowledge the gods'—and your—divine nature and ascribes it instead to their own leader. Their numbers have been growing, and it would be easy to blame them."

Cold shudders wracked Poppaea as she closed the door and hurried across the terrace and then inside. She knew the man she had married, his callous cruelty and depravity. Now she wondered about the other man in the room—the one her husband claimed was so like-minded. She had encouraged her best—her only—friend Cleo to marry him.

XVIII

"I wish it were over," Cleo said over her shoulder as she led Poppaea to her private atrium, nodding with a slight smile at Sayid as they passed him at the entrance to her domus.

Poppaea had been excited to be the hostess for Cleo's wedding—and would have chided her to look forward to it—but now had misgivings at what she had overheard between her husband and Cleo's soon-to-be husband. The joy of planning the festivities and the ceremony in Antium had dimmed. She had suggested to Nero in small increments that Florus be assigned to Judea so it would become his own thought. This assignment would restore order and provide what Cleo wanted, a return to a region she loved more than Rome. But it worried Poppaea that the two men of similar mind had discussed so casually the possibility of someone to "bear the blame and consequences" of their decision. But she knew how to manage circumstances and men so she would watch what developed and guide Cleo accordingly.

"All will be fine. Remember, as I told you, to secure the man, marry him... then appease—or allow others to soothe—his inclinations. Then set your own ways, but carefully." Poppaea arranged her robe as she sat. "And always know what's going on around you."

"What do you mean? Have spies?" Cleo knew Poppaea had spies placed in different households, even in Cleo's.

"Just pay attention to Gessius, what he is up to—even more so once you're married."

"What would he be up to that I should watch for?"

"The key to getting what you want, happiness, is to know how to create it. That means knowing what's going on in your life and in your husband's life." Poppaea felt almost guilty at saying that, because, for the first time, she knew Nero had set a course of action she did not yet know the details of nor understand, but she would find out. In the stillness, the soothing sound of water flowing into the impluvium, the central water basin in the atrium that served as the domus's cistern, ebbed and strengthened as the wind eddied through the opening in the roof. Poppaea noted the gilded cage close to the doorway of Cleo's bedchamber. Every morning she set the cage there with its door open so Cicero could come out onto the nearby roost and stretch his wings. "Have you taught him any new words since your return?"

"No, but he squawks in a peculiar way around Sayid."

"The Syrian boy you were rescued with?" Poppaea asked.

Cleo laughed. "Yes, I don't think they like each other."

Poppaea hadn't heard her laugh in a while. "Have you seen Yosef?"

"No. Not since you insisted on my archery demonstration."

"Don't you want to see him?"

"Poppaea, you admire the Jewish religion; your friend Aliturus, the actor, is one of them. And you know they cannot have a relationship outside their own religion. But I like Yosef."

"Just like?" Poppaea teased.

* * *

Florus had followed Cleo's father down the colonnade to his tablinum at the rear of the atrium and next to his own quarters. It was where he conducted his personal business. He heard voices carrying across the granite floor, and recognizing Poppaea's he paused. "Lucius, I'd like to step in," he gestured toward the atrium, "and say hello to Cleo and Lady Poppaea. I'll join you shortly." The older man continued to the exterior door into his room and went inside without looking back. Florus stepped closer to the side alcove and heard Cleo: "I know Yosef can't—won't—become more than just someone I *like*. I'm sure of that. We shouldn't even—not truly—become friends; he will leave for Judea as soon as he can, and we could never become lovers." Then Poppaea: "If you could, would you wish to be together, as lovers? Do you want that?" And Florus heard Cleo pause and reply— "Yes."

Florus considered Cleo's words. Theirs was to be a marriage of convenience—to him—but still a union. And above all, in every relationship he demanded respect. Cleo, not yet his wife, was already learning a woman's wiles from Poppaea. He would not have those deceits used on him. He had noticed the look exchanged—between Cleo and the Jew—the night of her homecoming party at the Domus Transitoria. Cleo was his link and access to Poppaea, and through her, Nero. But he did not need the Jew; he would only complicate matters.

* * *

The city heat was oppressive in the summer, but the discussion of her upcoming wedding was even more so. That and Florus's increasing distraction and decreasing patience with her made Cleo wish to be away from Rome. She sighed, thankful that Poppaea had offered her the use of this, her private villa, outside the city.

Most Roman nobles she knew chose second homes—retreats—on the sea. Nero and Poppaea had one in Antium, south of Rome and on the coast. Antium was his birthplace and where he and Poppaea would host the wedding. But Poppaea had offered Cleo a different retreat in the area—her private villa more to the east, nestled between Ariccia and Diana's Mirror, the Speculum Dianae, a small lake about twenty miles from Rome.

There, Cleo enjoyed evenings and early mornings when the crooked valleys between the surrounding hills filled with mist. Their coolness was a balm that settled her mind. Those moments—her favorite times of day—made the hours between acceptable, even though the passing of each hour brought her wedding day closer— and now only a few days were left.

Sayid was the only personal escort to accompany her there—she had insisted on that with both Poppaea and Florus. He brought a message for Cleo and found her on the long porch with peristyle columns from the doorway into the main room, sitting there in the late afternoon sun wearing a simple robe, hair not as tightly bound as usual, a woven reed basket full of feathers on her lap. The former owner of those feathers squawked noisily from its cage on a pedestal of stone near the lady. "Aliturus has arrived with your guests, my lady," he said, then bowed and backed away, smiling at Nicanor and Yosef as he announced them.

"Thank you, Sayid... and you, too, Aliturus." Cleo smiled at the handsome Jewish actor—one of Nero's favorites and a friend of Poppaea, who had asked Aliturus to handle discreetly bringing Cleo's two friends from Rome. She had convinced Cleo that it would be their last chance to meet before her wedding... and perhaps forever.

"You're welcome, Lady." The actor bowed and straightened; he knew Yosef from having brought him at Poppaea's request to Rome from Puteoli and then again from his cauponae to the Domus Transitoria the night of Lady Cleo's homecoming party.

"Do you now go to Antium?" Cleo asked him.

"Yes, Lady Cleo. His Highness, Nero, wishes me there to perform as he plays the cithara." Aliturus smiled. "I believe the emperor loves any stage, my lady, even your wedding." He bowed again, turned, and left.

"It's good to see you, Lady Cleo," Nicanor said, stepping closer to her and gesturing at the bundle of iron-tipped wooden shafts at her feet and the basket on her lap. "You fletch your own arrows?" The scar that bisected his right eyebrow created a chevron of its two halves as it raised and twitched with his question.

"Please, both of you sit. Sayid bring us wine, and then you sit with us, too."

Sayid brought a large clay jar and three simple cups to set on the low table between them. There were only three chairs, so he poured the wine, handed out the cups, and then sat cross-legged on the grass just off the floor of the marble colonnade. He looked up at Cleo, who was smiling in a way he had rarely seen, and not at all lately.

"Yes, Nicanor. I feather my own arrows and can even string my bow." She turned to Yosef, who seemed both glad and sad—at the same time—to see her. "And how are you, Yosef?"

"I'm well, my lady." He bowed his head.

"And your mission, how fares it?"

Yosef nodded, his serious look softening into a grin at Nicanor: "I've learned much, both about bearing arms and about Rome's military. It's been... enlightening."

"And your countrymen, the three priests that are imprisoned?"

"Empress Poppaea thinks she can arrange their freedom." He shook his head. "But it will take more time."

Cleo knew how subtly, and carefully, Poppaea handled Nero and nodded. "And then you will return to Judea?"

"Yes, my lady."

Nicanor had seen it before after their rescue on board the *Mithras,* and again the night of the small gathering at the emperor's palace. His sense of people, their manner and posture—what it said of them without their knowing—had served him well his entire life. And something, just beneath the surface, had passed between Cleo and Yosef, leaving behind the feeling of the air just before a lightning storm. He did not like to consider its depth or what it meant or would lead to if it were more visible—or worse yet, became known to others. "My lady..." He noted her hands had not stopped as she talked. "You truly know what you're doing." He lifted an arrow, the fletching completed, and turned it, testing the binding and gauging its balance. "I've never seen it done more finely, and"—his thick, calloused forefinger ran along its length—"never with such feathers as these." He glanced at the muttering bird, then back at Cleo. The eyebrow chevron appeared again.

Yosef knew nothing about the quality of arrows. But he had sat there watching Cleo's hands, too. The redness of sunburn from their time on the water had long faded, and now her skin tone was that of fine ivory. Underneath its surface played tendons that told of her hands' strength and deftness. He looked up to see she had caught him studying them.

Cleo smiled at Yosef and then turned to Nicanor. "I do it myself because I want them to fly true." She glanced again at Yosef and then back to Nicanor. "It's important to rely on what you can trust. What you know that will not let you down."

Nicanor nodded; he agreed with her on that. But he felt again—only stronger this time—that something had been exchanged, sent-accepted-returned, between this man and woman, who had oddly somehow become his friends. He looked at Sayid, who though young, also sensed it. The slight shrug of his shoulders and the look on his face likely matched his.

XIX

Gessius Florus was pleased. Nero had not only allowed him to travel with him in his royal carriage to Antium but had also provided a private villa next to his own Villa Imperiale that shared a grand view of the Tyrrhenian Sea far below its rocky promontory. The emperor's enclave spanned nearly three-thousand feet facing the water and followed the escarpment in a series of descending terraces bordered by long stair-stepped lengths of colonnades.

On arrival, Nero had entered his residence and left Florus to wander around the area attended by a servant. Poppaea and Cleo were to arrive later, just in time to prepare for the ceremony. Florus, having seen the location of his villa, waved away the slave and followed the colonnade's path down, past several terraces with their Greek-copied stoas and private pavilions, to the final plateau still high above the sea. The sun near its midpoint, in a sky so blue it almost hurt to view, shone down on quite a sight.

Antium had not been favored with much of a natural harbor, just a vestigial one. But where the gods had failed, Roman engineering had succeeded. Nero had used the stunted stone jutting from the seabed and reinforced and expanded it nine hundred yards for the western arm... and seven hundred yards for the southern projection into the sea, the end of which was affixed with a beacon visible day and night by ships at sea. Additional markers defined the seventy-yard-wide harbor entrance which was open to the southeast.

Florus stood there, feeling that his life—his career—was aligning as he had wished, as he had long planned. Caesarea and its man-made harbor would soon be under his control, as would all of Judea. He smiled. Tonight, was the night that set everything in motion and secured the future of which he had long dreamed.

* * *

The sunburst color of Cleo's veil matched the sun setting on the waters behind her. A girdle of the same color was tied around the waist of her white gown. The girdle's knot of Hercules would be untied by Gessius Florus, privately, after the ceremony. She approached him, doing what was expected of her, but felt that she

89

was betraying someone, a man who loved someone else he would never have. Yosef had explained to her on the raft the significance of the kinyan—Leah's gift—he wore around his neck; she had seen at sea how he often grasped it tightly in his hand—and why—and she understood. Both of them now had similar burdens to bear. Hers was before her now. Florus reached for her hand. Her eyes closed at his touch as the torches were lit to replace the dying sunlight.

* * *

The orange glow started low, and it showed at first through the alleys between the buildings. Capering, twisting tongues of flame flickered, then licked the edges of what he sensed were wooden tenements teeming with people. Yosef felt on his face the heat carried by the wind, the closeness of its breath a sweltering shroud that draped over him. Sweat formed and then poured from him. The blaze, now threaded with yellow, grew, and the surrounding air quivered and rippled. The edges of the buildings wavered, then ignited. The fire curled and formed a column, a roiling mass of smoke, vomiting clouds darker than the night. Within them, a thrusting hand—sparks flashing as if from jeweled rings on its fingers, glimpses of stones—pushed the fire toward him.

Yosef lurched from his cot, then staggered half-awake to the window and looked out onto a sleeping city quiet in the early morning hour. A ribbon of fresh air traced along the street and lifted, rising to tease his face. He wiped away the sweat, then returned to his bed, not looking forward to trying—again—to sleep.

* * *

Nicanor believed in the gods—in portents and their importance. And then sometimes he did not. He had seen too much of life, colored and formed by the intent, the motivations, and vagaries of men and women, to believe in any mystery in the cause of an event. In any such case, the forewarning—or anyone's prescience—was easily explained after the fact. What Yosef had told him was square in the middle of the range of his faith and doubt.

"And you say you dreamed of her—of Lady Cleo—before you ever met her?"

Yosef nodded. He had affirmed that the first time he had been asked, not five minutes before. He and Nicanor were in the tabernae near the Circus Maximus where he had eaten with Poppaea and Cleo not long after arriving in Rome.

"And last night you dreamed of a city burning?"

"Yes." Yosef still felt the heat of the vision on his brow.

"For the second time..." Nicanor studied his friend, then shifted to watch the young woman filling customers' cups from the large amphorae on the bar that ran along the back wall of the room. She was shapely and had a sparkle in her eyes as she returned the brimming cups to them. The honeyed-wine, massilitanum, was considered common, even inferior by some, but Nicanor enjoyed it. The girl nodded to confirm she had—as he requested—sprinkled their drink with chopped bits of the cheering euphrosynum plant. He hoped it would help lift his friend's spirits but doubted that it would. Cleo—even as they sat drinking—was wedding Gessius Florus in Antium. Nicanor knew that was on Yosef's mind. He turned from his friend and looked west along the broad avenue that the tabernae faced. Their table was in the small open area on the street and received the evening wind that offered relief from the day's heat. Further along, in the direction Nicanor gazed, the Circus Maximus, even in its immenseness, was lost in the darkness. Across the boulevard, to a coppery cast to the sky grow low behind the buildings. Strange, for the sun was already down. They had watched its orange-red orb sink below the long stretch of buildings to the west. A gust of wind came out of the night from the south, flowing along the equally broad north-south road that bisected the east-west avenue parallel to the Circus Maximus. The reddish tint brightened as he watched it, silhouetting the buildings—the shops and warehouses—densely packed in the most extensive merchant area of the city. As the light before them climbed, with the swirl of a crosswind came the smell of smoke.

Fires were frequent in Rome, Nicanor had learned. Most of the population lived in timber-framed, wood-clad apartment buildings. It was not uncommon for someone to cook a meal or to warm their rooms despite frequent proclamations against fires in collective dwellings. But those incidents were always small, confined to a single building or two. He turned to Yosef, who now stood beside him looking in the same direction.

* * *

Two men in the tabernae had taken the table farthest from the Jew. Both wore light cloaks cut long enough to cover them down to just below their knees. They kept the tails of their cloaks draped over their thighs as they sat at the table.

91

"We should've taken him before he met up with that big Roman," the smaller man muttered, rubbing the ridge of a scar from a long-ago poorly healed wound.

His companion—as big as the Jew's friend—laughed and rolled his empty cup between two large hands crisscrossed with the puckered seams of old scars. "He's a big, ugly one. But we have to give the others time to do their work." He pulled back the sleeve of his robe to rub the fish symbol tattooed just inside his right elbow. The skin was still red. What the symbol signified mattered little to him, or to any of them hired for the night's work. It was some new sign, the meaning of which he was told was not important but a requirement for the job. He remarked to his companion, "When it's caught and fed by this wind, which won't take long, that fire will scare the piss out of everyone in this quarter of the city. In the chaos, we'll separate those two, and then kill that stinking Jew." With a quick glance at their target, now seated, the man set the cup down and crooked a finger at the girl to refill it. As she did and then turned away, he scowled at the man next to him. "Don't squirm so. You look nervous."

"What if we can't separate them? What about his friend? He looks like a soldier."

The big man shifted and slapped his left thigh, feeling the gladius strapped to his leg. "He's not that big," he replied, a grin twisting his scarred face as he turned toward the front of the tabernae, eyeing the target and his companion. "I've killed bigger"—he looked over his shoulder, appraising the man—"for less money."

* * *

Aliturus drew his arms and hands into the long-sleeved tunic and wrapped his cloak around him. Cleo thought his expressiveness overdone—the gestures and hand movements of his performance ended with that motion just as the last chords from Nero's cithara echoed across the emperor's private theater. A murmur of appreciation rippled through the crowd. Aliturus was renowned for his artistry, which had been complemented by his patron Nero's strumming. The moon above, waning and approaching its third quarter, shone down on them. The light from torches and lanterns aided and did not override its beams. Soon she and Gessius would go to their villa, their bedchamber, to consummate the marriage. She looked up at the moon-governed sky, so bright that the stars in much of it were not visible. She looked north and east... wondering about the moon over Rome and who might be watching it there, too.

XX

JULIUS 64 CE

ROME

Yosef watched the billows of smoke pile up to the sky, the moon revealing their bunching into a dark underskirt beneath its pale beams.

"It's spreading fast," Nicanor said, not slowing as they ran from the fire.

The fire had sprinted toward Palatine Hill and then spilled across its base like a tide coming ashore creeping up its slope and that of the nearby Caelian Hill. The low area between the hills served as a spout for the funnel of flame.

Yosef and Nicanor felt the wind push and fuel the fire, as they sought a path to flank the flames and get ahead of them. But with each gust, the fire outpaced them. They had already encountered men stopping others from fighting the fire—no time to think about why, but with nothing to hinder it, the fire had become a raging beast, feeding on everything in its path, and it was headed straight for Cleo's domus. She wasn't at her residence, but Sayid was, and they intended to make sure he was safe.

Yosef had never felt such heat. The wind-whipped flames that lashed out had already scorched the hair from parts of his arms. He had stayed with Nicanor so far, following his lead, but was now falling behind. Yosef saw him glance back and slow down.

"Let's stop," Nicanor called back to Yosef, "catch our breath." The air had the taste of embers and ash, and he breathed shallowly with one large hand cupped over his mouth. Nearby he spotted two leather buckets that must have been dropped by firefighters who had turned and run or been chased away. "I believe there's a public cistern ahead"—Nicanor studied the cross street and buildings nearby, trying to recall its location from his travels through the city. He handed one bucket to Yosef. "We'll douse ourselves. It'll help turn away the heat—for a while—and protect us."

A few minutes later they were at the well. The basin was empty, with just an inch—maybe—of silt-laden water coating its bottom. He went to the well that capped the end of the rectangular cistern. But the hand crank mounted above the opening was missing its rope. "Futuo!" Nicanor muttered and slapped the handle, which turned uselessly. He leaned forward and could barely, in the smoke-veiled moonlight, detect the glint of water below, just out of reach. "Futuo!" he cursed again and then handed his bucket to Yosef. "Stay here, and I'll find rope." He turned toward the still-smoldering row of storefronts.

* * *

"That took long enough!" The small man who had been following Yosef and Nicanor elbowed his larger companion, who was flicking a piece of burning ash from his shoulder.

The big man looked beyond him at Yosef, who was now alone standing in the raised square at the center of a street crossing. He ordered, "You keep an eye out for that Roman. I'll take care of the Jew."

* * *

Yosef rubbed his more painful forearm and felt the blisters rising along its length. Incongruously, the sensation brought a flash of memory of once when his mother had been preparing dinner—roast lamb, his favorite—and he had steadily pestered her: "Is it ready?" Then not two minutes later, "Is it ready now?" No, his mother had told him each time. And he had finally reached a hand out to check the meat. His blistered fingertips had elicited no sympathy from his mother. He blinked away the memory. The blisters forming on his forearm were much larger, stinging and making his whole arm ache. For the sixth or seventh time, he scanned where Nicanor had disappeared into the smoke and shadows. Nothing. No sign of him yet. A voice behind him made him turn.

"Hey, Jew!" The bulk of a man-shaped shadow separated from the darkness and came forward. The fire's light caught him, and its shifting pattern twisted the man's features, distorting his expression. He had a jagged arcing scar that ran from jaw to brow, torn diagonally across his face. "Maybe this fire," he raised an arm and a blackened hunk of wood that he carried in his right hand like a cudgel, "will cleanse the city of the likes of you and your kind." The man charged at him.

Backing up quickly, Yosef fell over the basin's low wall and rolled as he landed, which saved him. The man's fire-scarred club came down—the embers of its edges fanning into flame—with such force that black splinters struck his face. On all fours at first and then scrambling to his feet, Yosef evaded the man's crashing swings. Around them, the wind picked up, and the fire thickened and coalesced, sweeping the area around the cistern. The only clear path out of it was through the man who was trying to kill him.

Yosef danced and weaved as Nicanor had taught him. The cudgel still landed burning, grazing blows on his shoulders and once across his back. But the assailant had lost his room to maneuver—the encroaching flame encircled them, except for a narrow lane behind the man, who stretched a broad, crazed smile as he readied to drive the point of the splintered beam into Yosef's chest.

Behind the man came a voice. "What in all the gods' hells is going on? I find water, and then some malignant little piss ant tries to knife me in the back. And now..."

Nicanor was off to one side, just behind the man, as he set down two full sloshing buckets of water.

The man turned from Yosef to face Nicanor and dropped his fire-blackened club. "This will be easy," he said. "I can use my blade on you, Roman."

Nicanor pulled his own dagger from its sheath at his belt, beckoning with the other hand to draw the man away from Yosef. "Does your lanista know you slipped your leash, dog?" Nicanor taunted. "The owner of your familia gladiatorium will lose his investment... ave imperator, morituri te salutant." Nicanor recited a twisted version of the customary salute gladiators offered the emperor in the games: "You who are about to die," he said, "I spit on you." He gestured again at the man. "Fight me." The grin Nicanor flashed was the same he had given the sharks in the Ionian.

The barbarian's sword flashed as he slashed at Nicanor's chest— a crude attack that proved a feint to force the Roman back and shift him to one side and closer to the flames.

Yosef watched helplessly as the tail of Nicanor's cloak caught fire. Nicanor swatted at it as the barbarian thrust again. He backed away until his heels were in the flames and his cloak ablaze for half its length. Nicanor grunted in pain as the fire lashed the back of his legs.

Yosef had to do something. Grabbing the charred piece of wood, the brute had intended to use on him, Yosef rushed at the barbarian a full head taller than he and twice as broad. Memories of his time with the Essenes—of his labors required to contribute to the community—rushed upon him. The heft of the wood felt like the handle of the scythes used at harvest. He brought it up in an arc to crash across the barbarian's thick neck in a shower of sparks. The man staggered, giving Nicanor an opening to thrust his dagger under the man's chin and then drive it upward with all his strength. The blow lifted the barbarian onto his toes before Nicanor pulled the blade out and the body crashed to the ground. The shower of blood smoldered as it landed in the fire spreading around them.

"There, you bastard," Nicanor grunted as he breathed heavily. "— What the?!"—water sluiced cold on his burning skin. He turned to Yosef who had grabbed one bucket and thrown its contents onto his back.

"You were on fire," Yosef explained unnecessarily as they both moved quickly out of the area closing in with fire. Once they were clear, he panted at Nicanor, "You said someone tried to stab you..."

Nicanor stooped for the other bucket and dumped its contents on Yosef's head and back, soaking his tunic and cloak. He nodded with satisfaction at having returned the favor. "Yeah, when I bent over a water barrel—and I found more buckets." He rubbed his brow with a bloody hand, leaving a streak of red smeared with soot. "And then I come back to you to find that big bastard trying to bash your head in." He bent to wipe his face and hands with the tail of his wet cloak, then gestured at the barbarian's body, now half in the flames, with his right arm flung out and away from them. "I grow tired of Rome." He straightened and squared his shoulders. "I'll be glad to be out of the city and back where I belong."

Yosef understood. He missed home. Even though Cleo was here in the Rome he so admired, he knew that neither the city nor the woman could ever be his.

XXI

"Are you sure this is Lady Cleo's domus?" Nicanor asked Yosef. Except for a smoke-filled path along the wide lane leading to the city center—all its topiary now burned and the pavement creating a firebreak—the Palatine was encircled with fire. The wind had abated, and the fire had slowed to a crawl, but the house they stood before was mostly in flames.

"Yes. Just inside the main entry—as I recall—was a Venus." Yosef pointed at the now-smoke-darkened statue of the goddess, standing as if surprised coming from a bath and modestly covering her breasts and groin with her hands. The entrance door and the decorative wood surrounding it had burned away. "I think that's it."

Nicanor eyed the statue and then Yosef. He shook his head and then entered the domus. "Sayid told me that the lady had quartered him near her own chambers."

"Which way?"

"The atrium in most domuses is surrounded by the bedchambers, so it must be..." Nicanor paused at a nexus of hallways and then chose the largest, thick with smoke and flames, heading toward the rear of the residence. "This way."

Moments later Yosef almost fell over Nicanor who had nearly fallen over a body. They knelt together and turned it over.

"It's the majordomus," Nicanor said, putting a hand on the gray-haired man's chest, feeling its slight rise and fall. "He's alive, but we have to find Sayid." He rose.

"We can't leave him behind!" Yosef protested. "We have to carry him with us."

Nicanor looked down at Yosef. "We?"

Yosef got his arms under the man and attempted to stand, but he couldn't. He lowered him back to the floor.

"Futuo!" Nicanor muttered, knelt and gathered the man's wrists together, then used his other hand to grab a handful of the man's tunic at the waist. With a heave and a loud grunt, Nicanor stood with the unconscious man now draped over his shoulder. "Let's go." He headed toward where he believed the atrium to be.

They heard squawking and cursing ahead of them. The high ceiling of the hallway they had just entered was filled with clouds of smoke. A unique configuration of polished metal mirrors brought faint moonlight into the room, cast upon the far wall by light from the blazing courtyard shining through the colonnade. Through the haze, Yosef saw Sayid in a struggle with an animated and angry creature of gray and blue and green. Sayid had grasped the bird by one yellow-clawed foot but cursed as its other claw was tearing ribbons of red from his forearm.

"Sayid!" Nicanor called in his sharp, booming centurion's battlefield voice. "Let go of that damn bird and come with us. This place is burning down around us." He shifted the unconscious man to ride better across both shoulders.

"I need to save Cicero!" Sayid cried. "Lady Cleo loves him!" It was clear that Sayid did not.

Yosef ran to Sayid's side, and better saw his soot-covered face, black streams running from his nose, and scratches from the bird's claws.

"I can't stand this... this creature," Sayid declared. "I hate it but can't let it die. Lady Cleo's grandmother gave it to her." He bent to hack and cough as Cicero bucked and then twisted free from his loosened grip.

As Yosef reached his side, Sayid collapsed and the bird shot off into what he assumed was Cleo's bedchamber. He half-carried, half-dragged Sayid to where Nicanor waited.

"This man is not getting any lighter," Nicanor grumbled and turned back to the way they had come, seemingly the only way out. "Stay behind me but close."

Bits of burning decorative trim fell on them from the second floor, mostly wood, that was now an inferno. Behind them, Yosef heard the bird scream.

"Can you walk?" Yosef straightened Sayid and steadied him.

Sayid was still coughing and retching but standing straight. "Yes," he gasped.

"Then go." Yosef clasped Sayid on the shoulder and pushed him toward Nicanor. "Follow him." He turned back.

"Are you crazy?" Nicanor looked up as larger flaming fragments dropped around them. "Arrow feathers be damned. Yosef, we must get out of here now."

"Go—both of you—I'll be right behind you." Yosef ran across the atrium and into Cleo's room. As he entered, a large section of the ceiling crashed down behind him.

"Stick with me, boy, grab my cloak," Nicanor said, leaning toward Sayid, "and don't let go."

* * *

The courier arrived late in the evening and was brought directly to Nero. At the interruption to his private discussion with Gessius Florus, Poppaea, and Cleo, Nero's face blanched. The feather affixed to the spear the courier carried as a staff showed that he brought bad news. With the empire's treasury so depleted, an unexpected event—any bad news—was not welcome.

The messenger, white-faced with fatigue, trembled from having ridden through the previous night and all day, exhausting five horses. The feather at the tip of his spear twitched as he faced his emperor. No one in the cursus publicus wanted to deliver such ill tidings, especially to an emperor as mercurial as Nero. He, the youngest and newest messenger, had been ordered to deliver the news.

"What is it? Speak," Nero commanded.

"Rome is burning," the youth blurted without preamble, "Your Highness"—added as more sweat formed and slid into his eyes.

Nero's experience on stage helped him maintain the concerned look on his face as his fear vanished but not entirely. His gaze shifted—just a flash—to Florus, then back to the messenger. "How bad is it?"

"It's terrible, Your Highness. The fire still rages, and many sections of the city have been destroyed completely."

Nero's eyes flicked to Florus again. "What parts of the city?"

"Almost all the merchant areas, sire, but as I left—" The messenger paused and swallowed.

"—Tell me." Nero leaned forward with an intense look.

"The wind... it was like a demon, sire. It was driving the fire north across the Palatine as I left Rome..."

Poppaea and Cleo gasped in unison.

Florus was no longer the relaxed figure from before the messenger's arrival. He glanced at Nero to find the emperor studying him, the two fingers tapping his lips. "Sire," he said to answer the prompt, "we must return and organize aid for the victims... and assess the damage."

The fingers tapped and tapped and then stopped. Nero's eyes now locked fully on Florus, "Yes, we must."

XXII

JULIUS 64 CE

ROME

It was the most extensive and destructive fire that Rome had ever experienced. Fanned by the wind at its beginning, the conflagration swept over most of the city, reaching five of the famous seven hills. No walled mansions or temples or any other obstructions could arrest it. First, the fire spread violently over the level spaces. Then it climbed the hills and returned to ravage the lower ground again. It outstripped every countermeasure, and the city's narrow winding streets and irregular blocks encouraged its progress. Terrified, shrieking women, helpless old and young people intent on their own safety, people supporting invalids or waiting for them, and fugitives and lingerers alike—all heightened the confusion. When people looked back, menacing flames sprang up before them or outflanked them. When they escaped to a neighboring quarter, the fire followed. Even districts believed remote were not safe. With no idea where or from what to flee, they crowded onto the country roads or lay down exhausted in the fields. Some who had lost everything—even their food for the day—could have escaped but in despair preferred to die. So did those who had failed to rescue their loved ones.

* * *

Nicanor caught the arm of a man hurrying past them, and the man spun with a gladius in his right hand, ready to strike. His scorched paludamentum, the cape of a Roman army officer, swirled and settled, still smoking. "Ho, centurion!" Nicanor called, releasing his arm and stepping back. "Do you have any word on how far the fire has spread and where safety can be found?"

The man, one side of his face singed and soot-covered, a swath of hair at the crown replaced with a blistered area where the flame had bitten deeper, breathed heavily. "Gangs are keeping many from fighting the fire, and others are plundering shops and homes." He rubbed his face. "Do you have water?" At Nicanor's head shake, he continued. "I'm told that soldiers—some Praetorian Guard—have gathered men to save the emperor's palace. They've regrouped in the lee of the Esquiline Hill and hope to stop the fire there."

Nicanor, now numbed by the weight of carrying Cleo's majordomus, staggered as he reached a hand to steady Sayid, who weaved beside him. He turned back to the officer, "What direction is that? North?"

* * *

Yosef blindly stumbled out of the conflagration that had been Cleo's domus. Cicero had quieted, but Yosef did not want to unwrap the blanket he had caught him in to see if the parrot was alive. With his singed wings the bird might never fly again. The way back to Nicanor and Sayid had been blocked, and with the ceiling coming down on him, Yosef chose to burn outside rather than be trapped and cooked—slowly—inside. He felt for and found the bank of windows along a wall of Cleo's bedchamber. Eyes closed against the smoke and heat, he opened the wooden shutters by feel and was relieved at the relative cool and smell of the smoke-laden air. Climbing out, he landed on what seemed a level path. He followed it, guided only by a sense that the heat at his back was receding. Any direction that led him away from that was good.

After several minutes of lurching in darkness over the estate, he tripped over something and crashed to the ground. His splayed fingers felt what had entangled him, and he opened his eyes. In the moon's light—what little of it that came down through the clouds and a haze of smoke—and the glow of the fire behind him, he could see that the wrapped bundle he carried had become caught on something. He tugged it free, and the angry, pain-filled squawk from within told him that Cicero lived. A long rod stuck in the blanket came free in his hand. His fingers ran along its length to a point. One of Cleo's arrows. He recalled that her private archery range had been on the northern side of her domus, as he had discerned from how the sunlight and shadow had profiled her face that day she showed off her archery skills. Maybe further north was safe. A loud crash and flare behind him confirmed that Cleo's home was done for. The second story had collapsed and was now on top of the burning rubble of the first floor. In the bloom of light created from the collapse, he saw the remnants of the thick hedge bordering the northern perimeter of the grounds. The heat on his back was growing again and now starting to envelop his sides as well. North was his only choice.

* * *

The Praetorian Guard and the firefighters—many of them conscripted—had stopped the fire at the crest of the Palatine, but only after it had consumed most of the Domus Transitoria. The blazing beast had been turned away from this now-small piece of imperial ground but was diverted just to ravage the more open and level sections of Rome. Countless temples and pleasure arcades had been destroyed. On hilltops where the fire had been subdued, encampments of sorts had been set up. Nicanor turned to scan the area at the end of the second day of the fire. Sayid was slumped at his side. Lady Cleo's majordomus had been taken to a medic's tent and was no longer his responsibility. The wail of the wounded and those still dying carried on the wind—a sound he was familiar with... and the stench, too. But the aftermath of a battle is raw—the odor of burned flesh does not rest so heavily. And as you and your unit—survivors—moved on, you left it behind. But not this. He had never seen such a scale or smell of destruction and death.

"Do you hear that?" Sayid was on his feet next to Nicanor.

"Yes, too many times, boy." Nicanor shook his head and looked away.

"No"—Sayid tugged at Nicanor's tattered cloak, and the centurion turned back to him. "That sound!"

The sameness—the thrum—of countless laments was all around them, and then Nicanor heard what differed from that droning: a periodic squawk—an angry squawk.

"I know that sound. I don't like it or what makes it, but I know it." Sayid, his ears sharper than Nicanor's, had identified its direction.

Nicanor followed the boy as he weaved through a scattering of tents, some taut, erected with army precision, and others sagging and as exhausted-looking as the civilians lying within them. They came upon a curious sight: a man in what had once been a white tunic now blackened and burned in spots, sitting with his back to them, his head seemingly replaced by the spread of wings—barren and blistered in spots along their length—that extended to either side. But as he circled, Nicanor saw the unruly human head that smelled of burned hair even from a distance.

"I keep finding you alive when I don't expect it," Nicanor said from above Yosef. "The gods must protect you."

Stiffly and sorely, Yosef rose, and Cicero shifted to sit on his shoulder. "And you two as well!" Yosef cried. He grinned at his friends.

"Water and fire, my young friend. We have been nearly done in by both water and fire, and yet, we live." Nicanor's scowl broke into a matching smile. "We live."

* * *

The morning of the sixth day, Nicanor heard from the senior officer of the Praetorian Guard that Nero and his entourage had arrived. He wondered, for likely the seventh or eighth time, whether he should give that commander their names as survivors, that he might pass the information on to Lady Cleo. If it weren't for that damned bird and Sayid's assignment to Lady Cleo's household, he wouldn't have. He would have let their former connection, even friendship, with a Roman noblewoman—now a married one—fade into the past. Nothing good would come of it for his friend Yosef. If he turned in their names, it would not only be the bird, and Sayid reunited with Lady Cleo but all of them. But he knew that he had no choice.

* * *

"Ah, Florus. Do you know my prefect of the Praetorian Guard?" Nero motioned toward the man at his side, hair graying at the temples and a calculating look in his eye. "Tigellinus, this is Gessius Florus. He is to become my new procurator of Judea once we have this tragedy in hand and Rome is recovering."

Florus knew of the man whose outstretched hand he grasped in greeting. "I've heard of him, sire, and it's a pleasure to meet you, Tigellinus." His smile for the man was one of equal to equal. Tigellinus Ophonius's reputation was that of a cold, callous leader and friend to Nero.

"Tigellinus has news of most interest to me," said Nero, "and some of interest, I believe, to you. Well, some of it was for your wife."

Florus knew it was men from the Praetorian Guard that had prevented the Domus Transitoria from being completely destroyed and that Nero already had ideas for the construction of his new golden palace. He had also heard that morning that a fresh fire had broken out at Tigellinus's Aemilian gardens. So perhaps the man was the opportunist he was said to be, as many were who surrounded any emperor.

"What news, sire?" Florus looked from Tigellinus to Nero.

"The people are not happy. I have brought grain from our stores at Ostia and neighboring towns and cut its cost to only one-quarter sesterce a pound. I've opened the Field of Mars and Agrippa's public buildings... even what remains of my gardens—for the homeless.

Temporary insulae and smaller emergency accommodations are being erected for the many who've lost their dwellings. But still, the people seek to blame someone other than the gods' whims. A rumor has spread that the fire was started by someone who would gain from it."

Nero turned from them to look out over the city. "Of my city's fourteen districts, three have been completely devastated, their every building—public and private—destroyed. Seven more have been reduced to remnants of scorched ruins." He half-turned, his eyes cast sideways at them. "Only four were undamaged." He looked past them to survey the area to the north and east. "Among the victims, Tigellinus's men have found the bodies of men bearing the markings of the sect that some believe are against Roman rule and have their own religion and religious leader they follow—Christians."

Florus smiled inwardly but expressed concern: "Sire, there are two prominent men I've heard of... Christians—Paul of Tarsus and Yohanan ben Zavdi—who should be held most accountable. Paul was recently released from prison and has been spreading his seditious message over much of the empire. The other one, Yohanan, seems to be the origin of rumors spreading among this cult that the end of the world is near and that Rome will soon burn. Of course, there has been a similar prophecy spreading for years from Egypt—that a fire would occur in summer at the rising of the dog star. So perhaps they are just encouraging people to believe that one. I would say these Christians were trying to help along Rome's prophesied demise."

Nero shook his head as he remembered. "Yes, my wife is constantly persuading me to go easy on these religious sects, including the Jews. I gave in last year by having this Paul of Tarsus released. But it looks like we will now need to bring them all to justice. Begin looking for all of the leaders, including the one here in Rome called Simon Peter."

Florus nodded to Tigellinus and said, "Well done, Prefect. This cult, I hear, practices secret rites in which they consume human flesh and human blood. The vileness and treachery of these Christians should be made known, and they should be punished severely!"

"It shall be made known, and they shall be found and punished, sire," Tigellinus replied. Nero nodded to Tigellinus, who, with a nod of his own to Florus and a bow to Nero, spun on his heel and left. "I think I can prophecy what's in store for the Christians the prefect rounds up," Nero said. "Something in keeping"—Nero spread his arms and slowly pirouetted—"with what happened to Rome."

Florus could guess the punishment Nero contemplated for the Christians. He reviewed the past days' events as a success. They had worked out just as he had planned—well, almost. But once recovery was well underway, and Rome was being rebuilt, he could go about his further business in Judea. "Will that be all, sire? I'd like to check on the Lady Cleo. She's seeing to what can be salvaged from her domus." He recalled what Nero had said with his greeting, and added, "Sire, you said Tigellinus also had news of interest to my wife?"

"Yes, I'm sure she was very pleased."

Florus paused, expecting a further explanation, but when there was none, he bowed. "Thank you, sire."

XXIII

JULIUS 64 CE

ROME

Florus saw that there was nothing left of Cleo's domus but blackened stone and the charred stumps of trees that had bordered its grounds. He could see through the structure to where its foundation ended at that area where Cleo had childishly played with her bow, a distinctly unladylike pastime he disapproved of and would change. The level patch of formerly manicured lawn at the northeast side of the domus contained three large army campaign tents set up by legionaries, as they had done across the city. The tents now dotted the surrounding hills. As he approached, he heard the squawks. That was it, then. The news must have been that somehow Cleo's bird had survived and been returned to her. A slave pulled back and held the entry flap of the tent, and he ducked inside. Chairs aligned north and south formed a sitting area on makeshift flooring covered by woven mats. The sides of the tent had been rolled up and tied to allow the fresh wind to pass through. Five people were seated around the parrot on its perch: Cleo, Poppaea, the centurion and the Syrian youth that had been rescued with Cleo. And then he saw the Jew.

* * *

"Is it true that the Temple of Jupiter Stator is gone?" Poppaea asked from where she and Nero stood, watching workers clear debris to recover slabs of stone and marble to reuse for the new Domus Aurea.

"Yes." Nero glanced at her and then returned to his study of the laboring men, none swearing—under their emperor's eyes—as they normally would. "Our eight-hundred-year-old temple, the sanctuary founded by Romulus himself, is no longer there—except for its base stone. Gone, along with the House of Vestals and its sacred grove." Caught up in a drama of his own making, Nero's mind had shifted—easily, and now convincingly—to single out the Christians. "I should never have listened to you."

"About what?"

"Freeing those Christian who persist in spreading discontent and their religion. They brought us to this"—he waved his hand over the scene—"this destruction. They were spreading rumors of a prophecy of a fire that would burn Rome down." He turned to Poppaea and lowered his voice. "And then they moved to make sure their own predictions came true."

* * *

Cleo did not know if another opportunity would come; the look in Florus's eyes told her likely not. He had, the evening before, seemed disturbed as he briefly greeted Nicanor and Yosef. His demeanor had ended their visit abruptly. That morning he had appeared less disturbed when he was called to meet with Nero. As soon as he left, she had asked Graius to find Yosef and Nicanor and invite them to join her.

* * *

Cleo's majordomus came upon them at their cluster of tents, as Nicanor read a message that had just been delivered by courier. Seeing the man, he stopped after the first few lines and rerolled the parchment, slipping it into his tunic.

"Well, I see you're on your feet," Nicanor said. "That's a good thing. I hope I'll not have to carry you again."

The gray-haired man, with much of his hair still singed to stubble, smiled. "I've yet to thank you for saving my life," he bowed to Nicanor, "so I do now. Thank you."

Nicanor grunted and stood. "I only carried your body... This fellow," he cocked a thumb at Yosef, "felt a higher purpose that led to that. He was willing," he grinned at Yosef, "but the flesh was weak. So, I did the lifting for him. But you're welcome." Nicanor's mind moved from accepting the thanks he thought was the man's only purpose to the contents of the message he had just received.

"My lady," the majordomus continued as Nicanor and Yosef both looked back at him, "my lady requests your presence."

* * *

Nero had gulped four goblets of wine to Florus's one, and said, "Yes, but once you become settled in Judea, how soon can you take... as we discussed, collect more from the Jews?"

"Sire, I've given this much thought. And I know how to accomplish the two things important for that task. But you must trust what I do, and should I need to invoke it, I will need your authority."

"You're sure that what you contemplate, what you need from me, will provide results?"

Florus smiled. "I'll tell you exactly what I plan, sire. I know men... what they yearn for... what motivates them." As he said that he thought how well he knew what emperors wanted, too. "And I can use that to deliver what you ask."

"Which will begin once you are in Judea?"

"There's something I must do here first, sire. But yes, it will come to fruition—for both of us—in Judea."

* * *

"So, like you told me on the raft... you also dreamed... had a vision of the fire?" Cleo leaned toward Yosef. She had felt from the beginning that some power—the gods, some divinity—had brought this odd group of men to become her friends. Yosef had yet to speak. *If only...* she wondered.

"Twice he dreamed of it, Lady Cleo," Nicanor answered, for Yosef was still disconcerted at what he had told Cleo on the raft.

Since the fire, Yosef had grown increasingly silent around them, something that concerned his friends. But everything that had happened to him in the nearly two years past had made him question what had once been deep-held beliefs. Seeing Rome and its economic and military might, coupled with Nicanor's running narrative—for weeks on end—about the empire and its reach, reinforced his admiration for Roman accomplishments. Then came the fire and destruction of a city far more substantial and grander than any he had ever imagined. Then he watched the city rise again before his eyes.

When he left Judea, he thought there could be a way for his people to coexist within Roman rule, but over the many months since his absence, he had heard of increasingly violent acts against that rule in the provinces and learned of how any rebellion was treated—how swift and harsh Roman retribution could be. He raised his eyes to look at Cleo without seeming to. It was almost too much. Do the gods—Roman gods—or did the God of his people inflict things on Man at random? Or was there some plan? He could not help but remember his teaching under the Essenes, who believed the Jewish prophets had predicted the end of the world was coming soon in a war between good and evil that would last seven years. "I'm sorry, Lady Cleo," Yosef said, having missed her question. "What did you ask me?"

"Do you believe in providence, Yosef?"

"You mean fate? That everything is preordained, that homo proponit, sed Deus disponit... That man proposes, but God—the gods—disposes?"

"—I believe"—they all turned to the voice of Sayid, who sat as far from the sleeping Cicero as he could and still be in the conversation—"that one day I'll see my father again."

Cleo smiled at the boy. He sought family and the approval of a father he barely knew. Nicanor had told her about Cicero and Sayid the night of the fire. The claw wounds on his arms and face were still healing. He had tried to save her parrot, at such risk and injury, and that said much of how he cared for her as if she were a beloved sister. She glanced at Yosef, who had faced the fire to save one of the few things she truly loved. His face remained cast down, and he seemed lost in thought again. Sayid's wistful tone made her a little sad. "Do you dream of that, Sayid? Of seeing your father?"

"No, my lady." He glanced at Yosef. "Not like that. I just know, I feel that one day I'll be able to show my father that I've become a good man and a good soldier."

Nicanor coughed into his sip of wine. "Boy, you're braver than many grown men I've served with. A lot of them talk much when deep in their cups, but in battle or when it is needed, their bravery runs down their leg. You hold your water and stand your ground."

Yosef raised his head. "What was in the message"—he looked at Nicanor—"that the courier brought you?"

Nicanor considered Yosef for a moment, then Cleo, and then Sayid. Each got a long and steady look. Something passed across his face that Yosef had never seen, but it vanished as he spoke: "I'm ordered to Ostia and then on to Antioch."

"What about the Praetorian Guard and the position promised you?" Cleo asked.

Nicanor rubbed his chin. "I've seen enough—perhaps too much—of Rome; I asked that my reward—my orders—be changed to remain what I am. A soldier in the field."

"So..." The deep voice from the doorway cut like a knife into the lull in the conversation. "Is this a goodbye to your friends, Lady Cleo?" Florus stepped into the circle of light from the lanterns. He walked closer and looked down at Yosef, who straightened in his seat. "And as the new procurator of Judea, I look forward to meeting your family and thanking them for all you've done... for Lady Cleo."

XXIV

ROME

The prison had been damaged in the fire but only superficially. As Florus waited, he considered briefly what the Jewish prisoners had thought as the heat rose around them and their guards abandoned their posts. He knew jailers, though often feeble-spirited men themselves, recognize which prisoners are the weakest. They know which one will do something—anything—in exchange for even the most trifling rewards, perhaps better or more food, cleaner water, or a dry blanket. And the longer they are in prison, the more willing they become. As he awaited the administrator commanded to bring each of the priests—one at a time—to him, he caressed the scroll that bore an imperial seal. He was attuned to power—addicted to and enamored of it—and felt its emanations course through him. He was here to find the one who most wanted to be free again and, therefore, would be the most useful to him.

* * *

Sayid prepared to travel with Lady Cleo and her party, who would stay in Antium until leaving for Judea. Poppaea would join her at the seaside retreat later to give her a sendoff. Yosef and Nicanor were with their friend, and Nicanor had a new sarcina at his feet holding his military gear. He would travel with Cleo's entourage until just outside the city, and then his journey would take him west to board a warship at Ostia as they continued south. Yosef rested a hand on Nicanor's shoulder. "If—when—I return home, I hope my path carries me close enough to stop and see you."

Nicanor turned to his despondent younger friend, understanding his mood. "We have been thrown together more than once, Yosef." He rubbed the side of his nose with a calloused finger. Finding greater meaning in events around him, much less those in the far greater world, was not a task that occupied Nicanor's mind. But he sensed those things, and more personal ones weighed heavily on this Jew. And he suspected that all things Roman perplexed Yosef. And now the only people in Rome familiar to him, true friends, were leaving him behind, a stranger in a strange land. Nicanor took in one hand the reins Sayid handed him and clasped Yosef on the shoulder with the other. "Perhaps the gods will bring us together again. I wish you well."

* * *

"You crucified the Christian leader, Simon Peter, after the fire, and since then, you have been targeting other Christians, detaining them and imprisoning even more of them, for what?"

Nero ignored Poppaea's question as he watched the workers. They moved like an army of ants, busy on his Domus Aurea. It would be the most splendid palace of any emperor of Rome. "I'll soon agree to release the Jewish priests—what your friend Cleo wanted to be done, a reward for the Jew she was rescued with—don't deny that she asked you to intervene—and then they'll be on their way home."

"And why have you decided to do it now?" Poppaea asked. "I've talked to you about that for months."

"I know that you're fond of Jews, their religion. But do they not dislike—even attack—the Christians, too?" Nero smirked. "It's so like them... kind begets kind, they fight and fall out, which weakens the whole. It seems all degraded and shameful practices gather and flourish in Rome." Nero smiled, and it sent a chill through Poppaea. "We do not have to always tolerate them, and it serves me well—and the empire—to do to the Christians as was done to Rome."

He glanced at Cleo and then turned his attention to the workers again. "As for the imprisoned Jewish priests, releasing them will put things more at ease in Judea—so Gessius Florus believes. And likely will please your friend Cleo."

"So, what will you do with the Christians?"

"Those I collect to punish will serve as a warning but also another purpose. The citizens of Rome need a distraction, and I shall give them one at the Circus." He leaned forward to rest his hand on Poppaea's thigh. The touch, more proprietary than affectionate, did not bother her, but his tone prickled her skin. "There they will be covered in animal skins and torn to death by wild beasts." He straightened and slid his hand from her. "And a select group of them are reserved for something I have in mind—an even more proper punishment and statement."

"Sire!" called out an approaching exploratore, a senior officer of his personal guard, as he neared the imperial carriage. "Sire, your architect and engineer are here."

Nero stepped out as the two men advanced. "Severus, Celer, tell me what cunning artificialities have you come up with? Something impudent, which nature cannot do, perhaps?"

* * *

It wasn't a purge but persecution of the Christians, starting with those deemed most unsavory by all the accounts Yosef had heard. They had been arrested and held. Some were said to be destined for death in the arena, according to rumors on the street and endlessly talked about in the merchants' shops and stalls. Over the weeks and months following the fire, Yosef had watched and perceived a growing hatred. It became a crime to bear the label Christian. He knew many in Judea, influential leaders in Jerusalem, pillars of the community and the Temple, that had also attacked the sect that had splintered from Judaism. The Christians had suffered at the hands of Jews, but Roman enmity—Nero's malice—was on a scale beyond measure.

"I wasn't there," said Aliturus, "but Lady Poppaea told me, and tales of it have spread as fast as the fire that caused such a vengeance." He handed Yosef the message he carried. "She asked me to give you this."

Yosef took it without opening, noting the actor's pale face and self-consciousness. "And Nero burned them—those Christians—in his garden?"

"Yes, to light the gardens at night. Emperor Nero said he had their lower bodies covered in tar—to make them suffer longer—and then set them afire, just as they had set fire to Rome." Aliturus pointed at the parchment in Yosef's hand. "Lady Poppaea told me that all Jews are safe. But I can't help thinking that even though Rome has always been open to a pantheon of religions from all parts of the empire, who's to say, if they do this to Christians, that they won't turn to Jews next?"

Yosef unrolled the message, holding it closer to the lantern's light so he could read:

> Yosef, do not be afraid of what is happening here in Rome. I know Cleo would want me to put your mind and heart to rest. She is well. And I have news for you about your imprisoned countrymen. My husband—I'm told he does this at Gessius Florus's request—will soon release the Jewish priests that are being held and will absolve them of any acts against Rome. On their release, they and you can return to your country. I know you have missed your family, and I wish you safe travel back to them.

It was signed, Poppaea Augusta Sabina.

112

XXV

AT SEA

On the bone-rattling ride from Rome to Ostia, Yosef let a familiar daydream of home occupy his mind. Dwelling in dreamland was far better than being present on the rough wooden bench of the raeda, a large cloth-topped wagon with its five benches now crowded with him and the twelve priests, as it bounced and shook for twenty-five miles. The sight of the port stirred him out of his reverie even more than the iron-shod wheels over the rough road. Nicanor had sailed from here, a place Yosef had not visited while in Rome.

Ostia was the Roman Empire's primary port and received an average of five four-hundred-ton cargo ships a day. The port was bordered on the east by at least twenty massive horrea that held much of the discharged freight. He had heard in Rome of Nero ordering the expansion of these public warehouses, adding a second story and doubling their storage capacity to nearly ten tons. It was from those warehouses that much of the grain had come from to feed the people in the months following the great fire.

As Yosef and the priests clambered from their conveyance and reported to the port master, Yosef handed them the sealed imperial order granting their passage. He wondered at the sight of so many ships. Within hours they had been led to and boarded a vessel departing with the tide, the first one headed south with space to accommodate the Judeans. He had hoped his return would retrace the route the *Salacia* had taken to Rome, only without the shipwreck this time. He also hoped to replenish stores and remain overnight near Antioch long enough to find and visit briefly with Nicanor. Once in Caesarea, he thought perhaps he could get word of Cleo and Sayid to learn how they had fared since arriving in Judea. But that was not to be.

The ship was headed to Aegyptus, by far the wealthiest eastern province of Rome, and to Alexandria, the second-largest city in the empire. From there, they would have to travel the Roman trade road some three-hundred-odd miles, another twenty days, by a combination of plaustrum cargo wagons drawn by oxen and then, once they left the major Roman road, by mule to Jerusalem—a tiresome and no doubt uncomfortable means of travel, but worth it to finally get home.

* * *

Yosef was in pitch dark, and the sound of movement came from something, someone ahead of him. He stretched his arms out in front, fingers splayed and reaching... feeling his way toward whatever was there, should something be there. The roughness of stone rasped his right shoulder, and he moved away until he was an arm's length from it. He had traveled several feet, and it remained dark. He could feel nothing to his left, so the passageway must be wide. Its floor—no, the ground, because he felt the looseness of small rocks on hard-packed earth beneath his sandals—was relatively level.

Again, in front of him some distance away, came the rustle of fabric, and then of something sliding, dragging, and kicking. Small rocks rattled and echoed as they struck stone. Louder now, he heard grunts from what must be men and sharp cries from what sounded like a woman—a woman hurt or injured. She cried but cut each cry off, as you do when they escape your lips, but you don't want others to know your pain. The sound grew more distinct as he got closer. The surrounding blackness was now graying, getting lighter and lighter with each step. Ahead he saw a pool of light that revealed a nexus where passages intersected.

He recognized it even though it had been years. One passage led to the Temple, and the other directly opposite it, to the fortress. The one he walked approached the intersection at an angle—it must be one of the hidden routes to and from the outer court. The fourth, the stub of which was all that could be seen from his view, was where the sounds came from. He did not have a clue where the passage came from or went and could not recall a fourth tunnel joining the other three. He slowed just before the crossing and moved left until he could touch that wall, hugging it close until the spot where the intersection opened into a wide area. Leaning to get an eye around the corner, he saw in the spill of light from two lanterns—one of them overturned or dropped and now burning in a puddle of oil—two Roman soldiers wrestling with a woman.

As he watched, one of them tore the light woolen mantle from her. As she was twisted to the ground, a clasp or pin came free and spun in an arc of tumbling glints to disappear into the shadows. Then came the ripping sound of cloth as they tore her outer tunic. As she kicked, her shoe flew off to land before Yosef. The fragrance of balsam and myrrh came from the closed-shoe of an affluent woman. He looked up, and she was now underneath one soldier, her fine linen sadin was now ripped, split in half. The other soldier had pinned her arms and shoulders as he laughed and urged the first man on.

Yosef surged forward, shouting "Stop!"

A shudder shook him, and he opened his eyes to see the fabric of a dingy tent. Just as on the *Salacia*, his accommodations on this vessel—and that of the priests returning with him—were on the deck. The ship pitched, rolled and trembled again, and then settled in a trough, riding more easily with the wind from square astern. It was early morning.

The night before he had left the circle of priests and their discussions. Many of their words were biting commentary for and against the actions they planned on their return to Jerusalem—the kinds of actions that had landed them in prison in Rome. Some had listened to what Yosef had added to the debate: a petition to think and act differently to avoid the same outcome or worse. Others, most of them, had shaken their heads, casting stern glares that flared hot in the arguments and sarcasm that had filled them once their gratitude at being freed had emptied. Now most of them disregarded his opinions. After hours of their circular logic and discussion, he had left them and wandered off where he could watch the moon and think of home.

That first night at sea, he remembered the last Shabbat dinner with his family before leaving for Rome two years before. Rebecca, his mother, had that morning asked him to accompany her as she bought fresh flour and other items for dinner. He remembered thinking how thankful he was that she and Miriam—unlike many Jewish women—did not have to spend their early morning hours grinding grain. He recalled that he carried the foodstuffs that morning, including a wrapped bundle of pungent goat cheese. In Rome, the scent of goat cheese—one of his favorite foods—had always made him think of home. For two years he had found it difficult to comply with the kashrut dietary laws his faith called for. He looked forward to the familiarity of home.

It had been hardest to leave his mother and Miriam. His little sister doted on him, and at that last dinner, he had felt so proud of her. She had grown tall and strong. Though his father had disapproved, Yosef had shared his reading and studies with her, especially studies of the Greeks and the Roman women who enjoyed a level of freedom most Jewish women did not. Miriam had worked hard to do the chores expected of females in a Jewish household, to get them done quickly but well, so she would have time to read or could follow her brothers Yosef, Matthew, and their friends on their explorations of the city and the nearby countryside and hills.

That night at Shabbat, Miriam had sat next to Yakov—her betrothed—as an equal, but still showed respect for custom and tradition, only without deference. She wore her jet-black hair in a thickly braided twist that draped over her left shoulder as she easily poured goat's milk from the heavy stone pitcher, a twinkle in her eye and a smile on her face. He missed her most of all. His father was stern and bound by rules and tradition that defined his life and expectations for his sons. Sometimes, Yosef thought, they were too restrictive. His older brother Matthew was a younger version of their father. Yosef was more like his mother in his curiosity, his intellect, and his interest in the far larger world. That she would never fully realize her potential drove Yosef in the decisions, he had made. Miriam was full of lightness and joy, and though probably married and possibly with a young child now, she was still that little girl he had teased, taught, and loved so much.

Yosef sighed as the warmth of that memory of home replaced the quickly fading vestiges of the dream he had just escaped. He looked up at the sky—so different from that darkness in the dream—now turning orange-red on the horizon off his left shoulder as he rested his forearms on the railing of the ship. Ahead, south and east, was Alexandria, which would be reached midmorning of the next day. Then would begin the last leg of his journey, north, and east through the Judean Mountains to Jerusalem and home.

ACT II

XXVI

JERUSALEM

Yosef and the priests had branched off the main Roman road that hugged the coastline and turned east toward Be'er Sheva; they followed an ancient route until it bent and climbed northward up the Judean hills to Hebron and through Bethlehem to Jerusalem. The Romans would not dignify it by considering it a road—in truth, it was a worn way of packed earth, widened by countless hooves and feet over centuries, and it skirted the heights, ridges, and deep chasms that shielded Jerusalem on all sides except the north.

Jerusalem is situated on an uneven, rocky plateau, mostly limestone, at an elevation of nearly three thousand feet. Built upon two elongated hills that are positioned side-by-side, the city stands at a point where the hills' three steep-sided flanking ravines join and form a single, broad valley. Encircling and protecting the city were high, thick stone walls that were erected, damaged, repaired, and enlarged over the centuries. They were also dotted with towers that rose even higher, and at intervals interrupted by massive gateways. Just inside each gate was a customs station where taxes were collected on all goods coming into or leaving the city.

Sore and exhausted, Yosef and the priests entered through the Jaffa Gate at the west side of the city near Herod's palace. The gate was situated at the western end of the Upper City, the section of Jerusalem where many affluent citizens and priests lived. They were relatively close to their homes but arrived unannounced. They seemed just another group of dusty, road-weary travelers entering the city in a hurry before Shabbat began. As they moved into and through the upper agora, surrounded by its graceful porticoes, some of the priests were recognized and soon were overtaken and borne away home with family and friends.

Yosef took closer notice of Herod's palace. It had once seemed very impressive, but his eyes that had seen so much in Rome now judged it more critically. At the Roman barracks next to the palace, he turned to cross through the heart of the Upper City, past the palace of the Hasmoneans, and then toward the Temple. His family came from a long line of kohén, and there, in that last residential area before the Temple grounds began, was his home. To the south was the Lower City, a crowded grouping of cheaply built houses, yellow-brown from years of sun and wind on narrow, unpaved streets that sloped downward toward the Tyropoeon valley that ran north-south through the center of Jerusalem.

The broad avenue through the Upper City ended at the two arched passageways where they crossed into the Temple. The late afternoon sun slanted down behind Yosef, casting his shadow before him as he walked past the dozens of white stone and timber villas that stood out against the well-kept reddish brown and green grounds. About halfway to the arches and the Temple grounds, he came to a two-story house with thick walls built of well-trimmed limestone, its foundations laid on the limestone bedrock that was Jerusalem's foundation.

Yosef paused at the entrance to his family's home. Should he just enter or announce himself as if he were a guest calling upon them? As he reached for the door, it opened. His mother stood before him, the lines on her face more pronounced than he remembered and the frosting of gray now threaded densely through the coils of her thick hair. "Yossi!" she cried and reached to hug him a long moment before drawing him inside. There he removed his worn sandals, and she brought a bowl of water and a cloth for him to wash his feet.

"Let me get you something to drink," she said and disappeared.

The reception hall on the first floor of the house was large and elaborate. Its high ceiling and walls were covered with white stucco, modeled in relief as a series of panels. Yosef followed her from the hall to the kitchen. "Just water is fine, Mother." To one side of the reception hall, the living area comprised three rooms, their walls decorated with frescos that ended at the entrance to an inner courtyard. At the eating and sitting area adjacent to the courtyard, he sighed as he reclined on a divan, its cushion the softest thing he had felt on his skin since Rome. Closing his eyes, he took in the feel of it, the sensation of finally being home. "Where's Miriam?" he asked.

"She's not here."

Something in her tone made Joseph sit up and look at his mother. "Is something wrong with her?"

"Your father and Matthew"—she glanced at the fading afternoon sun that still cast shadows in the inner courtyard—"will be home soon. They're at the hall... more and more often it seems."

Yosef knew how long and entangling the discussions—arguments—could be in the Hall of Hewn Stones, before and among the Sanhedrin. "And I think we both know were it not for Shabbat," he commented, "they'd likely be there even longer today."

119

"We heard the priests were on their way home. Were they with you?" She looked over her shoulder and caught his nod as she placed candles for the coming evening.

Every Friday, Shabbat began a few minutes before sunset. The meal started with the Kiddush, and another blessing recited over two loaves of challah. Yosef remembered sitting on the roof terrace of their home on a Saturday evening when he was a child as his father explained that Shabbat ended at the appearance of the first three stars in that night's sky. Before he left for Rome, on his last night, he had watched for those stars with Miriam.

As his mother turned to him, he saw the look in her eye. Something worried her that was beyond the squabbles his father and brother brought home with them from a typical day spent dealing with dissension and the combating characters in local politics. "What has happened to Miriam?"

"Miriam didn't marry Yakov. It was an ugly scene with your father, and the erusin—the betrothal—was disrupted and broken. Your father managed to petition for her divorce. And it's complicated, but your sister has changed."

Leah, his cousin, and first love had been abused—and likely still was—by her husband, Yonatan. And he knew how headstrong Miriam could be; she would not tolerate such mistreatment or disrespect. "Was Yakov mistreating her?"

Rebecca studied Yosef and heard the iron in her son's voice and the resolve in his demeanor. He had changed, too. Leaner, sterner... something had happened to him that had aged him far more than the two years he had been gone. She hoped he would tell her of what had happened over those years. She shook her head and said, "Yakov still loves her. She's broken his heart, and no one knows why."

A loud metallic clank and then a rasping sound of wood pushed across stone came from the far side of the courtyard, from the off-street gate to a long winding path behind the homes of Jerusalem's elite that led to the outer court of the Temple grounds. Yosef rose from the couch and took a step toward the courtyard.

"Miriam?" Yosef didn't glance back at his mother's call and watched as a figure wearing a dun-colored cloak entered the courtyard. Pale arms and hands flipped the hood back. "Your brother's home."

Miriam came forward a dozen steps closer as Yosef crossed from inner shadow into dwindling sunlight that revealed his face. He almost missed the flash of joy on her face as it shifted instantly to a startled look in her eyes that turned sad. Behind them, Yosef heard the entrance door rattle, open, and then close. He heard the familiar sound of sandals coming off feet and then of footsteps crossing the hall to join them.

"Rebecca! The priests imprisoned and held in Rome that we heard were to be released—they're back! Three of them entered the hall as we were discussing the—"

Mathias's voice trailed off as he saw his younger son. The delight that eased the lines of his face held steady, and his smile broadened as he hurried to embrace Yosef, half-spinning him with his strength.

Over his father's shoulder, Yosef saw Miriam had not moved but stood as if rooted in place, and now her eyes glistened. Tears silently ran down her cheeks, and one that dropped from her chin was caught in the day's last sunbeam behind her—as she backed away, then twisted and headed for her room.

XXVII

JERUSALEM

The table had been cleared following the evening meal. The conversation had been light and more subdued than he had imagined it would be, with only a few questions about Rome that he had answered without giving the more upsetting details.

Yosef had scanned his family as they ate. Matthew's and his father's faces showed there was much that they wanted to say but had refrained from during the meal, deferring until later. And he knew his older brother, Matthew, who sat across from him, had deferred to their father. After leaving so abruptly earlier, Miriam had joined them for the Kiddush, and had sat next to him during dinner but had not spoken, not even seeming curious as he talked of the splendor of Emperor Nero's palace and the many things he had seen in Rome.

Yosef's mother now sat in a nearby sitting area after cleaning up and putting the food away, probably sensing there would be talk that his father felt was not her concern. But Yosef understood his mother and her lineage—royalty was in her blood, and anything affecting her family involved her. So, she remained in reach of the conversation and would listen to everything and speak her mind later, alone with her husband.

Mathias glanced at Miriam, who remained at the table, and then darted a look at his wife and held it for a moment. Yosef caught and followed that exchange. His mother's return expression to Mathias showed a request: "Let her stay."

Mathias took a drink from his cup that he rolled between his hands before setting it down in front of him. "Yosef, the situation has become even more of a tangle. You know that before you left for Rome, Ananias, the High Priest, illegally seized control and ordered the death of Yakov, the brother of Yeshua ish Natzrat and leader of the Netzarim, who as you know have claimed this Yeshua was the Messiah. It's no matter whether the leadership believed or didn't believe that to be so—it was an unacceptable abuse of his power to carry out such punishment without Roman approval, so Ananias was deposed and replaced. But that did not settle the unrest. More priests were imprisoned for speaking out against Rome, and while you've been gone, opposition to King Agrippa has grown. Most now see him as simply Rome's puppet." He looked at Miriam again—and slightly shook his head—she had remained next to Yosef with her head bowed.

He continued: "Agrippa was hand-in-hand with Lucceus Albinus, the former Roman procurator whose actions had incited the Zealots to active aggression. But then he was recently replaced with what is rumored to be an even harsher man, Gessius Florus, and that has enraged the Sicarii. And they have now become the deadliest of all the Jewish enemies of Rome. And enemies of any Jewish officials or citizens who collaborate with the Romans."

Miriam raised her head, now watching and listening, as their father continued.

"Gessius Florus called on us—many of the Temple and city leaders—shortly after he arrived in Judea, during his first visit to Jerusalem. He and his wife seemed sincere about respecting our people and religion."

Yosef heard Miriam's breathing change and, with a sideways glimpse, saw her face tighten, and her eyes widen, more of the Miriam he knew before Rome and not the dull, round-faced girl he had greeted just a few hours earlier.

"These procurators—now Florus—have proven not to be respectful." Mathias paused and nodded at his older son, and Yosef saw that Miriam, too, studied her brother Matthew, her eyes glinting under the lantern's light.

"After his initial visit here and his return to Caesarea," Mathias continued, "Florus favored the local Greeks over the Jewish citizens. The Hellenists took advantage of his policies and insulted the Jews in Caesarea and the surrounding area."

"Has no one brought a complaint before Florus?" Yosef asked.

"I'm afraid what is building is more than a complaint, and something far more dangerous is coming," Mathias replied. "Your brother is now one of the three in command of the Levites of the Temple guard." He nodded at Matthew to continue—"Tell him of the others."

"The captain of the Guard, my superior, Eleasar, son of Ananias—"

"The former High Priest?" Yosef interrupted.

"Yes, and he is truly his father's son. His views about Romans and their treatment of Jews are uncompromising. His hatred grows every day."

"Matthew and I have tried to talk to him and the Sanhedrin about petitioning for a dialog with Florus," Mathias interjected, "to reverse the course that things are taking. Now that you've returned," he nodded to Yosef, "and have helped free and bring home the imprisoned priests—we hope they'll listen." He sighed.

"But," Matthew held up a hand, "there are too many voices and agendas... others are stirring trouble. Yohanan ben Levi, who is the voice for those in Galilee, has aligned himself with the Zealots. Also, there is Menahem ben Judah and Elazar ben Yair... the Sicarii leaders"—Yosef felt Miriam stiffen and draw in a sharp breath—"and Simon bar Giora, who has the support of both freed Roman slaves and the common people. Many of the Sanhedrin dislike this Simon, thinking little of the lower class he represents." Matthew locked eyes with his younger brother. "You know these men, Yosef, you know their egos and that they don't change their minds once it is set if it serves their purpose—no matter the logic against them." Matthew shook his head and half-turned to his father, who now seemed even more worn and tired.

"What of Yohanan ben Zaccai?... Before I left for Rome, he was—and hopefully still is—a moderate?"

His father nodded, and his face eased slightly. "Yes, he still is a reasonable voice, and he advocates for a meeting with the Romans—whether with Florus or some other high-ranking official, perhaps Cestius Gallus, the governor in Antioch—and somehow, some way to find common ground to coexist under Roman rule."

"That's what I believe we must do, too," Yosef said and rubbed his eyes. The many days and sleepless nights of the road were upon him. "I'm tired, so perhaps we can discuss them—and the situation—more tomorrow." But he first had to ask the question that he wanted to ask earlier but had not been able. He rose, and his father and brother stood with him. "How are our cousins?" he asked as he turned from the table, "Leah and Rachel?" Matthew's eyes flashed down to Miriam, who had remained seated and then back up to his brother.

"Leah is well, I believe... but Yonatan her husband has become one firebrand who hopes to ignite an open conflict with the Romans. I do not trust him—he is a Zealot on the edge of becoming a Sicarii."

"She's afraid," Miriam spoke for the first time.

"Of the Zealots or the Sicarii?" Yosef asked, looking down at her. She shook her head, not looking up. "Of him... she fears Yonatan."

XXVIII

JERUSALEM

Miriam picked up the sparking stones, struck them together over the wick, and when it caught, she carefully carried the lamp, cradled in her palm, from the table by her bed to the window that opened onto the courtyard. The flax wick glowed at one end, held in place by the groove of the lamp that ran into the olive oil that fed the flame. Burning brighter now, it gave off a sweet scent. It was a simple design, made of fired clay, while finer bronze lamps were used in the rest of the home. She liked this one for its simplicity and because the old man, Zechariah, had made it for her. Meeting him had been the only good thing she remembered from that day. Had it not been for him... she shook her head and studied her hands in the light. No tremble. She tested them with the memory. Seeing Yosef so unexpectedly that afternoon had shaken her. He, more than anyone, could get her to talk about what she had sworn to never tell anyone. Since he had left for Rome, she had prayed for his safe return. Now he had returned, and she wished him away—still safe but anywhere apart from her.

What had happened to her on that day that had changed her life was Yosef's fault. He had always included her at every opportunity in his exploration of the city and even outside the walls. But it was within the walls, and under the city, that she found something most fascinating—the tunnels. The sense of discovery when in them, laced with threads of fear and the uncertainty of the unknown, was always present when she and Yosef—often with Leah and Matthew—walked and sometimes crawled through them. They all delighted in finding lost chambers and passageways and imagining treasure they never found but dreamed was always possible.

Her engagement and family duties had set those adventures aside, and with Yosef gone, they seemed to be a thing of the past. Then one day near the outer court, a gust of wind had lifted her scarf and carried it away. Chasing it had led to a place Yosef had shown her had a hidden entrance to a series of tunnels that had connected the Temple area, the fortress, and the Northern City. The scarf that had blown along until it was trapped against a wall at the bend of the alley, where she saw the tracks of sandals with studded nail soles: Roman soldiers. Two sets went straight to the blind dead-end and behind a shoulder-height dense shrub thick with thorns.

That shrub had been planted—Yosef had told her—decades, if not centuries ago in that overlooked corner. It served as the guardian of a cunningly fitted trapdoor in the ground. When she was smaller, she could more easily get around the shrub, avoiding its barbs as Yosef held the door open from inside, and slip in after him. Now her robe and flesh had caught on thorns as she opened the door and looked down. There had been enough sunlight to show the top part of the ladder. Below she had seen the last of someone's lamplight pull away from the base of the ladder and into a tunnel. Curious, she had recalled that Yosef had cached lamps and skins of olive oil at different areas of the tunnels, including near the foot of every access and exit point. If they were still there, she could find them by feel. If not, she would climb back up and leave her curiosity behind in the dark. She wished now—for the thousandth time—she had.

The lamp and stones had been there. In the dark—just a square of light above—she had lit the lamp, pocketed the stones, and slung a small goatskin of oil over her shoulder. A clanking and clink of metal on metal had determined her direction—following the soldiers. She had walked for some time, remembering only some of how the tunnels were situated, because she had been young and mostly just followed Yosef before. Ahead was the broader glow of more than just the one or two handheld lamps she expected. She had heard a voice, a Roman's, and slowed, shielding her light with one hand as she had edged closer. Stumbling slightly on crumbled chunks of stone that had likely fallen from overhead, she had slipped behind a pile of rubble just ahead of her, near the circle of light. She had blown out her lamp and listened as the Roman's voice had grown distinct and imperious.

"These are men I trust, and they are our couriers. They'll post and retrieve messages between us, here."

She had peeked over the stones to see a Roman, a nobleman or official, to judge by his robes and bearing. He had pointed at the two soldiers and then on a spike driven into the stone wall just above shoulder height he hung a cylinder of leather—sealed at one end and open at the other. The man had turned his head, his face now in the lamplight. It was the Roman procurator who had visited them!

"I expected you"—the Roman now spoke with a figure in the shadows in one of three or four adjoining tunnels—"to live up to your side of our agreement. Or..."

126

The man in the shadows next to him had replied, "I will not fail you."

The man had sounded Jewish but spoke Latin—and she had thought his voice familiar, but the slight echo on stone made it difficult to tell. She moved a little, and loose rocks she brushed against rolled and clattered. The shadowy man had then whirled further back into the darkness, and she had then seen the flash of Gessius Florus's ring and arm cuff as he waved a hand at the two soldiers. "Find out what made that sound and take care of it," he ordered. Then he too had spun toward another tunnel opening and faded away.

Miriam had turned and run blindly back the way she had come. Over her shoulder she saw two bouncing lights—their jostling and jumping revealed brawny hands and harsh, coarse faces—that came after her far faster than she could stumble into the pitch black ahead of her. Then the two men—they had caught her, dragged her back to the broad area of the tunnel junction... and... and...

She was now on her knees in her own room and shook her head, trying to loosen that part, to cast that memory from her mind. The lamp's light flickered but not from the whisper of air through the window. She studied the flame and her shaking hand. After a long while, it steadied. Turning to her bed, she feared the shadows would come to life in the night, but she willed them to be still. She quenched the sputtering wick. Sleep would come eventually. So would another day... when she would have an unwelcome certainty to face. Yosef would not accept her silence. She would have to talk to her brother.

* * *

"And Matthias ben Theophilus is the High Priest now?" Yosef heard a scraping sound above them and saw the wooden shutter of Miriam's room move slightly from across the courtyard.

"Yes, Ananias's choice, Joshua ben Gamaliel, was quickly replaced by Agrippa." His father sighed.

The courtyard still held the morning's coolness, but the rising sun would soon warm it. An array of bowls was before them, most filled with fruit, but two with the porridge his mother had prepared for them. Yosef pulled a porridge bowl to him. "So, what drove Ananias to execute Yakov ben Yosef, Yeshua ish Natzrat's brother?"

"What do you mean, Yosef?"

"I mean the Netzarim are not rebels at heart. Didn't you tell me once you remembered him, Yeshua ish Natzrat?"

"Yes, he was put to death the year your mother and I married. Crucified by the Romans. We had heard of him at the time—all the stories. An earthquake shook the city the day he was crucified... the day he died. Many buildings were damaged."

"But of course, the Netzarim say he didn't remain in the tomb, and that he rose and still lives."

His father scoffed. "Stories... kept alive by his followers."

"In Rome, his Greek and Roman followers now outnumber the Jewish ones. There they are called *Christians*. Nero blamed them for the great fire I witnessed—it nearly destroyed the city of Rome."

"It could well have been them," his father suggested.

"I have my doubts." Yosef reached for the stone pitcher of fresh water and filled his cup. "I have this feeling Nero hates them because they refuse to acknowledge his divinity. They prescribe that only to their Christos—their anointed one."

"Well, the Romans would not be Romans without finding some new threat to the empire that they can react to. And some of our own people are no better. It seems every year there is some new rebel claiming to be anointed by God, to lead us to freedom. And the people are easily swayed. They want to believe."

A draught of wind swirled through the courtyard, rippling the leaves of the fig tree that had been planted when Yosef was a child. He watched it now in contemplation, with the sense that people and events around him and he, himself, were leaves blowing in a wind that fanned deadly flames. "You say that some—the Sicarii—are now retaliating also against people who simply want to work with the Romans?" He caught the movement above; Miriam's shutter was now fully open.

"Yes," his father answered. "Only a few incidents have taken place, but I worry it will get worse as I don't see Rome, especially Gessius Florus, backing off." Mathias straightened and rubbed his forehead with the palm of his hand. "It's the same for some of our own people. The Zealots and Sicarii now consider those they think are collaborating with the Romans to be threats to all Jews. Even if they don't. Even if they're not in a position to aid the Romans and benefit from that."

"What do you mean, Father?"

"Like those who use Roman goods. I know households destroying their redslipped plates and bowls... anything that's been manufactured by Rome or provinces it controls. The Sicarii deem that these objects taint the user. I've heard stories of that alone marking people for their punishment."

"That's ethnic allegiance taken to an insane degree," Yosef said, shocked that anti-Roman sentiment had grown so much while he had been gone.

"Yes. I'm meeting with the Sanhedrin tomorrow, and that will be discussed." Mathias stood. "Will you join me?"

Yosef saw Miriam's face now in her window, her countenance pale and puffy again. She had been listening. "No, Father. Today I want to talk to Miriam... and tomorrow, maybe walk the city... and just think about what's ahead."

"Ahead for us... for Judea... with the Romans?"

"Not that just yet, Father. I need to think about what's ahead for me." Mathias nodded and turned away to his own room.

Yosef sat alone after his father left. Miriam had been listening, and he hoped that now she would come down. And she did, hesitantly at first. She stopped to say something to their mother in her sitting room and then paused at the courtyard entrance.

He stood and walked to the fig tree, remembering when it had matched his height at five or six years old. It now towered over him. He looked up at the sky through its branches, the shifting leaves obscuring and then revealing the brightening blue of the sky and a string of clouds clustering above. Her footsteps on the stone came closer and stopped next to him.

"Yossi, remember how you would eat the green figs and then get sick?"

"Oh yes. It's hard to forget that," he turned to his sister. "Will you sit with me awhile?"

XXIX

The Temple and Fortress Antonia rising some distance behind them, Yosef and Miriam sat on the terrace atop their home and watched the sunset behind the three towers. The southernmost, Phaesel, was the tallest at nearly one hundred fifty feet high. The next was Hippicus, and then the northernmost and most decorative, Mariamne, was half the height of Phaesel. All protected the western side of the city. Herod had built and named the largest for his brother, the second for a loyal friend, and the smallest but most beautiful for the wife he had loved but murdered out of jealousy.

As the sunset turned to deep gold, to orange-red, and then to a purpling that darkened to shadow, their view of the towers at a slight angle revealed the tinting on the limestone blocks, where torches and lanterns sprung up as flares of light around and within the towers. With no more red left in the western sky and the three stars brightening above them, Shabbat ended.

Much of the day Yosef and Miriam had sat silently, enjoying being together after such a long time. But their silence was also awkward, with interludes of a brief conversation to answer Miriam's questions about Rome and his journey. Yosef told her of the good things, the spectacle and beauty, he had seen. She did not quite relax, but he sensed a sharpness of thought behind her eyes, and the tilt of her head toward him revealed that engaged listening he knew so well from growing up together.

"And what about you, Miriam?" He did not need to be specific. Something had happened to his sister, something severe enough to break her engagement to a man he felt she loved, enough to smother—seemingly almost extinguish—her spirit. But she was still that smart girl so quick to learn and to discern things and to form her own opinions. Given time, she would speak for herself and—he hoped—answer his unasked questions.

"Are Roman and Greek women so much freer than we—Jewesses—are?" The light from the lamp on the stand next to her cast the near side of her face in shadow as she turned to Yosef.

"In some ways, they are—many more ways for the noble or highborn."

"But still, even for them... men have power over them. Right?"

Yosef did not know why she asked these questions, but he answered, "Yes, in both cultures and societies, it's usually that way."

"Matthew told me that Yonatan beats Leah."

Her abruptness startled him. "What?!" Yosef knew Yonatan was overbearing and harsh and callous toward Leah but not that he had struck her.

"Rachel told me one day after you left because Leah wouldn't, and now she avoids Matthew and me." Miriam rested her hand briefly on his forearm. "Yosef, don't try to see her. She doesn't want you to know, and if she realizes you do, it'll only be worse for her."

"Someone has to do some—"

"—And someone will, but it can't be you." The silent moment that followed turned into minutes. Mariam knew Yosef must move on. "What do you have planned for tomorrow?"

"To walk..." Yosef shook his head and straightened up. "And to think. I haven't done that here"—he glanced out over the dark city speckled with spots of light—"in a long time. Why don't you join me?" He saw the flash of concern cross her face. "What is it?"

"Nothing... I... okay," she sighed, "I'll go with you."

* * *

Yosef and Miriam had wandered the city extensively as children and learned so much it seemed adults overlooked in their busy routine of daily life. Yosef wanted to see it all again with that childlike focus for the first in a long time.

The two elongated parallel hills of the city had corresponding rows of houses. The higher, Zion, was the Upper City, also called the "Citadel" by King David, the father of Solomon, who had built their first temple. The lower hill was slightly curved, like a crescent moon, and its northern section held the Fortress Antonia, the Temple enclosure, and a courtyard between them. That courtyard was the site of the former Akra, the Greek citadel that had been situated upon a rocky knoll, both of which had been cut down two hundred years earlier. The southern section held the oldest section of the Lower City. The two hills were flanked and divided by three deep valleys or ravines, up to three hundred feet deep and with sheer walls in some places.

The city's walls had been built over the centuries in three stages. The oldest—the first—wall would be the most difficult to breach because of these valleys, the hills on which it was built, and the fortress and defenses above them. That wall extended from the

Hippicus tower due east to the western wall of the Temple enclosure near the Xystus and the council house. Also, from the Hippicus it extended southward to the gate of the Essenes, and then eastward to the fountain of Siloam, and then northward to the Ophel, where it turned to join the southeastern corner of the Temple enclosure. The second wall started next to the Gennath gate in the first wall and extended around and enclosed the Northern City, terminating at the Antonia Fortress.

The third wall, which protected the New City, also began at the Hippicus, and ran north to the tower Psephinus and then extended east past monument of Helena and the caverns of the kings and to the northeast corner tower near the Monument of the Fuller. It then continued south to form the eastern wall that enclosed the section called the Kidron valley, and finally ended at the first wall at the Ophel. Agrippa had encircled the city with this third wall as it grew more populous and gradually crept northward. Now considerably larger, the newly enclosed region was called the New City and included the hill Bezetha, which was north of the Fortress Antonia and mostly separated from it by a westward arm of the Kidron valley. The site between them had been further excavated to more completely separate the foundations of Antonia from Bezetha. This increased the fortress's effective height and made it more formidable and defensible.

The city had eleven gates, nine along the outer walls and two passing through the second wall. They all were fortified and did not allow direct entry into the city without a sharp ninety-degree turn. This prevented enemies on horseback from charging full speed, straight ahead through the gates, and made it difficult to use a battering ram to break them down. Above some gates was a hole through which boiling liquids could be poured on attackers.

* * *

On the boulevard outside their home, Yosef and Miriam walked toward the upper agora, the open market. Ahead, more to the east, the Temple and Antonia with its corner towers, rose above them. The agora, surrounded by porticoes, was the forum of the city, the place where affluent citizens assembled for business, most often waited upon by the commoners. Parts of the agora had grown organically and unplanned, and there were myriad paths and alleys. Most people knew the ones that took them from one specific area to the next or to locations important to them. But the children, especially those full of curiosity like Yosef, Miriam, and their friends, knew all the windings—where they started, led, and ended.

The marketplace was filled, just as packed as Yosef remembered. But there were ways to avoid the throngs and crowds. "Where are we headed?" Miriam asked.

"Toward the arches and then down the steps into the Lower City." Yosef slowed so she could walk beside him. Glancing down, he noted her pallor that was so startling the day before was diminishing, and some color had now risen to her face. "Remember how we used to explore?"

Miriam nodded with the trace of a grin, the first he had seen since his return. "Want to look at something first—before we go to the Lower City?" He slowed even more.

She looked up at him. "What do you mean?"

Yosef pointed ahead to where the alley forked. "Remember? To the left leads to where I first took you down into the tunnels." He stopped at her look. "What's wrong?"

Miriam was stationary and not looking at him. "I'd rather not." She shook her head and looked at the way they had come. "Maybe I should just go back home."

Yosef saw some of the expression he had seen days before, steal back into her face. "It's okay," he assured her. "We need not do that— maybe another time is better." Yosef walked on to the right instead, and after a moment, she followed. She caught up and was beside him as they took the branching alley toward the southwest corner of the Temple. There they arrived at the terraced series of steps that began at the Ophel and went first down and across the Tyropoeon valley, then across the Lower City, and finally up to Mount Zion and the Upper City.

* * *

On the southeast hill was Jerusalem's oldest section and, on its slopes, the crowded houses of the poor, the ordinary people. This had been the fortified city occupied in King David's time, supplied on its east flank by the Gihon Spring, which strengthened it that much more. Early in the mornings, farmers headed to work in the fields outside the city walls—most of those fields being rich olive groves that covered the surrounding hillsides and provided the city's only major export.

Just past the gate into the Lower City, Yosef and Miriam entered a maze of dusty streets and alleyways, running uphill and down in every direction, and full of the sounds of hundreds of voices, the clatter of hooves, and odors of cooking food. Many taverns and restaurants here supplied fresh or salted fish, fried locusts, vegetables, soup, pastry and fruit, and patrons here could purchase or drink local wine or imported beer.

Then they came to the bazaar where merchants sold perishables like fruits and vegetables, dried fish, and sacrificial animals, and nonperishables like clothes, perfumes, and jewelry. The market street was always crowded and busy, especially on Mondays and Thursdays, the primary market days, when citizens and visitors came to buy goods. Shabbat was the only day that the street was empty.

Along the small market street, they passed open-air shops where Jerusalem's craftsmen sat at work: the city's weavers, dyers, potters, bakers, tailors, carpenters, and metalworkers. Craftsmen had been organized into professional groups for a long time, and most of them worked in public shops. The members of each group lived in a cluster of houses in their own neighborhoods and usually had their own synagogue. There were dozens of synagogues in Jerusalem.

As Yosef and Miriam passed through the market area, off to one side was where Miriam knew Zechariah had his stall. As they neared it, she saw he was not at his potter's wheel, which was a good thing—even nearly blind, his milk-white eyes always turned her way when she was near. In the months following her attack—after he had saved her—she had visited him, but he did not know she lived in the Upper City.

Yosef's family lived outside of areas where vendors and craftsmen plied their trades. Yosef could not help but see the similarity here to the poor areas—the tenements—of Rome. Each city had its transition from the community of the upper-class to the common people who lived below. Different cities, different people... same circumstances. When Herod's projects had ended, thousands of men were out of work, and that had caused hardship in many areas, like Galilee, where many had turned to banditry. Jerusalem had remained fortunate, but still, there was an undercurrent of tension that ran deep. For now, Roman taxes went to Rome. Before at least much of Herod's taxes had gone back into salaries that employed the people in his building projects.

* * *

Hours later, with the sun sinking, they had circled the city. This time as Yosef walked the avenue home, Miriam's shadow was cast alongside his. "Tomorrow at noon I have to meet Father and Matthew at the Hall of Hewn Stone." He paused before opening the door. "Do you want to go with me in the morning—before I meet with them—and check out some of the places we discovered?" He teased her: "You used to beg me to take you." Yosef smiled at her, but she did not return the smile. They had talked throughout the day, but nothing had come out about what had changed her so. Still, it had been good just to be with her.

Miriam shook her head, "No, Yossi. We're not children anymore. We have to deal with mature things now." She touched his arm and then left him to go to her room.

XXX

FEBRUARIUS 66 CE

JERUSALEM

Miriam heard Yosef in the courtyard telling their mother he would not be back until the evening meal and she turned away from the window. His repeatedly asking her to visit the tunnels with him had frightened her. What was only a dozen feet beneath the streets of the much of the city was a constant reminder of when she had thought she would never see sunlight again. Then from the black edge of her terror had come a voice.

"Let her go." The man's bass rumble had been sharp in the tunnel's confines, the words ringing on the stone. Her eyes had tried to find the source, but the light had been too dim to see much of the speaker.

The Romans—the second one now atop her—had frozen for a second. Then the one between her legs had risen, and the other, the first to take her, had pressed even harder on her shoulders to keep her pinned down. His hands had at first slipped in the blood from the long cut across the top of her breasts and then dug in with long fingernails that gouged her soft flesh. Not deep enough to kill, but painful, her chest wound was oozing blood. She was slick with it and had also bled below her waist, and that had been—still was—the pain that shrieked in her mind. She had cried out, and the standing Roman had kicked her.

"Quiet, bitch." He had spurred her again with his heel and then, with his dagger out and in hand, he had stepped toward the man at the rim of the pool of light. "Whoever you are, you picked a dark place to die." As one lamp had gone out, he rushed at the man.

The deep voice had replied, "Darkness doesn't bother me, Roman."

The man had come closer, and in the remaining light, she had seen that he wielded a six-foot wooden staff, and the thick ferrule end had jabbed into the soldier's throat. Hard. The Roman had croaked and staggered back. The man had moved further into the light, and his staff had flicked out and back to align along his forearm and then dart out. The other hand carried a large crescent-bladed dagger whose razor edge arced forward like the waning moon's glow crossing a night sky. The man had sliced the Roman's arms to the bone from shoulder to wrist, first one, and then the other. The Roman's weapon and arms dropped, and then his scream had been choked off by the sound of gurgling blood as the man twisted because the blade had shifted from a forehand hold to a reverse-fist grip that had punched the blade at the Roman's exposed throat. The tip had scored a long, arcing red line, and the flesh had held together for a half-second then gaped wide as it pumped a jet of scarlet seen even in the fading light from the single lamp.

"Now you are the one who dies in darkness," the man said as he looked down at the twitching body, then stepped over that Roman toward the other still holding her.

"Stop!" ordered the Roman who now held his own blade under her chin. The last lamp's wick had sputtered, withered, and gone out. In the pitch black, the sounds of their breathing had been amplified. One's breath had been fast and harsh, like the panting of a feral dog over prey. Hers had been filled with wracking sobs, and the breaths of the third had been deep and steady until the man spoke.

"As I said—darkness doesn't bother me, Roman."

The three or four heartbeats of silence afterward had seemed much longer than they had been before she had felt the blade pulled away from her throat and the arm crushing her chest removed. Then the Roman had screamed just before she passed out.

Later—she had not known how long at first—she had opened her eyes to sunlight streaming and a breath of fresh wind coming through a high window. She had been placed on a low cot on one wall, and on the opposite wall was a workbench with a potter's wheel stained in splotches by red clay. The room was filled with an earthy smell.

"Where am I?" she had asked the man hunched over a nearby table. Sitting up, she had felt the tightness in her chest and realized that all around her had been bound a cloth compress, and blood had seeped through its center. The pain was so sharp it shallowed her breathing to a thin whistle in and out. She winced as she swung her legs off the cot. Her torn gown and shredded undergarment had been replaced with a long, simple gray tunic. She gently pressed her fingers through the fabric to sense the likely bruises on her lower stomach and upper thighs. But someone had washed the blood away... the stranger! She looked at him again and shuddered at the thought of what had happened and that he—a man—had tended to such private and personal wounds. "Who are you?" she asked.

"You're in my home, young lady." She watched him, his back to her, reach for a clay pitcher to his right. "You were hurt and needed care." He turned and held out a full cup to her. "I thought it best to bring you here, quietly."

She had cast her eyes down, not able to meet his. "You killed those Romans?"

"Yes." He lowered the cup closer to her, and she watched the cords and tendons on his gnarled hand relax as she took it from him and then looked up into a rough, seamed face with clouded eyes, so opaque and veiled white she had no idea of their original color. "You're... you're blind!" she had gasped.

"Yes, young lady... mostly. I can see dark shapes, shadows of things, but only in the brightest daylight."

"But how... how did you...?"

"Miriam?" her mother's call shook her from the memory of meeting Zechariah, "please come down and help me."

"Yes, Mother."

* * *

Yosef crossed the Tyropoeon valley that ran almost straight north and south and split Jerusalem in two. He climbed the stairs that ended at the Temple enclosure's royal porch, the royal portico where he would walk past several columns before turning sharply to cross the Court of the Gentiles and past the low wall with engraved stones stating "No outsider shall enter the protective enclosure around the sanctuary. And whoever is caught will only have himself to blame for the ensuing death." This low wall surrounded the entire Temple. He passed the entrance to the Hall of Hewn Stone where he would soon meet his father and brother. Walking along the landing next to the Temple wall, he thought of what Miriam had asked him about the freedoms granted Roman women, then he entered through the southern gate into the Court of Women. This square courtyard, a little more than two hundred feet on each side, was as close as Israelite women could get to the Temple. Within the court stood four massive lampstands, each almost ninety feet tall. As he walked across, he passed the Nicanor—or Beautiful Gate—on his left. He paused a moment. Only now did it occur to him that the name was that of his Greek-Roman friend. He looked up to where he could see farther off the highest corner tower of the Fortress Antonia visible above the Temple enclosure's northern wall.

Fortress Antonia was built on an adjacent rocky hill that peaked at the northwest corner of the Temple mount Herod had constructed. From the top of its wall, the fortress towered almost eighty feet above the valleys to the north and west, with those northern and western walls built mostly upon the edge of cliffs that overlooked the valleys. The southern and eastern walls were surrounded by a deep, waterless, moat that had been dug for defensive purposes. Given the fortress had been built on elevated bedrock, those rock areas that were not sheer cliffs were covered with blocks made to be flat at a steep angle with smooth faces and joints so tight no attacking soldier could possibly get a foothold.

The stronghold had square towers at each of the four corners. Three of the turrets were almost eighty feet tall, with the southeastern tower being more than one hundred feet tall. There it commanded a view of the entire Outer Courtyard and into the Temple's Court of the Gentiles. Antonia housed most of the Roman garrison in Jerusalem, usually a cohort of about five hundred men, and there they also stored the High Priest's vestments. Covering nearly the same area as the Temple's fortress enclosure, there was room inside for shops and many rows of troop tents in its open courtyard. Another broad— almost fifty feet across—double cloister ran along the western wall of the Outer Courtyard, which lay between the two fortresses. Yosef had been part of many discussions about this cloister's purpose. King Herod, to satisfy the Romans, had included it in the Second Temple's construction so the Romans could keep watch over the Temple with sentries patrolling from Antonia to the walkways atop the four walls of the Temple enclosure. There they could preserve order, posting sentinels to guard against insurrection by those Jews who still bristled under Roman rule.

Yosef noticed the sun was almost directly overhead. It was time for another meeting, and his father had said the High Priest and Eleasar ben Ananias would join them. Word had come that Cestius Gallus, the Roman Governor of Syria and the Judean Provinces, would visit Jerusalem during Passover. There would be much argument again and dissent about the Roman's visit, its purpose, and what should be done about it.

XXXI

Just beyond the Court of Women, at the entrance of the Priest's Court, the meeting hall and chambers for the Sanhedrin were built into a wall of the Temple—half-inside and half-outside the space designated as the sanctuary. Separate from the sanctuary that had been constructed according to ritual and tradition from uncut stones untouched by iron, the Hall of Hewn Stone functioned as a sovereign court and the center of political and religious leadership in Judea.

Except—Yosef thought, as he passed its rows of low block seating for students and the tiered blocks for the seventy other members of the Sanhedrin arced around the High Priest's chair— *Judea's leadership was not unified*. Loud voices greeted him as he entered a small side chamber.

"Agrippa is a tool of the Romans. He cares nothing for *his* people," sneered Eleasar ben Ananias, captain of the Temple guard. "He has asked Cestius Gallus to Jerusalem at Passover to hear our complaints about Gessius Florus—but that is a meaningless token effort."

"Would you rather him—or anyone—not attempt to resolve our issues with the Romans?" Yosef asked as he entered the room. They turned and looked at him as he joined them.

"My son is right," Mathias said and directed his words to the High Priest, Matthias ben Theophilus. "And, Your Honor, we must present the Romans a single—rational—voice in any meeting with Governor Gallus and the procurator."

Their body language and expressions had told Yosef their opinions without their needing to speak. Eleasar was stiff with anger, his head up with a hard look in his eyes. The High Priest listened with his chin down and lowered eyes that darted beneath his heavy brows to Eleasar and then away, as if their roles were reversed and the captain of the Temple guard his superior. Yosef's father, shoulders squared, stood with feet planted as he gestured earnestly with his hands as he did when most impassioned. Matthew, one of the Temple guard officers now, matched his father's stance but remained silent.

Then their father's last words caught up with Yosef's thoughts. "So, Gessius Florus will be here with Cestius Gallus for the meeting?" Yosef asked.

"Yes, accompanied by his wife, who I'm told appreciates our religion," the High Priest answered. "She wishes to observe Passover while here."

"What she wishes doesn't matter," scoffed Eleasar. "But these discussions with Gallus"—he gave Yosef a dismissive look—"must bear fruit... or—"

"—Or will some of our more aggressive factions," interrupted Yohannan ben Zaccai, "perhaps Menahem Judah and Elazar ben Yair, use their particular means of communication?" His tone was sardonic, but his expression benign. He stood in the doorway, inclined his head at the room's occupants and then stepped inside. "Letting Zealots or Sicarii speak for Judea is not the exchange with the Romans that best serves our country."

"When what has been done," said Eleasar, "... what is being done to Jews by the Romans gets beyond our control, then we are not a nation. We live under the Roman heel and at their sufferance."

Eleasar's words—directed to Zaccai, a respected tannaim, sage, and teacher—were impolite and harsh, but Yosef knew many felt as Eleasar did, and that number was growing. He turned to Zaccai on the block next to him and said, "It's good to see you here from Galilee. Do you still live in Arav?"

"Yes, and I'm surrounded by the unruly whose anger is inflamed," he sighed, "by both the leaders here in Jerusalem and the Romans, except for Sepphoris. I think they follow Rome to a man." He shook his head and raised his voice. "I heard of Gallus's coming visit." He nodded at Yosef's father, a smile on his lips. "And perhaps a tannaim should be part of the discussion about that meeting, and the kohanim," he nodded at the High Priest.

"My son, Yosef," Mathias said, "you all know has spent much time in Rome. And"—he looked at Yosef—"did you not meet Gessius Florus while there?"

"Yes, Father." Yosef knew what was coming. His father had already mentioned it privately.

"Then he should join us, Mathias"—Zaccai directed his comment to the High Priest as well—"as one of the men that speak with the governor and procurator."

* * *

Yosef had left them when the discussion became more each person talking and less all listening and agreeing. His final comment to them had been this: "One thing I learned while with the Romans is that they have built—and continue to keep—their empire through the weakness of other countries' leadership. They exploit them, and that's their leverage. If we argue in front of them and are intransigent, they will sit quietly and watch us defeat ourselves." He had then paused before adding, "I stand with my country in pressing for redress, for our relationship with the Romans to improve and become based on mutual respect and tolerance. But if we strike out at them— if what are now small slights and protests against them grow—the Romans will bring upon us a punishment you cannot imagine." Unlike when he had entered, Yosef's words left them in momentary silence and—he hoped—considering what he had said.

Minutes later, as Yosef went down the steps from the Court of Women—descending six feet—into the outer court, he looked across the open expanse and through the colonnade that ran the length of the Temple enclosure. Just beyond was an array of merchants and money changers and the side street that paralleled the outer wall of the Temple. The road itself had been built and completed even as the Temple was under construction. Yosef, Matthew, Leah, and Miriam had played among the stalls and small shops to the raucous sound of the merchants' calls for customers to stop and sample their wares and services.

Just before passing under one of the connecting arches, Yosef looked behind him at the magnificence of the Temple enclosure. It seemed a series of foothills leading to a dazzling mountain covered with snow, where it was not overlaid with plates of gold. The afternoon sunlight reflected from the Temple in a fierce blaze that forced him to blink and turn away. It was nearly like staring straight into the sun. He turned his back on the glare and walked deep in thought until a small boy chasing another cut in front of him and brought him to a stop. He recognized the junction where two animal sellers were situated and heard their calls cast back and forth to persuade or dissuade buyers to one or from the other. The shop across from him was for a seller of lamps and fuel, olive oil. Next to it, semi-blocked by several large, broad-bottomed clay urns, was the dead-end alley he recalled led to one of the hidden entries to the tunnels under the Temple. The apparently useless alley had now become a storage area for the shops closest to it.

Yosef turned into the lamp seller's and minutes later slipped into and down that alley, carrying a lamp and a small goatskin of oil, with two sparking stones held in its attached pouch. It seemed he walked much further past the right-hand bend than he remembered before he reached the bush that he saw had become a larger tangle of a thorned tree. Looking back the way he had come, a reflex from his childhood, he then knelt beside the tree. Behind it was the open area he remembered Miriam being so excited to see after he described to her what he had found.

His smile at that memory dimmed as he thought of how resistant—how nervous—she had been when he had asked to visit the tunnels the other day. Careful of the thorns—some of them dagger-sharp and inches long—he swept a half-inch-thick layer of dirt from the trapdoor, always so camouflaged by the swirling, dust-laden wind deposited there at the end of the alley. Beneath his fingers, he felt the edges of the metal frame of the door that led below. Sliding closer, he hooked his fingers under the notches and lifted. With a soft squeal and spill of dirt, the door opened. He could see the top handholds that led to the long ladder still secured to the wall of the rough vertical tunnel that sank into the darkness below. He filled the lamp with oil, fastened the lid and strapped it to his chest, and then swung his legs over the lip and headed down.

In the darkness broken only by the circle of light from the lamp, his mind wandered back to hearing his father say Cleo would be coming to Jerusalem. He had conflicting thoughts and feelings. He half-searched for the wall markings he knew would show an upcoming branch or small chamber ahead. Holding the lamp high, he did not see the pile of rock before him and stumbled over it. The flailing arc of light briefly revealed a crossroad he remembered. Then—at the same time that he dropped the lamp to catch himself with his hands as he hit the ground—it came to him. That dream on board the ship returning from Rome. This was where he saw the woman attacked. That dream had faded quickly and never returned, but he was sure that before him, in this blackness, was the junction of tunnels that ran from just outside the outer court to join two others. One of them led to the fortress and the other to the Temple. Carefully, on his knees, he felt around for the lamp. Nothing. He shifted and reached. Still nothing. He was reasonably sure he could retrace his steps to the alley exit even in the pitch black if he had to, as he had done so once by necessity years ago.

Something sharp pricked his right-hand palm, and he yanked it back. Then slowly, he lowered it, and his fingers grazed a flat, odd-shaped piece of metal with a long point protruding from one side. Wondering what it might be, he held onto it as he continued to search for the lamp with his left hand. Minutes later, about to give up and to feel his way back down the tunnel he had passed through, he felt the still-slightly-warm wick end of the lamp. It felt light as he picked it up and shook it next to his ear—empty. The olive oil had spilled.

Letting out a breath he had not realized he had been holding, he switched to a sitting position from his knees and set the lamp and metal object between his outstretched legs. Fumbling fingers lifted the goatskin lanyard from around his neck, removed its stopper, felt for the lamp's reservoir and filled it with oil, and set it before him. The wick, thankfully, was still secure in its groove. Sealing the goatskin, he then took out the two stones from the pouch. Three strikes yielded ribbons of sparks that failed, but the wick caught the fourth and the tiny flame took hold and grew.

In the glow of light, he now saw what had stabbed his hand. He picked it up, and the tarnished metal gleamed dully as he turned it over. It was a hamsa, a depiction of an open right hand, its four fingers and thumb palm out—the hand of God that protected the wearer from evil and a sign of power and strength. It had been used as a clasp for a cloak or robe. Its retaining pin, affixed to the back, had been bent away from its closure at an angle. He pushed it back flat and into place and looked closer at something scratching or engraved on its back. He rubbed at the dull metal with the corner of his tunic, and stains came away to reveal silver and an inscription: "For Miriam."

XXXII

Caesarea

Caesarea Maritima—the city proper—was in its own way as impressive as the man-made harbor that made it a valuable asset to the Roman Empire. Herod, Rome's client-king, had not only constructed the port but also designed a well-planned grid of streets with a sophisticated sewage system underneath the city. Then he erected a theater, amphitheater, royal residence, and a temple, all of which he dedicated to Rome and Augustus.

The basilica, his palace complex on a jutting coastal promontory, was comprised of two levels. One looked upon the sea and included a vast seawater pool cut into the rock, and higher up, the main house was built of local kurkar stone and coated with a layer of bright white stucco. The complex included a large central courtyard bordered with peristyles and many strolling gardens, viewing knolls, towers, basins, and pools called naumachiae, where famous naval battles were reenacted in miniature as a spectacle for the king and his guests.

With the waters of the sea so close, the panoramic view from the palace—especially from the vantage point of the upper level—was spectacular. Cleo took in the lovely setting, the breathtaking sight of the sea and coast with the seaport just in view to the north. Her first night she had watched with delight as the flames atop the two towers marking the harbor's entrance danced in a swirling wind where sea met land. But she no longer saw its beauty.

Cleo had felt the tension in the land from the minute she set foot in Caesarea with Florus. As she rode along the route to Herod's palace—now the procurator's residence—the stony and occasionally angry Jewish faces turned their way as they passed. The only smiles were from the Syrian Greeks who made up a sizable part of the local population. She knew why they smiled and welcomed Gessius Florus.

Before leaving Rome, Poppaea had told her something she had not known before. Five years previously, Beryllus, one of Nero's tutors, had appealed to Nero on behalf of the Syrian Greeks in Caesarea, to revoke the equal-rights status of the Jews. He had done so, and so the Syrian Greeks now controlled the city government and worked hand-in-hand with the Romans. Florus publicly stated his support and preference for them upon his arrival, and emboldened by that support, the Syrian Greeks increased their disregard and disrespect of the Jews each day.

Not long after their arrival, Cleo had heard a courier delivering to Florus the administrative dispatches from Rome. The messenger had said Empress Poppaea had died and stunned, Cleo had not caught the courier to ask him for details. Trying to learn more from her husband had led to a disturbing incident—the first of what were to become commonplace conflicts.

"Did that messenger say Poppaea has died?" she had asked her husband.

When Florus had turned to her, the message pouch in his hands and still sealed, a smile had been on his face. It vanished as he spoke without answering her question: "Don't skulk about, listening at my door." He had then turned away from her to sit at his worktable strewn with scrolls of parchment and pages bound with twine.

She was startled at the tone he used when dealing with others, especially those she knew he judged beneath him, but had never used with her. She had paused before asking him again. "Gessius"—she had stepped further into his private office and closer toward him—"what has happened to Poppaea?"

The smile curled into a sneer on his lips as he looked up at her. "She's dead." Then he had looked back down, ignoring her as he broke the seal on the pouch. "Leave me," he had directed.

* * *

"What is it, Jucundus?" Florus looked up at his cavalry commander, who seemed both angry and nervous. "And stand still when you are before me."

"Lord Florus, there's been an incident in the city."

"What?" The procurator's head went back down to study the ledger spread open on the table. At the centurion's delay, he looked up again. "Tell me."

"At a Jewish synagogue"—he hesitated as Florus eyed him—"one of their places of worship." Jucundus did not like the unblinking stare. He shifted his weight from foot to foot and stopped at the scowl on the procurator's face. "On their Sabbath—the Jews' Shabbat—a Greek burned several birds in a pot of burning wood."

"You're interrupting me for something this stup–"

"He burned the birds at the entrance of the synagogue, my lord."

"So?" Florus spread his hands over the ledger and calculations he had been making, documenting how he was squeezing more tax revenue for Nero from Judea. "*This* work is important. I don't care about Greeks burning birds in front of Jews."

"My lord, this is not a trivial matter. I have served here for many years. What the Greek did is more than a petty insult to the Jews. It defiles their place of worship and makes it unclean."

"So, then they can clean it up."

"I... I removed it." At the dark look from Florus, he explained: "They can't, my lord—won't—touch it, so I did. I took it away and then returned as quickly as I could to the site to ensure the peace."

"Centurion, you don't serve the Jews—you serve me." Floris rattled the sheaf of tally sheets in his hand. "But what's done is done." He turned back to his work and stopped. "Is there something else... more to this... affront?"

"Yes, my lord. Young, angry Jews had attacked the Greeks. I returned to the scene to intervene because there were more Greeks than Jews, and the Greeks badly beat several of them."

"Good."

"Not good, sir. There is already much unrest. I hoped to quell the violence before it got out of hand." Jucundus was used to official indifference, but he had wanted to convey that adding more fuel to a fire that could burn indiscriminately and grow out of control was a danger to Rome and Romans. Watching his superior's face, he realized his warning was falling on deaf ears.

"And what do you want me to do?"

"My lord, I thought you should know about it, and that the local Jewish leaders seek justice, to have the Greeks punished."

"When they petition for that and request to meet with me, then I'll talk with them." Florus studied a long scroll of items and numbers.

Jucundus cleared his throat.

"Aren't you done? You've reported the incident—now leave."

"But, the Jews, my lord..." The centurion shifted nervously. "They've followed me here. They are in the antechamber and wish to speak with you now." Jucundus did not look at the procurator's face. He saluted, spun on his heel, and hurried to the door.

* * *

"Eight talents of gold to hear their complaint against the Greeks?" Cleo shook her head. She had taken Poppaea's advice and now realized the importance of knowing what her husband was up to. Only what she had learned—was learning—disturbed her, and now she had no one to turn to or to count on.

147

"Listening at my door again, dear? Florus studied her, a flat look on his face.

"No, Gessius, but even I hear things from others. And the Jews look forward to you reviewing their evidence of how the Greeks have persecuted—still persecute them, and they trust that you will address the injustice." Cleo shook her head again. "That's the right thing, what Roman law calls for in its provinces. And yet you told them that a 'contribution' would help their cause."

"This Jew, Levi ben Hitta," Florus glanced at the notes in his hand, "understands how things work. They have many grievances beyond this burned-bird offense. They wish much of my time to be used on their behalf. For instance, the Greeks that follow their religion are reciting the...," he held the note closer, "the Shema— whatever that is—they're reciting it aloud as is required, but in Greek." Floris shuffled the next note to the top. "And a Greek owns the building where their synagogue has been located for some time and will not sell to them, though they've offered him many more times than its value. Instead, the Greek has erected more buildings around it, leaving only a narrow and difficult access to their place of worship." He tossed the handful of complaints on his desk.

"So, will you help them in exchange for the eight talents payment, for your—for Rome's—time?"

"The Jews have far more gold than they let on." Florus stared at her until Cleo turned and left. Then he thought *and far more than they need.* He swept the notes with details of the Jewish leaders' complaints into the basket that held scraps for burning.

XXXIII

NEAR JERUSALEM

The noblemen were on horseback, as was the heavily armed and armored escort of forty men—legionaries, cavalrymen from one cohort in Caesarea—with a signifier at the head of the formation bearing the standard. Twenty of the cavalrymen were behind the two-person carriage that carried the Lady Octavia, wife of Governor Cestius Gallus, and Lady Cleo, wife of the procurator—and twenty men in the lead. The decurion leading the unit had to stop his horse at the rough sections of the path and direct eight to dismount, detach the donkeys from the carriage, and shift it out of ruts or guide it through or onto even more worn roads, much to the men's silent discontent.

Nicanor reined his horse to a stop before the two noblemen. "Governor, Procurator, the two scouts report the road ahead is in good condition—much better than this last stretch—and that we're close to Jerusalem. We should enter the city mid-afternoon at the pace we can make from here on." He glanced at the carriage, its side curtains and back canvas covering raised and open to let air flow across the passengers. The women wore light robes and veils to block the dust, but a dried-sweat rime of it had formed on their brows above the veils. Gallus nodded and smiled at his wife, who lifted a hand and smiled in return.

Nicanor studied Cleo sitting across from her. She had followed Octavia's gesture to grin briefly at Nicanor next to the governor, dashed a glance at her husband, who was not looking at her, and then she turned away.

Cleo's face had lit up in happy surprise as Nicanor stepped off the ship at Caesarea with the governor and his wife. Nicanor had been surprised at the assignment as well. Called to his office, the governor had told Nicanor "I understand that good fortune accompanies those who travel with you, Nicanor... that you're quite the protector. My wife joins us—and you know of the reports of Jewish unrest—so that's important to me. It's a concern as well for the procurator I'm sure, and I've heard that you saved his wife once before they were married."

And that's how he had learned he would see Lady Cleo again and Sayid, too, probably. Although he had felt embarrassed at their enthusiastic greetings, he was glad to see them. And who knew—ahead in Jerusalem he might see Yosef. It was strange how the gods, or fate, were bringing them together again. Nicanor glanced over at Cleo in the carriage. After that moment of their meeting on the dock in Caesarea, he had noticed how subdued she had become, guarded even, and had hardly spoken of or with her husband. When asked later, Sayid would say little to him about that, as if he had been told not to.

* * *

"Do you think Nero killed her?" Octavia asked.

Cleo was glad that Octavia had come along, though hearing the details—rumors really—had been as painful as the ride. But at least she now knew more of what had happened to her friend.

"Poppaea was pregnant and far along," Octavia said sadly, shaking her head. "Some say he kicked her in the stomach, rupturing something inside her." She shook her head again. "Others say it was an accident."

Cleo closed her dry eyes; she had cried them out in Caesarea. Everything, everything, she and Poppaea had talked about for their futures was gone—it would never happen. She touched the letter inside her robe that the ship's captain had brought her after he had docked and Cestius Gallus and Octavia had debarked. Heavier than the weight of the parchment it was written on, it pressed on her heart. The letter had not been signed, but she had recognized Poppaea's writing.

> Cleo, I hope you are well. There's much I want to tell you but have only a short time. The captain, a trusted family friend, must sail tomorrow morning. And from here, he will ride all night so that no other person handles this message. He will deliver it to you when he arrives at Caesarea. Here—in Rome—the persecution of Christians increases, but I fear it is driven more by stories—and schemes—and not facts. Aliturus came yesterday to tell me of a man he had met. The man had a curious scar on his inner forearm, and Aliturus had asked him, "Did that happen in the fire?" The man had replied, "Yes, but afterward." He then—deep in his cups—told Aliturus that he and a dozen others had

been paid to have the Christian mark tattooed on their arms and then to stir the chaos that first night of the fire. And now with all the Christians being hunted, imprisoned, and killed, he had slashed and then burned the tattoo from his arm with a hot iron. The man was rambling, but his words and other things I've heard make me think someone set the fire to serve a purpose. And I fear your husband may have been involved. I will find out more. It will be an unpleasant conversation, but I must verify my suspicions before saying any more. I will write again soon. Please be careful and watchful my little sister!

The captain had apologized as he handed the letter to her: "Lady, we were delayed by repairs and then a command to divert and pick up Lord Gallus and Lady Octavia, or I would have delivered this sooner." He had bowed and then left her.

* * *

JERUSALEM

Gallus's advance scouts—the vanguard—had become heralds. The first arrived that morning to advise the city leadership on a more precise time to expect the governor. The second arrived on a frothed horse and was himself in a slurry of sweat and dirt, ordering a fresh mount as he reported, "My lords are an hour away. Be prepared for their arrival." Then he had galloped to return to his unit.

Yosef was with the senior members of the Sanhedrin and the city councilmen that would greet the governor and procurator. Happy thoughts of seeing Cleo and possibly Sayid had been replaced with worries. He had taken home the hamsa he had discovered in the tunnel, and that evening, with his father and mother away, he had knocked on Miriam's door asking her to the courtyard, where an evening wind had freshened the air. She had joined him, and when he took out the hamsa and asked her, "Is this yours?" she had paled and run to her room. And she would not respond to his calls asking her what was wrong, and would not open her door that night. But the next morning, before dawn, he had awakened to a knock at his door. It was Miriam. She had held her hand out and said, "Give it to me, please." She had taken it and returned to her room and had been silent ever since.

The sound of metal on metal, the whinny of horses, and the rattle of wheels over rough stone made him look toward the northwestern gate. The watchmen atop the 100-foot-high Psephinus Tower had seen them a mile off and given the welcoming entourage ample time to prepare to greet them. Some watchmen claimed they could see the beacon from the lighthouse at Joppa from the tower on a clear night. The first Roman through was the signifier, and he bore the vexillum, a square woven flag of *textilis anguis*—a cloth with tassels—mounted on a gilt staff. It designated the legion, cohort, and unit number. Then—and the sight made Yosef smile despite his worries—came a large, grizzled and rough-looking figure he recognized-Nicanor. He slowed—his raised fist a signal for those behind him to stop and wait—and scanned the area around the gate. His eyes moved across the group arrayed to greet them, and he saw Yosef. His nod and half-grin would be all the acknowledgment he would give, but both knew it was good to see each other.

Yosef watched as Nicanor twitched his heels and his mount moved ahead as he directed the men behind him to fan out and clear the gate area. Next came the two noblemen and the carriage with their ladies. The women got out, and Yosef knew one was the wife of the governor, but he looked only at Cleo. She was singularly beautiful among the women he had met, her bearing regal without conceit or arrogance. She stood there in the afternoon sun with a sweeping look that took in her surroundings. Her eyes stopped on him and widened and then looked away.

Florus, beside her, glanced at his wife and then shifted behind her to align with her line of sight. He spotted Yosef in the second rank of Jews. He cast his eyes down to Cleo and then up again to lock on Yosef. He half-turned to a man just behind him, his voice low--"The tall Jew in the back is Yosef ben Mathias—watch him while we are here."

Yosef saw Florus's piercing stare and his comment to the man at his side. Cleo's eyes had darted away from him and not returned. He had no expectations, not really. But the look she gave him and then so intentionally abandoned had stung. He wondered again at how his heart hurt when he believed it could not hurt anymore.

The High Priest and city elders had stepped forward to lead the governor and his entourage to Herod's palace, where they would stay. Yosef did not wish to join them, so he turned away. The next day their meetings would begin, and the day after that was Passover. Lost in thought, he stepped around those still milling about and bumped into

Rachel and Leah. Heeding Miriam's warning, he had not seen either of them since returning.

"Yosef!" Rachel's hand was on Leah's arm. "Your mother has invited us to Passover Seder," a blush came over her face, "and it will be good to visit with you and your family."

Leah's expression seemed in disagreement. He did not know they had been invited but was not surprised. His mother bound their family together, and she worked—even silently sometimes—to fill any breach and repair any rift.

"It will be good to visit with you, too." Yosef smiled at Leah and then Rachel. "Both of you." He turned his eyes from them and saw that not all the Romans had left. One remained—the one Florus had talked to—and he wore the harness of a retired soldier but likely now served in civil service. His eyes squinted in the bright sunlight and took in him, Leah, and Rachel.

XXXIV

Jerusalem

"The complaints are many, Lord Gallus," Yosef said, looking from him to Florus seated next to him. He pointed at the document underneath Gallus's hand. "They are listed before you."

"I have seen these previously," Gallus said, passing over Yosef to address the High Priest. "You know your courier delivered them to my hand." He slid the parchment to one side without looking at it.

"My lord, it is not just us," Yosef's gesture included the High Priest and Yohanan ben Zaccai. "Outside this hall are thousands in the city... and beyond Jerusalem's walls are many times that who experience what seems increasing injustice and intolerance. The pressures of added taxes have forced many to mortgage their homes and land. Many of our people are on the edge of bankruptcy and financial ruin." His eyes again went to Florus, who sat there unblinking—seemingly disdainful—and had yet to speak. "And the situation has worsened since Lord Florus arrived." He turned back to the governor. "I have seen Rome—lived for a time among citizens in its capital city—and know its splendor and military might."

A bark of laughter came from Florus. Yosef saw Gallus's sideways glimpse at him and then continued. "We of Judea ask that Rome show an equal measure of respect and treat our people fairly." Florus's lip curled in derision, and then an image of Cleo's face flashed across his thoughts, and he wondered if such a man was good to... good for her. He brought his mind back to Gallus. "We ask for a stop to all injustices against the Jewish people. Punish any of our individuals when there is evidence of wrongdoing"—he shook his head and focused on the governor and not the procurator—"but do not target the Jewish people collectively."

"I've spoken with your procurator, and I can assure you that Rome"—his eyes cut a quick look at Florus—"that Rome is fair and shall treat Judea in a better manner."

* * *

Yosef watched as the Romans formed up before the western gate, only half the former number of men with Gallus, his wife, Octavia, and Florus.

"The governor and procurator return to Antioch and Caesarea," announced Mathias.

Yosef asked, "Do you think things will improve?"

Mathias shrugged. "The governor says it will be so. We have to see and pray that they do."

"But what of the procurator, of Florus? I didn't hear that guarantee come from his lips." Then it struck Yosef. "Where's Florus's wife, the Lady Cleo?" Yosef had not seen her since her arrival.

"Did you not know? I thought your mother had told you. The Lady Cleo wishes to attend a Passover Seder. It seems she has an appreciation or interest in our faith. He put his hand on Yosef's shoulder. She will join us this evening. And if the procurator does not intend to become more moderate, why would he let her stay?"

* * *

Yosef had expected that Cleo, being familiar with the Jewish religion, would respectfully sit through the two hours of passages in Hebrew before the dinner's beginning. That Nicanor sat beside her and also did so was surprising. The centurion had shaved and wore a dress tunic of fine quality. And for the first time, Yosef did not see a pugio at Nicanor's belt, though he suspected the centurion had one somewhere on him. He wore two silver armillae above his elbows, the ornaments formed as solid, hinged cuffs incised with legionary emblems, the overlapping ends terminating with a metal-formed knot. Yosef knew those had been awarded for bravery. Nicanor wore them not as a boast—he knew the man too well by now—but as a statement for those who understood what they represented. Odds against him did not matter, for he would protect Lady Cleo. He and Nicanor had talked briefly on their arrival at Yosef's home, and he had seen that Sayid and another legionary, both carrying blades, were seated comfortably near the entrance and out of sight of the dinner party.

At the table, Cleo—as their special guest—had been seated across from Yosef, with Nicanor on her right. Rebecca had tried to seat Miriam next to Nicanor, but his sister had moved past him to take the chair furthest from everyone else. In the two spaces between them now sat Leah and Yonatan. Yosef had not been pleased to see him, and Matthew had openly bristled at Yonatan. No words had been said... yet. Yosef felt there would be words later, or soon. Rachel, who had helped his mother serve the food, sat on Cleo's left and beamed at Yosef. He smiled at her in return. She had grown into a lovely young woman and was no longer in her sister's shadow.

155

All the traditional and loved recitations done, casual conversation sprang up among them. Cleo had not spoken directly to Yosef apart from a greeting and a few pleasantries at the beginning. He overheard her talking to Rachel.

"Your story of the exodus..." Her words, spoken in her clear Greek, came during a lull in the table discussions and all heard. She paused when it became clear that all were now listening.

Yosef encouraged her. "Yes, my lady?" He saw Yonatan stiffen, and a scared look flashed in Leah's eyes at his use of the proper courtesy. The Zealot had not greeted, nor even acknowledged, Cleo or Nicanor, and that had drawn Nicanor's attention. As the dinner progressed and Yonatan appeared more agitated at the Romans being there, Yosef noted how Nicanor watched him without seeming to.

Cleo continued-"The bravery it took," she shook her head, "the pain they bore, and that they endured... that they persevered." Her eyes moved from Rachel to Rebecca and stopped on Mathias. "How noble they were... you are."

Mathias nodded. "Yes, we have that quality as a people... that respect for ourselves and what's right... and some of us are noble. As are many Romans."

Cleo bowed her head and raised it to look into Yosef's eyes and hold there for a moment. It shook him.

"But enslavement and oppression continue." Yosef had expected such indiscreet and disrespectful words to spill from Yonatan, but they had come from further down the table. Miriam had been silent all evening, continuing the pattern of recent days. He watched as her hand stroked the hamsa pinned on her robe. "Yes, and cruelty." Miriam looked down at her hands, canted her head to the side, staring into the darkest corner of the room, then stood and left.

XXXV

Jerusalem

In her room, Miriam opened the shutters and breathed in the clean air. She had not been that close to any Romans since her attack. The smell of them made her shake inside, and her mother had tried to seat her next to the big, coarse man with the metal cuffs that cut into his biceps. Stout arms like those had held her while the other Roman soldier had... she closed her eyes and felt for Zechariah's lamp. Holding it steadied her.

That day she had been attacked she rested as long as she could—the bleeding from the shallow cut across her breasts had stopped—then Zechariah had escorted her home. One thing about following Yosef and Matthew all over the city--it had taught her a valuable lesson. Always know where you are, keep your directions straight, and stay oriented. Look for distinct landmarks on the streets. And so, as they had left Zechariah's shop and home, she had fixed its location in her mind. On the street, they moved slowly--seemingly a young maiden pacing herself to an old blind man's gait—but in reality, just the opposite. He had walked her home, and they arrived just as the sun faded beneath the towers and western city wall.

Calling to her mother to let her know she was home, she had claimed illness and spent the next three days and nights recovering so she could move around her parents and brother without revealing she had been attacked and injured. Thankfully—and any laugh at that painful truth would have soured in her mouth—her hurts could be covered by clothing. Her face was unmarked save for where the edge of the Roman's blade had left a thin red line underneath her chin and across her throat, but that was easily hidden.

The fourth day after her attack, she had gone to the Lower City. Zechariah was owed thanks and a reward. In a small purse tied inside a fold of her cloak were five silver shekels. She knew from her father it was two weeks' pay for an unskilled laborer and had hoped he would accept it. It was all she had and only because that was what Yosef had left her when he departed for Rome. His traveling currency had been in denarii, Roman coins, and he had left the last of his Judean money behind with her.

Zechariah had not been there. Her mother and father had taught their children to pay all debts and never forget those who had helped them, but her regret at his absence was shamefully tinged with relief. She had turned away not knowing if she would try to find him again. She felt the weight of her despoilment and knew she now faced breaking her engagement with Yakov. The thought brought tears to her eyes. She wiped them with a corner of her robe.

"So, are you better, young lady?"

The voice coming from the shadows of the building's alley had startled her. She had tried to hurry away, but the next words had stopped her.

"May I offer you a cool drink before you go?" Then Zechariah had stepped into the sun, his staff held loosely. As he passed her to open the door and step inside, she had followed him. That decision had changed everything for her.

Her room was dark above the bright room where the Seder was going on, but her eyes were still closed. That was part of what Zechariah had had her practicing daily. She found the lamp, fingers touching the wick, and her other hand traced what had been etched deeply engraved on the flat bottom of the lamp. She set the lamp down without lighting it and touched the clasp on her breast. In Zechariah's shop that second time, she had not thought to ask him how he had recognized her—that would come later, at another time. That day she needed too badly to talk about what was inside her that others could not know. And Zechariah was the only one she could speak with without consequence.

"You're frightened." The blind old man with the milky eyes had somehow known.

"Yes, of the dark, of... of men," she had told him.

"But not me." His voice had been soft, not how it had sounded in the tunnel, yet still distinct. His hands had been sure and steady as he poured water into two cups and brought her one. "Perhaps you are not afraid of me because of what happened, what I prevented happening, which would have been much worse." He had looked into her eyes with his unseeing ones, "Or is your fear that darkness is all I know and yet somehow cope with that?"

"How do you deal with what could be in the dark... or when something dangerous is there in a place where you can't see?"

"I let the shadows tell me what's there, what it is, and whether it is dangerous... and then I act."

"But—"

He had cut her off—"In the light, you can see what's before you to step around or over it... and are aware it's there. It's the same with people or surroundings. You see them, and then you know what to do or not do."

"How do I..."

"See into and through the darkness?" Zechariah had chuckled. "You don't always need eyes for that."

She had then been silent for a while, and Zechariah had been comfortable in letting her have that silence. She had shifted and heard the clink of coins in the pouch. "I have something for you—a reward." She had untied its strings and placed the small bag in his hands. "Please take this with my thanks."

Zechariah had rotated the pouch in his hand slightly, rocking the purse once or twice, hearing its sound, and then his cloudy eyes had met hers again. "Five silver coins. I didn't help you expecting anything in return." He had held the purse out to her. "Besides, five is too much."

"Please, keep it. I must repay you." She had not taken it from him.

With a sigh, Zechariah had turned to the long worktable behind him and set the bag of coins on its corner. "I had just fired this the day I met you and left it to cool, and that's when I came upon you in the tunnel." She had watched as he reached for and found a wooden-handled blade with a triangular-beveled bronze tip. "I have not asked, but will now—what is your name?"

"Miriam."

"Ahhh..."

She had watched his shoulders, still thick with muscle, move under his work tunic as he worked with the blade on something before him on the table.

"There..." He turned and, in his hands had been a finely shaped clay lamp. He had handed it to her.

Its weight had been—still was—pleasing. It was not a delicate thing easily broken, and the workmanship was exquisite. The lumps and roughness of hand-formed earthenware had been buffed away. She had turned it over, appreciating the texture of the pottery, and seen the carving in the thick base of the lamp. "It's... it's a—"

"It's the Hand of Miriam, a hamsa, to protect you on dark nights." He had then picked up the bag, taken a single coin from it and handed the rest to her. "One coin for the lamp, but the rest you must keep."

"But!"

"One is enough." He had sat down. "But maybe you'll visit me from time to time, and we can talk. And perhaps I can show you how not to be afraid."

She had come home with the lamp and only then had realized—she had not touched the clothes or cloak she had worn that terrible day, stuffing them under her bed with a plan to burn them—that her other hamsa, a silver clasp for her robe, was gone. And that she must have lost it in the tunnel. But now Yosef had returned it. She took it from her robe and turned it over and over in her hands as she sat and thought deep into the night.

* * *

A voice—a loud Roman voice—in the courtyard made Miriam peek out. The morning had come. Through her shutter, she saw it was the large Roman from the Seder. Yosef and Matthew were there with him. She sat and listened as they talked.

"Well, it was good to see you. And I learned something about your faith I'll always remember." Nicanor stood, and his eyes scanned the courtyard, lingering near the fig tree, noting the hidden watcher above—no threat to them—and then studied Yosef and his brother. He could see how they resembled one another, but the brother—Matthew—had a stiffness to his bearing that Yosef did not. But then, Yosef was his friend.

"Yosef says to fill his days in Rome, you trained him," Matthew said.

"I did." Nicanor nodded and glanced at Matthew's thick wrists and forearms, the signs of someone who often worked with a sword or staff. He turned from him to Yosef, about to tell him goodbye.

"Are you a good teacher?"

Nicanor looked back along his shoulder at Matthew. In Rome, Yosef had told him he had never been able to best his brother. "Why don't you test him?" Nicanor answered, nodded at Yosef and then gripped him on the shoulder. "I must go."

Nicanor paused. A pained expression came and went as he took a deep breath. "Lady Cleo asked me to tell you goodbye and that she wishes you well." His eyes slid from Yosef to his brother and then back. "As do I."

Yosef followed Nicanor to the door where the centurion—with a twist of hand and wrist—lifted his cloak from a peg and with a turning motion slid it over his shoulders in almost a dancer's pirouette. How smoothly Nicanor moved had always surprised Yosef, who now opened and held the door for him. "You said you had learned something... about my religion. What?"

"That your Pesach, your Passover, you call it, does not begin until your barley crops are ripe." A grin split Nicanor's sun-leathered face, with its broad nose, bushy brows and short-cropped hair above, and teeth framed by a gray-stubbled jutting rock of a chin below. "And you know how fond I am of my malted barley beer, so I can relate."

* * *

Miriam watched as Matthew went to a shed behind the fig tree, opened it, and pulled out two long wooden swords wrapped in a blanket. She knew he still practiced but had not seen those swords in years. When Yosef came back, Matthew tossed him one with a challenge--"Let's see what the Roman has taught you."

She watched as they sparred, knowing what to expect. However, the outcome was much different than it had been in the past. The Roman—who Yosef seemed to like—had taught him well. The brothers were now evenly matched. Her father's call to them echoed through the house and courtyard. Minutes later she heard them leave the house. Her mother was at a friend's, so she must be alone now. A good time to leave without questions and go visit Zechariah. She had finally decided—Yosef returning the hamsa had triggered it—that there was something she must ask him.

Yosef sat in his father's study. He had been thinking of Nicanor... and Cleo. The steps coming down the stairs were light, just a low scuff of sandal leather on stone. If the house had not been so still, he doubted he would have heard it. He saw Miriam slip by and ease the door open, step out, and close it carefully. Now, he thought, was the time to talk to her about the tunnel and his dream of the girl who had been attacked in it. He went out of the door after her. She was moving fast and already far down the street. He hurried to catch her, but turning the corner he ran into Leah.

"Yosef, I was coming to see you!"

"What?" Nearly in each other's arms, the two awkwardly parted as he looked over her head and Miriam moved out of sight. "I'm sorry, Leah. Why are you here? I mean, it's good to see you, but..."

"I came to apologize for how Yonatan behaved. I know those Romans were your friends." She looked up at him and pointed below his neck. "You still have it."

Yosef looked down and the coin on the leather cord around his neck—the kinyan he had joked about when she had given it to him years ago had pulled from his tunic and now lay outside it. "Always," he smiled and tucked it back under. "No matter what I've gone through, it has rested near my heart... and you have been, always will be, in it." Tears filled her eyes, and he stepped back, but she moved forward to remain near, her hand reaching to rest on his forearm. He gently took her hand. "But for us," he added, "that closeness can never be... now there's Yonatan between us."

XXXVI

JERUSALEM

"People speak of a new star in the sky... that it seems to just hang there, over the city."

When Zechariah talked about the sky, whether the day's or the night's, it was the only time Miriam heard any wistfulness... or sensed any longing in his voice.

"It's been there for some time, but now arcing overhead," added Miriam, who had heard Yosef and her father talking about it. Its tail has the shape of a slightly curved blade... a scythe in the firmament above Jerusalem. They had both sounded worried about its significance. "And now there are stories of a light—at the Temple— that came down over the Holy Altar, settled around it and lasted there for thirty minutes. It was so bright it seemed broad daylight there, even at three in the morning."

Zechariah scoffed: "Only Temple guards would be there—in the sanctuary—then... that time of morning... and they don't tell tales of what goes on in there. That's just a wild story, Miriam." He shook his head as he worked on a leather harness with a curious arrangement of what seemed like flat, slit sleeves or long, narrow pockets. Miriam had asked Zechariah before about what he was working on, and he had just smiled at her.

"Men on the Mount of Olives saw it, too, several of them at different spots. My brother, who's an officer of the Temple guard, denies it. But I know when he lies... and I think he's lying... and a little unnerved." She watched as Zechariah took a flat case from beneath the worktable, without searching for it. Somehow, he always knew when she hovered too close, so she only raised herself on her forearms from where she sat and stretched her neck to catch a glimpse. Dull flashes of something, maybe metal or polished wood, disappeared quickly. "Many people think the light was the Shekinah glory, the presence of God."

"Even people who can see... often understand very little. They misinterpret, or maybe it's just they want to believe a certain thing... and so that's what they see."

Zechariah half-turned and she saw the last glint, as whatever those things were slid into a sheath. She counted six, and each had a short handle, as thick as the somewhat curved scabbard affixed to the harness. With thumb and forefinger, Zechariah raised each slightly, and with a small thin rod he dipped into a jar of oil, placed drops where the handle entered the sheath. Setting the rod down, he then pulled each handle to reveal a dagger's blade. The oil gave their dark metal a deadly sheen.

"What is that?" she asked.

He looked at her—and she always knew now when he did that, he genuinely saw her—and nodded. His smile was gone. "It's for someone who hates Romans."

CAESAREA

"What did you think they would do, Gessius, only days after Cestius Gallus told the Jews your treatment of them would improve?" Cleo looked over her shoulder at her husband and caught his questioning look. "Yes, Octavia told me what was said. She and her husband actually have conversations and discuss what's happening that affects their lives, especially given the circumstances here in Judea." Cleo shook her head and turned from her husband. The mocking expression he now favored when speaking to her had been replaced with an underlying rage she did not care to see surface. "Demanding seventeen talents in gold from the temple in Jerusalem," she continued, "was sure to be protested." The slam of his ring-adorned hand on the tabletop behind her did not make her flinch as it once had.

"The people laugh at me... Jerusalem's young men carry baskets with signs that read, 'Collections for the poor procurator, Florus.' But they also cry out... 'Only Roman coins... no Jewish gold accepted.' That's far too valuable for them to part with." Another slam rattled even the heavy wooden table's legs on the stone floor. "They mock me at their peril."

Cleo heard the clatter of a soldier's nail-studded uniform sandals coming closer, and she recognized the stomping of the man's previous meetings with her husband. He was a brutal centurion that many local Jews—even in her household—had complained about. As he entered to stand before her husband at his desk, she turned to face them.

"Capito," Florus said, addressing the centurion, his once-heated tone now frigid. It was the precipitous drop in temperature that hunters feared when they had chased game too far from shelter and the warmth of a fire when a winter nightfall's killing cold settled upon them. "One cohort to accompany me, two more support cohorts in readiness here in Caesarea," he ordered. "We leave at noon, march with combat packs, and each man is also to carry a set of sudes to form caltrops for defense once in the city. We will be at Jerusalem's gates in the morning, day after tomorrow."

BETWEEN CAESAREA AND JERUSALEM

"A dozen men cannot move silently, Lord, much less a cohort moving quickly over this terrain." The centurion Capito was sweat-stained and dust-caked from the forced march over rough roads. "All the Jews between Caesarea and here knew of us as we moved... and feet much faster than ours must have warned them. And they can spot us from their towers more than a mile off." He stood before Florus, who looked little better, even though both had ridden. "It's a party of six, their priests and city leaders. They claim to wish to welcome you before you reach Jerusalem." Capito's sneer broke the mask of dried sweat and dirt over the three-day stubble. "They don't look happy— more scared than welcoming. They hope to appease you before reaching their gates."

"Tell them to return to their city and clear the way for us. No one is to be on the streets between the northwestern gate and Herod's palace, where we'll stay. Tell them to be there with the seventeen talents tomorrow morning. I'll meet with them in the palace hall, the large one used for spectacle." Gessius Florus smiled for the first time since receiving the reports of the Jews' mocking protest of him in Jerusalem. "If they don't have the gold for me, I will impress on them the fault of their ways."

JERUSALEM

Matthew looked over his shoulder at his father, his face a pale blob in dim moonlight and in the arc of light from a handheld lantern. "At the sixth hour last night a watchman in the Court of Women saw the eastern gate swing open," he told his father, who followed hurriedly. "Wondering at the sight, he passed through into the Court of Men and up to the Holy Altar, thinking there must be men on that side— with a reason to open the Gate of Nicanor at that hour. He found no one and even checked behind the thick twenty-foot-high polished bronze doors now set against the walls on either side, as they were during the day. Still no one, yet the heavy iron bars used to secure the gate every evening had been pulled back and released. And the large bolts set in the threshold stone had been raised.

"He ran for the captain of the guard," Matthew continued, "and Eleasar returned with him because he did not believe the report. But it was just as the watchman said. He commanded the man to remain there while he woke twenty men from the guard to get the gate shut again and ordered me to wake the Sanhedrin leaders and ask them to come to the Temple. So, I came for you first, Father. Do you think this is some kind of miraculous sign?"

Mathias looked ahead to see a knot of men put their shoulders and backs to the gate's doors, which they moved ponderously to shut just as father and son arrived. There was no way that this huge door could have opened by itself. The High Priest and Eleasar were standing off to the side, so Mathias headed toward them and bade Matthew return to his duty.

* * *

"Matthew, wait, and we will join you," Mathias said a few hours later, then turned and called toward the courtyard of his home, where they had been discussing the early morning hours' events with the Temple gate. "Yosef, come here!"

"Eleasar ben Ananias is gathering the Temple guard complement," Matthew reported to his father, "and all will be at the Hall of Hewn Stone with the full Sanhedrin to receive Florus's messenger."

"Why weren't we told before now that the High Priest knew Florus had left Caesarea and that he had picked the city's emissaries to meet the procurator outside the gates?" Mathias asked.

"Eleasar does not trust some of the leadership"—Matthew's expression told Mathias more than his words—"and demanded that only a few be told. And he determined that only a handful from those he trusted should meet Florus before he entered the city."

"To accomplish what?" Mathias demanded.

"I don't know, Father, but Eleasar had thought originally it was the procurator with only a token escort and not a full cohort. That development has changed a lot of thinking about what to do. I must go."

"Was that Matthew?" Yosef asked, coming from the back part of the house as the door closed.

Mathias turned to Yosef and replied, "Yes. Those rumors you heard at the market are true. Florus force-marched from Caesarea with a cohort of soldiers, and they just entered the northwestern gate. His representative has a message for the Sanhedrin."

* * *

The Roman centurion stood alone before them where the accused usually stood for the hearing of the court. Protected by his arrogant surety that no one would touch him, the procurator's surrogate at that moment became the accuser.

"So, the procurator expects the seventeen talents for the emperor," Capito declared with a scowl, "... as well as the protesters that mocked the empire." Capito's glare hardened as he turned and panned the assembly surrounding him, stopping on the High Priest. "He expects both tomorrow morning at the procurator's palace, here in your city, in the main hall of the Caesar wing." He pivoted and marched out, glancing at the captain of the Temple guard and his men, alert and at attention. With a laugh, he left the chamber.

XXXVII

JERUSALEM

Herod's palace was constructed on an elevated platform that ran north-south for one thousand feet and almost two hundred feet running east-west. The size of the building stones was unusual—not the common kind that men could carry, but large, heavy, white marble stones. Each was thirty feet long, fifteen feet wide, and seven-and-a-half feet thick. They were so precisely joined that each tower looked like one entire rock protruding naturally from the ground and afterward cut by the hand into its present shape. The palace rested on a series of retaining walls rising thirteen to sixteen feet above ground level and was comprised of two main buildings, named after Agrippa and Caesar. Each wing had its own banquet halls, baths, and accommodations for hundreds of guests. In the center of the palace were gardens with porticoes, and several groves of trees where visitors could take long walks. The gardens were filled with deep canals and cisterns that in several parts were filled with bronze statues through which the water ran out into ditches and ponds, and dovecotes along the canals held tame pigeons.

All this grandeur had been turned into a Roman military encampment with little regard for respecting or protecting the beauty of the grounds.

After a futile night of discussion and debate, Yosef, Mathias, Matthew, the High Priest Matthias ben Theophilus, and Eleasar ben Ananias arrived at the palace at the time specified by the centurion.

Capito waited at the entrance. The centurion's eyes searched over and beyond them as they climbed the steps toward him. "I don't see bearers with the talents nor a group of men who would be the protesters unless it is these," he remarked. The Roman jabbed a finger at Yosef and his father. "Only two?" he asked, glaring at them.

The High Priest was pale in the morning sun. "We must speak with Lord Florus."

Capito, five steps higher on the level area before the entrance, looked down on them. "You'll find that talk has little value, but you can have your say with the procurator and learn that for yourself." He crooked a finger to beckon him to follow. "But just you, priest."

Eleasar climbed one step toward the centurion. "The High Priest cannot go unaccompanied."

"I saw you in your judgment hall. Who are you?"

"I'm Eleasar, captain of the Temple guard."

Capito studied him from sandal to head, disdain on his face and in his tone: "Only you, then." He turned to the legionaries at the entrance. "Turn all others away and keep this area clear."

* * *

"You don't have the seventeen talents nor the protesters." Florus sat on the throne on a dais where King Herod would have sat in the great hall before hundreds of guests. Behind him, row upon row of Roman armored infantry stood at attention. He studied the two Jews before him without speaking.

"Lord Florus," the High Priest began, "what you ask for is not a 'known' tax. The former procurator Albinus never asked for such an amount and so unexpectedly. You must understand—"

Florus cut him off. "You—your people—are the ones who must understand. Now you know it is a tax, priest... one that it is owed to your emperor. The protesters must be punished. Bring them to me or name them, and my men," he glanced at Capito, who bowed his head, "will find and bring them before me."

"You cannot have them, Procurator," snapped Eleasar. "They have done nothing against the empire. They only object to your abuse. The legate Cestius Gallus—in this hall not weeks ago—gave his word that your treatment of us would improve, Lord Florus. It has not. We cannot give you those citizens of Jerusalem who rightfully protest your demand for gold from the Temple."

White-faced, taut with anger, Gessius Florus stood. "Hold them outside, with any others." He gestured at Capito: "Centurion, ready the men." Florus came down the steps of the dais to eye level with the two Jews. "My men will take what is owed in another form—in other ways—until you provide what I want."

* * *

"What is that?" Rebecca asked when she heard the shouts and then the screams from her courtyard. Not one, but dozens. Then a pounding on the front door. Miriam heard her mother's call and was coming down the stairs. She turned to the entry and opened the door.

"The Romans are killing people in the agora," Rachel gasped. "They're pulling the shopkeepers from the market and slaughtering them, and then stealing their goods." Rachel scanned the street behind her. "Soldiers are entering houses now. I saw them cut down a young boy and his mother where the market ends at our street."

"Inside, quick!" Miriam backed away to let her in and shut the door. "Mother, we must hide!"

* * *

Yosef and Mathias had been moved from the steps of the entrance to a corner formed by one of the series of retaining walls and the foundation of the palace. Five legionaries guarded them. Not more than fifteen minutes after entering to speak with Florus, the High Priest and guard captain had been escorted out to join them. They had watched as what seemed the entire cohort—hundreds of men—marched from the palace grounds. A third of them spread out and secured the palace perimeter with the Roman sudes, forming a line of the X-shaped arrangements of sharpened hardwood stakes that protruded outward once erected. Those soldiers now lined the barrier at intervals, their short, stabbing gladiuses in their hands. After several minutes, the clamoring of a crowd, discordant and uneven, came from the upper market, the area the bulk of the legionaries had poured into. The sound sharpened and became laced with screams. Eleasar started forward, and a soldier slapped him across the chest with the flat of his sword and brought him to a stop.

Yosef grabbed his father's arm. "Isn't that Berenice, Agrippa's sister?" Two Roman soldiers coming toward the palace held by the arms a crying woman dressed in elegant robes, and walked her up the steps and inside.

"Did you know she was in Jerusalem?" Mathias asked the High Priest.

"The king's sister is here—in the city—on a personal matter. She asked for no ceremony or notice."

"And she deserves none"—Eleasar spat—"She's the sister of a Roman puppet."

Mathias put his hand on Yosef's shoulder and shook his head as a warning to his son to not get into it with the guard captain in front of Roman soldiers. With a glare at Eleasar, Yosef turned to the High Priest. "Now is not the time for fighting against—and among—ourselves. We must—"

"They're bringing her back out." Yosef pointed at the two Romans now dragged the Lady Berenice down the steps toward them at the edge of the foundation platform, then stopped and let her drop to the ground. Yosef hurried to kneel and help her stand.

The circlet she usually wore on her brow was gone. Her head was down and her hair, now loose, veiled her face. She straightened and pushed it away and back over her shoulders. Tears still poured down her face to drip from her chin.

"They are killing our people," she said, "even the equestrians, the Jews with Roman citizenship, in the upper market. I saw dozens murdered in minutes and ran here. But he"—she stopped as a wracking breath shook her—"Florus will not stop them, though I begged him on my knees. All he said was, 'Be thankful it is not you.'" She wiped her face with the palms of her hands. "And I heard the centurion tell him that the messenger on horseback had left earlier this morning with his order to bring two more cohorts from Caesarea."

* * *

They heard the front door and its frame splinter, then give way with a crash. Rebecca held Rachel, who still softly whimpered, in one corner of the basement that ran the length of the house. Its access— behind a movable set of panels depicting plants along the shore of the Lake Gennesaret—was not well hidden, but they hoped it might be overlooked. In the pitch black, the sound of heavy footsteps above gave the women an idea of where the intruder was... the entry... then Mathias's study... then back across the entry to the cooking and eating area. There they heard a crash of pottery and then the scraping sound of sandal nails on stone climbing to the second level.

"Where are you going?" Rebecca asked Miriam, who had squirmed from beside behind her mother and Rachel. In the darkness, a Roman so close... she could not breathe... and she couldn't sit and wait.

"I will lead them away."

"Miriam, stop!" Rebecca tried to grab an arm, but her daughter had already slipped by her. There was a flash of light at the opening, and then it was dark once more.

Slipping her sandals off, Miriam went upstairs... step and pause, step and pause... moving with the soldier's noise. She heard him go from her parents' bedroom to hers. The door was ajar; staying low, she opened it wider and saw—framed by the daylight through her window—a Roman with his back to her, his infantryman's thick legs like tree trunks leading up to a barrel chest. A glint of dangling silver flashed from something he held in one hand—her mother's necklaces. In the other, he held Zechariah's lamp. She rose to stand as she stepped into the room. The soldier spun around, his silver-draped fist pulling at his gladius. His face relaxed as a smile spread and showed missing teeth.

"You saved me from rooting you out of your hiding hole." He took two steps toward her.

"Please," she looked at the lamp in his hand, "please don't hurt us. We'll let you have whatever you want."

"Oh, little one," he said as he circled her, and as she kept her distance, he stopped in front of the bedroom door and planted those legs as thick as her waist and tossed the lamp in the corner. "I think I'll be taking what I want, whether or not you let me."

Miriam knew there would come the point when she would use what she had asked Zechariah to teach her. But she thought that knowing how to kill someone up close would be something she would have to use far in the future. Instead, with one session to draw upon, she faced what had frightened—what had hurt—her most since that day in the tunnel's darkness. She took a deep breath and saw the man's eyes drop to her full bosom. Slipping her right hand into her left sleeve, she felt the haft of the dagger in its thin sheath strapped to the inside of her left forearm. Her fingers around it, she settled her grip with a deep breath.

"Now don't run, little one," he said as his hand reached for her breast.

"I won't"—Miriam let the breath out and did exactly as Zechariah had instructed her. *Hold the knife in a firm fist grip, draw it from the sheath, and punch straight ahead and up under the chin in one smooth motion.* The blade went in like it was stuck in a block of goat cheese. The Roman's mouth filled with blood as she stepped closer and shoved harder. He shuddered, looking at her like a large tree stunned at being felled by so small an ax. As his blocky body sagged and dropped, the dagger pulled free from her hand. She knelt to retrieve it and looked into his eyes as he died. "I won't run." She wiped the blade on his tunic, hearing Zechariah's warning: "Blood is sticky, so clean and oil your blade every time after you use it."

She trembled and then steadied as she stood and walked to the corner, expecting to find fragments. But the lamp had landed on the soiled clothes she had planned to clean that day. She wiped the blood from the blade with a hem of a tunic from the pile. Pouring a little of the remaining oil from the lamp on the knife, she ran a finger along the blade to spread it evenly on both sides, then slid it back into the sheath inside her left forearm. Through the window, she heard thousands of her countrymen—men, women, and children—being massacred.

* * *

They had been held all day as the Romans plundered and killed. Yosef looked at Eleasar ben Ananias and knew the white-hot anger and shock on his face was the same as on his own. Mathias had finally sat on the ground, head down, next to Berenice, who had stopped crying but shuddered with each scream that now infrequently echoed from the area of the agora and the residences of the Upper City. Roman soldiers, some with bloody swords still in hand, carried into the palace in a steady stream what they had taken. The air was a fitful wind heavily laden with the coppery scent of blood... the odor of death he had not smelled since the days after the fire in Rome. But that had been a far cleaner smell than the miasma settling on the city with the sunset. He looked up at the heavens, wondering how their God could let such things happen.

He rubbed his eyes, not believing them and knelt next to his father. "In the sky, do you see it? Do you see what I see, Father? The chariots and men in battle—they encircle cities made of red clouds and all hang over the city!"

Mathias looked skyward. "God save us..."

XXXVIII

CAESAREA

Sayid carried the cage down the steps at arm's length. With Florus gone, Lady Cleo would want Cicero brought down to the atrium and then taken to her chambers for the evening. It was something that Florus had forbidden since the parrot had become upset—loudly—whenever he raised his voice to the lady. So, Sayid kept the bird in a second-floor room above the atrium and the palace offices. From that room, next to his own, he could hear the bird flap and talk throughout the night.

"Temple gold..."

Sayid looked at the bird who had already squawked that phrase several times as he came down the stairs and across the courtyard through the colonnade into the atrium. He called to the Lady Cleo as he entered: "This bird has learned some new words, my lady."

Cleo rose from the divan. "Have you been teaching him, Sayid?" she teased. "What's he saying now?"

"I try not to talk to it—to him, lady," Sayid said, quickly correcting himself. "Well, say it..." He shook the cage lightly. The bird remained silent, looking from him to the lady.

"Here"—Cleo opened the cage, and Cicero carefully stepped from the small rod that spanned the inside of the cage to the lip of the opening. The parrot bobbed his head once and with a lurching flap flew the few feet to the pedestal, his customary perch before Florus had exiled him. "Speak, Cicero," Cleo commanded the bird as she smoothed his feathers. The bird preened but remained silent. Cleo turned to Sayid: "What was he saying?"

Sayid set the empty cage at the base of the pedestal and shrugged his shoulders. "It sounded like... 'temple gold.'" He shook his head. "But I'm not sure."

"My lady"—a young household servant entered the atrium—"Centurion Jucundus is here and says it is urgent that he sees you."

"Show him in, please," Cleo said, nodding to the girl. Sayid moved to leave her. "No, Sayid. You can stay."

The clatter of metal greaves preceded the centurion, who was equipped as if ready for combat. "My lady," the centurion commander said as he bowed.

"No formalities are necessary, Jucundus," Cleo said as she noted the tense lines of his face. "You seem rushed."

"I am, Lady Cleo, but I swore to Lady Octavia to warn you of any"—he paused and swallowed—"any alarming events." He eyed Sayid with an unasked question.

"I trust Sayid," Cleo said, following the meaning of his look at the young man, "and Lady Octavia... and through her, you. So please, speak freely."

"A message—an order—has arrived from Lord Florus. I am to mobilize a cohort of cavalry and one of infantry and march on Jerusalem to support your husband's efforts there."

"What efforts, Centurion?" A chill crept over Cleo.

"I'm not sure, my lady, but it seems something has gone wrong, and Lord Florus needs more men." Jucundus had the look of a man faced with doing something he knew would lead to more trouble. The look quickly passed as his Roman resolve replaced it. "That's all I know, but I had to tell you, my lady." Jucundus bowed again and left.

Cleo stood and walked toward her husband's office, smoothing the tuft of feathers on Cicero's head that showed he was agitated. In the office doorway, she stopped to scan the room and Florus's worktable, now clear of any documents.

"Temple gold..." Cicero croaked behind her.

"What?" Cleo looked back at Cicero, who, shifting from foot to foot on his perch, had his feathers up again.

"Temple gold..." Cicero bobbed his head.

Cleo heard him that time. "Sayid, come here, please." He joined her in Florus's office. "Does the aqueduct—one of its channels, anyway—flow into the atrium fountains through this wall?" She pointed, and her hand went from floor to ceiling. "And is some access to that structure through the room above?" Cleo remembered all the meetings here in Florus's office—at all hours—between him and the centurion Capito. "Is the room where Cicero now stays above us?"

Sayid had come closer to stand by her side, next to the worktable. "I don't know about that opening lady, but yes"—he pointed up—"the bird's room is there."

"The temple gold..." Cleo murmured, then turned to Sayid. "I have to ask you to do something hard and dangerous, Sayid. I need you to ride to Jerusalem ahead of Jucundus—get there as fast as you can—and find Yosef and warn him. Warn his people that my husband is after all their treasure."

JERUSALEM

"Miriam says a man—a Zealot, she thought, on the street—saw the Roman break in and then came to see... to protect us. He killed the soldier and then left." Rebecca, still pale, had regained her composure after Miriam had opened the cellar door to tell them it was safe to come out. But then she lost it again as Mathias told her of the massacre.

"As Florus pulled his troops in, securing Herod's palace as the night deepened, he sent that brute Capito to release us, and he delivered another message as he did: 'Obey the procurator's will and avoid further bloodshed. Do not stand against any Roman soldier, and do not resist.'" Mathias studied his wife. "Where is Miriam?"

"Upstairs in her room. She's upset." Rebecca wiped her eyes, afraid of what had happened and what was to come. "Is Yossi...?"

"Yosef's fine. He's taking Rachel home and will check on Leah." Mathias held his wife, feeling her trembling slow and then stop.

"What now?" Rebecca breathed deeply; her face buried in his chest.

"We care for our wounded, gather our dead... mourn them." Mathias gripped her shoulders. "In the morning we meet... and decide."

* * *

"There's a young Syrian at the northern gate," the Levite guard announced and then pointed at Yosef, who stood between Eleasar and the High Priest. "He barely makes sense, but he says he must speak with Yosef ben Mathias."

"Bring him here," Eleasar ordered, "to us, in my office." The guard captain had taken command, and the High Priest had let him. Yosef signaled his brother and father to follow them.

The Syrian was a slight figure, reeling from exhaustion and covered in dirt and sweat—both his and his horse's. He seemed gray-haired until he shook a cloud of bone-gray dust from his head, revealing the coils of oily, dirt-plastered black hair.

"Sayid!"

Eleasar snapped his gaze to Yosef, then went to stand before the youth. "You know him?" he asked Yosef, over his shoulder.

"Yes, he and I were companions on my journey to Rome and while I was there. He serves the lady who became the procurator's wife."

"Why is he here, and why does he ask for you?"

Yosef ignored the guard captain's glare and his demand. "Sayid, has something happened to Lady Cleo?"

Sayid shook his head. "More Romans are coming, Yosef." He straightened. "A cohort of mounted soldiers and one of infantry. But I traveled faster to—"

"We know that the procurator had called for them," Yosef interrupted. "We think he means to use them to suppress—"

Sayid cut him off, shaking more dirt from his hair. "At the gate, I learned of the killing of your people... but the extra men... Lady Cleo's warning is that they're not just to prevent you from fighting back. She thinks Florus wants to attack your temple and take all its gold."

* * *

The Romans had ventured out of Herod's palace only to crucify dozens of the people captured and brought before the procurator the day and night before. Across the once-beautiful grounds were a scattering of dying Jews. Their calls for mercy, for help, and their screams of pain came from beyond the barrier and the line of Roman legionaries manning it. The sound carried to the Temple enclosure.

"We need arms," Eleasar said as he paced. They were in the Outer Courtyard facing toward Herod's palace. "The only place to get them is Antonia."

"You think you can take the fortress with just the Temple guard?" Mathias looked from the guard captain to the High Priest, who remained silent.

"Father," Yosef touched his shoulder, "those aren't legionaries in Antonia. They're auxiliaries and, likely, conscripts forced to serve. They will not fight like Romans." He had learned that from Nicanor, who had a low opinion of conscripted troops.

Eleasar nodded—grudgingly—at Yosef. "Since Florus's attack they haven't budged, and he has sent none of his men to join the two strongholds. It's as if he disregards them," he snorted, "and us."

"But can Antonia be taken with just forty men?" Yosef asked.

"Yes," Eleasar rubbed his brow, "but an open attack against its entrance will be noticed by Florus's men, and they won't let that go without retaliation. If only we can move swiftly and strike unseen... but I don't know how we can do that."

"I know a way into Antonia," Yosef said and looked at his brother. "Through the tunnels."

Matthew nodded. "The Romans—these auxiliaries—they likely know nothing of Herod's hidden entrance to the tower. I can lead them, and we can make a raid on the fortress without Florus knowing it. We don't need to hold it, only stay long enough to obtain the weapons."

* * *

The advance scout returned with someone Jucundus did not expect.

"I have instructions from Lord Florus for you and your men." Nearly two days later, Capito was still flushed with the killing, and with the promise made him by the procurator—a share of the gold, if he served Florus well. That much gold made him a loyal soldier. "Approach the city from the northeast—toward what they call the Bezetha Quarter—to enter at the gate nearest the Fortress Antonia. But wait there. Lord Florus has demanded—as a gesture toward stopping hostilities—until a group of Jews welcomes you into their city. But you and your men must not acknowledge them. Do not return or respect their greeting. If any respond with insolence, ride them down." Capito scanned the formation of men that extended off into the distance as the road wound around hills and ridges. Half were mounted in front and half at the rear of the infantry between them. "Make rough camp here overnight and then close on the city at dawn." The centurion, with one rider accompanying him, spun around to return to Jerusalem.

* * *

After they heard from Florus himself about his proposal to step back aggressions, letting the city settle down, and to arrange for the Jews welcoming the two cohorts who would arrive to help restore order in Jerusalem, Yosef had wondered where Florus's spokesperson was— the centurion always at his side. He knew many in the Sanhedrin, even his father, wanted to believe that peace was Florus's intent, that he wanted to improve matters, and that the massacre was just an unfortunate situation. And that Florus was surprised the tensions had led to such widespread killing. But after hearing Cleo's warning, Yosef doubted Florus's word.

Yosef, Mathias, Eleasar, and the High Priest looked down as Capito, with fifty legionaries at his back, gestured for the group of Jews to exit the gate to greet the Roman cavalry and foot soldiers. From the wall, they could see the mass of Romans formed in rows and columns that arced in front of the gate as they awaited the Jews. A sprinkling of welcoming Jewish calls—complying with Florus's wish—came to their ears as the Jews drew closer to the Romans. Then the Romans moved forward and through the group, forcing them to split off to the side and get out of their way.

"Why are they doing that?" Mathias asked Yosef.

A shout from outside the wall made Yosef turn back to the scene before the gate. Anger at the discourtesy had prompted one man to curse the procurator. The mounted Roman closest to him swung a cudgel, and the man fell. Remembering what had happened just two days before, the Jews ran toward the gate. The riders surged forward and quickly trampled several before they reached it. Yosef watched as Capito and his men then moved to block the gate. The Jews outside were pinned between the charging cavalry and the wall. Soon, only the Romans stood on their feet or sat in a saddle to enter the unobstructed gate. Behind them lay a dozen Jewish bodies.

"A ruse to lull us!" Eleasar shouted and grabbed Yosef's arm. "Your friend was right. We must plunder Antonia to protect the Temple."

* * *

"Mathias," Eleasar said from behind them as they stood atop the third wall, "your son's signal now flies at the tower. We've taken the arms from Antonia." Yosef and his father looked and saw from one of the towers there now flew a white pennant—the signal that had been agreed upon.

XXXIX

JERUSALEM

Miriam knew she should not leave her home, but the Romans had disappeared from the streets, and in the dimness between dark and dawn, she could get to the Lower City unseen. What she had done... killing that Roman soldier... had felt right. Like the blade in her hand had chipped away part of the stone sealing her in, trapping her in darkness. She must talk to Zechariah.

On the street, it smelled of death... the smell of blood seeping into the earth of Jerusalem. She wondered what roots it would reach and feed. It seemed there was still blood on her hands even though she had scrubbed them clean. It made her feel strong.

Miriam reached to knock on Zechariah's door just as it opened. "How do you always—"

"Inside, Miriam. It's not safe out there."

"Zechariah, there aren't any Romans on the—"

He hurried her. "There will be today."

She followed him into the main workroom, surprised to see it well-lit with two large lamps, and touched his shoulder. "I killed one, Zechariah!" She stopped at the sight of a man standing in the corner. In his hands was the leather harness of sheathed blades she had seen Zechariah fashion.

"You killed one... one what?" the man asked her.

Miriam turned to Zechariah. "Who is this?"

"Please sit, Miriam. Why did you come here? It's not safe on the streets now." The blind man touched the chair opposite hers and lowered himself into it.

"I"—she shifted to look at the other man—"Who is this?" He now leaned against the worktable, his eyes dark and steady on her.

"You said you killed one, young lady." The man set the harness on the table behind him and turned back to her. "One what? Perhaps a deadly scorpion that crept inside?" One hand pulled at the tail of a beard that reached mid-chest, and then he slouched back against the worktable.

Miriam ignored him and leaned toward Zechariah. "They were killing people," she whispered. "Even women and children... one... one broke into my home. He was... he was going to..."

180

Zechariah took her hand and held it with gentle pressure. "It's all right, child."

"I'm not a child." She pulled away. "I did what you showed me."

"What have you shown this girl, Zechariah?" asked the man, now standing straight.

"Who is this?" Miriam asked again, gesturing at him.

Zechariah sighed, and his clouded eyes shifted to the man, who nodded, and Miriam knew the blind man somehow saw it, too. "He is someone who hates Romans," the older man said. Those eyes came back to Miriam. "This is Menahem ben Judah, and you can tell him anything you would want to tell me."

Miriam studied the man she had heard so many stories about— his hatred for Rome's rule over Judea. Her father had spoken of him many times, and of the Sicarii, he led. After her attack, she had dreamed of him or one of his followers finding and killing the Roman who had ordered the two soldiers to "take care of her."

"Zechariah showed me how to use a dagger to defend myself." She reached for and squeezed the blind man's hand. "And I did... to kill a Roman soldier."

"Ahhh!" The assassin's eyes brightened, and the white teeth of his smile split his heavy brown-gray beard. "So, you really have killed a scorpion!"

"Miriam is unlike anyone else I've trained."

"Even me, Zechariah? Menahem snorted.

"Yes. She strikes fast, faster than even you—and quicker than any scorpion's sting." Zechariah patted her hand.

"Interesting..." Menahem said as he tugged at his beard.

* * *

"Father, go home. Stay there with mother and Miriam." Yosef said these words as he walked away, then added over his shoulder, "Sayid is there, too. He's my friend, and he'll help you."

"No, I'm coming with you... we have to see how Matthew—"

"He will be fine." Yosef stopped and turned to face his father. "And I'll be fine. But you must protect mother and Miriam." He gripped his father by the arm. "Tell me you will!"

"I..." Mathias looked down from the northern wall of the city at what seemed an endless tide of Romans pouring through the gate. "I will."

Yosef ran after Eleasar, who had not waited, and caught up with him as he descended the wall's steps and slowed to push through people fleeing the Romans.

"Stop! Turn and slow these Romans!" Eleasar called out to them. But only a few slowed long enough to recognize him as he enlisted their help. "The Romans plan to take the Temple," he said. "Gather people to block the streets. Slow them down, so we have time to get ready to defend it." Several of the men nodded and separated to tell others. Their calls mingled with the roar of the crowd but were still distinct enough to catch a growing number of people's attention.

Yosef and Eleasar sped through the portion of Jerusalem referred to as the New City, between the second and third walls. They climbed the steps to race along to where the wall joined the aqueduct that was the base of the Upper City's entrance to the Temple enclosure. Four Jewish guards in the Outer Courtyard rushed to them as they crossed under the colonnade.

"Did you see them as we passed?" Yosef bent to catch his breath, looking sideways at Eleasar.

"—The Romans surging from Herod's palace? Yes. Now they'll attack us from two directions." He turned to the guards: "Get every man to help close the gates into the Temple." Then he looked at Yosef—"And our men will escape rather than attempt to defend Antonia.— So the soldiers could enter the Temple from there."

Yosef scanned the area behind them and saw several men carrying axes strapped to their backs—these were the hewers of wood that had just delivered cords to the Temple. "You men... come with us to the fortress!"

Ignoring Yosef, they turned to Eleasar, whom they recognized. "Yes, we need your help to defend the Temple," Eleasar agreed. "Follow us."

They ran as a group the full six hundred feet across the enclosure Yosef had walked many times before. Yosef felt bile rise in his throat. He watched as Eleasar, not slowing down, spat his own mouthful out. Yosef did not agree with the man's viewpoint on many things, but Eleasar was no coward.

Eleasar nodded at Yosef and then at the group of men with them: "Lead them up to the cloisters, and I'll join you."

"What?" Yosef called to him. "Where are you going?"

"I have to get something."

Somehow Eleasar had the energy to speed ahead, and he entered the passageways built within the wall of the Temple enclosure that led to private rooms for priests and the guard captain, offices, and the storage rooms for items used during ceremonies and festivals.

Minutes later, now atop the western wall with the handful of men beside him—hands on knees and breathing heavily—Yosef watched a flood of people fill the streets. The Romans were slowly fighting their way through the people and moving toward the Temple. On some streets, a hail of stones thrown from rooftops pelted the soldiers. Yosef felt a swell of pride for his people, but then a fist of fear clamped down, and his heart stuttered for a pace. There was no going back now.

A loud sound, a plaintive moan, made him turn toward the southwest corner of the Temple enclosure they called the Place of Trumpeting. What he heard first was out of the normal order. It began with the shevarim—three short blasts that then led to what should have been the third sound—the teruah—nine short bursts—a staccato blast. But together the sounds were like souls crying... a long, shuddering sigh followed by short, piercing cries, the sounds of pain and suffering. Yosef had never heard the shofar blown so loudly nor used for what it surely meant right now—a cry for Jerusalem.

Then it ended traditionally, with what should have started the trumpeting—the tekiah—meant to be a sound of joy. But now it was a call to battle, to defend what was the most precious thing to all Jews. It seemed to last forever, to ring off the surrounding hills and roll through the valleys. The echoes created a ripple of movement—like circles from a stone tossed in water—that passed through the city as the call faded. Then he saw a figure running toward them. As it quickly got closer, he saw it was Eleasar, with the curved ram's horn cradled in the crook of his arm. Yosef knew why he had blown the call customarily used at Rosh Hashanah, the Jewish New Year: Eleasar now had what he had repeatedly called for, a war to throw off a Roman yoke and become a Jewish people under their own rule.

"Bring down the cloisters..." Eleasar gasped, gesturing at the men. "The ones between the Temple and Antonia, along the Outer Courtyard. Take your axes and cut down the walkways." The colonnade beneath them supported the elevated walkways by marble pillars that held up the cedar beams that spanned them. Carved and decorated wood made up the railings and underside, the decking which became ceilings for the spaces underneath. The planks laid crossways as a walking surface were also sturdy wood but not too heavy for the supporting pillars. The men cut away lengthy sections of the decking and cut through the cedar beams below. Now, there was no way for soldiers to get from Antonia to the Temple easily. Eleasar knew the forty men in Antonia would not resist that many Roman soldiers very long, choosing instead to escape through the tunnels.

* * *

Jucundus and Capito stood before Florus.

"What do you mean you cannot get into the Temple?" Florus's face was that dangerous shade both men had learned to watch for—where sun-browned changed to a tinge of red. "Surely you have enough men, and these Jews have hardly any weapons."

"Some do, Lord Florus... they raided the armory at Antonia Fortress—"

Florus cut him off. "There's not enough to equip them to repel three cohorts of armed and armored legionaries!"

"If you'd just let me and my men deal with them, my lord," rasped Capito with a contemptuous look at Jucundus, "we'll reap them like barley at the harvest."

"Lord Florus, killing more Jews will not get you—us—into the Temple. They have closed those massive gates and chopped away the passage atop the cloisters, from Antonia into the Temple." Jucundus stepped forward. "There's no easy way in."

"I came here to get what's owed our emperor!" Florus paced in front of the two centurions.

Jucundus glanced over his shoulder and saw the curled lips that transformed Capito's scowl. He knew the man—only two things made him smile: killing and coin. "Lord Florus"—Jucundus paused until the procurator stopped and turned to him. "You—we've"—his eyes slid to Caputo and back—"killed thousands. Killing more Jews will not accomplish what you—we—want... for the emperor."

Florus shook his head, glanced at Capito, then studied Jucundus. "What do you suggest, centurion?"

"Stand down our men, withdraw, and bring their king into this—make him do his duty to Rome—to settle the dissension and return things to the way they were. And ensure that is how they remain."

* * *

"Have the Romans left?" Miriam asked her father, but he did not answer and had spoken little to anyone since the cloisters came down and the Temple was sealed. The omens... the killing... the attack on the Temple... but most of all the sound of Eleasar blowing the shofar—had pierced something deep within him. It all heralded something, a desolation for his people... for the Jews. Dark days were coming, and he had no idea when they would end. He looked up at his son and daughter, thinking of his wife distraught in her room. He could still hear her crying.

"Some have left. And Florus has returned to Caesarea," Yosef answered her. "A cohort remains, to help 'restore' order to the city."

"Will they? Can they?"

Miriam's sharp and biting tone made Yosef look at her. Those were not the soft words of sweet Miriam from before Rome. And not the sad, unsure tone of the Miriam after his return. Something had changed. He watched as her fingers touched the hamsa on her robe. How it got in the tunnel and was abandoned was still unknown, a question to come later, with the conversation between them. But so much more had happened. "We have petitioned Cestius Gallus again, demanding that something be done about Florus. We've asked him to come and speak to the city and its leaders. So, we'll see what that brings."

His father, still silent, was shaking his head.

XL

Caesarea

Cleo could hear Cicero shuffling with an occasional click of claws on his perch as she stood at Florus's desk, head back and listening. Without looking up and focusing, her husband would never have heard the bird above him. At least he had not yet. Anyway, she would ask Sayid once he returned safely from Jerusalem to move Cicero to his room and keep him there for now. She smiled at how he would respond to that request.

As she turned, the drape of robe over her right arm brushed the stack of correspondence the couriers had delivered for her husband's attention. The topmost, a square larger than those underneath it, spun off to land on the floor. She noted its difference before her touch confirmed it. It was a little heavier and not the typical parchment or vellum used by Roman administrators and officials. She had seen and felt something like it before. Straightening, she fingered the cord wrapped around it, then loosened the knot and flattened the document on the desk. Then she remembered Poppaea showing her Jewish stories written on what the Jews called *gevil*, the material Jews often used for their holiest writing. This piece before her contained writing in a language she was not familiar with, though she thought she had seen it before.

Always interested in the language and culture around her in Antioch, she had asked Octavia about an inscription carved on a plaque in the market with what—she guessed—was the same in Latin beneath. She had learned it was a language used by some in Syria and elsewhere in the region. But who would send a message to Gessius using an obscure language written on Jewish gevil? She looked closer. At the bottom of the sheet was a smudged symbol, an eye. Could that be the Hebrew letter ayin, which she knew meant to watch... to know? Shaking her head, she refolded and retied it, then started to return the message to the stack and hesitated.

"My lady" echoed through Florus's shuttered windows from down the colonnade that separated the house from the courtyard.

Cleo heard the calls grow stronger as the man drew closer. It was the servant Gessius had chosen to replace her old friend and household manager, Graius, who—at her husband's insistence—had

186

been pensioned and left in Rome. She quickly slipped the square of gevil into her robe, securing it in a fold. Not wanting to be found in Florus's office, she hurried out and into the atrium. She stopped by the fountain just as the man crossed from the outside portico to face her there.

"My lady"—he bowed and as he straightened glanced from her to the procurator's private office—"Lord Florus's escort has just entered the city."

* * *

"Cleo!" Florus's loud voice, accompanied by the clatter of soldiers entering with him, rang through the palace's main entrance.

Descending the steps from the second floor, she paused and saw her husband, Capito, and two—no, three—men behind them. A smaller man without a helmet was half-hidden behind Capito, between two large legionaries.

"See who I came upon... Well, he was trailing behind us, and the centurion's rear guard spotted him in the distance and brought him to me." Florus gestured at Capito, who nodded at the legionaries as he stepped to the side. The two men, each with a hand on the shoulder of the dust-and-dirt-covered figure between them, pushed the slightly built young man to stumble toward her. "Imagine my surprise at who it was"—Florus's laugh cut off sharply—"is."

Cleo knew that sound signaled trouble. She now knew he saw things as if written in a ledger—two columns with one side listing events (planned or real) that helped him, and the other listing events (assumed or real) or people that had hurt him or were in his way. He spent time scheming, weighing, and judging everything to place it in one of the two categories that formed his life. He laughed just when it suited, usually only when he saw something as leverage—or that could be twisted to become so—to benefit him. Humor never factored in. In his upturned face, she saw the deep lines carved on either side of that genuinely Roman nose, crevices that straddled the thrust of a mountain's peak. Beneath—she could tell—was anger that gathered, pooled, and simmered.

"My lady," Sayid said with a dry-throated rattle and cough, "I delivered your gift." Wide eyes slid to Florus, who still stood with his back to him, then looked up to Cleo. His thick eyebrows wriggled, trying to say something to her he could not speak.

Cleo took the last four steps down to stand before Florus. "It's good you're home, Gessius." She turned to Sayid and hoped that her real pleasure at seeing him did not betray a feeling in contrast to what she had just told her husband. "And thank you, Sayid, for doing that for me."

The boy nodded his head. "I told Lord Florus that Yosef's mother appreciated your kindness." Sayid—his arms in front of him now—shifted so Cleo could see his hands form a shape. "And your thoughtfulness."

"Yosef?" Florus asked. "Ahhh, the closeness you have with those"—Florus glanced over his shoulder at Sayid, who had dropped his arms to his sides—"who saved you, it now extends to their family?"

Florus was a good talker who always seemed to plan what he said, and the delivery of those words benefited from his smooth baritone. But Cleo sensed small cracks that showed when he was most tense or angry—as in what he had just said. "Yes, the gift for Yosef's mother was for her hospitality at the Passover dinner."

Noting the fixed, blank expression on Sayid's face, Florus shook his head, and his eyes moved back to Cleo. "Your appreciation for the Jews..." he murmured, then his tone sharpened: "What kind of gift?" Florus half-turned to look again at Sayid. "Your boy seemed confused at first and then told me." Seeing Sayid begin to speak, Florus cut him off—"Be quiet, boy"—and then turned back to Cleo.

"It was... a box." She saw Sayid's fraction of a nod. "At the Passover dinner, Yosef's mother showed me the fig tree in the courtyard, and it has meaning to them... to their family. So, I sent her an olive-wood jewelry box carved with a fig tree—I found it in the market here."

"And she loved it, my lady," Sayid said.

"A box..." Florus looked from Cleo to Sayid. "Yes," he said, turning to Capito. "Your men may go, but I need you, Centurion. I likely have dispatches that may contain matters I'll need you to tend to."

Once the men entered Florus's office, Cleo let out the breath she had been holding unaware. "Come with me, Sayid," she said. She saw the tension leave him, too, as he followed her into the courtyard, to the farthest corner, where the high wall offered shade from the setting sun. They sat on a small bench next to one of the long, shallow basins fed by three fountains.

"Lady Cleo, you must go to your room and get that box you bought recently, and I'll get rid of it." Sayid stood. "That was all I could think of when he asked me where I'd come from and what I had been doing."

Cleo smiled up at him. "It was good thinking. I'll get the box, but first, tell me of what is happening in Jerusalem." She scanned the courtyard, "And I have something I need you to translate if you can." She reached under her robe. "This language might come from your home region in Syria."

* * *

Cleo heard the curses long before reaching the office entry and waved away the frightened servant girl who told her with a shaking voice, "Lord Florus wishes to see you, my lady."

"Idiot!" Florus slammed his desk with an open palm. In the other hand, he waved a scroll from which dropped the last piece of crumbling wax from a Roman administrative seal. "Giving in to the Jews' complaints and sending Neapolitanus with Agrippa to Jerusalem..."

Cleo had stopped just inside his doorway. "Agrippa is their king, and he should be able to resolve the issues between you"—Cleo paused—"between Rome and the Jews in Jerusalem." But she feared no one could. Not if what little of that message Sayid had been able to read was accurate—the plan to set Jerusalem and Judea afire just as Rome had been.

"Gallus should send an entire legion." Florus set the scroll down. "Your Jews are a stubborn lot." He reached underneath the map spread halfway across his desk and pulled out a polished, carved olive-wood box. Jeweled rings caught light from the lanterns on the pedestals in the four corners of the room as he held it up to study the detail. Florus lifted the lid off and set the box down. He turned it in his hands.

Cleo saw the tree as it rotated. The box! Shocked at what little Sayid could translate of the message, she had forgotten to go to her room to find the box and give it to Sayid to get rid of.

The hands kept turning the lid, but his eyes were locked on her. "The Jews must be taught a lesson... and they will be. But now we— you and I—must talk about many things." Casually, almost too easily, Florus snapped the thick lid of hard, durable olive-wood in half. "And where is your little Syrian friend?"

XLI

Jerusalem

"I hope you've listened to me." Agrippa stood before the Sanhedrin. "I'll have more to say on this—what we've discussed—for the people of Jerusalem, who should hear it, too... and all who are willing to hear me beyond its walls. Because what has happened here between you and the Romans has consequences for all of Judea... for all Jews."

"—Which you are not, King Agrippa." Eleasar ben Ananias glared at him. "You are not of—you are not with our people. You may be a Jew, but you are a Jew in name only."

"Yes, that's true. I do not hold close to your faith... and I rule"— Agrippa paused as several rows of priests rustled and shifted on their stone benches, and the Temple guard captain's bark of a laugh interrupted him—"I rule, but I serve Rome, too. If your faith, your God, is superior, then why does Rome have such an empire and such power that other nations serve them?" He slowly turned to scan all the men in the Hall of Hewn Stone, stopping when a Levite guard appeared at the chamber's entry.

Seeing the guard's eyes search for him, Eleasar rose to meet him and listened to the message he whispered. He turned to Agrippa. "The people are gathering as you wished."

Agrippa focused on the Temple guard captain.—"Eleasar, you blew the shofar to call your people to battle. You and they have taken up arms against Rome. You've knocked down the cloisters that were an assurance to Rome that the Temple would not become a fortress to start a rebellion." Agrippa shook his head and now spoke to all of them. "You cannot unblow the ram's horn, but you can lay down the sword... you can repair the cloisters, and you can restore peace. We must discuss that and decide after I speak to the people."

* * *

After Agrippa left, the hall was filled with the sound of the rabble—a discordant sound—few of the voices in concert.

Yosef, who sat between his father and brother, watched as Eleasar leaned down and whispered in the High Priest's ear.

"Quiet!" The High Priest then called from his chair. "All of you. We must go and listen to what King Agrippa has to say. The people will no doubt have many questions to ask us about it in the days to come."

The members of the Sanhedrin and city leaders began to file out of the chamber, still talking.

"Wait"—Yosef put a hand on his father's and on his brother's shoulder as they started to rise. He had watched and noted that Eleasar and the High Priest had not moved to leave. They remained still. Soon the hall was empty but for those few. The guard captain looked at them—the longest at Yosef—and then, shaking his head, left the chamber, followed by the High Priest.

As he exited, instead of turning as all the others had toward the outer court to go to the Xystus where the people gathered to hear Agrippa, Eleasar and the High Priest went the opposite direction, toward the sanctuary. Mathias and his sons followed them into that magnificent cubic structure, one hundred and fifty feet high and wide—as tall as a fifteen-story building. Viewed from without, the sanctuary had everything that amazed both mind and eyes. Overlaid with stout plates of gold, the wider eastern frontage reflected the first of the sun's rays in so fierce a blaze of fire that hands shielded eyes as they approached that time of day. The five men entered the massive entryway and walked through the Holy Place until Eleasar stopped before an area partitioned by a veil. Sixty feet long, thirty feet wide, and one inch thick, the curtain was so massive and dense from the embroidery containing threaded gold that three hundred priests were called upon to carry to its place when it was first mounted.

"Even though you—as High Priest—are the only one of us who can enter it once a year on the Day of Atonement, can you feel it, the spirit of God within?" Eleasar asked. "I know what's behind this shroud is an empty space. It should contain our holiest treasures, like the Ark of the Covenant—but those are no longer there, lost when the first Temple was destroyed. This"—Eleasar gestured at the area before them protected by a heavy curtain of fabric and faith—"is still a sacred place, the Holy of Holies."

He turned from the High Priest to Yosef, Mathias, and Matthew. "My father—after he was no longer High Priest—told me that he could feel God filling him when he entered that place, and now it's like a soldier who has lost an arm or leg... a part of his body... but it still aches." He looked at each of them, his eyes holding theirs for a moment. "I would not have our people feel the pain of what they've lost... or will lose. No matter what Agrippa says or tells the people"— he walked toward them—"we cannot let the Romans steal or tear away who we are... even if it's only gold they want, and not to destroy our faith." He glanced at the High Priest. "Have you told them about what happened in the night?"

The High Priest shook his head. "No, and I warned the other priests to remain silent until we can understand... until we can interpret its meaning."

"What's happened that needs such a determination?" Mathias took the High Priest by the arm. When his eyes cut to Eleasar instead of answering him, Mathias turned to face the guard captain. "Has there been another sign?"

Eleasar nodded. "Last night, in the inner court of the Temple, the priests discharging their ministrations heard a voice. They're not sure where it came from—it seemed all around them. It started with a great noise, a clash of metal striking metal, and then stopped. Then a voice—or a host of many, speaking as one—announced, 'We are leaving this place.'"

"What does that mean?" Matthew asked his father.

Yosef turned to his brother. The memories of his visions and dreams that had come true... and the hint of a waking one... the shadows of them passed through his mind. "I think it means a beginning or ending."

"Or both," Eleasar said and walked toward the exit into the Priest's Court and then onto the outer court. "The finish of Rome's rule over Judea and the start of Jewish independence."

As they followed him to hear Agrippa, all Yosef could think was that the sign, the portent, was darker, more foreboding... maybe it was the beginning of the end for Jerusalem.

XLII

Jerusalem

King Agrippa stood on a platform below the western wall of the Temple enclosure, where the upper and Lower City were separated by the Tyropoeon valley. He watched as the Sanhedrin filed from the outer court and crossed the path atop the viaduct that spanned the valley to descend to the Xystus, a terrace where thousands of the citizens of Jerusalem, certainly much of the Upper City, were gathered in tiers to hear him. A single servant, at his left, attended him.

The leaders of Jerusalem he had just spoken with had not wished him to speak directly to the people. But his words, if passed through those ears and mouths, might not have served the Jews as well as they should have. And the people must know, simply and clearly, what was before them. They must know what could be the outcome of their leaders' decisions—the fate of their city.

The afternoon sun angling toward him made the scarlet of his robe brighter against the stark white tunic underneath. Across from the platform was a sky-blue-garbed form—Agrippa's sister, Berenice. That the Romans could have killed her, too, had at first angered and then frightened him. Roman favor and forbearance for its client-kings was notoriously fickle, especially under Emperor Nero.

Florus's urgent messages to Gallus in Antioch, imploring him to deploy a legion to suppress the revolt in Jerusalem, had been acknowledged. But the only action had been that Gallus's senior tribune, Neapolitanus, had been dispatched to intercept Agrippa on his return from Alexandria and bring him directly to Jerusalem. Neapolitanus now stood next to Berenice to bear witness to and report to the Roman legate Gallus what had happened and what Agrippa had done to resolve things and put to rest any sedition.

Immediately upon their arrival, Berenice had told Agrippa and Neapolitanus everything that had happened. The butchery of Jerusalem's citizens was shocking, but that it had occurred under Florus was not. And now much worse loomed over the city and its people. Agrippa shaded his eyes with a hand to look for his sister in blue atop the House of the Hasmoneans, behind and above the thousands of Jews that sat or stood, awaiting him. The sound of their movements easily carried to him as he knew his words would reach them. He saw Berenice's white hand lift in a brief wave for him.

Agrippa's sharp and distinct voice rang out, his words slow and deliberate as he began.

"Had I known you were all zealously disposed to go to war with the Romans, and that most of you do not propose to live in peace, I would not come out to you so bold as to give you counsel. I do not know if I can persuade men to do what they ought to do when they seem agreed and resolved to do the contrary. Some want to go to war because they are young and without the experience of the miseries it brings, and others are for it, out of an unreasonable expectation of regaining their liberty. Some of you hope to gain and are therefore earnestly bent upon making war with Rome, hoping that in the confusion and chaos, you may take what belongs to those too weak to resist you." He wiped his brow with a swath of silk held in one hand.

"I have come here and asked you to gather to hear me tell you what I think is best for you, for Jerusalem, and for Judea. Once you've heard me, I hope some will grow wiser and change their minds, reconsider their actions and how they may plan to act, and that the best men may come to no harm by the ill conduct of others.

"Many of you will hear me and disagree. Others of you already do—without listening. And nothing I say will please these. They are resolved to revolt and to fight Rome." He paused as a low undulation passed through the crowd. "And my words will then fall to the ground, unheard even by those that have a mind to hear me, unless you all keep silent as I speak.

"I well know of the tragedy of recent events and the injuries in the past caused by your procurators, and I know your desire for liberty. But think about who you are—you that must go to war—and against whom you wish to fight.

"First, I want to separate the reasons for the rebellion that are by some connected together. If you aim to avenge yourselves, to strike back at those that have done you injury, why do you pretend this to be a war for recovering your freedom? If you think all servitude—any, whether Rome's or others'—intolerable, what purpose is it to complain against particular governors? Even if they treated you with temperance, it would still be equally unacceptable to remain in servitude under them.

"Consider now the several cases—the incidents before what has just happened here in Jerusalem—that were of little reason for you going to war. The first was your accusations made against your procurators. You should respect those in authority and not give them any provocation. When you reproach, even offend, such men critically for small offenses, you aggravate and then enrage them, and they become true enemies. This will make—and has made—them retaliate and hurt some of you privately and to lay what you have to waste, openly. Now nothing so much dampens the force of lashes—of punishment—as bearing it with patience. The quietness of those who are hurt diverts the punisher from further, harsher methods." He motioned to the servant who poured and handed him a cup of water from the jar he held. He took two sips and gave it back and continued:

"But let us take it for granted that the Roman procurators that are inflicting pain and suffering on you are incurably severe and will not change their ways. Yet not all Romans injure or even suppress you and your religion... nor has the emperor against whom you wish to make war. He has not harmed you, and it is not by their command that any wicked governor is sent to you—because they who are in the west cannot see those here in the east, and it is difficult for them there even to hear what is done in these parts.

"Now it is absurd to make war with a vast empire because of one abuser. To do so against such mighty people, for a small cause, is folly—and this when Rome cannot know your complaints. Such crimes as we complain of may soon be corrected because the same procurator will not continue forever. It is probable that their successors will come with more moderate inclinations.

"But as for war, once begun, it is not easily laid down again, nor borne without calamities, which you do not want to have fall on this city or any city in Judea."

"And about recovering your liberty—it is late... this rush to reclaim it. Long ago you ought to have labored earnestly that you might never have lost it. The first experience of slavery was hard to endure, and the struggle that you might never have been subject to it would have been just. But those slaves who were once brought into subjection and then ran away are instead rebellious slaves and not lovers of liberty, because back then was the proper time for doing all that was possible to never have admitted the Romans when Pompey came first into the country. But so it was that our ancestors and their kings, who were in much better circumstances than we are—as to money, strong bodies, and valiant souls—did not repel, nor even resist, the onset of a small Roman army." A low rumble from the gathering started, failed to gain purchase, and then faded.

"And yet you who have not accustomed yourselves to obedience from one generation to another, and who are so much inferior to your ancestors who first submitted... you who are not as powerful now as they were then, you now wish to oppose the entire empire of the Romans. Think about this. The Athenians, to preserve the liberty of Greece, did once set fire to their own city. They also defeated Xerxes, that proud Persian prince, when he sailed with an army so vast the sea and could hardly be contained by it—these same Greeks made him run away like a fugitive in a single ship. These Greeks are yet at this time servants to Rome. And now Roman law rules Greece and its capital city. And the Lacedaemonians, the Spartans who had great victories at Thermopylae and Platea, are content to admit the Romans as their lords. The Macedonians, who still fancy what great men their Philip and Alexander were and see that the latter had promised them an empire over the world, they now pay their obedience to Rome because its fortune has advanced. Many other nations have greater reason than we to claim their liberty, and yet they submit to Roman rule.

"You are the only people who think it a disgrace to be ruled by those to whom all the world has submitted. Where is the army you rely on? Where are the arms you depend on? Where is your fleet that may defend your coast against the Romans upon their sea? And where is the money for your war? Will you empty the Temple of all its treasures? Will you not carefully reflect upon fighting against the Roman Empire? Will you not estimate your own weakness?"

The front two rows of the Sanhedrin shifted, and their muttering rose. Agrippa raised both hands, palms outward toward them, and they subsided.

"Hasn't your army been often beaten even by neighboring nations," he continued, "while the power of the Romans has been invincible? And they seek for more still beyond. All the Euphrates is not a sufficient boundary for them on the east side, nor the Danube on the north, nor Libya to the south. Cadiz, the coast of Hispania, is their limit on the west, but even now they push beyond the ocean and have carried their arms as far as Britannia, as it is now known.

"What do you pretend to? Are you richer than the Gauls, stronger than the Germans, wiser than the Greeks, and more numerous than all men upon Earth? What confidence is it that elevates you to oppose the Romans? Enduring oppression is hard. Yes, but how much harder is it to the Greeks who were esteemed the noblest—freest—of all people under the sun?

"It is the same with the Macedonians, who have more reason to claim their rights than you. What of the five hundred cities of Asia? Do they not submit to a single Roman governor? What of the Heniochi and Colchi and the nation of Tauri, those that inhabit the

Bosporus, and the countries around Pontus and Meotis, never united by a single ruler but now subject to Roman rule under three thousand men, and where forty longships keep peace in the sea, which before was not navigable because of danger?

"How firm a plea may Bithynia and Cappadocia, and the people of Pamphylia, the Lycians, and Cilicians put in for freedom! But they are made a tributary without an army. What are the circumstances of the Thracians, whose country extends in breadth five days' journey, and in length seven, and is much harsher and much more defensible than most of yours? And though its winter cold suffices to keep armies from attacking them, they submit to two thousand men of the Roman garrisons. Are not the Illyrians, who inhabit the country adjoining, as far as Dalmatia and the Danube, barely governed by two legions? The Dalmatians, who have made frequent insurrections to regain their liberty and had never before been subdued, they are now quiet under one Roman legion.

"If great advantages could provoke any people to revolt, the Gauls might do it best of all, as being so thoroughly walled 'round by nature—on the east side by the Alps, on the north by the river Rhine, on the south by the Pyrenean Mountains, and on the west by the ocean. Although these Gauls have such barriers to prevent any attack upon them and have more than three hundred tribes among them, they bear the tribute to the Romans—and prosper—because of the high regard they have for the power of the Romans and their good fortune, which is of greater efficacy than their arms. Additionally, the gold dug out of the mines of Hispania hasn't supported a war to preserve their liberty. These Gauls are kept peaceful by twelve hundred soldiers, who are hardly so many as are their cities." Wiping his brow, he gestured at the boy who again handed him the cup. He drank it off in one swallow.

"Vast distances from Rome by land and by sea do not assure success in rebellion. The Romans have extended their arms beyond the Pillars of Hercules and have walked within the clouds upon the Pyrenean Mountains, and have subdued nations.

"Who is there among you that has not heard of the vast number of the Germans? You have yourselves seen them, strong and tall, and you've seen them frequently since the Romans have them among their servants everywhere, even here in Judea. Yet these Germans, who dwell in an immense country, who have minds greater than their bodies, souls that despise death, and who in a rage are fiercer than wild beasts, are tamed by eight Roman legions.

"Do you who depend on the walls of Jerusalem consider what a barrier the Britons had? Yet the Romans subdued them even though they were encompassed by the ocean, and four legions are sufficient to hold and guard so large an island." The sounds now came from those at the lowest tiers, below the city leaders and elite. He raised his voice.

"Why should I speak much more about this matter, while the Parthians, that most warlike body of men, and lords themselves of so many, and with such mighty forces, send hostages to Rome? They—the noblest land of the east, desiring peace—submit to the Romans. Or the Carthaginians, who, amid their brags of the great Hannibal, and the nobility of the Phoenicians, fell by the hand of Scipio Africanus—defeated by that great Roman general. And so it is with the people of the Syrtes, a place terrible to those who merely hear it described, the Nasamons and Moors, and the immense multitude of the Numidians. None have been able to overcome Roman valor.

"But what occasion is there for showing you the power of the Romans over remote countries, when it is so easy to learn it from Egypt, your neighbor? Egypt has more than seven million men, besides the inhabitants of Alexandria, as we learn from the revenue of the poll tax. Yet Egypt is not ashamed to submit to the Roman government. Despite its vast city of Alexandria—so full of people and riches it has a grand temptation to revolt—it pays more tribute to the Romans in one month than you do in a year, and part of what it pays is sent as grain to Rome that supports the city for four months in the year. Egypt is also walled round on all sides, either by almost impassable deserts, seas that have no havens, or by rivers or lakes, yet none of these has been found too insurmountable as to defy or deny the Romans.

"When almost all people under the sun—many with far more resources—submit to Rome, will you be the only people that make war against them?

"Do you have allies? Where then are those people who will stand by you? Must they come from the parts of the world that are unknown? For all in the known world is under the Romans. Unless any of you extend hopes for help from far beyond our known world, then what remains is divine help. But even this is already on the side of the Romans because it is impossible so immense an empire could be established without God's providence.

"Reflect upon that and this--how useless it will be for the zealous observation of your religious customs to be here preserved, which are hard to be observed, while you fight with those whom you can conquer? How can you then, most of all, hope for God's help, when, by being forced to transgress his law, you will make him turn his face from you? And if you observe the custom of the Shabbat and will not be prevailed to do anything—even fight—on days with prohibition, then you, your city, and your country will quickly be taken, as it was from your forefathers by Pompey, who was the busiest in his siege on those days on which the besieged rested. But if in time of war you disobey the laws of your faith, I cannot tell on whose account you will afterward go to war, because your concern is that you do nothing against any of your forefathers. And how will you call upon God to assist you when you are voluntarily violating his religion?"

Agrippa waited through the loud cries of denial, the thrum and hum of the collective voice rising to him. When that ebbed, he took a step closer, right to the edge of the wall, where he could go no further. His head canted down and his eyes scanned them—the citizens of Jerusalem—hoping they believed what he said.

"All men that go to war do it either as depending on either divine or human support. But if you go to war, you cut off both kinds of assistance. Those of you that are for rebelling against Rome choose destruction. O my friends, it were best, while this vessel is still in its haven, to foresee the impending storm and not to set sail out of the port into the middle of the hurricane. We justly pity those who fall to such great misfortunes without foreseeing them. But for him who rushes into ruin, he receives reproach instead of commiseration.

"Know this. If you persist and war against the Romans, hoping that even should you lose, that once the Romans have you under their power again, they will use moderation or show mercy, know that they will not. As an example to other nations, they will burn your holy city and utterly destroy your whole country. And those of you who survive the war will not find a place to flee because all lands surrounding you have either Romans for their lords already or are afraid they shall have such hereafter. There would be no refuge. And the consequences of your actions here are not only for those Jews that dwell here but those in other cities as well. There are no people upon the Earth who have not some portion of you among them. If you war with Rome, every city that has Jews in it will be filled with slaughter for the sake only of a few men—those here who want war—and they who slay them will be pardoned by the Romans.

"Consider how wicked a thing it is to take arms against Rome and suffer the consequences for those you love and what you love. Have pity not merely on your children and wives, but upon Jerusalem and its sacred walls. Spare the Temple and preserve the holy house and all it contains. For if the Romans win—and they shall—they will no longer tolerate your faith and its worship."

The boy at his side lightly touched the sleeve of his robe and looked up and back toward the Temple. Agrippa followed the boy's eyes. At some point, as he spoke, Berenice had made her way to where he stood. Gallus's tribune, Neapolitanus, remained with her but stayed atop the wall as she descended the steps to join him. He saw her pallid face, the tears coursing from her reddened eyes. The thoughts of her tears began to stir his own as he turned back to the people. He was forced to pause and gather his emotions.

"I call as my witnesses your sanctuary and the holy angels of God, and this country common to us all—I have not kept back anything to sway your minds." His voice had now begun to falter, but he pushed through his last statements--"If you follow that advice, which you should, you will have peace. But if you indulge your passions, you will run those hazards and endure such punishment... and from the blame for all of it I shall be free."

An echoing cry rose as the angry shouts lessened. "You cry for us? For Jerusalem?"

He wiped his face and shook his head at the boy who offered the cup. "Yes," he answered. "For what you have done... and what it may bring down upon you."

A voice from the ranks of the Sanhedrin called out, "We do not war with Rome but fight against the procurator Gessius Florus!"

Agrippa shook his head. "The tribute you denied was not for Gessius Florus. You have refused Emperor Nero what is due him and have severed the connection—previously agreed to with the Romans—between their Fortress Antonia and your Temple. Unless the tribute is paid, and the cloisters rejoined, Jerusalem will be considered in revolt against the empire." He shook his head again. "It is up to you now what happens... or does not."

XLIII

JERUSALEM

Yosef noticed that some senior priests, the leadership of the Sanhedrin, had decided not to return to the hall and talk further with King Agrippa, who was now joined by his sister Berenice. And many of those who had returned now muttered among themselves.

Yosef leaned toward his father. "You see who is over there with Eleasar?"

"Yes. Menahem ben Judah, the most recent of our self-proclaimed messiahs," Mathias scoffed.

"But he's also the leader of the Sicarii, and next to him is Simon bar Giora, the Zealot."

"Another would-be messiah." Mathias shook his head. "Why are they here? For years, Agrippa has used his power to appoint high priests they despised. They'll not care—or listen—to anything he has to say."

"—Except that, as you know, this High Priest has discreetly aligned with them," Yosef said, nodding toward Matthias ben Theophilus, who was taking his seat as head of the ranks of the Sanhedrin. "Eleasar dictates his will, and that's in line with what the rebels want." Yosef looked toward where his brother stood in front of the Temple guard. "Matthew says Menahem and Simon are gathering men, bringing them from all around into Jerusalem, and they're camped nearby but out of sight."

"What of Yohanan ben Levi and his Galileans?" Mathias asked.

"He and his men aren't here. He remains in Galilee, says Yohanan ben Zaccai." Yosef patted his father's arm and pointed as King Agrippa and Berenice stepped to the center of the hall to face the High Priest.

"I've spoken to the people." Agrippa turned to the row of stone benches where students normally sat—it was now, as was the custom, used by guests and concerned citizens invited to attend council meetings or hearings. Front row, center, sat Neopolitanus, Gallus's tribune. "The Tribune has heard that speech and will hear what I say now... and await your reply. Then he will leave to report to the legate in Antioch." Agrippa looked at the Zealot and Sicarii leaders and then back to the High Priest. "I've given many reasons it would be a fatal decision choosing to war. Even though some Romans inflict the empire's rules in unjust ways that are both oppressive and injurious, it has not always been so. Many in this chamber are moderates and understand this." He paused as several whispers of acknowledgment passed through the ranks of the Sanhedrin. "In peace, you and your religion have prospered, and can—and will—prosper." His sister touched his arm.

"That is what my brother and I wish for you," she said. "Not just for those of you in the city... but across Judea. As I begged for mercy before Gessius Florus... to stop the killing, I saw the hardness on his face that was surely also in his heart. At that moment—that day—he was Rome being denied. Rome being told no." She wiped her eyes with a scarf and shook her head. "Listen to my brother. Fighting Rome won't benefit you... and death is not the freedom you want."

Yosef saw the faces of the Zealots and Sicarii tighten, their lips drawn into thin white lines framed by thick bristling thick beards and their jaws thrust out. But they remained quiet.

Agrippa continued: "I've spoken with the tribune, and he assures me that the legate hears you and your cries of pain. And he promises that if you step away from this precipice, this threat of war, he will work to have Rome replace Gessius Florus with a new, more moderate procurator."

More whispers of assent rippled through the Sanhedrin and city leaders. Yosef checked the faces of Eleasar, Menahem, and Simon—they were still unemotional and noncommittal as they studied Agrippa.

"But"—Agrippa raised his hand, pivoting it slowly as he scanned all of those watching him and then stopped to face the High Priest again—"The legate, Cestius Gallus, has received reports from the procurator stating that you—the leaders of Jerusalem—are responsible for the violence and the deaths of both Jews and Romans."

Yosef darted another look and saw there was still no expression, no red-faced restraint or holding back denials that would echo throughout the chamber. Many discussions in this chamber had ended that way, but still, the Zealots and Sicarii remained silent.

"You must prove your intentions to restore peace by three things. You must return the weapons taken from Fortress Antonia. You must repair the cloisters connecting Antonia to the Temple, so Roman sentries and patrols can resume their watches. And the annual tribute of forty talents must be paid. These things must happen soon. None who turn in the weapons will be punished. No Roman will enter the

Temple, but you must deliver the tribute. And you must not incite Gessius Florus further. He is the current procurator. Obey him until he can be replaced."

Yosef agreed with all that Agrippa had said. But once Florus was replaced, likely recalled to Rome, he would never see Cleo again. The fact was that the likelihood of seeing her again was already non-existent. He heard steps on the stone in the quiet chamber and looked up. King Agrippa and Berenice had joined the Roman, Neapolitanus, to exit from the hall.

"I'll await your answer," Agrippa said as he turned, taking his sister's arm.

"Wait!" Eleasar called out.

"What are they saying to each other?" Mathias asked Yosef, then looked back at the Temple guard, Zealot, and Sicarii leaders. With a nod, Eleasar left them and strode over to the High Priest, leaned down, and whispered to him.

Yosef saw the priest's eyes widen and cast a worried glance at Eleasar, who nodded at him and stepped away.

"King Agrippa," the High Priest announced, "we will repair the cloisters and make arrangements to gather the forty talents owed." He looked again at the guard captain. "And the weapons will be returned to Fortress Antonia."

In the silence, Yosef heard an equal measure of the exhale of held breaths and the intake of the surprised. He and his father were among the latter, and their faces surely matched the look on King Agrippa and Berenice's faces, and the brother and sister's surprise was soon replaced with relief. For Yosef and his father, though, there was no feeling of ease or that all would be resolved and peace would return. They had heard the rebel leaders and the talk they spread of their hatred of Romans. The rebels would rather have the walls of Jerusalem come down than bend a knee to Rome.

Yosef felt his father's stiff beard scrape his ear as he bent near to whisper, "What is going on, Yosef? Why were they so quick to agree?"

XLIV

CAESAREA

Korbanas, Cleo had learned, was a Hebrew word that referred to "sacred treasure" or treasury. She found it written on a scrap of charred parchment that seemed to be gevil, like the message taken from her husband's desk that she now carried hidden on her body. She removed it only when she bathed and then immediately reaffixed it as she dressed. Sayid had tried to translate it and thought the message contained words that indicated a coming event or its planning, an attempt of some type that would achieve their aim—she and Sayid assumed the writer's or recipient's aim. She must learn more about what the message contained. The scrap of burned gevil she held must be the remnants of a previous message, more from an ongoing correspondence between Gessius and someone—likely an educated or well-placed Jew, based on the material and symbol at the bottom. Not fully burned, the scrap with that one word, korbanas, still legible had—windblown—caught on the leg of her archery target. Her hobby had been an early confrontation with her husband, but she had been passionate, and he relented. The most recent confrontation, about the olive-wood box, had been more difficult to resolve in her favor.

She hated lies and liars. That her husband was such a person and that she had become one to protect Sayid and herself still did not sit well with her. But she convinced Gessius that she had bought two boxes engraved with a fig tree on the lid and sent Sayid with one as a gift to Yosef's mother in Jerusalem. It seemed to allay his suspicion at that moment, which had been interrupted by a courier arriving with new dispatches. She left him knowing he still had doubts about her. She had even more misgivings about him, and they were growing, for what he did seemed well beyond simple administrative tasks on Rome's behalf.

* * *

Gessius Florus wondered again at Nero's choice for contact and correspondence on their special arrangement. Tigellinus, the prefect, seemed to have broadening powers beyond those of just commanding the Praetorian Guard and spearheading the persecution of Christians in Rome. No doubt he was also benefiting somehow, and his latest message on behalf of Nero—taking away the obfuscating, the careful phrasing—had been a simple question: When?

Soon, he hoped, though he knew better than to reply with that vague answer to Nero via Tigellinus, and then not make it happen fast enough. He must wait for results from Agrippa, and he had not heard from his spy, which puzzled him because that was far more important. No matter what the Jews told Agrippa, it would not likely be the truth, at least not entirely. The factions in Jerusalem—according to previous reports—continued to work at cross purposes, which served his own agenda. But he needed a significant event—a major transgression by the rebels—to act against them and to create the conditions that would accomplish what he and Nero wanted. He could not confirm how vast the Jewish treasure held in their temple was, but he knew it was a far greater reward than forty talents in annual tribute. It was obvious even from the extent of the gold plating on the outside of the Temple that what was held within could be a staggering amount. And if they did not make some foolish step toward rebellion soon, he would have to create some issue to force them. So, for now, he continued to wait.

He put the message from Tigellinus into the basket set aside for burning and worked through the rest of the administrative documents that kept the far points of the empire connected to Rome. Done with that and the required official replies, he took out a fresh square of vellum and wrote for several minutes and ended the message with a command for an immediate response. Rising, he went to the doorway to find the servant always nearby to attend to him, but not too close to overhear or see anything he did not wish seen or heard. "Find the centurion Capito—he's on the grounds—and tell him to come immediately." He watched as the servant hurried away. They moved quicker if they knew they were scrutinized.

Back at his desk, he reread the message he had just written and then took out a small bronze bowl and set it into a holder above a small lamp, which he lit. He wiped the heavy gold ring on the middle finger of his right hand with a soft cloth, admiring its intaglio of the goddess Fortuna and her cornucopia set in the carnelian stone—a custom ring crafted before leaving Rome.

The red wax in the bowl had lost its dry, flaky surface and turned to a smooth red—a rich sanguine color to match the stone of the ring. He folded the vellum, bringing all four corners to the middle, and then folded it in half and again at the apex, bringing its point to the center. Checking that the wax had melted, he took a small set of tongs and lifted the bronze bowl, tipping it over the message and pouring from the small spout. It dripped and formed a blob that covered the inverted triangle tip of vellum. Setting tongs and bowl aside, he bent over and blew on it once to cool the wax and then pressed his signet ring down, holding it for a second or two. Lifting his hand slowly, he blew again, and the wax hardened, keeping the intaglio.

"Lord?"

Florus looked up at Capito who now stood in the entry. "Use your most trusted man, disguised, to get this to Jerusalem as soon as possible"—he held up the sealed message—"Tell him to wait for a reply. No excuses from our contact there. I must hear from him." He watched as the centurion spun and hurriedly clattered from his office, then made his way out of the silent palace. He wondered at the quiet and where Cleo and the young Syrian boy that attended her might be. Her explanation of the youth's purpose in Jerusalem seemed to ring true. But being so close to forcing events to align with his needs, he could not risk any mistakes or misplaced trust that could jeopardize his plans. He would watch them. His eyes caught the message atop the stack of replies just completed. That one to go to Cestius Gallus in Antioch. If only the bastard would do as he wished, what did it matter that it cost some Jewish lives? He was far removed from them. He swore again. If the legate would not act, then he would—soon.

XLV

Agrippa read the message from the Roman legate, Cestius Gallus in Antioch, to the assembled Sanhedrin leaders, the High Priest, the Nasi, court president Shimon ben Gamliel, and Yehudah ish Krioth, his assistant.

"Governor Gallus is pleased that repairs have begun and that you will soon have the full tribute collected for the emperor. He also grants your request that the tribute be delivered to a Roman official other than the procurator, Gessius Florus." Agrippa turned the sheet of vellum around to face them and held it out so they could see. "Signed and sealed by Gaius Cestius Gallus, Legate of Syria." Agrippa waved at an aide who came forward to return Gallus's letter to its dispatch pouch. "I'll remain in Jerusalem to report progress to the legate, and"—he held a hand up, knowing there might be a protest at what he said next—"and the same report will go to the procurator— as should be done until such a time that Gessius Florus has been replaced. I'll let you know who has been delegated to receive the tribute as soon as that has been determined."

Once Agrippa left, Shimon ben Gamliel turned to his assistant. "Yehudah, you'll find a small group waiting in the Priests' Court. Please bring them here, and we'll discuss what you mentioned to the High Priest and me. I hope it's unnecessary but will consider it once we hear what the others think."

A short time later, Yehudah returned with Eleasar, Matthew, Yosef, and Mathias.

"So, it does not seem that long ago we were on that ship bringing us home from Rome"—Yosef clasped Yehudah on the shoulder—"And may it be even longer before I have to suffer a long sea voyage again."

"But that was so much better than the prison, dark and dank Tullianum, in Rome." Yehudah shook his head—"I feared I would die there."

"But for my brother," Matthew, commented, "you might have. And we all still rejoice that you and the others are back home."

"Yes," Yehudah coughed, dipped his head, and then straightened. "I am truly indebted."

Shimon ben Gamliel raised a hand to get their attention. "Yehudah has suggested something we should discuss." He nodded at the priest to explain, but Mathias interrupted.

"Why did the Zealots agree to what King Agrippa asked for?" he asked. "I know, I know"—he looked at his sons—"Yosef, you and Matthew have already told me what you think, and I agree with you both, but I want to hear the reasoning from one of the Zealot leaders." He looked at Eleasar.

"Mathias"—Shimon put his hands out as if to settle the air between them—"perhaps we should—"

"I'll answer him... and any others." Eleasar looked at his subordinate officer, Matthew, then at Yosef. "I—we—don't trust the Romans to keep their word. The former procurator, Lucius Albinus, was barely tolerable. But he never ordered a slaughter of Jews... no matter the provocation. Gessius Florus has done that intolerable thing. As long as he is in some position of authority, he—Rome— cannot be trusted. But to stand against them, we need the time to gather more men and arms... and to find support from others who wish freedom from Roman rule." He turned to Yehudah. "So, I think your idea—and the High Priest agrees with me—is a good one."

Mathias nodded at Eleasar's explanation but with a frown. "I disagree with preparing for a war that could still be avoided." He sighed, "What's your suggestion, Yehudah?"

"We have seen that having the korbanas in a single location—no matter if it is behind stout walls—puts our treasure at risk. Were it not for Eleasar and Yosef"—he nodded at them—"and Matthew and many other citizens of Jerusalem, the Romans would've broken into the Temple and taken away all they could carry. We cannot risk that happening."

"What do you propose?" Mathias asked and studied the priest his son had helped free from a Roman prison. He knew this man had risen above the roots of his father's merchant family lineage, but still jostled others—perhaps understandably—for even more notice.

Yehudah smoothed his beard with one hand. "Distribute the treasure across Judea and hide it. Once we are free from Rome or sure that their intent is not to take it from us, then we can return it to the Temple."

"That's a colossal task," Mathias said, shaking his head. "That would require a great deal of planning and use of only the most trustworthy men."

"There are such men, and it could be done," Eleasar said. "And now, as we appease Rome and buy time, is when it should be done."

"Yes, but"—Shimon looked from Mathias to the High Priest—"who could we—"

"The Essenes." They all looked at Yosef, who continued--"They're ascetics who care little about wealth or treasure. The Essenes are pious, and they hold our faith as sacred and are adept at keeping secrets. I know this firsthand from my early years among them with Banus, my mentor."

Matthew and his father nodded. "Yosef speaks the truth," Mathias said. "They also could be counted on to control their emotions; they are devout and disciplined about remaining beyond anger." Mathias glanced at Eleasar and then studied Shimon and the High Priest. "I don't believe the treasure should be moved from the Temple, but such an undertaking can only be accomplished with success if cooler—humble—heads prevail."

"Then we'll put this for a vote before the Sanhedrin," Shimon said with a nod. "If we do, will you support this, Mathias?"

"If my sons are placed as leaders of this mission, I will. One should be the emissary to discuss and coordinate with the Essene leaders"—he nodded at Yosef—"and the other to represent the Temple guard and be in command of the relocation of the treasure"—he gestured at Matthew.

Yosef caught the look passed among the High Priest, the court president, and Eleasar, who then turned to Mathias and said, "I would support them in those roles."

* * *

Yosef and Mathias stood and watched the workers with a series of block and tackle raise the massive wooden beams into place. Scaffolding now framed what would become the repaired section of the bridge from Antonia to the Temple wall. Once the beams were in place and secure, they could affix the longer runners to form the base of the platform and then lay the planking for the deck of the walkway.

"They'll be done at month's end," Yosef remarked as they walked closer and looked up, remembering that day when the axmen chopped the former structure away. Yosef remembered too the cries of people—his people—rising as they were cut down by the Romans, and how the sharp scent of chopped cedar momentarily replaced the scent of blood on the wind.

"Yes, and by the end of next month the full forty talents will be collected without our having touched the Temple treasury," Mathias said with a sigh. "That will satisfy the annual tribute. Do you think that will placate the Romans?"

"I don't know, Father. I hope so. I'm more concerned about our own people. I wish the factions we contend with would relent and not force a war with Rome. But Yehudah is right—we must do what is necessary to protect the Temple and its treasure."

XLVI

Miriam faltered, a blush spreading across her face. "Why—"

"You know why." Zechariah reached behind to check his distance from the worktable and then leaned against it. "You're not as strong as a man, but you have two assets, and you were born with both." He stepped toward her. "You're fast... maybe quicker than any man I know. And the other thing is something no man can ever be—a woman." Knowing that she faced him, he pointed at the tabs of cloth that seemed decorative along the front of the man's tunic she wore. "We must check those and the one at your belt to be sure they work." He backed away to give her room, only stopping when he touched the wall of the farthest corner. He sensed that she still had not moved. "Miriam, why do you hesitate?"

Her face flushed, and Miriam took two steps toward the center of the room. "It's just... I can't take my..."

"Miriam I'm blind, and although I can sense people—even recognize them—and things, I cannot see you." His mild, soft tone was that of a father to a child, convincing her to do something she would rather not. Yet she remained frozen, so Zechariah gave her a blunt command: "Attack!"

That voice and tone was the man from the tunnel who had killed the Roman soldiers, and it drove her to act. Miriam stepped behind the life-size straw figure dressed as a man wearing a tunic and robe. With her right hand, she drew her dagger and punched into and up through the base of its melon head, which split open. And as the "head" fell, she spun and stabbed its heart. In the same motion, she pulled the blade free and slid it into her left forearm's sheath. She separated from the figure sprawled on the floor and ducked away while her fingers flew top to bottom and pulled the tabs. Her tunic separated. Shrugging it off, she pulled a woman's robe from around her waist and tugged it on over her head. Then—wiping spilled melon juice from her hands as she did— she rolled and stuffed the man's tunic under her breasts. Breathing heavily, she smoothed the bulk against her lower chest and stomach and then stepped back toward the fallen shape. Barely half a minute had passed.

"You won't always be where you can make an attack and change quickly, but by planning and preparing for where you'll strike, more times than not you'll be able to," Zechariah said. "Now—when you return to the body—is when you'll cry out as a woman. You will lament the killing." Zechariah came close to pat her shoulder. "Join your voice with others and become a Jewess distraught at the killing. Then leave because the sight has upset you."

He considered—not for the first time—what he was doing to her and what he was turning her into—albeit at her request. "No one will see you as a killer or a member of the Sicarii." He shook his head to free it from lingering doubts. "We will practice this over and over, and then when you can do it without thinking—without hesitation—we will practice it again in total darkness until you are as comfortable as you are in the light."

* * *

It was hot, but the afternoon sunlight felt good Miriam thought as she climbed the steps from the Lower City to the Temple and into the royal colonnade. She had spent most of the day with Zachariah in the tunnels. She had known of many of them from her days playing with Yosef and Matthew—those under the Temple enclosure and a few that branched into the Upper City—but Zechariah had shown her others that reached under and into the Lower City and that led to caves in the valleys that surrounded Jerusalem on three sides. The earthquake a little more than three decades ago had partially blocked some of them, but Zechariah thought that with work they could be cleared. Menahem ben Judah had plans to use them.

From the top of the colonnade, she could see to her right the rolling hills—the Mount of Olives—that rose above the Temple. And ahead in the distance to the left were the new cloister deck sections. A glint of metal from the Roman soldiers, at the end of their patrol close to the Antonia Fortress, twinkled under the sun. She felt solid. Thanks to training daily with Zechariah she was stronger, and keeping up with him no longer tired her out. Her mother had even commented that whatever she was doing during the days away from home, she looked better and seemed healthier. Running her hands over her arms and thighs, Miriam felt muscles that were now more defined.

The fear that once consumed her had turned into banked coals of anger that burned under control, and the sparks reflecting off the Romans' armor far down the western colonnade fed those coals, creating streamers of flame that climbed and then settled as she kept them in check.

She descended to cross the outer court to the viaduct that led to the Upper City. Down its terraced series of steps to the bottom, she paused near the intersection of a street and alley that led to one tunnel—the one she had not been in since her attack. A man standing there caught her eye. He carried a large goatskin pouch with an inserted rectangle of wood to flatten its bottom. The kind often used by merchants who walked the agora with samples of their wares— squares of cheese wrapped in large green leaves, spiced figs, and even smaller skins or jars of honeyed-wine—and he watched the shoppers wandering from stall to booth, table to table. He did not look at them as potential customers, but instead, he surveyed them as Zechariah had taught her to do. A judging, measuring... a sandal-to-head gauging of men as targets or threats. She felt his gaze sweep over her—a flicker of a pause and then his assessment of her as a non-threat, a woman—and then move on. After a full-circuit scan of the cross streets and shops, he turned and entered the alley.

After a minute, without thinking, she followed him. Beyond that vague feeling, that he was something—someone—not as he appeared, he also seemed familiar. Ten feet into the alley, just before it bent toward the western wall of the Temple enclosure, she realized that as he had scanned around him, his head had checked the rooftops. He had a scar shaped like an X—almost a hand's width—on his left cheek. She had seen it before. Months ago, right after Passover, there had been a man who seemed to follow Leah and Rachel in the market. She had been going to join them and slowed to watch the man for a moment and then forgot him as he turned toward the northern gate. She was sure it was the same man she now followed.

She paused and took a deep breath but kept a corner of her headscarf over her mouth to screen out some of the dust still in the air. Without a breeze around to lift and swirl it away, the dust was thick in the narrow alley. At the next branching and left-hand bend was the dead-end and entry to the tunnel. The muscles of her stomach clenched as she slowly moved forward. At the turn, she could see through the haze of grit to the thick-thorned tree and wall just beyond it that sealed the alley. The man was gone, and there was only one way for him to go—down.

Squeezing behind the barbed branches, she knelt to lift the platform door of the tunnel entrance—an inch at a time to pause and peek. She caught the soft glow of a lamp at the bottom of the ladder. Waiting for that to recede as the man got past the first bend, she moved quickly but carefully. She opened the door wide enough to slip in and swung her legs and feet onto the rungs as one hand closed the door, leaving her in darkness.

Soon she was far down the tunnel that she had nearly not returned from. If Zechariah had not come upon them that day... she shook her head. No, that thinking was over and done. She would never be their prey again, and she could thank Zechariah for that, too. She could still die, as could have happened in her own room that day of Florus's massacre, or would happen somewhere, sometime, in what was to come. Both Zechariah and Menahem were sure that no matter the talk of a desire for peace and resolution, the war was coming. But she would not die frightened of anything—of any man.

Moving steadily through the dark, she slowed as she heard voices ahead of her as she approached the crossing of tunnels and the place where she had been attacked. She listened. One voice spoke Aramaic but with a curious accent. The second one—softer but still clear—was undoubtedly a native Jew. She moved closer.

"I know he will go there as soon as he is done with his meeting, receiving the tally report on the collection of the tribute and confirming its delivery."

The accented Aramaic was harsher and harder to understand, so Miriam crept even closer, stopping at the corner of the passage. The Jewish voice replied to a question she could not make out.

"There is no doubt. Agrippa will be there. The merchant has a new stock of dyed silk Agrippa favors—the purple, scarlet, and silver—and a single bolt of blue he'll want for his sister."

Miriam knelt and then lay flat as she looked around the corner to where the voices came from. In the dimness of a single lamp, she saw the two men. One was taller, in fine robes but standing in an equinox of light and shadow. She did not recognize his features, but the Jewish voice was the same as that of the man with the Romans that she had overheard the day of her assault.

A flash of metal caught the lamp's radiance. A knife? Was the scarred man she had followed going to kill the man who sounded Jewish? In the light, a thick-tendoned hand twirled and spun the blade. Its elegant arc was familiar. She had one like it strapped to her left forearm: a Sicarii dagger.

"I continue to do as Lord Florus wishes, and I told your partner of the recent discussions about moving the treasure. Should you kill Agrippa, I cannot say what effect it will have on the Jewish factions, but it will force the Roman retaliation that Lord Florus wants and needs. Tell him"—the Jew paused and rephrased—"ask him what plans he has to protect me should that happen. I must know." He turned and disappeared into the shadows of the tunnel that led toward the Temple. A moment later the flare of a lit wick and then the bloom of a lamp cast a circle of light that receded.

Miriam had to decide. Follow the Jewish man, who was evidently working with the Roman procurator, or the man she thought was now on his way to kill King Agrippa. She felt that no Sicarii member—from what Zechariah had told her—would assist a Roman like Gessius Florus with anything. They would not serve a Roman agenda. And that man from the alley with the X-shaped scar was not a Jew. Killing Agrippa and making it appear that the Jews were responsible would bring the Roman army in insurmountable numbers down on Jerusalem and on the Sicarii. Sacrificing oneself for a lost cause seems noble until thrust on a person without choice or without an option to live to fight, to take more of the enemy, and perhaps to die another day.

She went after the man with the dagger. He had—thankfully—not backtracked into her and had entered an offshoot of the central tunnel that angled, she thought, toward Herod's palace. Within minutes the lamp's light went out ahead of her, and she heard climbing. Then a square of gray light above came and went just as she reached the foot of the ladder. She shot up the rungs without regard for noise or much else, and her head struck the closed door. Pressing one-handed, she lifted it and peered out to see that the tunnel exited behind a row of low decorative walls and a fountain girded by large shrubs that formed the perimeter of the palace, where it gave way to the luxury merchant stalls in the market.

Across the street before her, between two of his soldiers, was Agrippa, about to enter the silk merchant's shop. Trailing them was the man she was after. As Agrippa and his escort went inside, the man positioned himself at the corner of the entry, in the shadow of an alley that ran alongside the building. Miriam joined a group of women passing by, and once they crossed in front of the merchant, she ducked down another, smaller lane bordered by a wall. Going along the wall until it passed the back of the silk merchant's shop, she then crossed behind the building to the alley that ran up its side. Ahead of her, in the dim light that reached the alley's entrance onto the street, she saw the man. As she closed on him, she saw the telltale gleam of a metal blade in the hand he held low at his side.

She was an arm's length away when he sensed her. Her dagger was out as he brought his knife up and opened his mouth at the surprise of seeing a Jewish woman lunge at him. She thrust upward—

hard. His mouth closed with the snap of teeth on teeth, her blade pinning his jaws shut. Then he convulsed with a gurgling sound as she dragged him into the darkness of the alley. In the stillness of the man's death, she heard Agrippa's voice, well remembered by her from his speech.

"Such colors... the blue... Berenice will love it. And the scarlet, my favorite shade."

XLVII

Jerusalem

"It appears that Agrippa prepares to leave, lacking his royal demeanor." Yehudah ish Krioth studied the guard captain, who did not seem concerned.

"That he leaves Jerusalem, with or without it, is all I care about," Eleasar said as he paced the room.

"But perhaps it's best if he remains in the city longer. I—or perhaps the High Priest or Shimon ben Gamliel—could go to him and ask him to stay to help with further discussions with the Romans."

"Discussions?" Eleasar stopped and turned with a scowl. "The last of the annual tribute was delivered, so we've done all they asked." He paced again. "There will be no more talking."

"But there has not been any more abuse from the procurator. No one—at least not in Jerusalem—has heard from Gessius Florus. Isn't that what you wanted? A return to how things were, even though we remain under Roman rule?" Yehudah shook his head and looked at the young captain through lowered eyes. "The Romans will surely continue to treat us... acceptably." He stood and smoothed his long beard, clean and silky, a thought lingering on how foul it had become while he was imprisoned in Rome. "Though there is still no word on a replacement for Florus, we must hope we will be governed wisely, no matter who is the Roman procurator of our country."

* * *

"What about the High Priest?" Yosef asked Mathias as he set a bowl of fruit on the table, then half-turned and called, "Anything else, Mother?" Mathias stood to look out onto the courtyard as twilight turned to night. "Father," Yosef asked, "can't the High Priest request that Agrippa return?"

"Even before he became the Temple guard captain, Eleasar was arrogant and stubborn," Mathias observed. "Both are birthright traits from Ananias, who, despite being removed as High Priest years ago after he ordered the execution of Yeshua's brother Yakov, still wields power over many." Mathias uncrossed his arms, came to the table and sat at its head. "The current High Priest is as much a puppet as Agrippa—Eleasar and others know this well. Rome pulls Agrippa's strings just as surely as Eleasar and the Zealots use Matthias ben Theophilus like a puppet High Priest that says and does as they want."

"Did Eleasar actually insult Agrippa after confirming the final delivery of the tribute?"

"He did worse than insult," Matthew said as he entered the room, "when Agrippa responded to his report and commented as he walked away that he hoped there would be 'no further trouble with tribute or taxes.' Eleasar angrily put a hand on the king's shoulder, turning Agrippa to face him. Had I not stepped in to draw him away from the king, Agrippa's escort would have skewered Eleasar or at least tried. Then harsher words were said, and Agrippa replied that he was done dealing with angry children and that from now on the procurator and legate could handle any problems in Jerusalem." Matthew reached for a clay cup and poured water from the stone pitcher. "I've never seen Eleasar so enraged. He stormed from the chamber muttering he would show 'them' that Jews are not powerless."

Yosef lit the lamp on the table, and in the flare of light noticed—with concern—how his father's beard, once threaded with as much black as gray, was now mostly white, and that deep lines creased his face. "Father," he said as he touched his arm.

Mathias blinked, glanced at Matthew, and then studied his younger son next to him. "Yosef, when tempers are lost—when emotion overrides reason—lives can be lost. We've already seen that consequence and must talk to Eleasar and the other Zealot leaders and pray that no one acts rashly."

* * *

Eleasar, as captain of the Temple guards, stood before them, unmoved by the shouts and remonstrations from most in the stone hall. Yosef leaned toward his father. "He has half the Temple guard in here, and Matthew says almost all are with him in this crazy decision."

"I told your brother—yes, I know he was already conflicted—to go along with Eleasar and not argue against it nor confront him. He must just do his duty as a Temple guard officer. Perhaps having him close to Eleasar will allow us some leverage, or at least an opportunity to gather some information. We can take a lesson here from King David, who stayed close to his adversary, King Saul—closer than to his friend Yonatan."

"How can Eleasar decide to stop foreign sacrifice, especially the twice-daily offerings to the emperor? He doesn't have that authority.

Our continued offering of sacrifices at the Temple for Rome and the emperor has been part of our arrangement with them for decades. To stop those will surely be seen as an insult and an act of rebellion."

"Yosef, power is held by those who actually command, those who can sway or order the actions of others or form the reactions of crowds. Power does not come with a mere title."

Yosef scanned the chamber, noting that only the Sanhedrin president's assistant seemed unfazed by the Temple guard captain's abrogation of the sacrificial tradition and expected compliance with the established order. He felt his father shift next to him on the bench.

"Shimon ben Gamliel may be president of the Sanhedrin, Matthias ben Theophilus may be High Priest, but they," he pointed at the now-seated men, the Zealot, and Sicarii leaders, in the front row facing Eleasar ben Ananias, "are in command now."

Yosef rubbed his face with both hands and looked at the empty seat of the High Priest. "I don't want to think about what will come of this. It will be far worse than Florus turning three cohorts loose on Jerusalem. We must do something to stop them."

"The rebels have it in their heads that our glorious past should be our equally grand future. That we Jews will rise to prominence as the successors to Rome in the east. This messianic vision fuels their dreams and makes Rome the center of evil to be fought and defeated." Mathias rose from the stone bench, steadying himself with a hand on his son's shoulder. "It is men—not nations or religions—who are evil. Yosef, go home and check on your mother and sister. If your mother asks what has happened, you may tell her. I must find the High Priest and the Sanhedrin president." He glanced at his older son. Matthew stood in front of a dozen Levite guards arrayed along a wall of the chamber, and an equal number and the other junior officer lined the opposite wall. "We must figure out how to deal with this before it alarms the Romans. One of Gessius Florus's cohorts remains in Antonia, and once they know, they will be ordered to act."

Yosef stood to leave. "Any resistance to them—or worse, an attack on them—will bring more Roman soldiers quickly from Caesarea. I cannot imagine Gessius Florus is not watching what happens in Jerusalem."

XLVIII

Jerusalem

Miriam could feel the tension in the people change in tone. At first, they were in shock at the Temple guard captain's stopping the daily sacrifice for all foreigners. She saw the shock on faces and overheard the talk in the Upper City as men clustered outside the shops along the Xystus and western cloister of the Temple and could not help but still hear Agrippa's echoing voice that day. And then that shock changed to expressions of elation as she descended the steps into the Lower City. Jerusalem's working-class, those hardest hit by taxes and unemployment, seemed happy that something was being done about Roman oppression. They believed that throwing off the foreign yoke would make their lives better.

She walked faster. Her mother no longer asked about the plain robe and cloak she wore to fit in with other women in the Lower City. She had told her it was safer dressing that way—being less of a target. But there were only a few women on the street, and the men often stopped their talk to stare at her as she passed. Nearing Zechariah's, she noted that the heavy canvas cover was pulled down over the outer work area where he would spin and form clay as he chatted with passersby and the shop owners next to him. During the day that meant he was out, or, as she knew from her training sessions with him, that he did not want to be disturbed.

She entered the alley between Zechariah's and the leather worker's shop, and her nose crinkled at the smell of cured and uncured hides heavy in the stillness. She gave one–two–one–three knocks, the signal they had agreed on to show him it was her.

The door opened. It was Menahem ben Judah. "Zechariah said it was you." He stepped back and to one side to let her enter.

Miriam slipped past him and turned into a large work area to see Zechariah's broad back hunched over his table.

"Hello, Miriam," he didn't look up. "I haven't seen you"—the briefest chuckle—"in a while." He straightened, turned, and smiled at her. "But"—his head inclined slightly toward Menahem—"I knew you were okay." He stepped to the end of the table and picked up a piece of cloth to wipe his hands.

In the center of the table was a model. It was shaped—roughly—like the oval socket surrounding an eye, wider at the center and tapering at both ends. The lid was formed by a double wall around the perimeter with several structures both connected and separate—like buildings sitting atop the clay plateau. A few points along its base and a couple of projections along its height were marked with black stones. Zechariah used similar ones to mark entrances and exits for her in a rough model he had earlier made of the city to show her the many tunnel locations. "What's this?" she asked.

Menahem came over and pointed at a large square building toward the left side but separate from the furthest cluster at the edge. "Are you sure this is it—the right location—and that they're stored beneath?" He looked at Zechariah.

At the end of the table, Zechariah nodded. "My grandfather was a stone worker at its completion, and my father transported supplies there for many years. As a child, I helped him until I left to join the army." He set the rag down. "My memory is good—both of the stories told me and what I've seen—and my hands are true. It might've changed somewhat, but the structures"—his hand passed over the half of the model with the most buildings—"they will last until long after you and I are dead and forgotten."

"What is this?" Miriam asked again. When both Menahem and Zechariah moved from the table, she knew they would not answer. She followed Zechariah from the workroom to the front of the shop. Opening the door and stepping through, he paused near the wooden columns that supported the open work area now sealed by canvas.

"I can't train with you today, Miriam. I must work. But tomorrow, early morning, I can, if you wish." He looked over her shoulder to address Menahem, who stood in the doorway separating the front and back of the shop: "You can bring the others here later this evening. It's a two-day march, and they must time their arrival to locate the entrances when the sun is right."

"Zechariah"—Miriam touched his elbow—"the Romans—a Roman—tried to kill King Agrippa."

Zechariah let go of the rope he gripped to draw up the canvas. "What?!"

"Agrippa left the city," Menahem said as he stepped toward her and gripped her arm. "When did this happen and how do you know?"

Miriam had slept little since that night outside the silk merchant's shop. She thought every moment of how she crept upon the Roman dressed as a Jew, knife out at his side, and the smell of him as she got within a foot and pulled her dagger from its sheath. Her heart had been beating so loudly in her ears that she was sure the Roman had heard it, but he did not. Reliving that moment over and over—in fright—had not been what kept her awake. But the feeling of power that coursed through her with a blade in her hand, to decide the life or death of an evil man, had. She flexed those hands and turned to Menahem, who released her arm. "It happened days ago before the king left Jerusalem."

Zechariah's voice, softer, came from behind her. "How do you know this, Miriam?"

"Because I tracked the Roman and killed him just before he struck."

* * *

Miriam went quietly through the gate that led to and from the narrow lane running behind her family's courtyard. She had long ago adjusted it to open and close smoothly—no scraping if she kept pressure upward. Zechariah had taught her how to feel each step, even when moving quickly, to avoid anything that would make a noise as she moved—a twig, a dry piece of wood, a branch, or loose stone.

She paused in the shadows of the corner where the courtyard passed into the house and heard her mother's and Yosef's voices.

"Father is meeting with the Sanhedrin, and he and Matthew will tell us more when they get home," Yosef said. "He wanted me to tell you and Miriam and warn that you must be watchful on the streets."

"Miriam, I believe, is upstairs. Should I get her?" Rebecca asked.

"You can tell her later if I'm not here, Mother," Yosef said. "If we can't get Eleasar to rescind his decision to stop the daily offering for Emperor Nero, the Romans are going to consider Jerusalem—and all of Judea—in revolt. I pray the rebels to see reason and not make things worse by doing something even more foolish."

Hugging the wall to stay out of sight, Miriam went upstairs to her room. When she had left Zechariah and Menahem, both stunned at her news of the assassination attempt, Menahem's last comment before Zechariah told her to go home had been, "If the Romans are willing to kill their own client-king to send a message to Judea, we must move faster than planned."

Miriam lit Zechariah's lamp, taking a moment—as she did each time—to trace the carving in its base. That model on the table at Zechariah's... she didn't know what it represented, but she knew she must tell Yosef that something terrible—what he and father feared—

was going to happen. But she didn't know how to do it without revealing how she knew.

XLIX

MASADA

Herod built the giant fortress of Masada on an isolated plateau as a last defensible refuge should there be a revolt against his rule. Under Roman rule—after Herod's death—Masada had become a storehouse with large stocks of food, its cisterns fed and kept full by an ingenious rain-dew-collection system. Masada had all that was required to withstand a siege. Its armory contained bows, arrows, javelins, swords—enough arms and armor to equip several thousand men. There was even a stockpile of stones, perfectly-sized for handling and positioned to be rolled down the slopes and crush any attackers foolish enough to attempt to take Masada.

Menahem ben Judah knew the fortress held all these things, but not many Roman soldiers just yet. But since the incident in Jerusalem—though resolved by payment of the annual tribute and repair of the cloisters—more troops had been added, bringing it up to almost a full cohort. The size of the garrison would likely continue to increase by order of Gessius Florus because Masada would serve as a critical staging point for any Roman military action against eastern and southern Judea and along Lake Asphaltitis, a salt-laden dead sea.

That fact made the Sicarii's attack an urgency, Menahem also knew though that a Roman cohort could easily hold off five times their number from such a superior defensive position. He had only four hundred men, but they were determined to take Masada. And if they could, its weapons cache would equip thousands more. But they would fail if it weren't for the tunnels—that was the advantage that improved their odds. Were it not for Zechariah's knowledge and his model that had helped with the detailed planning, they would not stand a chance. Each of his leaders had meticulously diagrammed his steps and calculated his timing for the attack with Zechariah.

Menahem looked out over his band of men. Small groups of them had headed toward Masada without seeming to have an orchestrated purpose. Between and near the larger communities of eastern Judea, such travel was plausible and should escape the attention of the Romans. More than a day before, his assault teams had left Jerusalem and would pick up more men camped in the surrounding area. Then, starting at the base of the plateau's highest point, they would traverse the tunnels that rose 1300 feet over the arid plain—that would take time.

Following Zechariah's instructions, advance scouts had confirmed that the tunnels were clear of obstructions and that, with care, three hundred men—assigned across the three tunnels—could travel through them into the fortress through exits inside the casemate walls that secured Masada's perimeter.

The largest tunnel came up underneath the more elaborate of Herod's two palaces on the plateau, where it tapered to a narrow point toward the north. From there into the administrative area of the fortress, he and his men would soon be in and among the Roman officers—killing them and swarming their offices and quarters to converge with the other two teams at the soldiers' barracks that stood atop the armory.

* * *

It was late afternoon, and the setting sun created a halo on the mesa, a glow that caught the highest sections of the four sixty-foot stone towers at each corner of the fortress complex. Menahem had gathered the groups into a fake caravan to replace the regular replenishment and resupply for the garrison. This ruse would distract the Romans' focus at the end of a hot, dry summer day. Locals had reported that the Romans had let late-arriving tradesmen—especially those with fresh casks and barrels of wine or barley beer—remain overnight.

He looked at the rows of a dozen sturdy donkeys that pulled two-wheeled carts loaded with an assortment of fresh viands and the much-appreciated beverages for thirsty Roman soldiers. The donkeys and carts could easily make it up the sloped path that led to the fortified gate one thousand feet above.

"Shomer!" Menahem called to the man who would be at the head of the supply caravan—an actual wine merchant who strongly believed in their cause. "It's time. Your thirty men and the supplies will continue as you have done before, entering the western gate. Some Romans may recognize you, and that will put them further at ease. I and the rest will swing north to enter through the primary tunnel." He gestured at five nearby men wearing legionary uniforms. "These men—once we are in position—will station themselves near the tunnel exits and the gate you will approach. Two will watch to see if you are let in and permitted to remain overnight. They'll communicate with the leaders at the tunnel exits, who know we have only two choices. If you are allowed in to stay overnight, we will strike after the Romans are well into your wine and beer. If not, then at sundown we will rush from the tunnel exits, slaughtering as we go, and you and your men must take the gate and hold it. I'm told the Romans here are careless; they laugh at the thought some Judeans they consider rabble could be a real threat to them. Strike them down. No mercy and no quarter. We kill them all. Remember all the friends—patriots—we've known who have been crucified."

* * *

Menahem walked Herod's palace with the aid of the moon's light and that of two men accompanying him with lanterns to cast illumination on the luxury surrounding them. Their footfalls echoed on marble as they passed through the terraces—three of them—that interconnected to comprise the entirety of a lavish, sprawling private villa buffered from the fortress complex's administrative center and officer's quarters by a high wall.

The night was quiet now, but at its loudest, the screams and tumult of their successful attack and capture of Masada and all it contained had resounded among its dolomite-plastered buildings as the moon rose and the Romans fell. The morning sun would rise over Masada's gore-soaked soil and stone, but most of it was Roman blood. For now, a night wind cooled his face as he descended the staircase cut from the rock face of a hill rising above the plateau that took him from the middle terrace to the lowest. He entered a courtyard bordered by a portico of columns covered with fluted plaster and topped by Corinthian capitals. The walls, their lower half a series of colorful frescos, surrounded the courtyard and formed a square with chambers and passageways branching from it. The man ahead of him raised his lantern before an entrance. The current of air coming from it smelled and felt laden with water, a distinct difference from the breeze swirling over the plateau after passing over the vast, arid plain surrounding it. They stepped into a dressing chamber that led to a private bathhouse.

"Menahem," one man called to him and lifted his lantern to reveal a cabinet with stacks and bundles of dyed silk either overlooked or left behind by some noble or privileged high-ranking visitor.

"Yes," Menahem said as he stroked the material, a rich-hued, magnificent purple. "This will do nicely." Proper fabric, he thought, for a king's—or a messiah's—robes.

L

CAESAREA

"Where is Agrippa headed to? Surely not here, since there are no ships expected in at present..." Gessius Florus looked up at the centurion.

"Antioch, Lord Florus." Capito shifted uncomfortably. "That's two weeks overland, and we won't hear more until a message can be sent from there." Telling the procurator that the assassination attempt on Agrippa had failed—with the report of his leaving Jerusalem—was not pleasant, especially because the man assigned to do it could not be found to explain what had happened. And now word had come that Cestius Gallus had sent a request to Rome for a new procurator to be assigned to Judea.

"So, the two authorities in the region who want me gone," Florus said with a sneer, "have joined their voices and combined their complaints about me." He slammed the desk with an open hand. "And we don't know what happened to *your* man? Our spy—the mole—was to give him the 'when and where' to best strike down Agrippa."

Capito did not miss the way the procurator said 'your' man... The blame for the failure was forming at his feet. "Lord, the courier's orders—when he exchanged places with the other agent, as they have done many times now—were clear. One was to assassinate Agrippa using the information about Agrippa's timing and whereabouts. According to the other man who returned here with the latest news, it was solid information. No one else knew of it and *our*"—he couldn't help stressing that—"man was prepared to succeed and make it look like one of the Jewish factions killed their king."

* * *

Cleo held Cicero close to her chest in the farthest corner of the room as Sayid, kneeling with his head down and ear to the opening listened to the conversation below. She didn't know why, but the parrot was always restless and loud when her husband was in his office, even more so when someone else, especially Capito, was around. She wondered if it was the man's smell; it seemed he never bathed. She smoothed the bird's shock of fluffed feathers and tried to still his bobbing head. Cicero shivered and then settled. Minutes passed with Sayid focused on listening, though Cleo knew he was uncomfortable spying on her husband. Despite not holding a military rank, Florus could still cause problems with Sayid's auxiliary status within the Roman army. Cleo heard the echo of metal sandal studs on marble floors and the clack of greaves—a sign that the centurion was leaving.

Sayid rocked back on his heels and turned his head toward her. "They've both gone, I think," he mouthed to Cleo.

Cleo nodded and stood with Cicero still held close to quiet him. "Come with me," she whispered and turned to leave the room. At the door, she listened and, not hearing anyone, stepped out and looked both ways. To her left was the central landing from which a set of lavish marble stairs with carved-stone balustrades branched off. One set of steps led to the vestibule of the palace, and the other went down to the atrium with its adjacent bedrooms and her husband's office. To the right was a short hallway leading to another landing that ended at a simpler wooden narrow stairway that descended to the servants' quarters and work area, including the kitchen and pantry. Through those rooms was also an exit into the large courtyard at the rear of the palace. She turned right, casting over her shoulder, "Come with me," again to Sayid. "Quietly."

In minutes, they were following a path parallel to the colonnade along the courtyard the archery range she had set up despite Florus's mocking. It wasn't wise for her and Sayid to be seen merely standing as if having a casual conversation. Her husband and most Romans believed that talk with servants and subordinates was for giving orders and hearing from them that what one wished had been completed correctly. She placed Cicero on a tall stone pedestal, his perch when she practiced and gestured at Sayid. "Please fill this"—she handed a bowl to him—"from the fountain." He brought it back, and she placed it beside the bird.

"I missed the first part of what Lord Florus was talking about with the centur—"

Cleo cut Sayid off with a raised hand. "Wait." She scanned the area, studying the hedgerows between them and the palace; some were tall enough for someone to hide behind. All seemed clear, and she took two wrapped bundles from a nearby rectangular box made from woven reeds. The first, a quiver of green-feather-plumed and fletched arrows, she handed to Sayid. The second was a long bow with a small object wrapped in oiled parchment affixed to it with a leather cord. Her fingers untied and then unwrapped it. Within was a wooden dowel with a bowstring coiled around it. She strung the bow with sure hands, then motioned to Sayid, who handed her an arrow that she deftly nocked. Without looking at him and focused on the target, she asked, "Okay, what were they talking about?"

Sayid had his back to the hedges and kept his voice low. "I didn't hear the first part of what they said, but Lord Florus was angry."

"Could you tell what he was mad about?" Cleo let the arrow fly, and it sped through the air, striking the target high and right of its center marked by a large red circle.

"I think it was something supposed to happen to someone in Jerusalem, but it didn't go as Lord Florus wanted."

She took another arrow from him and nocked it. "What was it that didn't happen? Could you get any idea?" She drew in a deep breath.

"I think Lord Florus wanted someone killed."

Cleo released, and the shaft struck the target left and low as she breathed out. "He wanted who killed?" She took another arrow from Sayid.

"I didn't hear that part. We missed when they started, but then the centurion told Lord Florus that the Judeans—the leaders of the temple in Jerusalem—have stopped the daily offerings to the emperor. And"—Sayid paused as if still trying to figure it out—"and Lord Florus seemed happy to hear that."

Cleo was as puzzled. "What?" She lowered the bow with the third arrow at the ready.

"Why would Lord Florus be pleased to hear that?" He shook his head. "That makes little sense."

"I don't know, Sayid," Cleo raised the bow and sighted on the red circle. "What did they talk about next?"

"That a man—who must work for either the centurion or your husband—has been watching the 'Jew friend and his family'—that's the way he said it—and that another man, someone who was gathering information for Lord Florus, had been meeting with the Jew friend's father. They had talked about moving *it* to keep *it* safe."

"It? Did they say what 'it' was?" Cleo lowered the bow and shifted her grip slightly on the bow and realigned her pull fingers on the arrow and string.

"No." Sayid shook his head, and added, "But when Lord Florus mentioned the Jew friend—he and the centurion seemed intent on avoiding names—he sounded angry again. Like he hated whoever that person was." Sayid looked up at her. "I think that must be someone he wants to have killed, too. I think that may be Yosef."

Cleo shook her head, trying to settle the worry she felt building. She breathed deeply again, held it, and raised the bow and released in a single fluid movement. The arrow flew and struck the target dead center and vibrated. A green feather—one of the three fletching the shaft—came loose from its thin, deep notch near the nock's binding and floated to the ground.

She knew Florus did not have friends, or at least not any Jewish friends, but she did.

LI

Jerusalem

Miriam wondered how different her life would be were it not for her mother. The stories of her Hasmonean heritage, told quietly but proudly among the family, rang true. Rebecca had insisted that Miriam be educated, albeit at home. That streak of regal independence had convinced her father to agree to break her betrothal with her fiancé Ya'akov, despite not understanding why Ya'akov sought it. Maybe it was Mother's Hasmonean blood passed on that now led her into something that seemed to grow beyond mere revenge, to an aristocratic need for respect, even if just for herself. Ya'akov had guessed what had happened to her in the tunnel, and though he was empathetic, had lost respect for her. She was tainted through no fault of her own. But since the night she had killed the Roman stalking King Agrippa, she had felt a growing, strangely compelling sense that she was on the verge of something, but she didn't know what.

The buzz of conversation on the streets had lessened over the past days, but the tension remained as if Jerusalem held its breath. She had hoped to get back to Zechariah's sooner, but her mother needed her help to prepare for the upcoming Feast of Xylophory. Once certain responsibilities were met, her mother didn't question where she went but always cautioned her, "Be safe, daughter."

Miriam knew many mothers whose hearts and focus were always on their sons. Sons remained at home, and the girls married and became part of another household—daughters were little, if any, use to them in old age. Sons were a permanent part of a mother's life; daughters were temporary. *That is no longer the case*, Miriam thought as she stepped into the Lower City, *at least not for me, and maybe Mother knows that*. Resolve had long since replaced her regrets.

The street-side canvas was up, but she didn't see Zechariah in his stall. Turning down the alley, she knocked on the side door.

"Miriam, come in," Zechariah said as he half-smiled and stepped back to let her inside. He closed the door and followed her into the workroom.

"Why are you taking it apart?" Miriam stood over the worktable where the model that had filled it days before was now in pieces. At the end of the table on the floor was the basket Zechariah used to collect excess clumps of clay and the misshapen, failed or flawed lamps and clay-formed objects he would break down to reuse the material.

Zechariah swept more pieces of the model into the basket. "There's no longer a need for it." He shook his head as he bent to lift the full basket. Cords stood out in his forearms as the old man turned cloudy eyes toward Miriam. "So many things we set in motion to fill someone's needs." He shook his head again—"I've never questioned what I've done, who I've helped to meet whatever might be their need or mine." He walked over to the huge bowl he used for preparing his clay. "And I wonder, should I?" Emptying the basket, he stood there looking into the bowl as if it held an answer for him.

"Zechariah..." Miriam studied his face and the taut lines of tendons in his neck. He looked as if he still carried a heavy burden. "Is there something wrong?"

"I wonder if this one thing—a single thing I'm responsible for that troubles me, that I've started—if this one thing can be stopped."

"I don't understand what you mean." Miriam shook her head. "Does this have anything to do with Menahem... and that?" She gestured at the model's remnants.

Zechariah's milky eyes went to the table. "That? What that was for cannot be stopped. What's going to happen, what has happened already, can't be changed." He set the basket down and walked over to her. "But you don't have to be a part of what's coming." He gripped her shoulder. "I know why you asked me to train you, and I know why you killed those Romans. But has that done what you needed? Have you filled your need for revenge? I hope you have, and that you can walk away now."

＊ ＊ ＊

Yosef glanced at his father, who walked quickly beside him, and he called to his brother ahead of them—Matthew was already nearly at the small council house near the Xystus market terrace. "Matthew, what's the hurry? Why are we meeting here and not the Hall of Hewn Stone?"

"Eleasar is there now." Matthew wiped sweat from his face.

"So?" Yosef and his father had reached the entrance. "That's where you'd expect the Temple guard captain when the High Priest and Sanhedrin meet."

Mathias, breathing heavily, addressed his son: "Matthew, what's the hurry and what of Eleasar being in the Sanhedrin hall?"

Matthew opened the door and waved them inside. "He is with Menahem ben Judah, who returned to the city a short while ago—adorned in purple robes, and posturing as he came through the gates and into the Temple—from Masada."

"Masada. Why was he there?" Mathias asked.

"He and his Sicarii snuck into the fortress and slaughtered the Roman garrison." Matthew beckoned them in again. "Several of the senior leaders of the Sanhedrin are with him and Eleasar, but some are against them and have met here."

As Yosef entered, he saw several of the Temple and city leaders huddled in urgent conversation, both Sadducees and Pharisees, around a table. They quieted when they saw them.

"This is madness," Mathias said as he nodded at the men and approached the table. "Have you tried talking with Menahem and Eleasar?"

"The rebels don't listen—and now they no longer just talk or presume they have power... they have it and have wielded it!" Shimon ben Glamiel, Sanhedrin president, sat at the head of the table with his features drawn tight in anxiety.

Beside him, Yehudah ish Krioth seemed calmer and less strident. "It's true. The Sicarii took Masada by surprise and killed the Roman cohort garrisoned there." He pushed his chair back and stood. "It's good that Roman couriers to and from Masada are likely infrequent." Yehudah nodded to Yosef but spoke to Mathias: "And should one arrive, the men Menahem left to hold the fortress will kill them, which buys more time."

"Time? Time for what?" Yosef asked.

"To come up with some plan before the Romans find out," Matthew replied. "Menahem is not just arming the Sicarii—he plans to arm the rabble... looters. He is counting on them—when he turns them loose—to create disruption and distractions in and around the city."

"What purpose does that serve?" Mathias asked.

"Once he has enough weapons and armor moved here from Masada, he plans to take Antonia Fortress and then equip an army to defend Jerusalem."

"He's deluded," Mathias shook his head. "He cannot have enough men to follow him into such insanity."

"Father," Yosef said, "he believes he is destined to become the people's rightful king... to lead not just those in Jerusalem but all Judeans."

"He's lowborn," Matthew scoffed, "and hungry for power."

"Others have been lowborn, too, and that has not stopped the spread of their beliefs." Yosef paced as he spoke. "And he does not promise peace and forgiveness. He promises freedom, something Menahem says he can deliver to the people. That got their attention... the belief he will give them what they want. What they lack and blame others for—the Romans, and"—Yosef glanced at the other men—"and leaders of Judea. That's what draws them—fearmongers and nationalists—to men like Menahem and Eleasar. The rebels and Sicarii promise what tired men dream of at night and hold burning—angry—in their breast throughout the long days of not enough—not enough for them or for their families."

"We have to stop this," Mathias said.

"I and others have tried talking with them already," Shimon said, waving his hand at the other men around the table. "They had the Temple guards escort us from the hall."

Yosef said, "We must send a messenger to King Agrippa, asking him to return and to take control of the city to help put down the dissidents that will otherwise lead us all to ruin."

"I agree with Yosef," said Shimon ben Gamliel. He turned to the three men who had yet to speak. "Simon, Costabar, and Saul... Agrippa knows you, and I think he will listen. Will you go?"

Saul stood with a nod at the two other men. "We'll go, but it's two weeks to Antioch and two back... less if we push harder."

"You must leave now and push harder," Mathias said. "I agree with my son; we need Agrippa." He turned to Yosef and Shimon: "Should we also contact the procurator?"

"In Antioch, Saul and the others can also tell the Roman legate and show that not all rebel against Rome." Yosef shook his head. "But I don't know that Florus will do anything."

Yehudah spoke up as he stood. "I have to go, but I think as Yosef does. Gessius Florus should be told, but he will probably not send help."

LII

JERUSALEM

Throughout Jerusalem, the talk of Menahem ben Judah and the Sicarii supplanted the chatter about the Zealots stopping the daily offerings in the Temple. No matter where Yosef went, there was no escaping it nor the sweltering daytime heat. Summers always brought discomfort, often accompanied by short tempers. But Yosef had never experienced—nor heard his father speak of—a summer like this.

"I don't think Eleasar likes what Menahem ben Judah is doing," Matthew said as he sat at the table in the courtyard.

"What?" asked Mathias. "How he stirs people up—mostly in the Lower City—and how at every street corner the talk is of him?"

"No," Matthew said with a shake of his head, "his pretension. The factions of the Sicarii and Zealots have a common cause, to oust the Romans and make Judea truly independent. But that bond formed by their mutual belief is unraveling. Eleasar and the Zealots he leads want the Romans out, no matter the cost. But Menahem also wants to punish any Jew or citizen who may be perceived as a collaborator— anyone who cooperates or has cooperated with the Romans." Matthew looked at his father. "Menahem is creating a list of our leaders and affluent citizens he or his lieutenants feel either have helped or still help the Romans through the absence—or reluctance— of their resistance to Roman rule and that he considers supporters of Rome."

"What is his plan for those on the list?" Mathias asked quietly.

"To punish them once he's got his men fully equipped and positioned here within the city or nearby."

"And Eleasar is against that?" Yosef asked.

"He believes in raising and equipping an army"—Matthew rubbed his eyes—"but not as his personal strong-armed henchmen. Menahem's words and actions are splintering the bridge the two factions built for their joint effort."

Mathias held his head so low on his chest that his beard bunched around his chin as he chewed his lip, something he did when in profound thought—it made a tuft of wiry hair twitch beneath his lips.

"Father." Yosef waited a moment and tried again: "Father."

Mathias looked up. "Yes, what is it, Yosef?"

"What's wrong?" Yosef knew it must be the same thing that worried him, too—that their names were—or soon would be—on that list of Menahem's.

"What's not wrong, my sons?" Mathias looked from Matthew to Yosef and then into the shadows of the sitting room just inside the house. He could not see her from the courtyard in the growing dusk, but he knew that Rebecca sat there and listened. She, too, worried about their sons and daughter... and then worried for their city and people.

"We still must try, Father." Yosef reached to touch his arm. "We must do what we can."

Mathias took a deep breath. "We will do what we can do to bring reason to the unreasonable"—he straightened, and though he didn't smile, he was not as downcast. "We have a guest joining us soon, and we will talk about how to protect the Temple treasury. At least that does not have a human spirit to contend with."

* * *

Miriam was tired and hot. The day spent with Zechariah had been both mentally and physically exhausting. When he had asked how she felt—did she think the wrong done to her had been avenged—and she had tried to answer him, he had stopped her by saying, "Think long about it... consider that if you go too far down this path, you will reach a point where you can never turn back." He had shaken his grizzled head, then opened his clouded eyes to pierce her with their gaze: "I know this to be true." And then he had worked her harder than he ever had before. She looked down at her roughened hands. Her knuckles were scuffed, and one was still bleeding; the web of flesh between right forefinger and thumb was rubbed raw from the sweat-soaked leather straps of the dagger's haft. She now carried two daggers in sleeve sheaths on her forearms, and her left hand was even sorer than the right.

Arriving home at sunset with an "I'm not hungry Mother" reply to Rebecca's call, Miriam had gone up to her room with only a full pitcher of cool well water. She sat it on the table by the window and eased the wooden shutter open. The voices below carried on the soft breeze that eddied over the courtyard walls and up to her. The breeze soothed her flushed face. Taking a deep drink of water, she set the empty cup on the table sat down and leaned her head back against the wall and closed her eyes.

* * *

Matthew greeted and brought them—one man more than expected—through the house, pausing a moment for the guests' brief greeting to his mother.

Yosef lit the last lamp on the fourth post that illuminated the center of the courtyard. He was back at the table where his father remained seated as Matthew arrived with the visitors.

The extra guest was unexpected—Eleasar ben Ananias. *That explains*, Yosef thought, *the look on Matthew's face.* The same look, a flicker of apprehension, crossed their father's countenance.

"Welcome, Yehudah. It's been a long time—before you left for Rome—since you visited our home"—Mathias gestured to the seat on his right. "And Eleasar, you, too, are welcome." He cocked his head at the seat to his left and slid his eyes to Yosef with the same prompting.

Yosef understood and sat next to the guard captain, across from Matthew, who had taken the chair directly opposite him, next to Yehudah. Just before the glow of the lanterns blunted his night vision, he saw his mother watching from inside, framed by the light from a small lamp behind her, with her arms crossed. She turned away, and he lost her in the shadows. But her voice, what she had told him earlier, lingered in his mind. Then other words demanded his attention.

"I'm told you sent for Agrippa, asking him to return and intercede"—Eleasar held up a hand up to forestall an exclamation—or denial—that didn't come. At that point, his pause became awkward, so he continued: "We don't need him. But I understand your intent, and that you did what you thought was right because of what prompted it." He abandoned his calm tone—"But to send a request to Gessius Florus!"

"Eleasar, you have brought us to the brink of war by stopping the daily offerings for the emperor," Mathias said.

"To throw off the tyrant's yoke!" Eleasar slapped the table with his right hand.

"And now Menahem—the insanity of his taking Masada and killing all of the Romans there—has plunged us over that precipice into what will be a catastrophic war we cannot win—for all in Judea and not just Jerusalem." Mathias glared at the young guard captain. "Ask my son, Yosef, about the Roman juggernaut you and Menahem have awoken!" He bowed his head, hands on his brow, and kneaded his temples with his thumbs and then straightened. "Some of what he has seen is something you, too—we all—will soon see"—he raised his arm and pointed to the north—"arrayed before our gates."

"The Romans don't know yet"—Eleasar shook his head—"and we'll prepare."

"They will soon know, and it's better they hear it from a voice of reason from within the city than discover it through other means," Yosef said. "You could prepare for a year and still not match what they will bring to bear against us."

"What if Agrippa says no?" asked Eleasar. "And I hope he does."

"Then it's no different than if we hadn't tried, but it was worth the trying."

"And what if Florus, only two or three days away in Caesarea, says yes?" Eleasar locked eyes with each man, one by one. "He and the troops he commands will descend on our city like a plague of locusts."

It grew quiet, and Yosef heard the night sounds of the wind rustling leaves and of the insects and small creatures that stir once the sun is entirely down. Thoughts of Gessius Florus took him to thoughts of Cleo. Then to Leah. Two women he cared for but would never—could never—be with. And then there was Rachel. His mother had told him just that day about her infatuation: Rachel had feelings for him and he must talk to her soon about them. He looked up at the guard captain, who was still speaking.

"The possibility that Florus might say yes is why I'm here"—Eleasar leaned forward—"at Yehudah's invitation."

* * *

Exhaustion and the droning voices in the courtyard below had lulled Miriam to doze. Louder—sharper—words woke her. Something about Florus—she half-turned in her chair to peek through the shutter. From her angle, she saw her father's side profile and the chest and lower faces of the men sitting to his right. One was Matthew in his guard officer tunic. Next to him was a man with a long, luxurious beard; its silky sheen caught the lamplight. With their backs to her sat Yosef—her brother's unruly mop of hair was unmistakable—and a man next to him who wore a guard officer's tunic but one a little more decorative than Matthew's.

The beard next to Matthew rippled as the man's lips moved. "Gessius Florus is the reason I asked Eleasar to join us, Mathias." The man and beard shifted back slightly from her father as he talked. "When Menahem trumpeted the news, here within the city, of his Sicarii taking Masada, you were right to call for a meeting to plan what we discussed to protect the Temple treasury from the Romans."

A hand came up into the light and smoothed the beard. Then it rippled again, and the man's voice pricked at something—some memory she could not quite recall. "As the Temple guard captain, Eleasar must be involved." The hand did more beard smoothing. "And unlike others who are also responsible for where we are, and what we all fear we face; I believe he only wants to help defend our faith and treasure."

Miriam eased the shutter open wider and inched closer to the window. The man opposite the beard, sitting next to Yosef, seemed to bristle as he straightened, squared his shoulders, and stiffly bent toward her father and spoke: "Mathias, I know you love your faith and country as much as I do, but we must break free from Roman rule." The man shook his head—and before Matthew leaned back, she saw the wariness in his eyes when he cast a look at his brother—then continued. "What I do is not for me. Don't mistake my actions as the same as Menahem's self-aggrandizement."

The beard twitched. "No matter the reason or whose fault it is that we have to take such measures, we must develop a plan to move and hide the Temple treasury. That task and the need for secrecy are immense."

"My sons and I agree with you, Yehudah." *The beard now has a name*, Miriam thought as her father continued: "And Eleasar, we know you're not like Menahem. But your actions..."

"What I've done is done, Mathias, and we will not reverse that decision. Now we need to plan for what will happen next, especially if that becomes Florus at the gates of Jerusalem again with three or more cohorts of Roman legionaries."

"I don't think we should move and hide it all," Yosef said, and all looked at him.

"Why not?" Yehudah's voice still teased something within Miriam. Perhaps he was an old friend of her father's she had met before. But he was not one she could recall from recent years. Something in just the two words of his question seemed cool and cautious compared to the heat and demand for action in the conversation before.

Yosef stretched his arms and then tugged the sleeves of his robe higher on his forearms. She had seen him do this all her life when he was ready to debate or discuss a sensitive point. "If Florus or any Roman enters the city, takes Jerusalem by arms, gets into the Temple, and finds that the treasure is not there... a Roman like Florus will tear our country apart to find it, or he will punish all who are at hand and within his grasp."

"You mean we leave the treasure to appease them?" The unfamiliar guard officer stiffened and turned to Yosef. He looked close to the same age as her brother. "We should let them take it. Pay the Romans and pray they go away!"

"You didn't listen to him. No, Eleasar..." Matthew's face came into the light again. "My brother means leave them part of it and hope the Romans believe that is all there is."

"How much, then... a third... or half of it?" As Eleasar choked that out, Miriam followed Yehudah's hand stroking his beard.

"Even a third or half... is a lot. The treasury is... substantial." Her father coughed. "So those we enlist to help us must be trustworthy." He stood and stretched; his hands pressed at the small of his back. Miriam knew its ache troubled him when he sat too long.

Yosef moved his chair back and looked up at him. His face full in the light, Miriam saw lines that had not been there when her brother had left for Rome. He had returned with shallower versions of these lines, the tracks of his experiences that had now deepened, accented by the shadows as Yosef canted his head up and spoke. "The Essenes—they can help select good, secure locations, or locations that can be made secure to hide the treasure and then document what's been hidden and where. And they would be the safeholders and protectors of that information. They don't care about material things and have no greed."

Mathias nodded. "And you know them well from your years with them."

Yosef replied, "Yes, and I can go to Qumran to discuss this matter with them."

"The ascetics... hmmm..." Yehudah had spoken, his hand had stopped, and the beard lay still on his chest.

240

LIII

Caesarea

"Do you ever hear from your *friends* in Jerusalem?"

Cleo detected her husband's emphasis as he no doubt intended. Instead of turning to him to reply, she kept her eyes on the sea. Out beyond the large stones capping the escarpment that formed the seaward terrace of the Roman procurator's residence, King Herod's former palace on the water. She and Florus dined on the terrace during the heat of the summer and enjoyed the wind coming off the ocean. Now the sun, a molten ball of orange that shaded to scarlet and brown in places where it touched the waves, tinged the whitecaps with a reddish tint that matched the sky.

When she turned, she saw that ruddy cast was on Gessius's face, also, as he raised yet another goblet of wine. He was pleased with something or with himself, as was evidenced by the frequency the Greek servant girl refilled the cup. Cleo had learned her husband was not a man like many who drank when angry or when confronted with problems. He faced his problems sober and never muddled his anger with anything. Preferring to remain sharp and as keen-edged as any centurion's pugio, like the blade he always wore sheathed at his belt.

"No?" His eyes did not blink or slide away as they studied her over the goblet's rim as he drank. "Well, I have news from Jerusalem," he set the cup down, and the girl quickly filled it and stepped away, careful not to look at nor appear to look at him, "news that might interest you."

Cleo moved away from the edge of the terrace and sat at the carved-stone table with her back to the sea, facing him. The table's flat surface was pitted by the elements, but years of servants' work had kept it smooth. The edges of the thick tabletop top bore an elaborate design, an Egyptian frieze that repeated and spiraled around the columnar legs. *Another great civilization*, Cleo thought, *now ruled by Rome.* She looked at her husband, who was still watching her. He was a man, she had learned, who cared nothing about rules—except those that served his interests—nor about responsibilities, but he cared a great deal about riches. If she didn't respond to him, his mood would darken, and though he had yet to hurt her physically, others could suffer. "Leave the amphora, and you

241

may go, Agnes," she told the girl. Bowing, Agnes set the large two-handled jar near Cleo, and with a bob of her head, she hurried toward the residence. "What news do you have, Gessius?" Cleo's question brought his eyes back to her.

"An envoy told me that a Judean faction—not that of your friends—has wrested control in Jerusalem." He barked a laugh. "And they've asked me to intervene, to come to the city or send troops, and help the city leaders regain power."

"And will you?" Cleo asked.

"No," Florus said and laughed again without humor. "Me—help them?" He sneered. "I told this—emissary—they must quell their own uprising." He lifted his cup and drank. "Let them all kill each other."

The wind strengthened behind Cleo and blew her hair free and into a tangle. She swept it back with both hands as she rose from her seat. "And if all the people—the Judeans—are dead—who will pay taxes and tribute to the emperor?" She looked down at him as he slowly turned the goblet by its stem. He didn't seem concerned at that thought.

Behind him, coming from the residence along the winding gravel path to the terrace, was Florus's majordomus. The household manager was a man Cleo had to come to despise, and she knew that he spied on her. Stomping along with him was a stocky figure in full centurion regalia, Capito. She was glad to be upwind and lifted the amphora and filled her husband's cup. "You have a guest," she said as she set the wine down. "I'll leave you with him." She nodded in their direction, and when they gave her a curt greeting, she passed them without speaking.

JERUSALEM

Where is Eleasar now?" Shimon ben Gamliel turned from Mathias and Yosef to ask Matthew who was catching his breath.

"His men and most of the Temple guard are with Menahem as his lieutenants distribute the weapons from the Masada armory. They will close and fortify the Temple." Matthew had run from place to place, home to home to inform the Sanhedrin leaders that had not aligned themselves with the rebels and asked that they meet at the House of Caiaphas, a place where the Sanhedrin council—made up of senior leaders—had met in the past.

"Son, did you find Yehudah ish Krioth?" Mathias asked. "He should join us."

"No, Father," Matthew answered. "He's not at his home and not at the Temple."

Yosef looked at his father and brother. Mathias stood and rested a hand on Matthew's shoulder. The chatter of men, their cross-conversations, slowly subsided as he silently scanned the room, stopping—for a scant moment—to consider each man.

Until a year ago, Yosef had often wondered why his father had not accepted the Sanhedrin presidency or some other official position. Their family lineage merited it. But what he had seen since his return from Rome had given him the answer to that question. It was something his father abhorred in others—greed, whether for power or money or both because they often went together. Yosef and his brother had been fortunate coming from an affluent family. He realized that, and it had always kept him humble when judging others. Eleasar ben Ananias had also come from privilege; his father was a High Priest and although forced to step down, was still a rich and powerful man. But Menahem ben Judah and the other rebels, who were violent, were not privileged. They were lowborn into poverty, yet ambitious in a **class-conscious** society, and that society was ruled by a powerful and dominant—also class-conscious—empire; it bred anger and resentment. Thousands in Judea were unemployed—eighteen thousand in Galilee alone—since Herod's massive decades-long construction projects had ended. These men were ready to follow any charismatic leader who promised them something better. Even if all he had given them so far was a full belly and a sword to use against those they blamed for the wrongs that had been done to them.

"If the rebels are arming men to take the Temple, then we must arm men to defend it." Mathias's voice was low, and the room quieted further to hear him continue. "Some of you were once soldiers, and some"—he squeezed Matthew's shoulder—"some of you are young and have the skill but no experience. We must all do our part now."

"What of King Agrippa? Do we know if he is sending any help?" asked a man.

Mathias shook his head. "Two more days would be the soonest to expect any help—and that's if Saul and Costabar set a killing pace to get there and to return quickly."

"What about weapons, Mathias?" Shimon ben Gamliel's face was pale and slick with sweat.

"Son"—he tapped Matthew, who looked up at him—"what of Menahem's men, how many has he equipped?"

"The first pack train from Masada had only enough metal weapons for maybe a hundred men, but he had gathered more than two hundred when I left Eleasar. And the rest were given clubs and Roman hastas—these short spears lack iron tips but have fire-hardened points."

"Did they have any bows and arrows?"

"No, Father. But Menahem's largest pack train should arrive soon with more weapons and armor from Masada."

"Hastas are for thrusting, and the longer pilum is a spear for throwing," Yosef commented. "Without javelins or bows, it's all close-quarters fighting." Yosef looked around the room; many of the men—mostly his father's friends—he had known much of his life. Some were tense and afraid; some had a look of resolve and resentment. "All we have are personal weapons, kept by you former soldiers, and some training equipment, but we can make clubs and maybe even slings. And we must organize our men into disciplined units that proportion those weapons and are led by veterans. That's one thing I learned from the Romans."

* * *

Yosef looked upon bodies strewn across the Xystus, and the market terrace was mottled with puddles of blood yet to congeal. The day before, Matthew, leading men equipped with metal swords and slings, had taken the viaduct connecting the Upper City to the Temple, giving the slingmen an advantage to fire down on any rebels below. And that foothold had enabled them to push the rebels back.

But forcing them back further, here at the Xystus, and then down into the Lower City had been all they had accomplished. They held the gates, defending those narrow points that limited the point of attack and thereby securing the Upper City, but the Temple was still held by the rebels.

Yosef did not know if his assailant was a citizen of Jerusalem or someone brought in from outside the city by Eleasar or Menahem. He deflected the man's thrust and then spun to swing the hard olive-wood training sword—all he had at home to bring with him to the fighting—and strike him across the neck. He put all his flagging strength into it, and the loud crack made him think the tough but now-splintering wood had finally snapped. As the man fell, Yosef realized it was a bone, not wood, that had broken. It did not matter where a man came from if he was trying to kill. He took the hasta from the man's still-twitching hands and, breathing heavily, scanned the area for another rebel.

* * *

"We have strong points established," Matthew reported, "defended by men adequately armed with what we had and what we took from the rebels. We've secured the gates of all entrances and exits to and from the Upper and Lower Cities."

"And we wouldn't have them if Eleasar and Menahem had not kept the best fighters there, to secure the Temple and to seal off Antonia." Yosef wiped the blood from his hands and forearms. It had spurted—showering him—from the last man he had faced on the steps of the Temple's Outer Court. A leatherworker he knew and that his family had bought goods from had attacked him—armed with a Roman gladius in one hand and a small hook-bladed wooden-handled leather tool in the other. He had gotten above Yosef on the broad steps, and at the man's broad sweep of the short sword, Yosef had stepped in and done just as Nicanor had shown him—it seemed so long ago on that vast plain between two of Rome's seven hills. "Don't try to be a sword master," Nicanor had told him. "It's a basic jab and thrust—when the footing's bad or a fool leaves himself open." And "into the throat" was best. Yosef touched two fingers to the jagged red line scored across the width of his stomach. That man's hooked blade, sharp enough to slice strips of leather, had almost carved him. The shallow wound stung.

"I told your mother and sister you and your brother are safe," Mathias said, handing Yosef a fresh tunic he pulled over his head, working his arms into their openings.

"It smells of home," Yosef said, sick at the stench of sweat and blood, a sour blend that had broiled and then dried in the heat. But his father had not heard his comment. The noise from a huddle of men at the entrance to the House of Caiaphas had drawn him away.

"It's Saul!" someone cried and then Yosef heard his father's voice, now raised: "Clear the way and let the man through!"

An acrid odor of something more than sweat—that mingling of a man's perspiration and a frothing horse ridden hard—came with Saul as if it were an invisible, rank haze gathered close around him. He looked twenty years older than the man who had left Jerusalem, Yosef thought, but perhaps he was gray from the dry, dusty roads and paths.

Without preamble, Saul gripped Mathias's arm—hard. Yosef could see his father wince. Saul was a strong and sturdy man whose voice croaked at first, then loosened. "Agrippa has sent three thousand cavalrymen with me... to help secure the city." The room

245

erupted again with conversation; this time it had a more optimistic tone. Saul tugged Mathias's robe, pulling him to one side.

Yosef's father followed Saul and leaned down to hear him. After a moment's whispering between them, Saul turned and accepted a goatskin of water which he drank from greedily, then went to a basin of water and plunged his head into it.

"Father, what is it?" Yosef asked as he approached. "What did Saul tell you?"

The pleasure that had lit his face on the news of Agrippa's troops had been fleeting. "Saul said that as they got closer to Jerusalem, they fought off several attacks, and Costabar was killed." Mathias rubbed his face with both hands. "And there are thousands of men—most on foot—converging on Jerusalem."

"Rebels?"

Mathias nodded. "Find your brother and meet me at home. We must talk."

LIV

JERUSALEM

"Yosef's right, Father," Matthew said, rolling a pomegranate in his palms. "Outside the city—across the region—if you're alone in a cart or riding even the poorest donkey, then you have something to steal. He must go on foot and keep hidden from the bandits, or he must seem not worth their interest."

"I don't think he should go," Rebecca said.

Mathias had been silent at the head of the table, and his heavy brows contracted over tired eyes that glanced at his wife. "He must, Rebecca. It's an enormous task and complex—we must have help that we can rely on—and it can only come from them." He sighed. "Yosef is the only one who can arrange it."

Yosef looked at his mother. He had insisted with his father she should know why he was going to Qumran. "Mother, I'll be fine," he said, looked first at his father then back to her. "I'll leave here dressed as an Essene—one of their many travelers—and to all appearances, I'll seem to be one. I'll carry little, nothing of value—just provisions, some water, and food for the three days to get there from here."

Rebecca regarded her older son, who returned the fruit to the bowl, then said, "Mathias, Matthew should go with his brother."

"He can't"—Mathias shook his head—"There's much for Matthew to do here as an officer of the Temple guard, and we must be on alert. His eyes must help to watch the rebel leaders."

"But with King Agrippa's troops here now—with so many of them—are not things at peace?" Rebecca asked. "The Feast of Xylophory begins soon and lasts over the next several days. I've heard Eleasar will open the Temple's Outer Court for all to enter and celebrate."

"Yes, it is quiet"—Mathias nodded—"for now. But—"

"Mother, the city is like your cooking water—it's cooled, but it won't take much to boil over again." Matthew straightened and took his elbows off the table. "And either Menahem or Eleasar or both could rekindle the flame beneath the pot."

"When will you leave?" Miriam asked, tugging down the sleeves of her robe. Yosef, across from her, studied her hands. Their mother had mentioned what they'd all noticed, that Miriam was thinner since

247

her broken betrothal to Yakov, and that she had become more active—maybe too much so, their mother thought. She no longer spent hours on end in her room and instead was gone for half days at a time. But no one had noticed, he thought, the other changes that he had seen. Her forearms and neck had grown taut and lean, and although she spoke more than she had at first on his return from Rome, she also had long periods of silence. He realized how she had appeared, just then, at the table—without a sound on the stone steps of the stairs or floor. No stirring of noise indicated that she had left her room to join them. She was just—suddenly there. He rubbed his eyes and answered, "In the morning, before first light."

* * *

Yosef had left in the darkness and passed through the quiet avenues of the Upper City and into the less silent streets of the Lower City where each day except Shabbat started early and lasted long. The sky turned to a purpling gray as he crossed the Tyropoeon valley and into the city of David, the oldest part of Jerusalem that King David had once captured from the Jebusites who had fortified it and its spring— the Gihon—more than a thousand years ago. Across the Kidron valley, the dawn bloomed over the Mount of Olives. The growing morning sky had lightened further as he exited the city at the southern Dung Gate near the pool of Siloam.

As Yosef followed the path that continued down the valley and headed northeast, he saw how the rising sun cast its rays through the trees on the top of Mount of Olives and onto the high parts of the city, including the Temple. He settled the sling of the roughly made goatskin drawstring bag around his neck and right shoulder, so it rested on his left hip, and in his left hand, he gripped a sturdy six-foot staff. Its iron ferrule tip had been tapered to a point but blunted by use. Miriam had surprised him with it that morning. As he left their home, his goodbyes made to his father and mother and stepped outside, Miriam had been waiting in the shadows.

"A friend gave this to me," she had called out to him and then handed him the staff. "He says it has—had—been a solid companion to him for many years." Her face had been a pale blob in the waning moonlight, and he had wondered who this *friend* was, but that—and other matters, like the hamsa he had yet to ask about—would have to await his return. He had taken the staff from her, and as she hugged him, she had said, "And you'll need one... Be careful, Brother."

The staff, a handsbreadth at its center worn smooth, had nicks and gouges along its length but was thick and dense weighty wood.

He balanced it in his left and kept his right arm free near the broad-bladed dagger sheathed at his right hip. Ascetics believed in self-protection, though they disdained fancy trappings and finer clothing. His tunic and robe were the same he had worn when he had returned to Jerusalem after his year with his Essene mentor, Banus, at Qumran and Ein Gedi. They were travel-worn but well patched and still serviceable.

Yosef breathed deep the last relatively cool breeze of the day before the sun baked the land. Over the next two to three days he would descend the plateau that Jerusalem sat upon, high above sea level, to arrive at Qumran near Lake Asphaltitis, the dead sea thousands of feet lower, where the atmosphere was heavier, cloying in the summer heat.

QUMRAN

The community sat on a dry highland above a gorge only a mile northwest of the shore of Lake Asphaltitis. Constructed of large, undressed stones, the main building—used as an assembly hall, Yosef recalled—had a stout tower in one corner. On one side was a long room used as the eating room, and the first-story room in an opposite corner was furnished as a large writing room. A fat circular cistern and two rectangular ones sat above ground, next to the cluster of buildings, and were fed by an aqueduct rain-collection system connected by channels. Near the cisterns were flour mills, a stable, laundry, and various workshops. Qumran—as with all Essene communities—aimed to be as self-sufficient as possible. The settlement's inhabitants slept by the dozen in nearby caves—configured as residences—in the sheer cliffs overlooking the gorge and wadi.

The blazing sun had dropped below the mountaintops behind him as Yosef entered the community.

* * *

"Nahum, we need your help," Yosef said to the steward of the order at Qumran who had replaced Banus upon his death.

"We?" the leader of the commune asked as he removed his headdress and wiped his face and brow with a wet cloth. He slid the water bowl to Yosef and handed him a dry cloth. "The priests in Jerusalem—the senior leaders of the Temple—rarely have much use for us. Nor does the Sanhedrin." Nahum sat back and studied Yosef.

Yosef pulled the sweat-soaked wool from his head. He rarely wore such a headdress, and the whole journey from Jerusalem he had felt suffocated, though it shielded his head from the beating rays of the sun. He dipped the cloth in the water and sighed as it cooled his sunburned cheeks. The road had been longer and harder than he thought it would be, with many detours to deter groups of men who seemed of questionable purpose. It appeared that Judea, at least the stretch of land between Jerusalem and Qumran, was an anthill of activity with men crisscrossing from point to point and others clustered as if waiting for something or someone. "Yes, we need your help—the help of the Essenes—because it's a matter of trust... and the Temple treasure."

"Yosef, you know there are among us those who profess to foretell what is to come, and rarely, if ever, do they fail in their predictions. We continue to work on our war scroll, for the final conflict, the war of light against darkness. I feel as if the reason you are here is part of what is to come."

* * *

Morning purification was not something Yosef missed, but Nahum was—as he must be—an observer of all the rituals. Though Yosef had followed the Essenes' ways only a brief time and had been away from them for even longer, the look Nahum had given him said it was expected.

The series of stepped pools that descended from the commune were filled by water drawn from deep wells and the underground cisterns. The water felt cold, and for a handful of heartbeats, refreshing, but that rapidly turned uncomfortable, until he quickly dried with the rough woolen blanket Nahum handed him when he stepped out into the warm morning. It was not long before the arid climate made him thirsty again.

It was just as Yosef remembered. After the purification, they gathered in the eating hall and were seated in silence. The baker served the loaves and each person one dish of food—a gruel or porridge of barley. Then the priest of the community offered a prayer over the food. There was no talking as they ate, and at the end of the meal, the priest concluded with another prayer to honor God as the author of life.

As they rose to leave, Yosef turned to Nahum, who had followed him out of the building. "Did you speak with the young engineer you told me of last night?"

Nahum nodded. "All the teachers tell me he is the brightest to come through the Yahad in many years"—he glanced at Yosef and smiled—"since your year with us."

"You didn't tell him what the locations are for, right?" Yosef stopped just outside the classroom.

"No, of course not," Nahum shook his head. "If it was important to him, I would, but it's unnecessary. I told him only that he would scout secure storage areas—naturally formed, if possible, or that needed only a little modification—that will not be easy to find without specific directions."

"Nahum, this task is for all our people—the Jewish people. We have lost our treasure to conquerors before, a tragic event in our history we do not want to be repeated. I need you, and the young man we're about to talk with, to swear an oath on your faith that what we talk about doing—and do—will be kept secret and secure. No one will know but us."

"Yosef, you know we are servants of fidelity. And everything we say... I say... we promise... I promise... is more forceful than an oath. You know how we Essenes feel about false oaths; few things are worse, for they degrade one who then becomes unworthy of belief in God. We Essenes love truth and expose liars." A sardonic grin formed on his face. "That is perhaps why we are sometimes in conflict with Judea's and Jerusalem's leaders." He locked eyes with Yosef. "We will keep our hands pure from theft and our souls from unholy gain; we will neither conceal anything from you nor disclose anything of this— the task you ask our help with—to any others, even if one should apply force to the point of death."

LV

JERUSALEM

"We cannot let you in, Father." Matthew stood slightly in front of the line of Levite guardsmen that spaced the length of the western colonnade and turned some people away and let others through. "I'm sorry, but Eleasar says hewers and bearers of wood—especially those who cut the cloisters down with him and Yosef—enter ahead of any citizens, then all from the Lower City may enter—and then those from the Upper City."

Mathias could see the strain in his son's face, partly because of his own instructions to follow along and comply with Eleasar's orders as long as Eleasar could be reasoned with. Menahem ben Judah and his Sicarii could not be reasoned with at all. He watched as Menahem, leading a large group of men, entered the inner courts of the Temple enclosure. "And them?"—he pointed and asked Matthew, who had half-turned to watch them pass—"What about those with Menahem?"

"Eleasar's orders were to let Menahem and his men—even those believed to be Sicarii—enter also."

"So, he trusts them?"

"No, Father, but he's trying not to inflame them."

Nodding his understanding but thinking how futile that effort might be, Mathias left Matthew and walked to one of the low benches that dotted the two street sides of the Outer Court and sat upon it watching men approach with armloads of wood for the altar so that the fire never burned out. The Feast of Xylophory celebrated that hope of an eternal flame—and every man brought his offering. The hundreds of men he watched streaming by carried more fuel, it seemed, than could be burned at the altar in years.

"They bring a far larger offering than I've ever seen."

Mathias shifted around on the bench and looked up at Shimon ben Gamliel, who had just left the street and stopped behind him. "I was just thinking that, too." He moved over to make room for the Sanhedrin president. "Sit, Shimon—it looks like we will await our turn."

"If it comes," Shimon grunted as he settled his ample rump on the stone bench. "Mathias, your son does not look happy at his duty."

252

Mathias shook his head. "Not today—and not lately."

"I wonder if they"—Shimon waved a hand at the mass of men—
"give any thought that it's also Tu B'av, and we should also celebrate
the beginning of the grape harvest." He looked up and beyond the
walls to the rolling hills around the city. "My family has owned
vineyards for generations. My father made me work in them as a
boy—to learn what it took to sustain and profit by them and to
appreciate what we had—tilling the soil, pulling stones from the
earth, cultivating the woody vines to help them grow and produce. I
learned all the pruning requiring judgment—not too much and not
too little. And the watering never ends." He leaned to one side, closer
to Mathias. "My friend, I wonder if what's happening around us is a
pulling of the stones that formed our city, our very foundation—and
a pruning of who we are, but that now threatens to grow beyond our
control."

"Yes, and at the hand of those who don't understand that what
they do will kill the vine and end its yield. No more will come from it,
and then it is no more than wood to be burned. And when it is gone,
there is no more."

"On the days I worked in the field," Shimon said, "I beheld the
watchtowers where my older brothers stood their duty day and night.
I remember longing for when I would grow old enough for that to be
my responsibility"—he glanced at Mathias and sighed—"to watch
over the vineyard and to protect it."

Mathias looked at his friend and then away. "Are we the watchers
now, Shimon?" He stood and looked toward the colonnade where just
inside, a knot of men seemed to struggle with each other near his son
and the guards. "Powerless watchers that cannot prevent those who
wish to steal—that cannot protect from those who would harm," he
mused and squinted down at Shimon. "This gift from God was meant
to be enjoyed—and men were not to go to war until they tasted their
own grape harvest." Mathias raised his hand and pointed. "Shimon,
something is happening." He started toward Matthew, glancing over
his shoulder to see if Shimon was following. Shimon had recognized
the quote, and his face was as grim as his own.

* * *

"Your Sicarii are out of control, Menahem." Eleasar ben Ananias
raised his hand, palm out, toward the Sicarii leader. "They are too
many. They're pushing others out of the inner courts."

"What good is wood for a flame—fuel for a fire—that doesn't serve
a purpose?" Menahem responded.

"And the offerings are token, for the Temple altar. I agreed to let your men in for the Feast of Xylophory so they could honor its meaning and hope. Why are they bringing so much and what do they plan with all the wood?"

The two men stood atop the western cloisters midway between the Temple and Antonia Fortress, on the new section that had replaced what had been cut away not long ago. As they looked down, a rough-dressed group of men holding lengths of wood as clubs and as offerings forced clusters of better-clad men away from the Temple. Some of those being pushed away wore the uniform tunics of the Temple guard. They had been disarmed and were shoved along with the fine-garbed men.

"I've... we've forgotten nothing, Eleasar. The corruption of the priests, of the city leaders—the elite. All who benefit from Roman rule"—Menahem pulled a dagger with a curved blade from the sheath beneath his robe's left sleeve—"or the recent fighting and the men killed by them." He spun the knife in his hand and then gripped it to point at the Temple guard captain. "And I know you have met with them, Eleasar—and talked about who knows what—betrayal?"

Eleasar backed away, but behind him was Antonia, and they had sealed the fortress walkway entrance to contain the Roman auxiliaries within. He had nowhere to go. "We—you and I—and the city leaders agreed to a truce. Agrippa's troops will—"

"Not save you. Don't look to those that you despise to buy you more time—most of Agrippa's men are outside the city and right now are being attacked from all sides by the men—thousands of men—I've drawn to my side. They have been camped around the city, and all are armed with Roman weapons from Masada." Keeping one eye on Eleasar, Menahem went from side to side of the walkway to get a glimpse down over either side of the cloisters. He turned back to Eleasar with a broad smile.

Eleasar, closest to the western balustrade, could now hear the animal sound of the crowd filling the streets, and then a clear voice driving them: "To the record house—we will burn the records of all your debts, and you'll be free of them!" He looked at Menahem. "Is that your reward for them—for the rabble and looters you've armed and brought into Jerusalem—is that how you command their loyalty?"

"You're a rich boy and have never lacked for anything," Menahem retorted. "And that nationalism you believe in is for a country that lost its way when it let the Romans take control of it because a select few profited when they did. A new nation must arise, led by those who hate any form of bondage, who can be freed of any debt owed the corrupt owners of everything in the city and in this country—those who detest the feel of the Roman heel on their throats that holds them down." Menahem sneered and swept his arm, and the blade in his hand cast glints in the sun in an arc that encompassed all of Jerusalem and beyond its walls. "I will burn down anything—anyone—that stands against me. My followers know my time has come to rule them, and I will do so justly and fairly. And they know not only the Romans must die but also those who accept an overlord's rule or won't punish those who do—so we may start anew."

"Eleasar!" The shout made Menahem turn just as Matthew reached him, swinging a short sword to strike Menahem's forearm with the flat of the blade, forcing him to drop the dagger. Eleasar rushed forward and kicked the knife, which skittered to a stop a dozen feet beyond Matthew.

Menahem spun and pulled another dagger from a right-forearm sheath. He slashed at Matthew, who quickly stepped back, drawing Menahem toward him. "You're not a leader—not a messiah, Menahem," Matthew taunted. "You have to buy or bribe your followers. True messiahs gather them by their actions and their efforts to install a fair and free government, not under Roman rule."

"You, your Roman-loving brother and family will soon pay. We'll—"

Eleasar, his hands locked in a double fist, hammered at the base of Menahem's skull and shut him up. Matthew stepped forward as he fell, and with a left-hand punch that caught him on the bridge of his nose, sent Menahem down like an ax-fallen tree, and he lay moaning.

"The Sicarii have pushed your Zealots from the Temple," Matthew gasped, "and there are hundreds, maybe more, fighting in the streets. Agrippa's troops in the city have pulled back to Herod's palace." He glanced at the Sicarii leader, who had gotten to his knees, holding his head with both hands. "Menahem's men have lined the base of the palace walls with all the firewood brought for the Temple altar. And they're bringing quarrymen and stone workers from the Lower City to undermine the walls. Eventually, they'll breach them."

"What area do we hold?" Eleasar asked, following Matthew in a sprint down the walkway toward the steps descending to the street level.

"Nothing—nowhere I've heard yet. The public buildings in the Upper City are overrun by Menahem's men. The citizens' residences have yet to be touched. But"—he slowed to look over his shoulder at Eleasar.

Eleasar grabbed Matthew's arm and stopped him. "But what?"

"A group led by one of Menahem's lieutenants is headed to your father's and the High Priest's mansions. They will burn both down and plan to kill anyone trying to escape them."

LVI

SEPTEMBER 66 CE

JERUSALEM

Antonia Fortress had long stood watch over the Temple and over the citizens of Jerusalem—over those most likely to bristle at Roman rule and to act on their desire to break it. The towers at its four corners and the high walkways of the connected cloisters were the province of sentries dedicated to the sole purpose of preventing a rebellion. It had served its purpose—to assure order for the Romans—for which Herod had it built. But now Antonia—the men garrisoned within it— had failed, and blood ran down the long, gently sloped and stepped double walkway atop the colonnade leading from the fortress to the porticoes of the Temple court. Deep within its walls, armed rough-garbed men— Antonia's defenders—fought under torches or lamplight on stone floors slippery with gore. The echoes of metal striking metal, of blade on blade, were much louder than the deadlier sound of such implements against yielding sundered and riven flesh. The cries rang out in different tongues, men reverting to birth language as they died, but the cries faded with the end of the second day of Antonia's siege. Now its towers and ramparts stared emptily— dolefully—down on a city in revolt.

* * *

"What of Eleasar?" Yosef asked his brother.

"He's still searching for his father because the Sicarii—and the looters who have joined them—have burned down his house. Ananias ben Ananias is still missing." Matthew turned from the railing that bound the perimeter of the terrace atop their home. To the east, the large smudge of smoke over the Temple-fortress complex had thickened over the fortress's tallest tower, the spire now nearly obscured by a clot created by violence.

"Did he tell Menahem's men of the tunnel?" Yosef asked. Matthew had used the tunnel from the Temple grounds to the fortress to break into the small armory after Gessius Florus's massacre after Passover.

"No. He told me the Sicarii have long known of it, and many other tunnels in and around the city. They have some resource that knows far more of the tunnels than we ever discovered as children." He took a last glance toward the sky over the fortress, then faced Yosef. "And old tunnels—some the Romans did not know of—were the way they got their men into Masada."

Unlike natural clouds, the smoke over the fortress was distinct in the haze of a hot summer late afternoon like a blot or stain that spread toward them, darkening the blue skies over that part of Jerusalem. "Have they taken any prisoners from the auxiliaries manning Antonia?"

"I don't think prisoners are part of their plan. They killed them all, nearly five hundred men--mostly Greeks from Caesarea—and now Menahem's rabble thinks no one can stand against them." Matthew shook his head, then studied something in the direction of the setting sun.

"Well, auxiliaries—especially garrison troops—are not fighters like Roman legionaries," said Yosef. "Nor are King Agrippa's troops their match, barricaded as they are within Herod's palace. And the small contingent of Roman soldiers with Agrippa's men are too few to bolster their strength." Yosef followed his brother's gaze to see the other clouds—these of dust—billowing just beyond the Hippicus tower west of them. "What is that?"

Mathias stepped onto the terrace. "That's from the cartloads of dry brush Menahem's men are bringing into the city. I just came from watching dozens of them come through the Gennath gate."

The three distinct long trails rising from the earth to the northwest, west, and southwest were dirt brown shading to gray, and they narrowed to converge at the wall closest to Herod's palace. "I was there earlier," Matthew said, "but could not get close since the looks I received were not kind. I saw the Sicarii or the ruffians Menahem has recruited are digging trenches along the base of the palace walls." Matthew half-turned to Yosef. "If they want to breach the walls to attack the palace, why not just tunnel directly under them?"

"That's just a single point of attack, narrow and defensible," Yosef replied. "The Sicarii are going to undermine the bulwarks all around the palace, Roman style. First, they'll dig along the walls. Then they'll create parallel tunnels wider than the walls but shore them up at the same time with wooden planks or timber. Then when they have all the tunnels ready, they'll pack them with flammable tinder—that dried brush they're bringing into the city. They'll likely soak it in lantern or lamp oil and then, with coordinated timing, set it on fire. That way the walls will all come down, approximately timed, together. Then they'll have a broad breach, almost impossible to defend, and they can flood through with their men." Yosef paused while his father and brother took in the idea. "My friend Nicanor showed me how the Romans trained for such sieges. I watched them do that to a small fortress constructed just for training—they took the walls down just that way."

"Yosef, outside of the family, don't mention that you have Roman friends"—Mathias held up a hand—"I know—I know. Many already know your experiences in Rome and with the Romans—and are aware of your appreciation for them. But those threatening looks Matthew received are going to grow more plentiful. Don't provoke them." Mathias turned to the dark mass in the sky to the northeast. The wind from that direction now carried the smell of burning bodies into the Upper City, forming a pall, a shroud that would soon loom over the city. In the other direction, the bone-gray cloud from the caravans of donkey- and man-drawn carts stacked with brushwood and kindling flowed toward the city on a current of its own.

"I fear that once Menahem and his men take Herod's palace," Mathias said, "they are going to turn on those in the city they feel are against them or have too strong an affinity for Rome or Romans." Mathias gestured at his sons to follow him back down to the living area of the house. "Then the streets will not be safe for people like us. Come with me. I must talk to your mother and sister about this."

* * *

Twilight had hidden what the sky held but did not cover the smell. "Cover your faces with a wet cloth," Yosef directed Rebecca and Miriam. "It was the only way I could breathe—and sleep—in the days after Rome's burning." He wrapped his own lower face with dampened fabric. "Miriam, don't go off on one of your meanderings. Tomorrow morning Matthew and I are taking you to the Temple. The guard has taken it back now, and Eleasar says they can protect citizens who feel vulnerable or threatened by the Sicarii. You'll be safe there."

Rebecca looked at her middle child, the son she had worried most about over many years. Yosef had traveled farther than anyone in her family and seen things they would never see. He had aged beyond his years. She didn't tell him so, but she doubted that anywhere in Jerusalem, perhaps even in Judea, would be safe.

LVII

JERUSALEM

Miriam awoke with the birds that sang before dawn in the fig tree outside her window. Their song, familiar through the years, pierced even her recent darkest nightmares. Quietly she dressed in her training clothes, then donned a rough robe her mother would cast doubtful eyes on. But they allowed her to blend in on the streets of the Lower City.

She had to make sure Zechariah was safe. One-on-one or even a handful against him he could take care of. But the chaos of the streets over the past days, the flood of men to and from the Upper and Lower Cities, could overwhelm even him if he was caught up in a fight on the streets.

Barefoot, she crept downstairs, then carefully through the courtyard and out the back gate into the private lane that wound its way into the upper agora. She slipped her sandals on, securing the straps around her ankles, then set out and picked up her pace. She must get to Zechariah's and back before daybreak. The fighting had been mainly concentrated from around Antonia Fortress to Herod's palace along a skirmish line that ran just inside the older wall in the Upper City that separated it from the Northern City. It extended to the Hippicus tower near the western wall of Jerusalem. She knew from Matthew that there was still sporadic fighting in the Lower City and that it had spilled outside the walls into the surrounding area.

* * *

Few lanterns were lit, and no one was on the streets as she crossed the marketplace to the viaduct, across it, and then down the broad steps next to the Temple to the gates into the Lower City. The stench from the burning of Antonia's slaughtered garrison had carried and settled there, and there was not a breath of wind to lift it above the city and push it beyond. Miriam had done as Yosef had instructed the night before and kept the cloth covering her nose and mouth damp from the waterskin, she carried looped over her shoulder. The smell of the leather worker's shop grew stronger, the only odor more powerful than what had wafted from the captured fortress. She paused, for ahead of her, close to Zechariah's, at a small square of the open area formed by four intersecting streets, was a large lit lantern. It cast a glow for several feet around, and she saw a man stride through the arc of illumination. He moved without hesitation or secretiveness toward the alley that led to the side entrance into Zechariah's workshop and home.

She was about to follow him when two men came from the shadows behind the other man, paused at the edge of light and then separated, and each followed the perimeter of lamplight, gray shadows in the darkness. If she had not seen them just then, she would never have spotted them converging on the man they followed to Zechariah's. They moved fast now, with flashes of metal in their hands. She hurried after the stalkers but also stayed out of the lantern's glow.

Moments later she was in the alley, where the lantern cast two large shadows beyond the men, and by the light of a burning torch mounted on the back corner of the leather worker's shop she saw Menahem ben Judah. He had flipped back the cowl of his robe and was about to rap on Zechariah's door.

The two shadows moved silently, and the glint of burnished metal in their hands revealed each carried a short-bladed but deadly gladius. She shrugged her robe off and pulled the daggers from their forearm sheaths. With only a small bird's wing beat of sound, she closed on them as they reached Menahem, who turned toward the men in surprise. Changing her right-hand's grip on the blade, she took the shorter man with a mallet blow—the dagger in her fist—into the base of his skull. The taller man next to him slashed at Menahem, slicing through the sleeve of his robe and along the length of his arm as he whirled away. Pulling her blade out, she stayed with the shorter man long enough for a side thrust. Her left-hand blade entered his ear and tore along his head as she then spun on the balls of her feet, and her right-hand dagger arced to gash the face of the tall man as he lurched away from his fallen comrade. Pivoting to face Miriam, he brought his sword around in a sweeping flash in the torchlight. She knew she could never block it and dropped to one knee, praying she could get low quickly enough. With the briefest of tugs, the blade passed over her, and time slowed as she saw a cleanly cut lock of hair fall from her as he now brought his sword around for a straight-ahead thrust, Roman style. She had learned from Zechariah that this move would skewer her.

But the blow did not come. In that slowed moment, through the man's throat she saw first the tip, then inches of a curved blade. The man choked and frothed blood from his mouth, eyes staring at

Miriam as he fell face down at her knees. She looked up at Menahem, who had sheathed his dagger and was attempting to bind one-handedly the wound in his left forearm.

"Who?"—Menahem stopped as she stood and raised her face to the light—"You!"

Behind her, Miriam heard the scrabbling of hands unbarring the door and turned to it as it opened. Zechariah, bared knife in one hand, iron-tipped staff in the other, stepped out. Sightless eyes went from her face—his nostrils flared and brow furrowed—to the two dead men sprawled in the dirt of the alley, and from them to Menahem and then back to her.

"Both of you get inside while I drag them away," Zechariah ordered.

"To where?" Miriam asked him before following Menahem inside.

Zechariah gestured to the back area of the leather worker's shop. "To a rendering vat that's used to dispose of unwanted bodies."

* * *

"Once you are home, stay off the streets," Zechariah told Miriam, who had cleaned up and, with the sunrise near, had to go. He closed the door behind her and secured it.

"She told me she braved the streets to check on you." Menahem shook his head.

"Yes, that was foolish of her, but if she hadn't... well, it seems you'd be the one to regret it." Zechariah went to the worktable and placed his staff upon it and then picked up a sharpening stone, which he took to the iron tip with slow, steady strokes.

"Would you regret the outcome if she had not saved me?"

Zechariah turned toward him. "I believe in what you—what we—are doing, Menahem. So, don't take my concerns about you wanting to use Miriam as a sign I've grown weak."

"Perhaps you have grown weak, though, Zechariah"—Menahem winced as he flexed the muscles in his left forearm—"for her."

"I see her as the granddaughter I never had. I don't want her hurt or—"

"Killed by the Romans like your wife and daughter." Menahem straightened and paced the room. "And don't you want to continue to avenge them?" He paused for a step, "She was upon those two—Agrippa's men or Romans—before I even knew they were there and about to kill or take me. That's not just a skill, Zechariah—it's an art."

"You just heard her," Zechariah said. The Sicarii's mission to kill Romans appeals to her, but not what's happening with Judeans fighting Judeans, with the factions within the city tearing it apart. She saved you—but she fears you and your retaliation against her family."

"They've nothing to fear if they don't help the Romans or Agrippa, but there is one person—one high-placed Judean—that I will deal with once we've killed all of those hiding within Herod's palace. I'll bring the palace walls down around them, and that will show them our strength." He walked over and put a hand on the blind man's shoulder. "Zechariah, this girl can be a weapon for us that no one suspects."

LVIII

JERUSALEM

"Have the pack mules unloaded and distribute the bows and arrows, the slings and lead balls to the men most skilled with them," Menahem ben Judah told his chief lieutenant, who had accompanied the weapons from Masada. "We must target the Romans who are with Agrippa's men in the breastwork turrets and towers. Their aim is so deadly they are steadily killing or wounding the men digging the tunnels and trenches below the walls. They must have demolished an inner wall or partition in the palace and smashed it into chunks to throw down on us and to break through the wooden stoa we erected to shield the diggers."

Elazar ben Yair looked up at the sporadic rain of shafts coming from the defenders and heard the grunts of pain as a handful of arrows struck his workers. He and Menahem stood off at an angle and distance awkward for the archers to reach, as they continued to fire on the men below. Elazar studied Menahem and paused before replying. Every cause required a leader the people would rally around. Menahem was such a man. But Elazar's own desire for an independent Judea, for its true freedom from Rome, was as strong in him as in anyone, including Menahem. Both followed the movement of the heavily loaded mules coming through the Gennath gate and moving past them toward a staging area for the rebels' supplies and equipment—what they needed to bring down the outer wall surrounding Herod's palace. Menahem drew men to him, created followers, but Elazar wondered whether this man wanted people to follow the cause or just to follow him personally.

More of the defenders' arrows flew from the Mariamne tower, the most beautiful of the three Herod had constructed to protect his palace. Others arced from atop the palace itself, over its outer wall, with a skilled archer's precise pull to make them fall just beyond and onto the workers clustered along the base of the wall. Despite the flurries of arrows that had killed dozens, the men had excavated a trench running from the base of that easternmost tower, Mariamne, to a point about two hundred yards south. Then they had widened that channel to tunnel under the wall, shoring it up with timbers as they went. Behind them a team had unloaded the scores of carts full of dried wood and brush, packing it tightly into the trench, among and around the wooden shoring under the wall. Six young men—not much more than boys—were pouring amphoras of oil on the brush, soaking it as they raced, fleet of foot, along the wall. The smell of the oil, thick and heavy, followed them as they shuttled back and forth, evading the arrows, picking up full jars and emptying them, steadily working their way toward the southernmost end of the trench where the archers could not reach them.

"Right. I've assembled a unit," Elazar said. "Eight archers, eight slingers, paired up with men bearing bundled arrows and canvas bags of lead shot." Elazar half-turned to motion at the drayman who had headed the Masada pack train, a veteran warrior skilled with projectile weapons. "Equip the men and have the slingers target the turret and tower openings, for a ricochet can be as good as a direct hit. Position the archers to rake the breastworks atop the wall and force the defenders from it." He turned back to Menahem. "And then we'll work down to focus solely on the tower, the only vantage point from which they can safely fire upon us."

Menahem nodded. "And when the wall has been cleared, I will have men with torches in position to ignite the trenches at several points at the same time." He clasped Elazar on the shoulder. "Those walls," Menahem said, as he released Elazar and swept his arm the length of the wall they faced. "Those walls will soon come down—and we will sweep Agrippa's troops and the Romans from the city. And then, Elazar"—he gripped his shoulder again—"then we will force them out of all of Judea. Or they can remain... with the rest of their dead."

* * *

When he read the Soreg's inscribed warning, Yosef always felt its words were the unequivocal underpinning of the militant aspect of his faith and almost a challenge: "No outsider shall enter the protective enclosure around the sanctuary. And whoever is caught will only have himself to blame for the ensuing death." Those words posted outside the sanctuary formed the real separation—more than screens or walls—between the Court of Gentiles and the inner courts of the Temple, the sanctuary itself. As Yosef and Miriam stood atop Solomon's porch overlooking the Beautiful Gate and the Court of Women now dotted with tents and clusters of families seeking safety, he thought of those inscribed words, their warning for outsiders, for those not of the faith. He thought of what had happened recently within the walls of Jerusalem—of Jews killing Jews, and not because of differences in religious beliefs, but differences in opinions, which underneath were fueled by poverty.

The area surrounding them seemed safe. Temple guards and volunteers had secured the Hulda gates to and from the Lower City and the gates to the Upper City. The violence had moved on, and those packs of rabble and looters, the Sicarii and their heavily armed followers all now focused on matters elsewhere. The Temple enclosure had become an island, or more aptly described, a stone thrust up amid a wide and raging river, its turbulent rapids churning along the periphery but flowing around the rock.

Miriam looked past the Court of Women to beyond the Temple toward where the aqueduct and roadway crossed over the Tyropoeon valley. "Is Matthew at the aqueduct?" she asked.

"Yes, that's his post until the unrest is settled."

"And will it be... settled?"

Yosef glanced at Miriam. His sister didn't seem frightened by what had happened and was happening around them. "We hope so. Eleasar has said he believes Menahem ben Judah will stand down once Herod's palace is taken."

"You sound doubtful."

"I think we're past the point of a return to peace, nor even to what seemed to be a never-ending tension between factions, a tension we all wanted to resolve. Now I'd settle for even ongoing tension." Yosef shook his head and raised a hand to rub his eyes. "We may stop the actual fighting, the physical conflict among ourselves... but that's just a lull before the real storm."

"The Romans...."

A deep sigh racked Yosef. "They will bring a legion or more against Jerusalem. Miriam, we've awakened a sleeping beast we cannot kill, no matter how much we believe we can." He took her by the arm to lead her down to the court and back to their father and mother. "Look"—he pointed west—"the flames of Antonia Fortress are barely out, and new ones start." A growing light inside the western wall—at Herod's palace—had replaced the setting sun's dark red now shading to a deepening purple and then to the black of night higher in the sky. "Menahem's men have set their trench and tunnels afire."

"Do you think Agrippa's men and the Roman soldiers will surrender once the palace walls come down, as Matthew believes?"

"I'm told they will be offered that chance."

"You doubt that, too, don't you?"

"I don't know, Miriam. There have been so many on both Roman and Judean sides, and within Jerusalem, who say one thing but do another. Menahem styles himself as a would-be king—a messiah to return us to our former glory." They had descended the steps and passed into the courtyard, and they watched as men tended to the four massive lamps that now lit the broad expanse of the Women's Court in the deepening dusk. "But he lacks grace and compassion."

"Must he—must we—show any compassion for any Roman?" She felt the need to defend the man whose life she had just recently saved.

In the distance, Yosef saw their mother raise a hand to greet them. Miriam's words made him stop his return wave and lower his arm. The words from her were cold—remorseless—not like anything he had ever heard from his sister. He thought of the nagging questions he had yet to ask her. "Miriam, where have you been disappearing to?" When she didn't answer, he stopped and half-turned her to face him. "Miriam, I know you leave the house—to where or for what purpose, even Mother and I don't know—and this morning when I called for you to come down, and you joined us to come here, I knew you had returned home from somewhere not long before. Where did you go?"

She shrugged his hand off, matching his stare with dark, unflinching eyes. For a moment he thought she would speak and would tell him. Instead, she left him standing there as she joined their mother.

LIX

Jerusalem

Menahem, knowing he was near his destination, had paused in the darkness to listen. He heard the quiet breathing of what must be the person he was to meet. "I already know you can kill when you have to," he spoke into the darkness as he neared the spot he had described for their meeting. "But can you do it—kill a man or even a woman—when it's planned?"

Careful as he proceeded, his head pulled in and angled down, Menahem was aware of the rough tunnel ceiling of the storm drain with its jagged sections spiking down like long teeth. The glow of his small handheld lamp showed the drain's throat had widened into the mouth of a chamber. He entered what might have been a natural cavity further excavated by the same men who had dug Hezekiah's tunnel. It had been a long traverse from where he had entered under the Tyropoeon valley, below the base of the old west wall of the City of David.

This chamber had once been a waystation, an area where the ancient miners could rest, stretch, eat, and drink, yet remain close to the critical project. The round stone cistern in the corner was long dry, though the remaining benches and shelves on the wall next to him, carved from rock, were long and wide enough to lie upon.

The sound of metal on a striking stone echoed, and in the dimness ahead of him a streamer of sparks arced, landed, and caught. He had smelled the pitch-soaked head of a torch, and now it blazed. Held at arm's length toward him, it lit the chamber. He walked forward and could now see holding the torch the dark-robed and cowled figure sitting on one of the waist-high shelves next to where the tunnel continued its narrow way southeast to come out below Gihon Spring. His eyes met large bright eyes that studied him over a covered nose and mouth.

"So, you know the tunnels," he continued into the silence. "I had been told you did and assumed you must when you did not ask how to get here, nor for me to wait and lead the way." Menahem held his small, flickering lamp in one hand and waved the other over a series of holes bored through the rock walls. From the holes came a current of cool, moisture-laden air drawn from the nearby channel that they had diverted Gihon Spring to course through. "This tunnel's air remains much fresher than in the others in the city." He patted the walls, whose openings were set above the high-water mark. "Waiting in the dark did not bother you?"

"Darkness doesn't frighten me," Miriam answered, "and if meeting you here is part of testing me, then yes, I know the tunnels." She shifted and rose from the carved-stone bench. "And I've become accustomed to not waiting for others to decide—or for anyone to lead me."

"You know where they are, but do you know *about* the tunnels— their past? This is the site of a most important accomplishment, a crucial one in our history. It brings life—water—to Jerusalem." He paused, and with no comment or query in response, continued: "The Gihon Spring—the only permanent source of water around Jerusalem—brings life to our city. It comes to the surface just outside the walls, on the steep slopes that overlook Kidron valley. An extensive passage we call Hezekiah's tunnel was excavated seven hundred years ago to bring the spring's overflow into the city. And the spring itself has been covered with large stones and masonry so it could be sealed to protect it in the event of a war." Menahem gestured to the wall running east and south. "At the center of Hezekiah's tunnel is an inscription that recorded the making of the tunnel." He paused again. "And this is important to understand. The tunnel began from each end—one originates just north of where we are, within the city walls. The men worked for months, and as they neared each other, the men heard the picks of the others ringing against the stone, and that's what guided them as they got closer. When they came near to accomplishing their goal, they were only a few feet apart, and the more-distinct sounds led to their precise redirection. Soon they broke through the short expanse of earth and stone separating them—and what were two separate tunnels became joined.

"And that is what I have done with my purpose"—he searched those eyes for understanding—"though there are those who do not understand nor agree with me completely. I have started at one end— what I believe is right for our people—and those others, with what they see as a similar aim, are at their end. And though in some ways we are apart, with what is happening now"—he pointed up toward the city above—"we will be joined by our common goal and meet in the middle."

Menahem set his hand lamp on the wide lip of the cistern and sat next to it. He started to say something else but then paused as if he

269

had changed his mind, and he pointed across the chamber to where the tunnel recommenced. "There—just outside near the exit but still inside the city walls—lies the pool of Siloam. You know of it. It's not that far from us right now. But do you know the poor and sick still go there to bathe?" At the nod of her cowled head, he continued: "Then you've heard that Yeshua ish Natzrat, who years ago many thought to be a messiah, sent a blind man to the pool and it healed the man." Menahem studied the silent figure. "It is recorded among our writings of the oral law that this—the pool of Siloam—was described as the messiah's pool. "Do you know that story and meaning?"

"I'm not uneducated." Miriam stood. The writings state, in different ways and many times, that 'messiah' means the 'anointed one' sent by God. And the word 'Siloam' in Hebrew means 'sent.'

"So, perhaps you understand why I chose where we meet... for those two examples... and other reasons."

He straightened and took three steps to stand next to the silent figure. "Our writings also say the Messiah will come at a time when the scepter is taken from Judah, as the Romans have now taken it— we've lost our authority to pronounce a death sentence. So, the time must be now. I believe I have been sent to free our people from Roman rule. Many who believe as I do have joined with me. And I believe that you"—he gestured as if to tap her right arm—"have been sent to help me." He asked again into the silence, "So, can you kill when ordered and without regard for who the target is?"

"Romans?" Her voice was muffled, pitched low, and she stirred and turned toward the tunnel leading to beneath the Kidron valley. As she stood, the torchlight caught the hamsa clasp on her robe.

Menahem studied the gleam of metal. "Yes. Romans."

"I'll kill Romans for you," she said, her head dipping so that the cowl shrouded her eyes.

"Good, then we'll meet again—soon." Menahem's smile shone brightly in the torchlight full on his dark face and a grizzled, thick beard. "Our arrangement must be kept secret. I'll call you 'the Hand,' like the clasp on your shawl, and that is how all will soon refer to you." Her head came up, and they locked eyes. "You'll become feared," he said.

"—by Romans," she answered as she paused before exiting the tunnel. A few minutes later, she was outside looking up as the bright orange-yellow orb lighted the Temple and Ophel Hill that stood above the Kidron valley.

LX

Jerusalem

The blaze had grown from several clots of flame into a writhing serpent that climbed from the trenches to twice the height of a man. The fire coiled and struck at the timbers that now supported the eastern side of the wall surrounding Herod's palace. The wall had been splashed with lamp oil as high as a man could reach as he darted in to brave the defending archers, and the oil now flamed and smoked until it burned away. Fanned by a night wind from the west that spilled over the outer wall of the city and swirled through the streets, the flames and heat were fierce.

"I think they've exhausted their supply of arrows. Are your men ready?" Menahem ben Judah could not take his eyes from the spectacle of the six-hundred-foot-long fire now eating away at the base of the wall but knew Elazar ben Yair stood next to him.

"Yes, five hundred and more," replied Elazar, "most of them helmed and armored with Roman gear. One hundred of them are between Gennath gate and Mariamne tower, another hundred between the southern end of the fire and the House of Caiaphas. And here"—he gestured over his shoulder—"are the rest... three hundred men."

Menahem looked behind them. "They are the center point of our trident."

"Yes. When the walls come down, and you give the signal, we will strike from the outside points first. And then the center force will thrust straight ahead and through the breached wall."

"And how many men are in reserve?" asked Menahem.

"They're not as well equipped—we need more arms from Masada. But five hundred men, half on the other side of the Gennath gate and half outside the western wall—to prevent any Romans or troops of Agrippa that get atop the wall from scaling down to escape the city."

Darkness grew where the light of the fire did not reach, and all around them became a night filled with flashes of illumination from the twisting flames and shadows. As they watched, the thick piles of brush in the channel, the lower clusters now consumed, fell in on itself and showers of sparks and tongues of flame lapped the wooden shoring supporting the wall. Those timbers were smoldering and charred black on the edges of their length, and the smoldering spread ember-red with tongues of yellow-orange as they burned through. Thinner and thinner they became as the fire hungrily ate the wood and each piece burned, flared, and fell away.

A loud snap, greater than the crackling of the fire, cut through the air. Menahem and Elazar searched for the source of the sound but did not find it until—slowly at first—a section of the wall shook. It was not just the shimmer of waves of heat, but the sagging and then breakdown of the wall. Vertical cracks traced a zigzag pattern along where the stone blocks of the wall had been joined, the cracks quickly shooting out horizontal branches as large sections broke off. Chunks of stone and mortar filled the trench and flames trickled up amid the now-loose rubble. The cracking snap of timber cascaded and soon the wall, erected by Herod the Great several decades before, collapsed.

Menahem nodded to the young man next to him. He had wished for the shofar, but Eleasar ben Ananias and the High Priest had refused him. The young man who held a smaller ram's horn brought it to his lips. It would suffice. The young man blew, and the horn's shrill moaning signaled the attack. From north and south, they heard the rush of men, the clatter of metal and armor, and the curses and cries of their scrambling over the stone blocks atop the scorching rubble-filled dugout. The two endpoints of the assault swept toward their targets, the palace itself and the high towers at the northernmost end of the palace enclosure.

Once sure they were well in, Menahem gestured at the young man who then blew two more blasts on the ram's horn—the signal for the main thrust. Menahem watched as Elazar, with a single glance and nod at him, charged forward leading the three hundred men over the still-smoldering trench rubble and into the palace grounds. Once inside and over the fallen wall, the men spread out seeking opposition. Soon they and Elazar discovered that the palace grounds were undefended. Menahem looked back—east—across the broken wall and the scorching channel that flickered and pulsed with now-low flames nearly smothered by stone. Then he swept his gaze south, west, and north within the boundary of the palace. He spotted two men—his lieutenants from the outer prongs of the attack trident—as they slowed their approach from a full run.

"No sign of Agrippa's troops or of any Romans in the palace," reported the first to reach Elazar.

Elazar nodded. "The palace was too open and too accessible for what men they have... they've picked somewhere more easily defended."

The second man, breathing heavily, wiped sweat and blood from his singed face. A deep cut angled diagonally across his brow and bled heavily down one side to drip from his jaw. "They built a barricade by breaking up the decorative stone from the gardens, fountains, and terraces to fortify a perimeter that arcs out from the base of each of the three towers. Agrippa's troops hold Phaesel and Hippicus—the Romans hold Mariamne." The man palm-wiped his face again, clearing his eyes, then cut a strip of cloth from the undertunic beneath his Roman cuirass to bandage and bind his head wound. "We can't draw them out of the rubble, and I don't think they are fools enough to sortie from those positions. What are your orders, sir?"

"Find the officers commanding Agrippa's troops and offer them—all of them—a safe passage from the city if they lay down their arms." Elazar and the two men turned. Menahem still wore his robes of leadership, though he was armed with a short sword in one hand and his dagger in the other. He nodded at the sublieutenants. "Report back what they say."

The two men hurried off, one to Hippicus tower and the second to Phaesel.

"What of the Romans?" Elazar asked, turning back to Menahem.

"Many of Agrippa's troops are Judean. I think we can sway them to our side if we give them a reason—convince them of our cause."

"Menahem"—Elazar was used to the man's whims and musing, the politicizing and belief in his power to persuade—"But what about the Romans?"

"Find the Roman officer in charge of their contingent. I want to speak to him."

"Are you going to offer them a safe exit from the city, if they surrender?"

Menahem smiled. "I will convince him to accept that offer."

* * *

"This is terrible." Yosef shook his head. The battle for Jerusalem had reached an end.

"Did you not expect that the Romans would die?" Mathias looked at his youngest son. "Menahem and his men had already killed hundreds."

"Father"—Yosef looked at him and his brother—"Matthew... you don't understand. It's not that they were killed by Judeans—yes, that we are all considered in revolt against Rome is how the empire will treat us, and we'll pay the price for that. But it's the way they were killed—after surrendering."

273

"That was cruel," Matthew replied, "but then the Sicarii and that rabble army Menahem has assembled are fueled by their hatred of Romans."

Yosef objected: "For centuries the Romans have had a policy—in conquest and battle—to extend the right hand of surety to a defeated foe, or to one that faces certain defeat and surrenders, guaranteeing terms of submission. Surrender-to-live is an accepted treatment by all Roman military commanders and units. It prevents further needless loss of life. They saw that offered to Agrippa's troops and then watched them leave unharmed. Then Menahem assured them that they, too, could lay down arms and be allowed to leave the city. The Roman officer Metillus felt safe in accepting his offer, felt sure that 'we'—Judeans—would honor such terms.

"And then after they came out and laid down their weapons," Yosef continued, "Menahem's men suddenly leaped upon them and killed them all. The Romans just stood there in disbelief. They did not resist. We broke a most sacred code of military honor."

Matthew shot a warning glance at Yosef as Miriam entered the courtyard, passing them on her way inside.

"Metillus was the last Roman"—Miriam had slowed her pace, and Yosef paused until she moved out of earshot—"Rome—when they hear of this—will be outraged. What Menahem has done is unthinkable and a supreme insult to them—and to honor. And"—he leaned toward his father and brother, who shifted closer in their chairs—"Menahem ordered Metillus circumcised—by force, once he had surrendered his men—and then set free to tell the tale. Word of that will spread, and every Roman soldier who comes against us will bear it in mind. There will be no mercy offered us."

LXI

CAESAREA

As Sayid came into Cleo's sitting room through the inner court, he saw the back of a man in a bluish-gray tunic enter the atrium and disappear. "Glaucio must be reporting to his master, my lady," he said. He did not like Gessius Florus's majordomus, the head of household put in place upon their arrival.

Cleo noted the disdain in Sayid's voice, and she cared even less for Glaucio, with his spying and prying into her activities. She looked up from her writing desk. "Probably so. He came to tell me my husband had received dispatches that required an immediate reply, so the courier awaited them. He said for me to make ready any letters I wished to send."

"To the Lady Octavia in Antioch?"

"Yes. He thinks she is the only one left I correspond with, which is no longer correct. And he reads them before they go out, though he thinks I don't know he does it. But if I don't write Octavia, he will become more suspicious."

Sayid looked at the stack of folded vellum sheets bound by a cord braided from strips of blue silk, something she did for all her letters to Octavia. The bronze pen Cleo held dipped into ink in a small *terra sigillata* pot that had been given to her by her grandmother. Her hand flew across the sheet of papyrus, the writing in a language he did not recognize. The letters were like Greek and Latin, although not exactly either one, but she was writing them from right to left, as his mother tongue of Aramaic was written.

Cleo paused and with the back of her left hand nudged the strapped stack of vellum toward him. "Please take these to my husband for the courier."

Sayid paused. "Should I wait, my lady?"

Cleo looked up. "For what?"

He pointed at the papyrus sheet she had filled with her clear script. "For that one... that letter, my lady."

"No"—Cleo shook her head—"You told me of the man who trades in olive wood, cedar, and other wooden products, the man you became friends with..."

Sayid didn't understand the meaning of her comment but answered, "Yes, on the small trade route between Caesarea and Ptolemais and along the coast and up... all the way to Antioch."

"Can he be trusted to deliver this?"—she held up the papyrus sheet, blowing on it to dry the ink, and folded it into a square—"to no one but Lady Octavia in Antioch?"

"I believe so if he is paid well."

Cleo slipped the folded rectangle into a larger square envelope of scuffed, rough-stitched leather. She picked up a small piece of parchment. "Take the letters for Octavia to my husband and then come back for this. I want you to get it to your trader." As Sayid turned to go with the bundle of vellum in his hand, she took a small square of parchment, dipped her pen in ink and wrote on it: "Please get this to Marcus Otho in Lusitania."

Sending the message—the longer one to her brother Marcus was written in Etruscan—was a risk, but one she had to take. She didn't know if her brother could help her. They had been taught Etruscan at home, but the language was rapidly dying while Latin became so widespread in her home region. So Etruscan was convenient to deter prying eyes. Her brother had been in trouble—banished to the governorship of a small province—since Nero had taken his wife, Poppaea, to his bed and then had her divorced from him so he could marry her. But Cleo had to find someone to be on her side, someone she could share what was going on with Gessius. She inserted the parchment into the envelope, closed its flap, and secured the flap with a double-wound strap of leather.

* * *

Florus took the blue-bound document from the Syrian boy he knew Cleo favored to attend her—eyeing him with a look not returned by the boy—and waited until he left to slip the cord from the bundle and read each page. He refolded them, neglecting the silk tie to bind them together, and tossed them into the pouch for the courier. There was nothing in them but the banal chattering of women. His own correspondence was important, especially his reply to Tigellinus—no, really to Nero. The emperor communicated through Tigellinus, the prefect who handled delicate matters for him, that he wanted an explanation of what was going on in Judea. He also mentioned that the legate in Antioch, Cestius Gallus, was expecting the emperor's reply to their request for a new procurator to replace him in Judea. And this, the thinly worded demand from Rome, had been written before they received the latest news—what his agent had just reported to him—of the killing of Romans and auxiliaries in Jerusalem.

He prayed that his reply to Nero would reassure him the desired results would be achieved soon. Then he prayed that his next dispatch, one that would include teasing mention of pending details and information he did not have yet about the treasure, would appease him. With what had just happened, a full-out war was coming to Judea, and then he would have free rein amid the chaos to make good on his promise and take what he wanted—all that gold, silver, and other valuables—and send half to Nero.

He sealed the pouch and called for Glaucio. Only minutes later he handed the sealed leather pouch to him. "Give this to the courier who awaits it—and send someone to bring the centurion, Capito." He had to get the mole in Jerusalem to provide something tangible about the temple treasure.

JERUSALEM

The haze and smell of smoke from the rubble of Herod's palace wall still hovered in the Upper City. That site was so nearby it had drifted through the doors and windows to hang in the air within Mathias's home. *Will Jerusalem ever be clear again of such a stench?* Yosef wondered as he looked at the four men around the table. They still did not grasp the seriousness of the consequences of what Menahem ben Judah had done to Metillus and the other Romans who had surrendered at Herod's palace. The slightest sound, the dislodging of the smallest rock, could trigger an avalanche that buried all of them. Menahem had done something that would so alarm and enrage the Romans that it would bring down retaliation against the whole province—a people—in revolt. Rome had dealt with many of them. Revolt was a common matter for an empire built over centuries. But the Judeans—represented by Jerusalem—had just perpetrated an affront far beyond the proportions of normal dissent against a ruler.

"Son—"

Yosef sat slumped in his seat but looked up at his father at the end of the table. Next to him on his left was Shimon ben Gamliel, the Sanhedrin president. On his right was Yehudah ish Krioth, and next to him Matthew. "What was that, Father?"

"You returned from Qumran just as the siege and burning of Antonia Fortress ended—and then the final attack and battle started at Herod's palace." Mathias shook his head, and his right hand rubbed his brow. "Since those actions, we haven't been able to discuss your meeting with the Essenes."

"Father, it will take time for them to locate suitable sites, prepare any that need work, and document—securely—their locations." Yosef straightened. "We can't move any of the Temple treasure until they're ready."

"Surely, we can do something," Yehudah said. "Some of it could—"

"No, Yehudah," Yosef interrupted him, wondering where the man had been during the recent events. "We can't proceed without doing it right, and proper preparation is the best way to protect the treasure. And now"—his eyes went from man to man around the table—"understand that Rome—the empire—is like a large animal. It is lethargic, slow-moving, and even tolerant to a degree of smaller creatures, but it will not be disrespected and threatened by its subordinates. That's what Menahem has done—disrespect and threaten—and when Rome gets word of it, the beast, now provoked, will awaken and strike faster and harsher than we can imagine." He looked at Matthew. "Where is Eleasar? He should hear this, too."

"He's arguing with Menahem and attempting to get him to stop his search for his father and uncle and to cease his plans to strike against the citizens he believes are pro-Roman."

"I thought Eleasar said Menahem would stand down—moderate his actions—once Agrippa's troops and the Roman soldiers in the city were..." Shimon's voice trailed off, then continued: "I've been approached about the forming of a proposed new governing body, a free council. Does that not mean the rebels intend fair representation? That they plan to include the city leaders and to work toward a peaceful negotiation with the Romans, their leaders, when"—he glanced at Yosef—"when they arrive?"

Matthew snorted. "Menahem will not be part of that. He sees himself as our leader now—the true messiah and eventual king."

"And he will, even unintentionally, make a sacrifice of our nation," Yosef said, "a sacrifice to his own ego." The room grew quiet. "When the Romans arrive at our gates, they will not be here to talk."

LXII

"Recall your men, Menahem." Eleasar ben Ananias stood alone before the self-proclaimed messiah. The soldiers had stopped the two Temple guards Eleasar had brought with him, keeping them from entering the chamber. The Sicarii leader sat on a raised, almost throne-like chair in an open gallery within the Hasmonean palace, surrounded by his private guard and chief lieutenant, Elazar ben Yair. "My father and uncle," Eleasar said, "I, too, have differences with them, with what they've decided and done in the past. But you have burned their houses and forced them to flee for their lives. Let them go. Do not hunt them as if they were animals."

Menahem's look at the Temple guard captain reflected his scorn for Eleasar's father and uncle, the former High Priest and his brother. "What city would let a leper remain free and roam its streets? What king would wish to have such in his land?" He leaned forward with hands that gripped his knees. "And what leader who cares for his people would allow it?" Menahem shook his head, straightened and crossed his arms. "Your father, his brother, and their kind have long wielded power in Jerusalem and in our country. Now I"—he scanned the surrounding men—"and all my men outside Jerusalem's walls... cannot tolerate such haughty, gluttonous, and rapacious men. Corrupt leaders," he sneered, "who do not serve their country and must be brought to justice."

"They hold no power, Menahem. They can do no harm. Let them go. We have more important things to focus on. The Romans will—"

Menahem cut him off. "I will deal with the Romans when we face them. For now"—he stood and spread his arms wide as if encompassing more than those in the room—all that was beyond the walls of the building and the city, too—"we must clean and purify our house, our city, and our country."

He turned to Elazar, the lieutenant at his side. "It is taking too long, so I want you to take charge immediately. You must find Ananias ben Ananias, the former High Priest, and his brother Hezekiah, and bring them before me." Menahem sat and looked at Eleasar ben Ananias. "When I have them here"—he gestured in front of the dais—"I will call you to return." He dismissed Eleasar and turned to his lieutenant, bending down to whisper into his ear.

* * *

Elazar ben Yair had left the Hasmonean palace to supervise the search, but he did not agree with his orders from Menahem ben Judah. Some men had served their own interests above Jerusalem's and Judea's, and they deserved punishment. They could not build a nation on a rotted foundation such as those men, but Eleasar had been right about his father and uncle. They had fled, and without position and privilege, they could do no further harm. If they had not already escaped beyond the city's walls, then they were in deep hiding somewhere within them. The time and energy used to hunt them down could be better spent preparing Jerusalem and other areas that needed fortifying for the coming confrontations with the Romans. Elazar's own time would be better used to return to Masada and bring back more arms. Menahem's personal desire for retribution had overwhelmed rational thinking, and that could have deadly consequences in war.

Elazar had initially focused the search teams—men gathered by Menahem that he must use but would never trust in battle—on the Upper City. Ananias ben Ananias, who came from a long line of family wealth, was vain and arrogant. Hiding in the Lower City would be repugnant to him. But after days of searching without results, Elazar had sent more men into the Lower City as Menahem brought in citizens and merchants from the Upper City to question, hoping to find who was hiding the two men or to confirm they had left the city.

* * *

The boy was careful. He had two large water skins slung over one shoulder and over the other a leather bag filled with dates wrapped in leaves, pomegranates, and two smaller containers of boiled barley gruel. The incline into the deepest part of the Tyropoeon valley was steep and treacherous. The steps and footholds had worsened the path as he went deeper, the rocks loose as the rotten teeth in his grandfather's mouth. Halfway down the placed steps disappeared, and he had to rely on the natural stone outcroppings with an occasional earth shelf formed by the erosion of rain and runoff water. Many years had routed that water over buried stone that had carried the earth across, then dammed up into a pile over a cluster of larger rocks. Those clods of dirt had taken root and sprouted tough weeds that held them together well enough for a toehold. He had made this journey several times in recent days and on each trip—whether on his downward delivery of food and water or in the upward return—he had nearly lost his footing. Now, when he slipped or tottered on the edge of losing his balance and grip, behind closed eyes, he could see the rocks far below. They were man-sized, and though many were worn smooth by weathering, others were more recently sheared off from the escarpment he now clung to. He saw in his mind's eye the jagged edges and sharp points ready to rip and tear him should he fall. If that happened, he wondered, would anyone find his body?

He always started each descent as soon as it was light enough to see. After the first two trips, he knew that by the time he reached the bottom and picked his way through and around the rocks that littered where the slope ended, the sun would be over the hills. It slanted down, casting its first beams on the western side of the narrow valley. To the north and up the slope, in the far distance, he could see the terrace of the Xystus market that overlooked the valley at the edge of the Upper City, close to the wall that separated it from Bezetha, the northernmost part of Jerusalem. To the south, the valley extended further into the Lower City that overlooked it. He turned in that direction and in twenty minutes had arrived at the largest storm drain that emptied into the Tyropoeon. A dry summer's coating of dust and dirt rimmed the opening and formed a shallow but wide pile lying over old silt at the end of the drain. Beside the masonry-framed mouth of the opening, he bent to pick up a rock as large as his hand. He struck the frame of the conduit. Bang–bang–bang, he paused a moment and then bang–bang–bang–bang. At that signal, two men appeared in the mouth of the drain but did not step out. Even though the daylight was still faint at the base of the eastern slope, they shaded their eyes.

The two men looked only slightly worse than most men the boy knew. They wore once-fine clothing that was now dirty and torn, and they had matted hair and unkempt beards. But the silver coin they gave him—that he would then take to his father each time he delivered—told him they were not the same kind of men. Until his father had told him of this new task, instructed him how to get down into the valley, then where to go and how to signal, he had never held money—a metal coin—in his hand before. Though he knew it had great value to buy the things his family needed, he most enjoyed the bright flash it made when he held it up under the sun. The men took the water skins and bag of food from him and the tallest one, with a nod, handed over the small coin. The boy gripped it in his hand as he turned back for his long return climb, loosening it only long enough to polish it on the front of his dirty tunic and hold it up to the sun now nearly directly overhead.

* * *

"How did you find them?" Menahem asked, though he already knew that information from Elazar ben Yair. He wanted to hear it told by the rough-clothed man he knew must be a bursiyyon. The tattered and discolored tanner's apron the man wore as if it were regular attire revealed his profession. The man came closer, and the stink of him confirmed Menahem's conclusion.

"I saw a nubbin of a boy climb out of the valley 'tween here and down toward the Lower City." The tanner held up a coin between a large, stained thumb and forefinger. "Wouldn't have paid him no mind, but for this." He pivoted his wrist, and the coin caught the late afternoon sunlight from the bank of windows. "The boy was tossing it in the air and catching it, and the twinkle caught my eye. He wasn't far away but didn't see me. I stole up on him and grabbed him by the arm. It's rare enough for a grown man from the Lower City to have silver these days, so I asked him where it came from. He tried to run, but I got a handful of the back of his tunic, snatched him around, and with a bit more arm work, I had the coin, and the boy spilled where it came from. Then I let him go, and he ran off blubbering. I followed what he told me and went down into the valley, counting the drains and come to the one with the widest mouth. It was about high enough for a man to stand up straight in. I banged with the rock just as the boy told me and near-to-out of it came two men, one of them asking, 'What is it, boy? Why do you come back?' Well, when he saw me, he shut up fast. He spun around and"—the man paused, his eyes sliding from Menahem to Elazar who stood beside him and then back to Menahem—"I was told you were looking for two men hiding—that there'd be a reward—and you wanted them dead or alive. So I hit him with the rock I still had in my hand, and he went down. Then I went after the other man... he hadn't got too far—and got him with the rock, too."

The man wiped sweaty hands—one of them still holding the silver coin—on his apron. "I climbed back out and got a couple men to help me come back for them. I think it was dragging them up from the valley that did in the men you wanted."

* * *

When the messenger entered the Temple looking for the guard captain, Matthew pointed him out and watched as the man approach Eleasar.

Eleasar saw him and knew his father and uncle must have been found. Since talking with Menahem, he had thought long about an argument that would work to convince him to release them. He had not come up with anything, although he was still hopeful as he hurried from the Temple through the inner and outer courts to cross the viaduct and descend the steps into the Upper City. From there to the Hasmonean palace was a short distance. He passed the two men posted at the main entrance and turned into the main gallery.

As he entered, Menahem's voice rang out: "As I promised, here they are before me."

LXIII

Jerusalem

"Menahem ben Judah has tortured and murdered my father and uncle... and will pay for it."

Eleasar had gotten himself under control since the Sicarii brutes had dragged him to the guard office, where Matthew had held him—calming him—until the senior Sanhedrin members could be gathered to hear what had happened. Now Yosef watched as Eleasar, still white-faced and in a cold rage, denounced Menahem to the few who had come and to the face of Mathias ben Theophilus, who sat in his High Priest's chair—but likely not for much longer. Either Eleasar or Menahem would want him cast from that position in favor of someone more sympathetic to the rebellion. Yosef looked at his brother Matthew and father sitting beside him. Mathias had been approached more than once to take the position of Sanhedrin president, or possibly even that of the High Priest, and had decided not to accept. Yosef thought his father regretted that, but given the way factions had fragmented Jerusalem's—and Judea's—leadership, it was unlikely anyone could have resolved the issues and united the opposing factions to a common cause.

Eleasar's voice grew stronger and louder, and Yosef turned back to him.

Eleasar scanned the chamber, marking for memory those who were there and those who were not—a tally of his own, like Menahem's different list, for future retaliation. "We all chafe under Roman rule," Eleasar said. "It has become unbearable, and some of us have taken action to throw off that yoke. Whether you agree with what's been done or not, we must now stand together. We—together—now revolt because we and our country must serve no master but our God."

The scorn and hate now dripped from each word as Eleasar paced the room with all eyes following him. "Menahem is nothing more than a lowborn shouter in the streets, a rabble-rouser, and a raiser of false hopes among those easily misled, those without the will or wit to think for themselves. He projects his fears on them, and they respond as he wants them to." His hot eyes roamed the room, his voice now growing hoarse. "You know what and who I mean—those who stand with him, with Menahem, because they won't stand up for themselves or because it serves their own purpose. And they do it at the expense of all our people."

The High Priest twisted in his seat as Eleasar continued: "Menahem is no leader, much less a messiah. He is not an anointed one sent by God to unify and lead us to freedom. Mark my words judgment is coming for such a man, and it might arrive before the Romans get here with their own retribution."

* * *

"Father, Matthew, I'll join you at home," Yosef said and noted that Matthew had seen what he had seen. Ahead, just inside the Women's Court, were Leah and Rachel. Both had seen them, and their gaze had not wavered. He must stop and say something to them.

Matthew touched Yosef's arm. "Brother, be careful. Yonatan has returned from wherever he was—and was just with us in the Hall of Hewn Stone listening to Eleasar." Matthew looked over both shoulders at the clusters of men coming from the inner court, then back to Yosef. "He's become even more fanatical, and though he's aligned with Eleasar, he is more like the Sicarii. And he hates you."

"I know he does, and I'll be watchful Matthew." Yosef nodded to him and his father as they turned south toward the outer court and then on to home. He walked straight ahead to greet Leah and Rachel.

"I thought we might lose you to the Essenes again," Leah said, her smile as sweet as it had been more than ten years ago, but she lifted a careworn face. It had become the lined face of a woman older than she really was. Rachel's younger face was fresh and alight with joy, and she spoke as he reached them: "Miriam mentioned your visit to Qumran."

Yosef made a mental note to discuss that with Miriam when he talked with her about her own secrets. Leah's smile still tugged at his heart, a bittersweet pain, but he changed what he wanted to say, to say what he should: "I was just renewing an old acquaintance I had not seen since returning from Rome. I went during what I thought would be a quieter time here in the city." *Better to not suggest or confirm any importance to my trip.* "It's good to see you, both of you." He smiled for Rachel, too, and turned back to Leah. "I understand your husband has returned." Matthew's warning had his lips spilling what was on his mind, and he regretted it instantly as the smile and glow in Leah's eyes flickered and faded. He felt pain at that, but her eyes grew wide and looked beyond him.

Behind him, a loud voice called out: "Do you still have feelings for my wife, Yosef? After Rome—and all you have seen and done with—Romans?"

Yosef turned. Yonatan was as tall as he but much broader and thicker of chest, arms, and legs. Hands on his hips, Yonatan glowered at him. Yosef knew Yonatan had noted some of the looks Cleo had given him at the Passover Seder. There were not many, but a few throughout dinner that evening had planted the seeds of what he had just implied. "Leah and Rachel are old friends," Yosef said calmly. "And yes, Yonatan, I have feelings for all of my friends."

Yonatan shifted his bulk around Yosef and between him and the women, forcing Leah and Rachel to step back and make way for him. Yosef did not move but kept his eyes locked on Leah's angry and jealous husband.

"So, you have just friendly feelings, then?" Yonatan's thick arm came up with his hand palm out, and he shoved Yosef in the chest with the kick of a mule. "I don't believe you."

Yosef caught his balance within a couple of backward steps and then came forward after Yonatan. *Fighting*, he thought even as he responded in kind to Yonatan, *among ourselves and soon with the Romans. Why can't we get along and let things—let people—be?* Still, he could not stop himself as his own hand shot out to shove Yonatan away from him. He knew he shouldn't have done it—it would only escalate into something he wanted to avoid—but he did it anyway.

Leah latched on to Yonatan's arm, and her feet dragged on the stone of the courtyard as he surged toward Yosef. Rachel wrung her hands before Yosef to coax him in the opposite direction. Yosef watched Yonatan's thick chest heave with anger as Leah, in a low voice, talked to him like a shepherdess soothing a mad beast. But he, like a beast, was ready to rear and trample all around him. Yonatan's breathing slowed, and he stopped his pull of her toward Yosef. He pried Leah's hand from his arm—not gently. "Stay away from my wife."

Yosef didn't respond. The tears coursing down Leah's face as she mouthed the words "Please go" took the retort from his mouth. He let Rachel call him away. They were in the Court of the Gentiles, near the colonnade and the gate into the merchant's streets in the upper agora, when he realized two things. He still had Rachel beside him. And the looks she cast at him he had seen from the corner of his eye as they walked away from Leah—the look she was giving him was not some tiny, harmless, will-die-with-time flame of a young girl's fascination. It was the adoration of a now grown woman.

LXIV

JERUSALEM

Yosef scanned the room, one of many in the House of Caiaphas, and thought of his father's comment about the meeting location for the Zealots and those not aligned with Menahem. It had become their routine gathering place, and his father had commented, "This chamber is where we judge those of our own, we disagree with. Yeshua ish Natzrat, and many others since have been held here to be examined and judged—and now three decades later we sit here and judge ourselves." His father, already burdened with the creeping pain of age in his joints, was bent and bowed where he sat, saddened by the faction infighting and what it had brought to pass. A country and city were divided and now faced an enormous, deadly threat, the full wrath of the Roman Empire.

Word had come to Jerusalem of the anti-Jewish uprisings in other parts of Judea and the region, reprisals that came as news spread outward of the Romans killed by rebels in the city and the knowledge that such acts gave free license—in the eyes of Rome—for anyone to retaliate against Jews. Long-held, deep-seated racial and religious animosity now boiled over. Rumor had it the Greeks around Caesarea had slaughtered twenty thousand Jews, and Yosef wondered if Gessius Florus had had a hand in that. Other anti-Jewish protests were reported in Damascus, Tyre, Gaba, Sebaste, Ptolemais, Gaza, and Anthodon. In Ascalon, the Jews had felt loyal to their Gentile neighbors and had helped to protect them in the unrest. But then the anti-Jewish attackers drove the Jews from the town. And when those fleeing had taken refuge in a nearby sacred grove, their attackers had fallen upon them at nightfall and murdered thirteen thousand and stolen all their belongings, leaving their bodies strewn across the forest and glade.

Yosef tapped his father's knee and pointed at the entrance to the chamber. Eleasar had come in and now strode to the front of the room. Matthew had entered behind Eleasar but turned to sit with the two dozen men arrayed at tables and in seats around the chamber. Yosef shifted over to make room on the wooden bench where he and his father sat. As Matthew seated himself, Yosef leaned toward him.

288

"So, Eleasar has enough backing—and has he had enough of Menahem ben Judah so that he will denounce him?"

"Yes," Matthew nodded, "and Eleasar claims he has subverted the Sicarii remaining in the city, now that Elazar ben Yair has returned with his men to Masada. Elazar has gathered to his side most of the rabble that Menahem has relied on." Matthew shifted, "Move over more," he said as he nudged Yosef and Eleasar began to speak.

"We will not trade one tyrant for another, even if it is a purple-robed fellow countryman." Eleasar's eyes swept the room. "All of you—and I have heard from others beyond this room and our city walls—believe as I do, or you would not be here. Know that, from this point on, we don't just talk. We act."

* * *

"Just as you said he would," the filthy man said, spitting on the floor as his odor filled the room, "Menahem came to the inner court dressed in his finery and his guards with him. All done up and wearing those shiny Roman breastplates, helmets, greaves, and armor—but without the Roman insignia, though. But armor's not much good when you're buried under stones. The bunch of us"—he cocked his thumb at a mass of men behind him—"we each had a pile of stones ready to throw and drop on them. Once his men were bloodied and down, he tucked that fancy robe up high between his legs and ran. Just like you told me to, I held my men back a while to give him time to build up a good fear of the hunters on his heels. Then we trailed him. The silver coins you paid us worked, and the promise of more. I don't think citizens cared for how he styled himself—and they were happy to point out where he had run to hide." The man wiped his hands on a stained apron and nudged with the toe of his sandal the unconscious, bloodied man in torn purple robes at his feet.

"He fought a bit at first, cursed us, but we beat him down and dragged him all the way from a cave at the foot of the Ophel." The tanner, Apsalom, blew through his lips. He had learned that hunting men paid well. "So, here he is—alive as you wanted—for you to do what you will with him. And now"—he glanced at the cluster of dirty, rough-clothed men behind him and then back at Eleasar—"we'll take the silver you promised us."

* * *

"I don't believe your sister should hear this." Mathias frowned at his sons, passing his eyes over Miriam, who sat between them.

"Rebecca"—he turned to his wife who had also just joined them at the table—"you and Miriam should—"

"Sit right here with you all and be a part of this conversation."

Yosef almost smiled at his mother's directness, so typical of her. Miriam did smile. Matthew, who thought as his father did, squirmed in his chair.

Mathias sighed and looked at his wife for a moment and then at his daughter. Miriam had changed in recent months. Her face taut and eyes no longer dull or only showing a pain he could not help her with. They were alight with attention, and he was glad to see a spark of life. But he wondered as he studied her what had caused it to return. Miriam's smile at her mother's blunt statement had now faded to a serious and determined expression. *Never has she looked more like her mother*, he thought. He nodded to her and felt her smile near to surfacing again. But what was happening to their country, their city, and their family was nothing to smile about. "Is Menahem still alive?" he asked Matthew, who had just returned from seeing Eleasar at the Temple.

"Yes, but I don't think for long. Eleasar has seen to it that Menahem suffers from the same injuries Menahem had inflicted on his father and uncle: arms and legs broken, ribs caved in, and skull fractured. But he is ordering no damage to his mouth and jaw because—and he told me this—he wants to hear Menahem scream until he dies." Matthew shook his head and looked down at his clenched hands on the tabletop. "But all he does now is whimper and cry. And that not likely for much longer."

"It's terrible," murmured Rebecca.

Yosef did not look at his mother, who had grown white-faced at Matthew's words. With his head tilted to one side and a sideways look, he watched Miriam, who had become tense but did not seem upset. "Menahem brought it on himself," Yosef commented. That provoked a sharp side-eye glance from his sister, and then her eyes slid away from him. "Once it became apparent, he was more focused on fulfilling his own messianic prophecy than a true desire to unite and free our people from Rome in the best interests of all of Judea, there was no way to accept or even abide his delusion of leadership."

"Yosef is right"—Mathias reached his right hand out to his wife and his left across the table to take Miriam's—"And Rebecca, you're right as well. This is when we as a family"—he patted his daughter's hand—"must decide what we do in the future. The Romans will come, and though I fear what will happen then, we must stand with the rebels."

"I agree with Father," Matthew said.

Yosef thought of Cleo, Sayid, and Nicanor—whom he cared for—and of all the things of Rome that he had seen and admired. He already felt heavy-hearted about their certain loss. "Yes. We must stand together and fight."

Miriam watched her mother's hand grip her father's so tightly he winced, and then she nodded in silent agreement. Miriam straightened her chair, squared her shoulders and told her father, though her eyes flicked toward Yosef, "We fight and kill all the Romans against us."

LXV

JERUSALEM

The talk on the streets ranged from boasting that what Menahem had done could and would be done to any Romans threatening Jerusalem... to fear of the depredation to come. Those whose voices were the most optimistic at defeating the Romans seemed to be the ones who knew the least. Miriam had learned enough from Matthew and Yosef to know that. Those voices that were the quietest, most subdued, were of veterans that had fought and bled and understood the power of the Roman army and how weak the Judean forces were in comparison. She understood that, too.

She had dawdled along as the city awakened, listening for something she had not already heard. She picked up her pace. Menahem's death—as foretold by Matthew—had bothered her at first. Losing a mentor would disrupt her plan to do just what she had said in agreement with her father and brothers, to stand with them to fight and kill Romans. She sought Zechariah's advice on how she could still do that. She hoped he would still offer it now, with Menahem dead and the Sicarii having fled Jerusalem to encamp at Masada.

Just before dawn that morning she had heard her father's and brother's voices in the courtyard. A messenger from Yohanan ben Zaccai from Arev had arrived an hour before to report that a Galilean sailor who had just returned home on a coastal trader from Antioch had learned that the Roman Twelfth Legion was mobilizing. The only purpose for that must be that the legate, Cestius Gallus, planned to march on Jerusalem to break the revolt and resistance. When the news spread of the legion, would the brave words from some she'd overheard that morning still hold?

* * *

"Menahem is dead, and the Sicarii have all gone to Masada." Zechariah sat on the high stool at his worktable and studied her with an off-angled look that centered back on her when she spoke. "And what will you do now, Miriam?" he asked. "Now that the war is upon us."

"When the Romans arrive, I will fight."

Zechariah lowered his head, eyes cast down as if considering the staff his two gnarled hands gripped across his lap. "You cannot defend the walls or fight in the streets. Your father and brothers won't let you." He shook his head and then raised it toward her. "You should fight only to defend yourself... don't"—he shook his head again—"don't seek it out, child."

"I'm not a child, and I am not a timid and scared girl... not anymore. Menahem did not treat me as such—"

Zechariah cut her off. "And he is dead, as you will be in a real battle where strength matters and the fighting is won or lost in the daylight. I taught you to protect yourself, and you've done that and more—more than perhaps anyone but I will ever know. But I won't help you risk your life needlessly."

"Doesn't our country—our city—need every defender, every warrior?"

"Yes, but your life would be wasted. You must live, or at least have the best chance possible to survive what's coming. I have lost too many I care for—I've lost my wife and daughter to the Romans. I do not want to lose you, too."

* * *

Miriam left Zechariah's place midmorning. They had talked more, and she had realized why the death of Menahem had troubled her only for a while. What Zechariah had said would last much longer, and it made her dig deep inside for the right meaning. Menahem had seen her as a surprise weapon he could use—and probably use poorly because it would have been to serve his purpose, not a greater one, and not the one she would choose. Zechariah was right--she must consider things, and the coming war—differently.

Ahead of her, the northernmost gate leading up to the Temple enclosure and then to the Upper City was jammed with a mass of people. As she passed several of the streets that led to the western gates, she had seen a queue of carts, the kind used to haul stone and lumber in large quantities. Why were so many apparently headed to quarry outside the city walls? She tugged the sleeve of a woman ahead of her—one of the few in the crowd. "Has something happened?"

The woman turned, her seamed face looking ready to scold whoever had jostled her. She saw Miriam's young, fresh countenance turned up into the morning sun and gave a quick up-and-down assessment of her tidy, plain-but-well-made clothing. Her demeanor changed, and her voice was more pleasant than Miriam expected, though the voice trembled with fright. "The Temple guard is going about the city in pairs and gathering all the stone masons." At Miriam's quizzical look she continued: "Have you not heard? There are twelve legions of Roman soldiers in Galilee, and they are headed here." The woman clutched her chest as if Roman hands already reached for her breasts. "Many want to flee the city, but their men who are stoneworkers or woodworkers have been commanded to bring stone and lumber to reinforce the northern gates of the city and the wall protecting Bezetha."

Miriam knew from what she had overheard from her father that the Roman force, the Twelfth Legion, was still forming in Antioch, and was not anywhere near Galilee. And from Matthew and Yosef she knew that the only direction the Romans could attack the city from—with any sizable force—was the north. To the west, south, and east, Jerusalem was protected by deep ravines two to four hundred feet deep, and the city's high walls loomed over their precipitous slopes. No one could mount an attack of any serious threat from those sides of the city. She had seen the southern and southeastern approach recently herself—the Kidron valley was a deep rift in the plateau the city sat upon and carved south and turned west after joining the Hinnom valley, where all the city's rubbish was dumped and burned. Both valleys had steep climbs from the base to reach the foot of the city walls, and once there, no level ground to speak of other than a narrow, winding path that followed the walls but made no room for armored troops.

So now the Temple guard and rebels were readying the city for siege. She had started to change direction to find a less-congested gate if that was possible. She didn't like the jostling of the crowd, either. Then she saw a man in fine robes reach the lowest of the broad-tiered steps that descended from the outer court of the Temple enclosure. A well-manicured hand came up to smooth the long, silky beard against his chest in a gesture that prickled her memory. She watched him as his hand made two more palm passes over the beard, now flat against his breast. A rough-garbed man paused near him, and their heads bent toward each other for a moment. The shorter, grizzled man moved away, and into a street she knew bent and turned to parallel the southeastern wall of the city. The smooth-bearded man in the fine robes looked around, left and right, and then followed the shorter man. After a moment's pause, Miriam trailed them, wrapping her shawl around her lower face.

The alley soon broadened into a row of backstreet shops, and at a corner where the east-to-west street formed one side and would have led her toward Zechariah's shop, she saw the two men at a stall where cups of wine or barley beer were sold. They now sat beneath an awning that stretched alongside the building over a handful of tables and cast a slanting shadow over most of their table. She paused at the fruit vendor nearby as if a morning shopper checking the pressed bricks of dates and pots of honey. The short, grizzle-bearded man's sleeves were now pulled back from thick-muscled forearms to show the wide leather cuffs above his wrists. He pushed a small, greasy, full-looking purse toward the smooth-bearded man, who picked it up by its leather cinch cord and bounced it up and down twice, his head cocked to one side as if listening. Then he nodded and pulled a square, folded piece of parchment from inside his tunic and slid it across the table to the man. He took the purse and tucked it into a pouch at his waist, stood and smoothed his beard again, and without a word, walked away.

Miriam watched as the grizzled-bearded man's left hand stroked the cuff on his right forearm, fingers tracing a design or embossing she could not see. He picked up the folded parchment the other man had given him, folded it twice and wrapped it in a slip of cloth, then tucked it under the leather cuff on his left forearm. She looked off at the receding back of the smooth-bearded man moving slowly through the thickening crowd of people on the streets and considered following him.

"Young lady!" The stall vendor's bark startled her.

"What?" She turned to look at him.

"Are you buying or do you just wish to just play with my produce?" He gestured at the cloth-wrapped rectangle of pressed dates she held in her hand.

Miriam handed him a coin. The smooth-bearded man had disappeared in the crowd, but the other man had left the table and now walked to a set of exterior stairs that led to rooms above the building. She watched him climb the stairs to the landing, enter, and close the door behind him. Then the smooth-bearded man's name suddenly came to her.

* * *

Yosef looked up and caught the shutter of Miriam's room open a hand's breadth. He smiled. Miriam had been a nosy little sister, wanting to know and be included in every little thing her big brothers were doing. She had not lost that part of her personality as she had grown up. He turned to Matthew. "So, Eleasar has ordered the buttressing of the north wall and gates?"

"Yes, and he sent men back with Yohanan ben Zaccai's messenger to Galilee to ask the rebel leader there, Yohanan ben Levi, of Gischala, if he would work with us to set watch posts at the northern border. That would give us warning of Roman troops or any advance scouts."

"Did he also set the city patrols?"

Matthew nodded. "And that's probably a good thing."

"I guess we have been at the point where we cannot blindly trust everyone. We need someone watching our streets."

"That's not it, Yosef. In the early hours this morning, they found a man dead—killed in the Lower City."

"Couldn't it have been a robbery or a jealous or drunken quarrel?"

"His throat was cut, and the body dragged to sit upright against a wall, and beside the body, on the wall was left a bloody handprint."

"The killer's?" Yosef asked.

"No, the dead man's. Whoever killed him dipped his hand in his own blood and used it to place the mark."

"The city always has its share of violence, even without the added tension among the different factions, and now everything else that's happened."

"I don't think it's that, though, Yosef." Matthew leaned forward across the table. "They checked and found this man had not been in Jerusalem long. He was said to be a traveling trader, and not much was known about him. He would show up in the city for several days and then not be seen for days. When they checked his body, they found Roman legionary tattoos—those of a Thracian mercenary."

LXVI

CAESAREA

"Another man of mine killed in Jerusalem!" Gessius, who had paced away from his desk, roared as he spun on a heel to glare at the centurion who stood before him.

"L-Lord Florus, I—" the man stammered.

The procurator cut him off. "You have picked drunken incompetents to serve me. How many is this—two, three men?"

"Two, Lord, but—"

"Do they stand up in the middle of that city and announce, I am a Roman spy—kill me!?" Florus saw a flicker of movement just outside the entrance to his private office and walked quickly but silently to it and looked out. There was no one there, but a flowering plant—one of the many his wife favored, set in large waist-high pots and placed around the atrium—stirred at the corner, its petals and cluster of stalks settling as if brushed by someone passing it in a hurry. He felt a slight current of air and looked to the bank of windows that opened onto the seaward porticus and colonnade. Beyond were terraced gardens that led to an overlook and the sea below. The wind carried the tang of saltwater and sea spray, which freshened the air throughout the residence. Despite his aggravation and frustration, he breathed it in with appreciation. Only Roman power—the authority given him by the emperor—enabled him to live in such a palace. And only money would give him the means to continue to live similarly— but elsewhere, thank the gods—as he had become accustomed.

"Should I send the man back to Jerusalem?"

Florus turned back to the centurion. "Yes, and have him find out immediately what was shared with the man who was killed before he could deliver the information. Then he must bring the information directly to me himself, without delay. After you send him off, find me someone—a man harder to kill, one who can stalk whoever killed the others—someone that I can count on." He waved a hand to dismiss the soldier. As the man reached him to pass from the office, the procurator's hand shot out to the centurion's shoulder, abruptly stopping him. "And Capito, if this man dies or does not deliver what I need—the details on the Jews' plans to move and hide their temple treasure—I will have the word 'Roman' branded on your chest and have you delivered naked to the Jewish Sicarii." Florus watched as the centurion quick-marched noisily from the room and across the atrium.

"Is there anything you require, lord?" Glaucio had turned up as the centurion's clattering echoes faded.

"Where are the Lady Cleo and her constant companion?" Florus asked, wondering still whether it had been Cleo, the boy Sayid, or perhaps even Glaucio listening at his door, and not the wind.

"I believe Lady Cleo is practicing her archery, lord, with that Syrian boy in attendance." The majordomus paused and asked again, "Is there anything you wish, sir?"

Florus thought of the news he had received that morning and of all the waiting he wished to end. "Nothing you can deliver, Glaucio." He curtly turned back into his office. At his desk, he picked up a square of vellum. So, Cestius Gallus had received word that Rome had assigned a new Judean procurator—a Marcus Antonius Julianus—who should arrive in Caesarea in a month. That message in his hand... he paced again. He must plan how he could convince Emperor Nero to not recall him to Rome. There he would face questions he would rather not answer or would be forced to lie about; in Rome, he could not help himself. In any inquiry, he would be held accountable for events in Judea, and he would have no leverage he could use to save himself. To gain that leverage, he must remain here—in Judea, in some role, even if unofficial, but with Nero's approval and protection—until he could get his hands on the Jewish temple treasure. That the gold and silver it held was what Nero needed desperately right now was his only bargaining chip.

He set the sheet down on the desktop and picked up another. Gallus had readied the Twelfth Legion and would soon march to subdue the rebels and specifically to break the will of its leaders in Jerusalem. That legion—known as the thunderbolt of the Roman army—Legio Duodecima Fulminata—had been originally levied by Julius Caesar more than a hundred years earlier and had served throughout the Gallic Wars. Then it had become a hard-luck legion assigned to unappealing places within the empire. It was a veteran army—and seeded within its ranks must surely be some level of discontent—and it would be led by Cestius Gallus, a politician who had served only as an administrator and had no military experience.

Florus wondered, could his agent inside the legate's staff find a senior officer or officers there that could be bought with a promise of a share of the treasure? And could he give him some measure of control over the Twelfth that would enable him to dictate the pace of movements or strategy? Gallus would never know good tactics from bad—and could never tell what a marginal decision or action for Rome was. But such an action could significantly improve his opportunity to grab his share of the temple treasure. And if Gallus failed, the chaos of battle and of war would continue and still serve his purpose. That failure would be on Cestius Gallus, who would be held responsible. Florus smiled as he planned and thought, yes—that could work to achieve my purpose—and all while I sit here and wait for just the time to strike.

LXVII

Sayid hurried. He and Cleo had seen Glaucio watching them earlier. Cleo's morning archery practice had become routine, as had the man's spying on her. Sayid had noted that Lord Florus's majordomus had become enamored of the new Greek servant girl, and after checking on them, he dallied with her, each morning following her down several terraces to the large seawater pool King Herod had constructed among the rocks of the beach.

Sayid knew that Jucundus, the centurion who had served with Lady Octavia's brother and had known her family for many years, had done as he had promised Lady Cleo and always let her know when a courier was expected. And once the dispatches were delivered and the courier gone was when Gessius read and often reacted to them and regularly met with Capito, a man, and centurion Sayid had no liking for but he did as the lady asked and tried to listen to those meetings. He was nervous about being caught, but the lady worried more at the worsening situation—all the violence and killing breaking out around them—and he agreed with her that Lord Florus was responsible. A courier had arrived earlier that morning. So once Glaucio was away, he had returned inside the palace and lurked near Lord Florus's office to hear what he could.

"My lady"—Sayid caught his breath as he reported to Cleo—"your husband received two messages from two sources. One official, I think from Rome or perhaps the legate in Antioch. The other must be from Jerusalem. He sounded upset by both, but the most by the one from Jerusalem. Another of your husband's agents there has been killed, and your husband ordered the centurion Capito to find him a man more skilled, a more reliable mercenary, to hunt down the man who has killed his men in Jerusalem."

Cleo unstrung her bow, wiped it and the string with a soft, lightly oiled cloth, and handed them both to Sayid, who stowed them and her quiver of arrows in a large rectangular case made of light wood, with a broad leather strap as a shoulder sling. The case was a gift of thanks for her generous payments to the wood trader that Sayid had befriended. She had convinced him to become her private messenger to carry her letters sent via Octavia in Antioch to her brother in

300

Lusitania. She had not received a reply from him—prayed nightly that she would—but it was too soon to expect an answer yet.

"Sayid, there is something—a very important letter—I have to get to Lady Octavia. Do you remember that strange message I found on my husband's desk that we couldn't read?" Not waiting for his nod, she continued: "I need to get that letter to her along with one I will write tonight. And Lord Florus cannot know about them." She sat on the stone bench, and a chill passed through her. Maybe it was caused by the cool, early fall breeze that smelled of the sea, or more likely it came from what she was doing and what she was about to ask Sayid to do. "The only one," Cleo murmured and looked beyond him to the palace and across the grounds to the seaward overlook and terraces descending from it, and then on toward the east as if at something or someone she sought but did not see. She shook her head and looked up at him. "You're the only one I can trust to do this, though I hate that it must be done."

Sayid bowed his head. Cleo was his best friend, yet he had no illusions that they were equals. He would do anything for her, but he knew Caesarea, Jerusalem, and all of Judea was dangerous now for anyone found alone and among others not of their kind, not their people. Anti-Jewish Syrian Greeks, anti-Syrian Greeks, and anti-Roman Jews—he had also heard of the factions of Jews in Jerusalem fighting among themselves: Greeks killing Jews, Jews killing Greeks, Romans killing Jews, Jews killing Romans. Everyone, it seemed, had cause to slay one another—and recently had been doing so. All he wanted was to live, and one day to find his father and make him proud. And he hoped to see his mother again. It had been three years. He felt Cleo waiting for him—and sensed her need to know if he was that one person she could trust, someone who could do what she asked, no matter the risk. He sighed, and he knew she heard it.

The boy had lowered his eyes from Cleo, but when he raised them, it was as a man. She watched as Sayid nodded once as if to himself and then answered the question she had implied but had not asked him.

"I will do it for you, Lady Cleo, though traveling in these lands does frighten me."

The tightness in her chest loosened, and despite fearing herself what was to come and that she might be sending him to his death, she smiled at her friend.

"But how will you explain my absence to Lord Florus?" Sayid asked.

Cleo's smile faded.

* * *

"I had nothing to do with the Greeks or the half-Greeks—whatever they are here in Caesarea—that killed all of those Jews." Gessius Florus stopped his pacing and glared at his wife. "And I had—and have—nothing to do with stirring up the Jews—the Judeans—in Jerusalem, or of inciting them to act as they have." A jeweled hand slammed down on his desk. "They've killed scores of Romans in open rebellion, Cleo, and disrespected Roman rule, laws, and traditions. And by the gods even the hand of surety. They deserve any punishment or retribution coming to them."

Cleo did not flinch at his stare and did not shrink from him; she was long past that. She met his look until he turned away. She thought of Poppaea—a wave of sadness washed over her—and her suspicion that Florus somehow had been involved in the great fire and how it had been blamed on the Christians. She thought of Florus's massacre of thousands of Jews in Jerusalem after Passover. And of his greed, which was the driving force behind every choice and decision he made, even his marriage to her.

Only she no longer offered him anything of value. The evidence of that was in the way he had treated her after learning of Poppaea's death. Only if she reached her brother would she be safe, if with his reduced authority Marcus Otho could protect her. Her risk of not having that safety would increase with what she was about to do. But she, in good conscience, had no other choice. She would have Sayid take to Octavia Florus's secret messages, the Syriac letter, and the scrap of gevil with the Hebrew word korbanas, sacred treasure, written on it. Cestius Gallus, the legate and senior Roman administrator in the region, must know what Florus was suspected of by Poppaea. Her belief that he had a hand in planning the intentional setting of the fire in Rome and instigating the reprisals against Christians to serve his purpose. Of his agents in Jerusalem, and what Cleo believed he was now doing to create war and chaos in Judea. The only way to reach the legate's ears was through his wife—Octavia.

"I don't accuse you, Gessius, and it doesn't matter now who was or is at fault. This country is tearing itself apart, and the status or nationality of a person—of anyone—is no longer a protection. Now it's more like it paints a target instead. I would like, with your permission, to send Sayid to Antioch with a letter to Lady Octavia." Florus's head came around sharply back to her, and she continued: "I want to ask her that if things get worse, as I fear they might—might I come to stay with her." She studied her husband's lined, stern face. "May I, my husband?"

Florus stood still as he thought: I cannot control what that boy carries as a message—not like I can with what goes with the couriers. But the boy will probably be killed, anyway, between here and Antioch—a good outcome. And if he isn't, there's nothing she can give him to bring or tell Octavia that will change anything. The Twelfth Legion is coming, and more people will die. Cleo could be one of them. He willfully softened his look and took a step toward his wife. "I want you to be safe," he lied.

LXVIII

JERUSALEM

It was only the second or third time since Yosef's return from Rome that the full Sanhedrin—all members from all factions—had met. And the first since long before that to be so quiet. Yosef felt the impact of Menahem's death, too. Though the man was not revered or even liked by most within the chamber, his death had cast a pall over them all.

They had collectively given Rome sufficient grounds for war, and all was beyond remedy. The portents in the sky and within the Temple, observed by so many, *even my own eyes*, thought Yosef, had foretold what had come to pass for their nation. They had offered the Romans in Herod's palace the hand of surety and then had slaughtered them, and the stench of the dead and burned bodies now smothered the righteousness many had felt when they fought back after Gessius Florus's massacre.

The blood drawn by Zealots and Sicarii stained them all. It colored them individually, as citizens of the city, and as inhabitants of the country—as rebels. In Roman eyes, there would be no distinction of who among them might be presumed to be innocent. All were guilty and must be punished for their transgressions. And the devout among them feared more ill-omened visitations from heaven as much as or more than the vengeance of Rome. Yosef had never felt or seen his city and his people more dejected.

His father was speaking with Shimon ben Gamliel, the Sanhedrin president, with his assistant, Yehudah ish Krioth, at his side. Yosef was surprised to see Eleasar in his customary position as the Temple guard captain, beside his brother Matthew and the third guard officer. He, too, looked severe and sober. The mantle of rebellion weighed heavy on those who had—through act or omission—set Judea on its current path. Nearby, the High Priest's seat was empty, and Yosef did not see Mathias ben Theophilus among the members within the chamber.

"Attention... attention everyone," Shimon ben Gamliel announced, as though there was the usual side chatter or arguing that needed to be silenced so the meeting could begin. "We all know what has happened and we cannot change the past." His eyes scanned the room. "We must now discuss the future." He put a hand on Yosef's father's shoulder. "You all know Mathias and value his experience and wisdom, his and that of our Temple guard captain"—he gestured toward Eleasar. "They have accepted leadership roles in the newly formed Judean Free Government. They will lead us, our city and country, as we face the Romans."

Yosef saw the concerned but not quite doubtful look on his father's face. It was the same expression he had worn as he explained his decision to him and Matthew that morning. He had said, "If I have a prominent role, then I have a voice in assigning roles and responsibilities in any discussions or negotiations that I hope we can have with Roman authorities or leaders, or in choosing the commanders of our forces that I fear will be in combat against them."

The chamber stood to congratulate the two men. As Yosef watched, he saw Yakov, Miriam's former betrothed, and Yonahan ben Zaccai come forward and shake his father's hand. A large, bulky man stood and approached Eleasar and cast a sour look at his brother Matthew, who ignored him. It was Yonatan, Leah's firebrand husband. Yosef knew he had been petitioning for a role as a combat leader and feared for anyone led by that man. He settled back in his seat on the bench as others returned to theirs. He would listen to all about the new government but felt there was little that could or would be said that would make any of them feel better at facing the reality of war against Rome.

ACT III

LXIX

ANTIOCH

The residence of the Roman legate of Syria and the Judean provinces was not as ornate or extravagant as Florus's in Caesarea, though his rank was higher than that of the Judean procurator. Florus lived in a palace constructed by a king such as Herod who had built many edifices to celebrate himself. With a handful of messages, including that procurator's latest, now at his side, Cestius Gallus turned to look at his own home. The most palatial in Antioch, it had been constructed by order of two senators sent by Emperor Caligula nearly thirty years before to inspect the area after a massive earthquake had destroyed much of this city the Roman emperors favored. The third-largest city in the empire, behind Rome and Alexandria, Antioch was an excellent capital for the eastern part of the empire, and they wanted to shape it into an eastern Rome. A great temple to Jupiter Capitolinus rose on Mount Silpius with two long colonnades constructed nearby, and a forum of the Roman style had been laid out. They had built other colonnades and vast numbers of baths—named after the Caesars—with new aqueducts to supply them. The Roman client-King Herod had erected a long stoa on the eastern slopes where the city rose in stages above the river. The Circus of Antioch, a hippodrome used for chariot racing, was a replica of the Circus Maximus in Rome and measured sixteen hundred feet in length and one hundred feet in width. Eighty thousand spectators could attend the races, and other events held there matched the entertainment available in Rome.

Gallus turned back to look out from the bow's point of the extensive terrace that jutted from his domus and commanded a stunning view of the city from the heights that climbed Mount Casius. He and Lady Octavia next to him watched as the sun sank into the western horizon. The city with its sprawling population of a half million people had long ago recovered from the earthquake's devastation. He took great pleasure at the view, and in his lucrative position as a career politician. His ambitions had not run to intrigue and guile—the jostling and positioning of Roman politics. He had been content to rise no farther than where he was; he did not need to sit or live astride the political mountaintop. Now all he had enjoyed was likely ruined by events he could not stop and now must confront in a way he had never expected when he had assumed his duties as legate.

"King Agrippa is right, Cestius, and you have made the right decision about ordering the Twelfth Legion to get ready for a forced march."

He did not look at her but said, "My men and officers don't know yet what the preparation is for nor where they will fight." He noted that the yellow-orange sun had now shaded to a crimson that tinted the sky and underbelly of the clouds. "But I've called an officer's briefing."

The legate gauged the fall of the sun and thought, *Not long, and I will have to tell them.* He was not comforted by what Agrippa had said to him a short while ago, here in the late afternoon sun that seemed to have lost its warmth. Agrippa and other leaders from the independent states and free cities would march with him and contribute another fourteen thousand men, gathering them as the Twelfth Legion mobilized and moved south. The number of auxiliaries assembled from the free cities, men who were not as skilled in war as legionaries, made up for it with their readiness to give free rein to their hatred of the Jews. With them, the Twelfth and the supporting units pulled from other legions in the area, he would lead a force of more than thirty thousand men against Judea—against Jerusalem and its rebels.

Still, combat was not something he relished—he had no experience of it, but some of his peers and officers did. Gallus looked at the sheaf of messages he gripped. On top was the most recent from the Judean procurator, Gessius Florus, asking again—almost demanding—that the legate bring a legion to Jerusalem to take the city and impose Roman rule on the rebels. It was what others wanted, too. Agrippa and the leaders of the free towns in the region had experienced the disruption and violence brought about by the Jewish rebels, and that had resulted in their anti-Jewish elements rising in anger, which threatened their own leadership. He shook his right fist holding the sheets of parchment as if that could change their contents and rearrange the words to form what he wished. Instead, the last but most important item at the bottom was the message from Rome advising him that a new procurator for Judea had been selected. He was heartened to hear that but dismayed that he would not arrive for another one to two months. Rome had also pointedly told him the Jewish rebellion was his problem and his responsibility to fix when now it seemed only force could be the solution.

* * *

Though well into the beginning of fall, with an occasional stray cool breeze swirling for a moment's respite, Nicanor sweated. A week before, the legate's staff officers had ordered a full training cycle, including all officers and men in full armor and field equipment. He could have donned the lighter lorica hamata, chain mail made of iron and bronze rings. But his thirty-thousand-ring mail, which had taken an armorer a month to make, had gone down with the Salacia, and its replacement—what had been on hand at the time of their rescue— had been the lorica segmentata armor he had worn for so many years in the heavy infantry. Made of iron hoops fixed to leather straps, the two semicircular sections laced together with hinges, tie rings, and buckles made of brass, enclosing his torso. The shoulder guards and breast and back armor plates added further protection. The padded undertunic relieved some of its pressure points and abrasion but was now pounds heavier and sodden with perspiration. Still, he wore the segmentata effortlessly, long accustomed to its weight and discomfort. Careful of the leather cuff, he wiped his forehead with his right forearm. Maybe—as a medium between the two types of armor—he should switch to lorica squamata, made of small overlapping metal plates like the scales of a fish to give it strength. That style was not as weighty as segmentata but also gave less protection. So, if—as he suspected—the Twelfth was being readied for some purpose or mission, he would stick with what he wore, as uncomfortable as it might be.

Nicanor patted the rump of his horse which he had become fond of, and the horse—after working through a fiery reluctance to being ridden—had granted him grudging respect and seemed to even like him in return. Abigieus, a roan, was the largest horse he had ever seen—easily two hands taller than others—and he had caught the trader in dire financial straits and willing to sell to him directly instead of at the Antioch auction. There he feared his money lenders would take the horse as payment—though its value would be far more than what he owed. Abigieus had since proven he could bear without strain or loss of endurance both Nicanor's weight and that of his armor and equipment. He and the horse stood together on a hillock, one of many that dotted the great plain five miles across and ten miles long, between Mount Taurus and Mount Lebanon. The river Orontes, winding its course, split the plain unevenly.

Twenty miles from the sea, Antioch itself sat on the eastern bank of the river. It was now behind Nicanor, at some distance, as he faced his men. He had been a soldier for most of his life and had always believed the Roman army, its legionary were the finest fighting men of any country anywhere in the world. They were the elite, and the scope and size of the Roman Empire—and its longevity—proved it. And as he had worked his men through the week's series of drills, he realized that the men he had assumed command of a year ago had finally met that ideal.

Reshaping the focus of his centuria's young optio and its jaded tesserarius had taken a lot of sweat and even blood. He was not as lax as the unit's previous commander and far more physically demanding, and after several months of hard training, the lieutenant and sergeant were leading men who were now looking like real Roman soldiers.

Cupping his hands around his mouth to channel his command, he barked out, "Cuneum formate!" one of the core movements Roman soldiers were expected to execute immediately and smoothly. He watched as the men formed a wedge, its point formed by his best men, to focus the formation's offensive—and killing—power. He called out to them what he had said more than a thousand times in months past: "A sharp point drives deep into the body, and the widening mass behind splits your enemy's line, separating them and breaking their defense." He had thundered that at his men until they got it down to a precision movement.

When he had been in Rome—one of the unexpected benefits of having been stuck in that metropolis for months—he had spoken with veterans who had served in other provinces and regions. One, a retired centurion with an eye gone and missing half of his right arm below the elbow, had told him of how—only four years before—in a battle between Londinium and Viroconum, in provincial Brittania, his wedge had broken an Iceni charge with a volley of spears. Then they had advanced through the packed lines to break the much larger force and defeat Boudica, the Queen of the British Celts. He had not forgotten that, and though he never thought he and his men would face the likes of the raging Iceni, he had also learned in battle to always expect the unexpected.

"Triplex acies!" he ordered, and his men quickly shifted from the wedge and into three rows, a centuries-old formation he believed was still practical in battle. The hastati, in light chain mail, were in the first row, followed by the principes, in heavier armor, then the most veteran of the unit's men, the triarii, wearing the heaviest armor and armed with the best weapons. At the front of the formation and ahead of the hastati, in a Roman improvement on the Greek phalanx, were the newest men—bare or lightly armored recruits armed with pilum.

Their javelins were seven-foot-long wooden shafts that had pyramid tips and soft iron shanks that deformed when used once--so the enemy could not turn the weapon on them. On order, these men would hurl their pila at the enemy and then quickly get behind the triarii.

He nodded at his men as they settled into position and awaited his next order. "Testudo." The rows pulled in and formed close ranks. The front of the formation kneeled, interlocking their three-foot-high scuta. The second rank overlapped their own shields above the men in the first rank to form a cover for them. The third rank repeated this to protect the second rank. The men on the flanks and rear presented and locked their shields to seal the turtle formation, creating an intimidating defensive barrier.

"March. Forward." The ranks of men—a mass of shields bristling with spear points—moved toward him. "Halt. Sidestep. Right." The turtle stopped and then shifted sideways. "Halt. Sidestep. Left." He stopped them directly in front of him. "Rest." The men straightened, spread out, and settled their shields' bottom rims on the ground at their feet. Nicanor had seen a horseman leaving one of the nearby groups of men on the plain and now heading toward him. The rider and horse were covered in sweat-caked dirt, and the rider did not dismount but leaned down to him. "Officers meeting, all centurions at the commander's residence, horam prima noctis, the first hour after sundown."

* * *

Though Nicanor knew it meant hundreds, possibly thousands of deaths—maybe even his own—the sight of a full legion aligned, arrayed and ready to move out to fight a battle stirred him. In his lifetime he had not sought a wife or children. In truth, the army, his men, had long ago replaced thoughts of them. He pushed away any desire for a family until the day he would retire. But even as old a veteran as he was, that day seemed very far off at the moment.

He knew Cestius Gallus was not a military man, but Nicanor approved of what he had just done. He passed review of the legion, pausing to nod at each centurion and offer him a grim, resolved look. It was a moment of personal and professional connection he had not expected from the man. And then he had actually stopped to greet Nicanor, his brief comment recalling and thanking Nicanor again for escorting him and his wife to Jerusalem at the Jewish Passover.

A flashing thought of Lady Cleo, the boy Sayid, and Yosef came and went as he beheld the legate's ornate helmet—clearly rarely worn—glittering in the morning sun, and his elaborately decorated cuirass and body armor gleaming, unscratched and unscathed. It had never been worn outside of a convivium or epulum, private banquet or public feast the Roman nobles enjoyed and sometimes attended in full regalia. Nicanor always thought such events to be an excuse to emphasize the difference in the classes of Roman citizens, so he avoided them unless ordered to attend. Gallus's scarlet paludamentum was attached to one shoulder by a silver fibulae in the shape of an eagle to match the legion's aquila, pinning the cloak in place. His crimson sash, the formal cincticulus, was not frayed, its edging still clean around his waist. Though untested and never bloodied, the man appeared earnest about his duties as the legion's commander.

That moment passed, and Nicanor watched as the legate returned to the front of the legion. With a signal from Gallus to the tribunus laticlavius, the second in command, the standard-bearer lifted the aquila. Orders cascaded from one to the next as each unit moved out.

Nicanor now focused on the primus pilus, the senior-most centurion in the legion who commanded the first cohort immediately ahead of his. That officer's movement would signal him and his men—a cohort of heavy infantry—to move out. Alongside them on Abigieus, he could envision the legion in the shape of a thrusting spear as it pivoted west toward the Roman road, the trading route that hugged the coast and ran south all the way to their first destination. The cavalry rode up front and, on the sides, where they could protect the flanks. In between were two rows of five cohorts of infantry and supporting mounted troops. Behind the main body of the legion were equipment, siege engines, and supplies, and then reserves followed by a rearguard mix of seven veteran units of heavy and light infantry capped at the end by two cavalry units. All formed the spear pointed at Ptolemais, twelve days away at a forced march. From there they would work their way to Jerusalem.

LXX

NEAR DAMASCUS

Sayid was more afraid than he had ever been. Even more than of the sharks he had fought while adrift at sea with Nicanor and Yosef. He rubbed the scar on his leg without thinking. It was not the bands of anti-Roman rebels that prowled the countryside, or the bandits and looters that would attack and kill anyone who had better sandals or maybe a cleaner tunic than they wore, that worried him. He had expected that kind of danger.

It was the four men that Lord Florus had insisted accompany him, men hand-picked by the centurion, Capito. Florus had told Lady Cleo the morning they left Caesarea that they were to protect Sayid and to see he arrived safely in Antioch with her letter to Lady Octavia. He had not needed to see the flash of warning in Lady Cleo's eyes as she faced him—her back to others—and handed him the message to take to Lady Octavia. The night before she had given him the most important ones, and he had secured them in a thin goatskin pouch the color of his skin that he had wrapped and bound like a bandage around his chest.

Once they had left Caesarea and made it to Damascus, the plan was to join a well-defended caravan on the major trade route from there to Antioch. As the four men were legionaries, he understood there would be contempt for him from them. He was only a Syrian auxiliary who had somehow been favored by a Roman noblewoman. Back in the world he had known before meeting Lady Cleo, such disregard was typical, and he was not surprised at how they treated him. Still, he had trained with the short sword, spear, and sling even while with her, so he could show his bravery and skill in combat, though because of his service to Lady Cleo he had doubted he would ever see a battle. But now a fight might happen soon, and he wondered how long they would wait. He could defend himself one-on-one, but he doubted what he could do against the four.

The rebels and bandits had been reported thickest around Galilee, and it was there he thought something would finally happen. But a day and then two passed with Galilee behind them. The continually watching eyes of the four brutes had grown blacker until they seemed as dead and implacable as those of the sharks in the sea.

A day's march from where the road they were on joined the heavily trafficked trade route, he woke early and rose to relieve himself. When he returned from the brush, they were waiting. As they circled and then rushed him, he turned to run, breaking past one of them—hoping to find a place to turn and face them with better odds—only to stumble and fall. As he scrambled up, pulling his short sword, a dozen men, long on the road as judged by their dirty clothing and matted beards, stepped from a copse of scrub trees and thick underbrush with blades in their hands.

"I don't know about this one," said the large snaggle-toothed man in front who must be their leader, "but those"—he jabbed the tip of his sword at the four—"they smell and look like Romans."

The legionaries whipped their weapons out and formed a square. Before they could move again, a whistling sound and a rush of something in the air went by Sayid's head. Three of the four Romans dropped with fractured skulls. A sickening thud and the crack of their forehead bones attested to the accuracy of the bandit slingers. The fourth man, bowed over and cradling his head, remnants of a pulped eye oozing down his cheek between his splayed fingers, screamed and raised his sword. He charged the bandit leader closest to Sayid. As the legionary leaped to plunge his sword into the bandit's chest, Sayid spun and ran, crying out, "They tried to kill me!" in the same language the robber had used. He tore through the thick waist-high shrubs clotted with a tangle of weeds, and behind him heard the sound of butchers' work as the bandits closed in on the Romans. Sayid was the raggediest-looking of the group, and obviously not a Roman, so he prayed they would let him go. They did. He ran for hours until he collapsed.

* * *

"It is most of a half day's journey from here," said the fat merchant who had stopped his line of donkeys and carts laden with beams of cedar to check on the scrawny young man who seemed the age of his youngest son. Surprised to be greeted by such a shabby youth on the run from someone or something, he answered his questions instead of moving on. He gestured toward six younger, burly but not yet fat versions of himself who carried stout staffs, four with blades belted at their waist, two with bows and full quivers. "My sons and I are going there to deliver an order to a client." He looked up at the darkening sky, dusk upon them, and studied the young man who had staggered from the thicket along the road and stumbled to a stop to ask them how far it was to Damascus. "We were about to stop for the night and will begin again early tomorrow morning to be in the city before the gates close for the night. Do you care to camp with us tonight and join us in the morning?"

Sayid unconsciously clasped at the pouch with Cleo's messages still strapped to his chest and nodded. "Yes. Thank you."

* * *

ANTIOCH

The fat merchant had known another merchant with regular trade to and from Damascus whom Sayid could join for the long trek into Antioch. After the introduction was made, Sayid was at the southern gate to Antioch several days later. As they approached, he saw a Roman sergeant and another soldier carefully watching the steady flow of people, mostly traders, passing into the city. With a wave of thanks to the merchant, Sayid dropped off the tail of the donkey cart and approached the soldiers. "Sir"—Sayid stopped and came to attention as he had been trained.

The sergeant's eyes raked him up and down. "What is it you want?"

"I have messages for the Lady Octavia, the legate's wife."

The sergeant grunted, "I know who the Lady Octavia is, boy. But you're not a routine courier."

"I come from Caesarea, bearing letters from her friend Lady Cleo, the wife of the procurator."

The sergeant straightened and stepped toward Sayid. "And why are you"—he scanned him again from worn sandals to mop of dirty hair—"entrusted to carry messages for and from a Roman lady and why were they not given to a regular messenger?"

"I'm Lady Cleo's friend," he corrected himself, "servant and the letters are urgent. They could not wait."

"Give them to me, and I will deliver them to Lady Octavia." The sergeant held his hand out.

Sayid stepped back. "I can't. My lady told me they must be delivered—by my hand to hers—to Lady Octavia personally."

The Roman sergeant lowered his hand and took another step closer to Sayid, waving at the other legionary to come forward.

"Sir, all I ask is that you send word to Lady Octavia that Sayid— that's me—she has met me once in Caesarea—that Sayid, who serves Lady Cleo, has important letters for her." He took a deep breath and let it out. "If she denies knowing me, I will then give them to you."

Even as he said these words, he worried that he would have to run again and figure out another way to reach Lady Octavia. Perhaps through Nicanor, if he could find him.

Without turning from Sayid, the sergeant ordered the other soldier, "Do as he asks." The soldier pivoted toward the gate. "And don't go at your normal snail's pace or I'll have you out here all night and all day tomorrow." The soldier walked faster.

* * *

"Are you sure you do not want to bathe first?" Lady Octavia had told Sayid to sit but now regretted the dirt drifting on her furniture from the boy's clothing and hair as he shook his head.

"No, my lady. It's important that I give you this now." He reached inside his tunic and plucked at the wrapping around his chest.

The Roman sergeant who had escorted the boy to her surged forward, his hand on the hilt of his gladius, the sword half-drawn. Lady Octavia stopped him when she saw the pouch and watched as Sayid withdrew squares of folded vellum and some other parchment from it.

"Lady, I believe this one"—he held up the Syriac letter—"is one you can read or could have translated." Sayid handed it to her. "And this"—he held up the next square—"explains everything and tells of where my Lady Cleo found that"—he pointed at the letter written in Syriac on gevil, the letter she held in her hand.

* * *

Sayid was cleaner and felt better than he had in two weeks. Lady Octavia, who had looked at him so doubtfully the evening before, had let him sleep on the kitchen floor and greeted him that morning with fresh pomegranate juice. He also noticed that a Roman soldier was not present with her.

"What you brought me was—is—shocking."

"My lady wanted you to share with your husband what was in the letters as soon as you can. She fears what will happen if he doesn't learn what's in them, and she knew he would listen to you."

"I think it's already started, and it may be too late." Octavia refolded the letters, the one whose language she had recognized and, with some help from the old woman who cooked for her, had read the night before and written out a translation. Her husband and thousands of Roman soldiers were headed into a battle—manipulated into a war—that seemed could have been avoided. "My husband has already gone with the Twelfth Legion and allies to attack

Jerusalem, with orders from Rome to kill every rebel in Judea standing in revolt against Rome." She looked up at the boy who was still so exhausted she thought he would fall asleep sitting there. She reached for a sheet of vellum, a bronze-tipped pen, and a small jar of ink and began writing. "I'm sorry, Sayid, but you must get this message and the translation of that letter to my husband as fast as you can. Thousands of lives are at stake."

LXXI

Without roads, Nicanor thought, the Roman army could not wield its power. The gods blessed the empire when the first Roman leader set a firm mandate. Secure the land, then build the roads to connect it all. And so, throughout all the lands the army held, the roads ultimately led back to Rome. He turned to look again for the rear of the column, out of sight in the distance. He raised a hand to rub where the armor chafed his neck. The primus pilum had listened to his complaint about the baggage unit. The carts and wagons carrying the legion's equipment and supplies and siege machinery had, as they marched, drifted back until it was at the tail of the legion, exposed and vulnerable without their rearguard troops.

Nicanor did not know Decius Speritus, other than that the First Centurion had previously served under the prefect of Egypt, Tiberius Julius Alexander, in Alexandria. He had had field command of one of the two legions that on Alexander's order had killed over ten thousand Jews that summer in an amphitheater—they had been protesting during a public assembly. Speritus was a sour man, at an age when if he did not retire himself, would be forced out of the army. The man was a blunted pugio, a blade no longer of use, Nicanor thought, and the man had replied to his complaint curtly—saying the baggage units were fine and that the legate approved of his letting them remain where they were.

Nicanor disagreed—that unit carried not just important siege equipment but also much of the foodstuffs and supplies for the legion. But he had held his tongue and directed Abigieus, who snorted his own disdain, to return and ride alongside his men. He would speak with the camp prefect once the legion was settled just outside Ptolemais. That man's job—third in command behind the legate and the senior military tribune—was to organize the legion, maintain and update its equipment, and set the training of the men and units. Canus Velius Protus had served with him and would listen. And maybe he had already observed what Nicanor had and planned to correct it. Nicanor checked the sky, shading his eyes with the flat of his hand. The sun slanting down in the mid-afternoon was bright and strong. Two, maybe three hours, and they should be at the encampment site outside Ptolemais by nightfall.

* * *

Canus Protus did not look well to Nicanor as he turned from supervising the four men placing a large wooden table in the command tent for the legate, Cestius Gallus's briefing. "Yes, I understand, Nicanor," he said, as he pressed his left hand against his stomach and held it there. "I noticed the position when all the units closed in and entered the encampment site." Sweat beaded on his forehead, and it blotched his undertunic where the armor padding had swathed his chest and shoulders. Large damp rings under his arms showed as he wiped his brow and used both hands to push greasy hair back from his forehead. "You're right. I'll talk to the unit's officer, and"—a look of something more than stomach pain passed over his face—"and I'll tell Decius Speritus." He sighed. "The First Centurion thinks killing Jews is easy. I've heard him boast. But in Alexandria that was just a slaughter in the confines of a city amphitheater, where the Jews were unarmed." Canus shook his head. "He should understand that's not what we face here."

Nicanor nodded, and a fleeting glimpse of Yosef's face flashed in his mind. He closed and opened his eyes. "Who called this staff meeting?"

"Galerius Equititus Senna." Canus shook his head again then cupped his chin with his left hand as if to steady it. "The senior military tribune says there are reports that Simon bar Giora, one of the Jewish rebel leaders, is nearby recruiting men. He wants us to strike and maybe cut off one of the heads of the rebel leadership. I think the town is called Zebulon." He motioned at an orderly who was unrolling a large map and weighing it down at the four corners with soft leather purses containing lead missiles for the auxiliary slingers. The camp-prefect's head bobbed, and he swayed.

Nicanor gripped his elbow and steadied him. "Canus, you should see one of the capsariors. They can give you medicine to help."

"I'll be fine—just a bit tired." Canus blinked and gestured toward movement at the opening that connected the command tent to the legate's private quarters. Cestius Gallus stepped in and went around the table to sit at its center and face the gathering group of officers. Canus glanced at Nicanor and saw his concern. "Okay. I'll seek one out after this briefing."

* * *

Two days had passed. This time the intelligence gathering—Nicanor almost laughed at that thought—had been correct. Only the timing was off. Simon bar Giora had been there, raising troops for the rebel army, but he had come and gone. This 'City of Men,' as Nicanor had heard the Judeans refer to the town, had few remaining in it—only the oldest and infirm along with the women and children. One man, not a tooth in his bald, wrinkled head, had told him that all the fit men of fighting age had fled to the mountains. Then the First Centurion, leading his cohort and two others including Nicanor's, had ordered the town pillaged and burned. When and if the Jews, many of them probably Galileans, returned, they would find a once-thriving, and estimable city turned into ruins. Then another order had been added—and Nicanor wondered by whose decision—to kill all the Jews left behind. A doubt flickered as Nicanor saw the town's young women running away with their children in their arms or pulled along by their mothers, and the old men and women hobbling trying to follow them. A few turned to fight.

Nicanor was a Roman soldier, a centurion, and would obey. He knew the Roman fist would not unclench, and its blows would not cease, until someone much higher than he had decided that enough Judean blood had been shed to loosen it. He gave the orders to his men and noted the ones who responded with alacrity and a gleam in their eyes, and the handful that also obeyed but with what seemed downcast eyes, an expression matching what he felt but did not show.

* * *

Nicanor reined in Abigieus and motioned to the cacula assigned to him: "Watch his head, or he'll knock the brains from yours." He and the horse both grew irritable when tired. There had been no sleep overnight in the ashes of Zebulon. Just past the third watch, a large body of the inhabitants had returned to the town and foolishly attacked. They had been wiped out. With the deaths of those they had left behind, there were probably two thousand corpses now feeding the carrion eaters where Zebulon had once existed. "Kaeso, tend to Abigieus. I go to meet with the camp-prefect."

"Centurion," the boy began as he led the horse to a water trough made of ox hide sealed with pitch and stretched within a wooden frame. As Abigieus dipped his muzzle deep, the boy continued: "Canus Protus died during the night."

LXXII

After an interminable wait, things were finally moving, Gessius Florus thought, as he watched the man Capito had recruited leave his office accompanied by the centurion. Cestius Gallus was finally bringing the Twelfth Legion and more from Antioch and this man—Geganius Murena—had been both a hastilarius, a weapons instructor, and a quastionarius, an interrogator. There could not be a better combination of skills for his new agent to infiltrate Jerusalem. A veteran soldier, a beneficiarius with twenty years' experience in specialized and secret assignments, who was also an expert with all weapons and interrogation—that was the man who could keep his Jerusalem mole to task and also find and eliminate those who had been killing his men in that rebel stronghold.

Florus returned to his desk and picked up the bundle of messages received that morning. The emperor had named his replacement, a Marcus Antonius Julianus—someone he did not know and had never heard of—who would be irrelevant if Nero, through Tigellinus, replied with his approval of what Florus had just sent him. His proposal and plan to further enrich the emperor—and himself, though that had not been stated—was sent in an emergency dispatch with the imperial courier who would return via ship directly to Rome. Then, when he had the emperor's continued support, being the procurator would not matter.

At the clank and clatter approaching his office, he looked up as the centurion stopped at his doorway. "What is it, Capito?"

"As I was leaving, lord, a rider arrived—"

"So"—Florus cut him off and returned to rereading the dispatches.

"Lord, he's from Ptolemais, from the Twelfth Legion's encampment. The legate Cestius Gallus sent him with this"—he held up an unsealed square of parchment and approached the procurator's desk—"requesting that you report to him immediately."

Florus took the message from the centurion. It was not written by some actarius from dictation—he recognized Gallus's writing. He looked up at the centurion without expression. "Tell the messenger I cannot come but will as soon as I am able." Once Capito was gone, he tossed the message into his burn basket and returned to his reading and thoughts of what was to come.

PTOLEMAIS

Nicanor watched as more men—the balance of Agrippa's troops and those gathered from the independent city leaders loyal to Rome—flowed in and the camp grew to massive proportions. *Thirty thousand men or more now.* He shook his head. He had never seen such a great force in the field. He turned to Tyrannius Priseus, whose promotion to camp-prefect had not changed his dour expression, frowned at Nicanor.

"You're no longer a pilus prior."

Nicanor blinked. "What?" Emperor Nero himself had conferred senior centurion rank upon him, his reward for saving the Lady Cleo during and after the *Salacia*'s sinking. He knew Priseus did not like him, but his promotion did not give him the power to demote other centurions.

Priseus's frown hardened. "The legate wants you to become primus pilum, the new First Centurion, and has promoted you." He shook his head. "Remember that you still report to me. Assemble your men. You and the tribune Galerius Senna are to lead twenty cohorts, including cavalry, south, against Narbatine and Joppa."

Nicanor studied the new camp-prefect who had not said a word about his predecessor, Canus Protus. *My friend,* Nicanor thought, *found dead—suspiciously—in a pool of vomited blood.* Instead of saying something about his friend's death, he held the words and instead replied, "Yes, sir." He would report to this superior officer's rank, but Nicanor would never trust the man and would watch Tyrannius Priseus closely. He had learned that fools can gain status and position from mere circumstance and not merit, and Nicanor's responsibility was to prevent any mistakes that could get him or his men killed.

LXXIII

The big roan stood out next to Galerius Senna's smaller brown horse. It was not the size that made the difference in the horses but their stance... their look. The brown was placid, unmoving beneath its rider. Abigieus shifted his weight, ears up... listening, watching... still on alert from the fighting. Nicanor stood beside him, patting his shoulder, the horse's coat matted with sweat, dirt, and a streak of blood—from a rebel who had nearly unseated Nicanor, though Nicanor had stabbed him through the neck. The Judean had not wanted to let go. The coarse coat and undercoat, the black hair mixed evenly with the white, always made Nicanor see Abigieus as a creature of mist and smoke. More elemental than animal—even more so standing next to the smooth, parade-shiny, dun color of the tribune's horse.

Abigieus snorted, not caring for the other horse standing so close to him. "Shh... steady." Nicanor took a palm full of grain from a small pouch tied to his saddle; cupping it, he held it under Abigieus's muzzle and quieted him. Just as with men, horses respected a smart, experienced leader who used them well and treated and rewarded them fairly. Those were actions that created loyalty and respect. This was something he had learned from men he had served with, recognizing their wisdom. *Wisdom that others*—he glanced up at the tribune Senna—*have not learned.*

The tribune was not a bad man, but like most inexperienced commanders—especially if they were administrators more used to offices and ink than fields of blood—they didn't fare well when leading men in combat the first time.

It had pleased Senna to be in command—and evidently still did, judging how quickly his patrician manner returned—but in the first hours of engagement, he had lost two hundred men to the rebels. Positioned above the Romans, they cast arrows and spears down on the patrols the tribune had ordered—disregarding Nicanor's advice to secure the heights above the winding trails around Mount Asamon and its adjacent lower hills.

I told him, Nicanor thought, before giving that order. And Senna's stupidity, or pride, or both... got two hundred legionaries killed. And now he was mad because, during the ambush, Nicanor pulled the rest of the men out of harm's way and sent units to encircle and work their way up the hills to take out the rebel positions. Once the Judeans had been cleared from the mountain and ledges above them, again without his asking the tribune, Nicanor had directed a sweep of the area. Even the best-equipped insurgents wore only light armor, and his heavy infantry had chewed through them, and now two thousand dead rebels littered the hills and trails. Nicanor's only mistake had been in not asking the tribune before giving the orders he knew were necessary to both use the men well, not exposing them to more danger than warranted, and to maneuver them to strike the rebels.

"We should regroup, Tribune," Nicanor said, looking up at Senna, "and then return to the city." The tribune had left half their force in Joppa. It had surprised Nicanor how unprepared and unprotected that city had been. The rebel fighters, at the Romans' approach, had fled into the nearby mountains. Now their bones would remain there. Nicanor had selected the units—all seasoned veterans of the legendary Thunderbolt legion—to pursue the rebels into the surrounding countryside. But the men they left behind in Joppa were unknown to him—contributed by the allies the legate had gathered to march on Judea—and many of them had the eyes of the kinds of animals that skulked in the shadows on battlefields at night, picking over the dead bodies.

"Then order them in, Centurion." Senna was gruff as he put heels to the brown, startling it, and moved off without looking at Nicanor.

He's not a bad man, Nicanor thought, just as he believed about the legate, Cestius Gallus, *but he does not know men*. Nicanor mounted Abigieus—the solid feel of his steadiness lifted his spirits—and, bracing his thighs to rise higher in his saddle, he surveyed the surrounding area and below where it flattened into the plain that ran toward Joppa. Bodies lay in tangled clumps, twists of arms and legs, some splayed out flat and face down or on their backs, with a few some distance from their dead companions. Those were the runners who tried to flee and save themselves. He looked once more at the tribune's back as his horse carefully descended the rocky path. *Senna does not understand the maneuvering of men—they are not pieces on a game board*, he thought and hoped the man would learn. Shaking his head, Nicanor turned to the cornicen. "Sound the recall and regroup order."

The soldier raised his cornu, its crossbar supporting the weight of the instrument on his shoulder, and he drew in a lungful of air. His horn blast bugled and echoed among the hills. Nicanor watched as, from a distance at different points, the men slowly followed the sound's origin to form up below.

* * *

Thinking the tribune should check the men—for it was his responsibility—Nicanor had hesitated. But as the night deepened, after a while, seeing that the flap of Senna's tent remained closed, he did it himself. A commander walking the camp after sundown and the day's last meal was a good means to connect with the men. It gave a commander a feeling for the tone and pulse of their attitudes and even capabilities. What did they do? Gamble, slouch, and complain? Were they sullen or in a good mood? Did they tend to their equipment or help new recruits by showing them how to be a man—a professional soldier—in a Roman legion? Getting a sense of that was critical in a time of war—especially after recent events.

The units the tribune had left in Joppa had killed thousands of old men, women, and children—far more than in Zebulon, easily four or five times more. And the three cohorts of cavalry that had been split off had taken the handful of small towns the Judeans called Narbatine, and hundreds had died there.

As Nicanor walked through the camp, he heard the talk as he went from one man to another, through the middle of the throng and circling the perimeter. The Thunderbolts—the Twelfth Legion's most seasoned veterans—muttered about wanting to fight against real soldiers and not civilians. They were loyal and would do as ordered—many were still enraged at what they had heard of the Judeans killing the Roman legionaries and auxiliaries in Jerusalem—but killing women and children was hard to bear if that was all there was to this war. The clusters of men exchanging that talk among themselves paused as he approached, and then continued and nodded to him as he passed. They knew he understood what they meant and how they felt.

As Nicanor made the full circuit and stopped at his own tent, he looked up at the sky. As a younger man, he had never thought much about the future, what it might hold. Since the *Salacia*'s sinking, the rescue of the unlikely collection of those he now called friends, and events in Rome, he found he had such contemplations more often. Moonbeams outlined the night clouds, and he wondered if Luna, the goddess, looked down on him—on all of them—from her chariot... and if she really did... did she bestow peace or madness on the Earth touched by her light?

LXXIV

ANTIOCH

"Yes, Lady Octavia," staff sergeant Arruns Vulso said, nodding. He understood what she wanted and wished he had not been the tesserarius on gate duty when that scruffy Syrian boy had shown up. He glanced at Sayid who, now cleaned up, looked better than when he had brought him to the legate's residence at the lady's direction. The lady's orders made him regret he had remained in the army another year. A retentus who had served past his twenty-five years was often well rewarded by a good commander. But he had not expected a shepherd's job to escort this scrap of a boy, not quite a man, through a region about to be stirred up by the Twelfth Legion essentially jamming a stick in an anthill to bring the ants out to be stomped upon.

"Futuo," he cursed under his breath. "So I'm to pick five good and trusted men," he repeated to her, "and we are to escort him"—he cocked a crooked thumb at Sayid—"to the legate who is with the Twelfth Legion in Ptolemais. And no one is to know he has been here and seen you." Arrun did not know the reason for the secrecy, or what this Sayid—who claimed to be an auxiliary—carried that was so important to give to the legate. But it must be urgent, based on the stern look on the lady's face, which told him he must succeed.

* * *

Lady Octavia watched the legionary sergeant leave with Sayid and then went to let her majordomus know he no longer had to keep the other servants busy and away from her private rooms. She trusted the man—he had traveled with them from Rome—but she trusted none of the others. Cleo's letter had told of spies in her own household and suggested the same might be true of Octavia's, even so far off in Antioch.

* * *

NEAR DAMASCUS

Sayid was happy riding and not walking or running as he had been for much of the way to Antioch, but when he looked at the sergeant, he could see the man was not content.

Arruns Vulso regretted that the legion's cavalry had taken the best mounts. Even the Lady Octavia's nudging had yielded only the knot-headed or oldest horses held in reserve. "She could've used her rank," he muttered. Clenching his thighs for a better grip, he lifted his body to rub his rump, sore from his horse's disjointed gait. But then, maybe she could not mount them better without drawing attention, and she had not wanted that.

"I'm sorry about the loss of your men," Sayid had said, trying to engage the sergeant in conversation as he had several times since leaving Antioch, but without luck. That morning, a day north of Damascus, they had lost two of their company in a daybreak attack by bandits or rebels—it was impossible to tell one group from another.

Arruns looked at Sayid. The boy had cut one attacker down with his short sword, coming awake and responding faster than any of them. His two men had been skewered—with stolen or captured Roman cavalry lances—as they struggled up from their bedrolls on the ground. Arruns was a veteran of field combat but for many years had been garrisoned in cities. He had not heard the attackers himself, and the boy had been quick to secure their horses that the raiders must have been after, killing one attacker in the process. Arruns rubbed his hip again, halfway wishing they'd taken his mount.

"You did well, boy. Got one bastard," the sergeant growled. He saw Sayid press his chest. "Were you wounded?"

Sayid dropped one hand to a saddle horn. "No, I'm fine." The thick bandage holding the letters was slipping, and he would need to tighten it when they stopped for the night. "How far to Damascus?"

"We're not going to Damascus, boy." Arruns straightened, glanced over his shoulder at the two other men trailing three or four horse lengths back, and pointed off to the right, southwest. "We're headed that way and will pass Caesarea Philippi... then Kedasa, two towns inland of our route, then straight to Ptolemais. We can refill our water at the springs at Caesarea Philippi."

Sayid half-turned, bringing his hand up without the sergeant seeing him, and pulled his tunic tight to his chest, patting it. No stopping in Damascus meant they would camp out in the open again and not until past sundown. The sergeant had already told the other men, who had complained, "We make our distance while we have daylight... legionaries can rest when they're dead."

* * *

Sayid looked at them sprawled in the sun, a dead horse near one body. The blood had pooled under them and spread, soaking the dirt and forming a now-crusted, clotted brown blanket beneath them. They had all ridden into an ambush, and the two men now rested in Elysium for eternity.

"Will they come back?" Sayid turned to the sergeant who was wrapping around his bleeding neck a scrap of cloth torn from his undertunic. An arrow had struck his shoulder bone and bounced up to slice beneath his ear.

"You bet they will. And they weren't after horses, boy. I don't think they are bandits—maybe they once were—but now they've got Roman arms and equipment, and someone's been training them. They timed their attack perfectly." He looked over at his horse, the only one left. Sayid's horse had thrown him and taken off with the other when the two men went down, and they disappeared, more agile and moving faster than they did with a rider. Arruns's knobby, sway-backed creature didn't look so bad to him now. The boy had an arrow stuck in the thick part of his thigh, both hands around it, with blood puddling beneath them. Pulling it out would make him bleed faster, and there was no way he could make a run for it. Arruns looked at his horse again.

"Tesserarius Arruns, where are you going?" Sayid looked up from his blood-soaked leg.

Arruns thought about the years of blood and sweat—he was so close to retirement—*just go, run. Who would know?* Belly to the ground, he moved steadily under another volley of arrows toward his horse. He could make it before they charged.

"Sergeant!"

Arruns heard the boy's cry and then the louder voices of the Judeans approaching, taunting and insulting them. They would soon close in to finish them with blades. He shot a look at Sayid, who looked back at him. Who would know he had left some Syrian boy to die? And who would care? He felt the boy study his face and then let his gaze fall away as his head slumped to his chest. The feeling he had in response to that dejection hurt worse than the torn flesh that had gaped open again and poured blood down his chest. Arruns would know what he had done, and it would haunt him. Even after so many years... he cared.

"I'm coming to you, boy. I'm coming, Sayid." He stood and gripped his gladius, and a rivulet of blood mixed with sweat ran down his arm and onto his hand to flow onto the blade and drip from its hilt. Stepping toward Sayid and then past him, he moved to stand, legs spread shoulder width, weight centered and raised his sword as the first of the rebels came into sight.

NEAR GISCHALA

"Where am I?" Sayid was dazed and in pain, but he knew he wasn't with Romans anymore. "Where am I?" he asked in Aramaic again but louder, shaking off a vivid dream of his mother. Would he live to see her again or ever find his father? He sat up, wincing at the jolt of pain through his leg. But someone had taken the arrow out and wrapped a rough dressing around his thigh. His bound hands went to his chest, thank the gods the bandage-hidden letters were still there.

A high window set in the wall to his right let dim light in. His stiffness and the dried blood told him it must be morning. He raised his hands again, this time to his head, and discovered caked blood and pain there too. The gash seemed only an inch or two long, but he couldn't tell through his thick matted hair. He remembered seeing the sergeant—Arruns—with three arrows in his chest, then a javelin pierced him, and that did what the bolts had not. He had fallen in front of Sayid, facing the attackers. As the Roman dropped, something had crashed into Sayid's head, likely from a slinger. Sayid bowed his head to hold it in the palms of his tied hands. The legionary had not abandoned him.

"You don't look like or sound like a Roman soldier," someone said loudly with a voice that rang off the stone walls.

Sayid looked up, his eyes adjusting to the light, and he could see a man with a short sword belted at his hip and a Roman pilum in his hands. "I'm not," he replied. "They were taking me to meet someone. Who are you?"

"Who I am is none of your concern. But who you are, to be escorted by Romans, interests me, and I'm sure when my leader returns, you'll find out how much. He will find out who you are and why you would be with Roman legionaries, not in a force under an aquila or other unit standards. Who were you to meet and why?"

The man approached Sayid, and the iron point of the spear stopped an inch from his stomach. "I'm nobody." Sayid felt the tip touch his ragged tunic. "But it's important I continue on my mission."

"You were with Romans, so it may be important to them—or to you—but not to us." He pushed the tip in, found flesh, and held it there. "I sent a message to my leader, and we'll see how he wants to deal with you."

* * *

Sayid heard two men arguing in a Galilean dialect and kept his eyes closed. It had been days, and though they had brought him a little food and water, no one had spoken to him again.

"The traitors of Sepphoris just opened their city to them, those Rome-lovers... and the Roman Twelfth Legion just rode in like they owned it."

Another, deeper, voice commented, "Yohanan is furious that any in Galilee would embrace the Roman fist, after what the Roman procurator has done. He returns tonight from meeting with Simon bar Giora."

"He cannot stand that man."

"War makes strange allies. We must stand together against the Romans. Now, stop talking and let's get this done."

The two men entered the room carrying large buckets of water and a blanket, and one had a folded pile of what looked like clothing under one arm. They sat them in front of Sayid. "You are to wash up and put these on," said the smaller man with the deep voice, and nudged the worn tunic and robe with his toe. "Our leader Yohanan ben Levi will question you, and he has smelled enough Roman stink on the wind."

"I'm not Roman," Sayid said in Aramaic, as he cupped a handful of water to his mouth.

"Wash, don't drink." The large man picked up and dumped one bucket on Sayid. "I don't care who you are."

Sayid did not drink again and washed the dried blood from his leg, wincing at the red flesh surrounding the wound. He felt the water that had been poured over his head had loosened the letters strapped to his torso, and he grabbed at them.

"What is this?" The small man pointed at Sayid's chest.

"Nothing," Sayid gasped when he put weight on his wounded leg as he tried to move away. "It's just—"

The large man tore the strip of cloth from Sayid, and the flat, dark oiled-hide pouch fell at his feet. The small man bent to grab it as the larger man pushed Sayid back. The man opened the pouch and fingered the sheets of vellum and parchment. "Letters... messages!"

"Please be careful with them—they're important!"

The man put them back in the pouch and tucked it into his sash at his waist. "Yohanan, our leader, will decide if they are... to us... and whether you will live or not."

LXXV

NEAR CAESAREA

"The procurator Gessius Florus is here, Lord Gallus."

Cestius Gallus looked up from the camp desk that had been set in place only hours before and was already covered with messages and dispatches. "Bring him in," he said with a nod at his orderly. As soon as the legion arrived at the encampment site a mile east of Caesarea, he had sent a messenger to bring the procurator to him.

Gessius Florus entered, the orderly waiting outside the tent within earshot should the legate need him. "Lord Gallus, it is good to see you again."

"I sent for you hours ago." Cestius Gallus doubted that Florus was happy to see him. "And you did not report in Ptolemais."

"Your messenger—today—had trouble finding me, lord. I came as soon as I knew you asked for me. And"—Florus came closer to stand in front of the legate's desk—"unfortunately, local demands kept me from coming to Ptolemais. Then when I was able, I heard the Twelfth Legion was moving south, so I waited until I knew where." Florus's smile did not reach his eyes. "And here you are, and you have had some success, lord... at Zebulon and Joppa... and in Sepphoris without a fight. Do you now plan to march on Jerusalem?"

"Soon, Procurator." Cestius Gallus stood up. "Before I do, I want to know what you will do that aids our efforts."

Gessius Florus's smile—more a smirk—held, as he replied, "Lord Gallus, my replacement has been selected, and he is expected soon... likely within the next month. I intend to stay out of the way, and not incite the Jews nor the Judeans further. I will await the emperor's decision on my new role for when I am no longer a procurator."

"And do you believe you will have one?" the legate asked curtly.

"Surely, Lord Gallus"—Florus's smile was now genuine—"I have much value to offer the emperor—and to Rome—and I believe he agrees with me."

NEAR JOPPA

"You asked for me to join you, Tribune?" Nicanor shed his hooded, oil-treated waterproof cloak, a paenula, as he appeared before the man. He did not wear the hood, preferring to let his head get wet than to not be able to see from the corners of his eyes during the heavy October rains of Judea.

"Orders from the legate," Galerius Senna said, motioning to a soldier even more drenched than Nicanor. "Lord Gallus directs us to make a southerly sweep." The tribune waved Nicanor to a table littered with scrolls of parchment and a map held down by the tribune's spatha. The heavy long-sword held the center flat but left the opposing corners to curl. "First to Lydda... then Antipatris, a Jewish stronghold there, a fortified tower called Aphek. Then east and north of Jerusalem to join the legate and the bulk of the Twelfth Legion at Gibeon. From there, we will prepare for an assault on Jerusalem."

Nicanor studied the route and locations of the towns, the land they had to cover and the likely fighting within or around them... not to mention fending off raids and strikes while marching south. "When do we need to be in Gibeon, tribune?"

"What do you mean?"

"How long will it be before Lord Gallus is in Gibeon? If we are to clear Lydda and Antipatris of rebels, Lord Gallus's part of the legion can bypass those towns with no delay for action and head straight to Gibeon." Nicanor could see the tribune was not following his question or its importance. "Do we—will we—have the proper time to both cover all this territory," he swept a hand over the map, "and to attack two cities? Or does the legate expect us in Gibeon within a precise time?"

Galerius Senna's face stiffened. "Lord Gallus will move quickly from Ptolemais, stop briefly at Caesarea, and then go on to Gibeon. He expects us to do the same—move swiftly while following his orders and meet him there as soon as possible."

Nicanor knew by the tribune's expression he must watch how he spoke to him, not letting that "teaching-a-green-recruit" gruffness into his voice. "Yes, Tribune. I'll assemble the unit commanders and issue the orders. We'll move out as soon as we've formed up."

NEAR GIBEON

Nicanor was beginning to believe this Judean leader, Simon bar Giora, was nothing but a story. First, he had been at Zebulon and then he was not. And then at Lydda, where he was believed to be, they found the city mostly deserted and the few dozen remaining claimed all the other Jews were headed to Jerusalem for one of their festivals,

Sukkot. He rubbed the sweat from his eyes. No one journeys to a festival when at war; he shook his head and studied the tribune's back just ahead of him. He had not had time to talk to Galerius Senna since leaving Antipatris. "We burned Lydda as we should have since the Judeans more or less abandoned it," he said loud enough for the tribune to hear him. "And we should have destroyed their tower in Antipatris, though leveling it would've taken more time. But, Lord Senna, rooting the Judeans from the tower and the town was a minor accomplishment. We learned that this Simon bar Giora—again—had been there days before but wasn't there then. Now that we've left the area the Judeans will move back into that fortress."

"Not the dead ones." The tribune did not turn to look at Nicanor. They had neared Gibeon and just ahead was a group of riders coming into view. His attention was on them.

"Yes, Tribune, not the dead," Nicanor agreed. He reined Abigieus obliquely and goosed him, heeling him to come alongside the tribune. The sun glinting off armor was clear now and meant the horsemen were likely either the leading edge of the army's advance converging with them on the same road or the tail of the legion they were overtaking. He had expected to find them settled in Gibeon already. What had delayed them?

* * *

"And the Judeans were led by a man we have heard of," Tyrannius Priseus said as he lifted a scrap of parchment in his hand and read from it. "This man... is Simon bar Giora. One of the wounded Judeans named him and boasted before he died that he—Simon—would be the leader to kill more Romans than any of the other rebels."

The legate's command tent held only the most senior officers and centurions. Nicanor glared at the camp-prefect who stood before them. How could that man stand there and report that the Judeans had killed over five hundred Roman infantry and cavalry and lost only twenty-two of their own men, and not show shame? The baggage unit with the bulk of the legion supplies again lagged behind the formation and the raiders, led by this Simon bar Giora, had picked it apart. They took away with them much that the legion needed. Nicanor shook his head. Never had he heard of that happening to a Roman legion. Earlier they had also been told that the legate had secured a soothsayer in Caesarea who would read the signs and portents. He hoped the portents showed the gods' favor would return to them because things were not going as they should. No matter that the reporting came from someone he now distrusted—the new camp-prefect... facts were facts. So many killed and so much lost, and they had yet to reach Jerusalem.

LXXVI

NEAR GISCHALA

It had been a week since the two men had taken the letters from him. Sayid gathered the slack of the chain in his bound hands and hobbled to the wall with the high window to turn his face up to the morning light. It would not last long, as the sun would soon pass the opening of the narrow window. Lady Cleo had told him of the letters' contents, including her message to Lady Octavia. But even if he could escape—he rattled the length of chain—the legate, Cestius Gallus, would never believe a story told him by some young Syrian auxiliary unknown to him. Sayid had only verbal messages he would claim came from the legate's wife. Nicanor might vouch for him, but he doubted anyone else would believe him. And Octavia's seal on her letter to Gallus would certainly be broken.

A noise at the door caught his attention. Other than the serving of a meager ration and a little water once a day, he had been left alone—at least not mistreated, though the chain and shackle chafed his ankle. His thigh wound still pained him, but it was healing.

Depending on how the rebels interpreted the letters, his situation could change for good or for ill. Soon they would determine that the messages, in Latin, were to and from Romans, one of whom was leading the Twelfth Legion through Judea. Sayid had overheard the talk from his guards that the legion had already killed thousands of Judeans. Sayid hoped they would read the messages through enough to see—before they killed him outright—that one was a plea to Cestius Gallus. His wife and Lady Cleo asked him to consider the information the other messages contained about the procurator instigating events leading to the war. The women asked Gallus to stop all reprisals and military action against the Judeans so there could be a chance to resolve the issues between Rome and the rebels peacefully.

If only Sayid could have time to explain his mission... that might make the difference. On the other hand, if the rebels didn't want peace, the letters might not help him at all.

The door rattled again, its outside bar or latch shifted or released, and opened into the room. The two men from before entered—the large one with a high voice and the smaller man with the deep voice. The smaller man held a key.

"Come away from the wall," the large man ordered. "Stop in the middle... there... and don't move."

When Sayid stopped where directed, the small man knelt. Taking the bent metal loops that attached the shackle to his ankle and to their counterpart that passed around and through the loops, he twisted the padlock toward him. It was a type Sayid had seen before at slave markets and never thought would be used on himself. The Roman barbed-spring padlock that secured the shackle took a shaped key to release. The small man inserted the four-inch piece of curved metal in his hand into the side keyhole and turned it, and the lock popped open.

"Don't move," the larger man warned Sayid again.

"I won't..." The relief Sayid felt made him want to reach down and rub his ankle, but he stood still. "Are you taking me somewhere? Is your leader here and now wishes to question me?" He didn't regret the hopeful sound in his question. "I must speak with him—it is to his benefit and yours."

The small man stood as the big one gripped Sayid by his upper arm and squeezed tighter than the ankle shackle had, and the man push-pulled Sayid toward the door.

"I must talk to him about the letters you took from me," Sayid said again, worried at their silence. "Please."

The small man kicked him and gestured toward the door. "Move."

* * *

Sayid was not sure how long he and his two keepers waited in what seemed to be an antechamber while two men inside talked at first, then argued. One voice—the loudest—seemed to show the speaker's disdain.

"I cared little for the priests and politicians in Jerusalem before all this started... and your talk does little to change that. This new Judean government you describe sounds like more of the same."

"Yohanan ben Levi"—the answering voice now struggled to maintain the calm tone it had held up to that point—"you've heard the news. The Roman Twelfth Legion is a juggernaut unleashed on us. Towns have been destroyed, thousands upon thousands killed. We must all stand together... or we will die in pieces... one village, one town, one city at a time."

"—Like Sepphoris stood with you and the Judean leaders." Sayid could hear the contempt in the man's voice. "They believe in these men in Jerusalem?" The man's bark of laughter cut off his own words. "So far the only ones to fight against the Twelfth Legion—other than my men—are Simon bar Giora and his men. And I cannot abide him. He is too much a Judean."

"He, too, has been asked to come to Jerusalem."

"I know that, Yohanan ben Zaccai." Again, the voice dripped with contempt. "And if he should go to Jerusalem, I will as well, but not before... and only then to speak out against any untruths told about me and to advocate what I believe should be done to defeat the Romans."

That ended their discussion. Sayid heard footsteps, and his guards moved him away from the chamber's entrance. An older Galilean, portly and more scholarly looking than a rebel, came out. He glanced once—piercingly—at Sayid and his keepers, then quickly left.

"Bring him in!" the arrogant voice—still loud—commanded.

Sayid, still looking at the departing figure, felt that large hand squeeze and push him toward the voice. Inside the room, he saw the man it belonged to.

"You look little like a Roman, despite your auxiliary clothing," the man said. He held the bundle of parchment and vellum in his hand.

"Because I'm not one..." Sayid replied. He wasn't sure how to treat or address this man, so he bowed his head.

"That deference shows me you must not be one, then." Yohanan ben Levi waved the three of them forward—Sayid's two keepers now had claw-fingered grips on his upper arms. "But don't bow your head, boy. I'm not some Roman who assumes due respect because of his title or position. But these"—he fingered through the letters—"these are Roman. And now you fear you stand before a man who can determine your life or death. Tell me why I should not kill you. You're either some skulking spy or a courier, both of which serve Rome."

Sayid straightened, not trying to shake off the hard-handed holds on him but also no longer accepting them. He tensed his arm and stomach muscles and met the rebel leader's glare. "I am a courier—a messenger—but if you can read any of those"—he nodded his head at the man's fist full of messages—"you know it's important I deliver them to the Roman legate, Cestius Gallus, who leads the Twelfth Legion against you, against Judea."

Yohanan ben Levi stepped closer. Sayid saw in his face the severe lines, deep channels on either side of a hawk nose, the deep-set eyes, and ebony glint that flickered as if stoked by the man's hatred of Romans and their authority.

"I had someone who could read a part for me. And I'm not sure you must be alive to deliver these letters. Or—if we dumped you near the Twelfth Legion, someone could find them on your body."

LXXVII

The leaders of the new Judean Free Government had deferred to tradition. Though they needed to convene and make decisions, they would observe Sukkot while the Roman Twelfth Legion slaughtered their people and moved ever closer to Jerusalem. Yosef shook his head. The first day of the Feast of Tabernacles was treated as Shabbat, which meant no work was done, and on the next six days, the Choel Haomed, only certain necessary work was permitted. "The Romans will not stop, or even slow, for any holiday of ours."

His father's sharp look at him reminded Yosef of when, as a boy, he had questioned tradition when it made little sense to him. But he knew his father, too, was worried about forming a new government. He feared it would be little more than a new name for the old way of governing the Judean people.

"Yohanan ben Zaccai has not returned with Simon bar Giora and Yohanan ben Levi," Mathias said with a shake of his head. "And they must be a part of this, Yosef. We need to coordinate with them."

Yosef nodded, for his father was right. But those two men would not likely even agree to meet to jointly make decisions and to plan. They would remain at opposite ends of any discussion and challenge each other's intelligence and leadership. *And if we cannot decide... cannot plan... it dooms us,* Yosef thought. And maybe they would have the same outcome even with all the thinking and planning in the world.

"But we have decided about the new coins," Matthew said. "Gather all the silver, all the Roman coins and smelt them to re-mint. Right, father?"

Yosef couldn't tell if Matthew was making a joke to lighten the mood or was serious. Before their father could reply, Miriam spoke up.

"I heard they will have the words FREEDOM OF ZION on one side." Before their father could speak, Miriam continued: "And that will surely make a statement to all about our independence from Rome."

Yosef shook his head at Mariam's sarcastic tone and noticed the frown deepen on his father's face.

"Miriam, your words are disrespectful," Mathias said. "We must do things to establish that we no longer bow to Rome and are no longer ruled by the Romans."

"But coins, Father? That's one of the new government's first decisions? Silver is not the metal... and money is not the weapon to kill Romans." She hesitated. "Even I—just a woman—know that. And I know that killing Romans is the only thing that will make us safe and independent." Miriam rose and left, heading toward the stairs to her room.

"Rebecca!" Mathias called, and she came into the room. "I don't know what has gotten into Miriam, but—"

"She speaks her mind, Mathias, and I would rather have her do that than not have her own thoughts and opinions." Rebecca turned away, then paused. "All the decisions made in the past by our leaders, and those now... affect the lives of our children, Mathias, and the children of all parents in our country. The consequences will have an impact far beyond our lives and theirs. And yet there are people making decisions who assume we can defeat a Roman legion... one that has yet to arrive at our gates."

Yosef looked at his father's bowed head and agreed with his mother. And with Miriam, too. He wished—for the hundredth time—for Sukkot to be over and for Yohanan ben Zaccai to return with the two top rebel leaders. They—with Eleasar ben Ananias—controlled the forces their Judean provinces must turn into an army against the Romans, and somehow, they must defend their fortress city.

LXXVIII

OCTOBER 66 CE

GIBEON

At least he treats failure as a leader should, Nicanor thought as he listened to Cestius Gallus. "Not all the rebels have left for or are in Jerusalem for the Jewish holiday, Sukkot, as we were told," said the legate. "As we moved through the pass at Beth Horon, the rebels who had taken a position above, at its narrowest point, rained arrows and javelins upon us. The climb at that part of the pass was too steep, in the teeth of the rebels' fire, and we could not retaliate. As we pushed on, we killed a few of the rebels but lost five hundred men." He looked down at a scrap of parchment in his hand, continuing, "And those were mostly with the baggage and supplies units." Nicanor thought the legate's eyes slid sideways toward the camp-prefect, Tyrannius Priseus, sitting in the front rank before he continued. "Along with the men lost, the rebels captured some matériel." The legate paused and squinted at a man Nicanor had never seen before standing off to the side with the row of seated senior officers.

Nicanor, without seeming to, surveyed the other legion officers attending the briefing. Those men he knew well and respected had stern looks, showing the concern he felt. The legate was doing what he should, accepting responsibility without openly blaming who was truly at fault. But Nicanor knew that if you listen to fools... or bad advice... and act on it, then you own the consequences. The camp-prefect was responsible for the order to march through the pass and to keep the all-important baggage units safely in the middle of the formation. That had not been done, yet Tyrannius Priseus did not have one of the stern or concerned faces. He had no expression other than his shifting eyes, an elusive twitch as if other things were on his mind.

During the legate's lull, without planning to, Nicanor spoke up—"Were any units left behind to secure those key points in the pass?"

Cestius Gallus's eyes fluttered again toward his third in command, the camp-prefect. "No. It was determined best to continue at full strength to Gibeon."

"But Lord Gallus—"

Tyrannius Priseus—alert now—cut off Nicanor: "Why would we reduce the manpower needed to crush the rebels in Jerusalem, Centurion?"

"Because—and you know this—it's always prudent to secure a force's egress route. It's the legion's way out... behind us, Prefect."

"So, you expect the rebels will remain a threat once we have destroyed their largest city and their leaders?" Tyrannius Priseus shook his head, "Do the rebels instill such fear in you, Centurion?"

The man's taunt lay just beneath his words. Nicanor knew the strategic importance of the pass. From the plain of Aijalon, it rose twelve hundred feet to Beit al Tahta then ran along a narrow ridge between two valleys until it cleared into a widening that led to Gibeon. "It's a Roman road, Priseus." Nicanor had to hold his temper, but he refused to give the man the respect of his title. "As you saw, it is via glareta, gravel layered over banked and compressed earth in the ascents and descents, then via munita, stone-paved on its level sections. That road is the best means of moving men and equipment from our ports on the coast to the area surrounding Jerusalem." Nicanor locked eyes with the prefect. "It should be secured"—he turned to Cestius Gallus, who had followed their exchange—"when fighting a war."

"Thank you, Centurion," the legate said, stepping behind his work table to set the note down and motioning to the man who still stood off to the side, his head half-bowed—watching from under a tangle of black eyebrows with hands folded upon his chest. He walked over to join Cestius Gallus, who continued: "I have brought a haruspex from Caesarea—the diviner Spurinnus will tell us the will of the gods."

Nicanor reviewed all that worried him that tumbled around in his head. The poor decisions about the use and placement of units. Information promised to lead to the certain capture or killing of key rebel leaders that proved to be inaccurate or false. The two senior leaders of the legion, men who lacked field and combat experience, making decisions without the benefit of experienced veterans' advice, the current camp-prefect notwithstanding. And Nicanor now had doubts about that man's intent. He believed in the gods—and prayed to them in times of peril, mostly in battle—but like his misgivings about the camp-prefect, he had doubts about a soothsayer gleaning wisdom from looking into an animal's guts. He stood with the others and followed the legate from the command tent.

Outside, a thick rectangle of heavy stone had been stood on end and sunk a good two or three feet into the earth, with four feet of it still above the ground, and then topped with a flat stone that rested securely on the broad pedestal. Off to one side of the flat stone were two large earthenware bowls and a stone pitcher, likely containing water. A large curved-bladed carnifex, a butcher's knife, lay there, too, its edge glinting in the sun.

Spurinnus stepped up to the rough dais, poured water into a bowl and rinsed his hands, then dried them with a swath of cloth attached to his waist. He raised a hand, and a rooster was brought to him. The cock fought the auxiliary who had been designated the haruspex's helper. The youth had a hard time with the bird that twisted in his hands, trying to spur and peck him. The soothsayer darted a contemptuous look at the boy and took the bird himself. With a quick twist, he broke its neck, picked up the blade and within a minute had the animal sliced open, its liver removed, rinsed, and placed in the empty bowl. As he stood there, with a prod or two and a lift and shift of the slippery organ, intently studying it, Nicanor wondered if there should be more to the show—maybe a burning brazier of incense. He peeked at Cestius Gallus standing to one side of the pedestal. His expression was still serious—expectant—and maybe hopeful.

The haruspex's brow furrowed, and he flashed a squint from beneath them—at the senior officers arrayed before him. Another poke of the liver and then more scrutiny. Spurinnus slid the bowl away, gesturing at the boy he had instructed to remain close by, to take it away and empty it. Nicanor watched as the soothsayer took three steps over to the legate and murmured in his ear and then leaned away as if awaiting a whispered answer in reply.

The lines in the legate's forehead deepened, and the area around his eyes tightened. He nodded at the haruspex, who moved back to the dais. "Spurinnus shall continue."

Another opinion must be needed, Nicanor thought as the auxiliary brought the sheep forward. Minutes after docilely dying, the sheep's liver was in the bowl and under the soothsayer's eyes. There was longer scrutiny this time, but no shifting or repositioning. Done with it, Spurinnus went to the legate as before. At his whisper, Cestius Gallus's expression did not relax, and the glimmer of hope that had been there had vanished. He seemed resigned to what the entrails said.

"The legion and its allies will assault Jerusalem," he announced, nodding toward Galerius Senna, the senior tribune. "We will prepare tomorrow and leave the next morning at full strength."

Nicanor shook his head, but he realized how heavy the burden was for the legate. Unremitting and unyielding was Rome's pressure on him to punish the rebels and bring Judea under heel. And he would obey—he always had—and lead his men into any battle ordered. Still, the thought of Yosef and his visions that foretold both the shipwreck of the *Salacia* and the fire that nearly destroyed Rome came to him. He wondered at what the cock's liver had told the soothsayer, then what the seer had told the legate and thought, *I'd rather listen and act based on unprompted dreams or visions of men... at least their foretellings are somewhat specific.*

LXXIX

October 66 CE

Near Gibeon

"I watched the Romans all day, Simon," the man panted. "Earlier a man who must have been a soothsayer cut a chicken and sheep open and took a look, and then I saw centurions moving through the camp, readying men and equipment. Afterward, I saw King Agrippa's personal guard approach the Roman legate's tent, and a man in the most colorful clothing I have ever seen in a Roman camp went in the tent, leaving the guard outside."

The man wiped rainwater from his face, for a sheet of it had passed over him as he was relieved from his watch post. The bunching of clouds, now thick and gray, covered the sky and hastened twilight. "I think they will soon march, probably tomorrow morning." Niger of Perea knew Roman routine—he had experienced it as part of King Agrippa's troops before defecting to join the rebels.

"March to Jerusalem," Simon bar Giora said and saw Niger's nod before he turned. From the small hillock he stood on, he could see his lieutenant Silas of Batanea, another man who had chosen to fight for the rebels and not for Agrippa and Rome. His men—good men from Adiabene, stout and loyal—spread around him. Nearly two thousand spilled over the lower plateaus and up the bases of the surrounding taller hills, the Roman encampment behind and below them on the plain. He turned back to Niger. "Tell Silas to get the men ready but have them stand easy." He regarded the darkening sky. "Tonight, at the turn of the Romans' third watch, we'll strike."

* * *

Nicanor held a swath of gallic to his face, and the olive-oil-soaked old linen quickly turned red.

"Let me at it, Centurion," the medicus said, holding a bone needle and length of dried-gut thread for the suture. "Arrow or blade?"

"Arrow, Aulus," Nicanor replied, appreciating the capsarius's directness. A trained combat medic in one of the legion's contubernia, an eight-man unit, Nicanor had met him when he questioned him about the death of his friend, the former camp-prefect. "Hundreds of arrows were falling with the rain," Nicanor said. "I heard the shouts and the sentry's alarm and rushed out...

346

toward where the fighting was, down where they had staged the baggage units. On the way, one of them got me. Thought I'd lost an eye."

"You nearly did," the medic said, deftly closing the gash along the centurion's brow. The arrow had narrowly missed the orb, and the gash was shallower where it ended below the curve of the cheekbone and just above the centurion's jaw.

"Put them over there," the medic told the men coming in who carried more wounded for treatment, many with one or more arrows still in them. He turned back to Nicanor. "Keep it clean. Honey and vinegar poured over the wound, once in the morning and once at night. Try not to tear the stitches out. As it is, you'll have another scar... don't make it worse."

Nicanor nodded, twitching at the jolt of pain that motion brought as he stood, and went to see how many men had died.

* * *

It was a wet dawn, and the hours preceding it were not auspicious, *no matter what the animal guts said yesterday*, thought Nicanor.

The legate's face was pallid and drawn as he turned to Galerius Senna. "How many are dead?"

"Sixty-eight men, lord." The senior military tribune glanced at the camp-prefect and then back to Cestius Gallus, opened his mouth, and hesitated.

Nicanor did not hesitate. "As bad as losing those men is, Lord Gallus," he said, "more than half the mules are dead or gone. They were taken by the Judean raiders along with more supplies." He shot a look at the camp-prefect. "The mules are needed to pull our equipment, legate... our siege machinery. Our ballista, onager and scorpio... we need them to cast stone and arrows at a distance and with power."

"You said half of our mules, Centurion. Can't those remaining transport them?"

Nicanor waited to see if the senior military tribune or camp-prefect would answer Cestius Gallus, as was their responsibility. Senna and Priseus remained silent. He clenched his jaw, and a spasm of pain from the still-raw wound pulled down the eyebrow on that side. He blinked, sighed and answered him: "Yes, Legate, if that is all they have to pull."

"What of the supplies for our men, Centurion?" the camp-prefect asked.

"Divide the remaining foodstuffs and supplies among us all—we must carry it."

"Our allies already grumble, Centurion." Tyrannius Priseus cut a sideways glance at Agrippa, who sat near Cestius Gallus.

"They will complain more—as will we all, Prefect—if we arrive in Jerusalem and don't have what we need to assault the city and to press a siege."

"Other than these raids, we've not met any serious resistance."

"Lord Gallus," Nicanor said, ignoring the camp-prefect, "Priseus must not understand how walls like those of Jerusalem stiffen backbones and make men willing to die defending them."

"The Judeans"—Galerius Senna leaned toward Cestius Gallus— "are wracked with dissension and strife among their leaders." The military tribune shifted his gaze to Nicanor. "Walls are only as strong as the men behind them."

It's time to be quiet, Nicanor told himself. He would get nowhere being the one pointing out the obvious decision when it would not be acknowledged. The silence hung heavy in the tent. King Agrippa slid his chair closer to Cestius Gallus and whispered in his ear. The legate listened, paused for a moment, and then nodded.

The legate rose, and all stood. "Ready the men to march," he ordered the camp-prefect. "Half of the remaining mules are to be used for supplies. The rest will pull what siege equipment they can manage."

LXXX

NEAR GIBEON

Nicanor thought that the day had not started well, had not gone well, and was not ending well.

After the dawn briefing, the legion had formed up. The remaining mules had been assigned pack duty or harnessed to pull equipment. He was disturbed to see some of the heavier siege machinery being left behind and shocked at how heavily the mules had been loaded with supplies. Now in the daylight, he could see how little it came to, with so few mules. They had nowhere near enough supplies to feed a force of thousands of soldiers and conduct a prolonged siege. At some point, they would have to forage and take grain and other foodstuffs from the Judeans. This was not how they would support the peace offering Agrippa had convinced Cestius Gallus to make. He shook his head as he watched an overburdened mule, whipped to blood-striped haunches, try to pull harder and drag free a cart buried to the wheel hubs in the mud. So, it had been throughout the day. But one such delay had given him a chance to overhear the legate and senior military tribune discussing Agrippa's emissaries and offer of amnesty... Roman surety. Galerius Senna thought it foolish to waste time talking with the rebels. But Cestius Gallus was troubled and needed time to think—enough had happened to justify his concerns. That was likely his reasoning for agreeing to Agrippa's request for them to give the rebels a final peace offer.

The mule driver's cursing brought Nicanor back to the present. At this pace, the legate could do a lot of thinking between here and Jerusalem. He shook his head.

* * *

"Will they listen?" asked Phebus, a short, stout man. The taller and leaner man at his side carried a white staff angled across his chest, occasionally stabbing it to the ground on one side or the other to steady his gait. Their path had wound among the hills for hundreds of years. The gravel had washed away to ruts and wallows by rain in fall and winter, and then baked hard and permanent in the summer. Though uneven, it was the most direct route to Jerusalem.

"King Agrippa believes they will listen," replied Borceus. "We must stand before them unafraid." His face grew sterner.

"Shouldn't we have a larger escort?" Phebus pivoted his head to scan the eight legionaries with them, four in front and four behind.

"More would invite attack, without a chance to talk with the rebels," said Borceus. "The rebels can't see us as a threat, and these men are enough to protect us, so we get that chance."

"And we have these that mark us..." Phebus brought up his staff to balance across the bulge of his stomach. "Even the Judeans know this means we're emissaries... and you and I aren't armed." He lowered the length of bleached wood and called to the tesserarius leading them, "Tertius, watch for a good place for our overnight camp." Phebus eyed their lengthening shadows cast by the low sun as it shone between the hills and spilled across the road after the rain had finally stopped. They could not reach the city before nightfall.

Borceus looked down at his companion and nodded. "In the morning we won't be far from the gates of Jerusalem."

* * *

A clear dawn was on their shoulders with the sun just cresting the hills behind them as they stepped onto the road.

"Only eight Roman soldiers, a thin and a fat Roman in robes!" called out the man as he came from the thicket of head-high trees that skirted the road. His frame and clothing matched the tree trunks, and his bushy hair matched their tufts of foliage. He pushed through dense waist-high bushes to the road.

"Hold!" Tertius ordered his men, not moving the hand that gripped the hilt of his gladius. In the middle of the road, he widened his stance and studied the coarse man before him wearing the garb of a country chieftain, not a city dweller. "We escort two emissaries—from your King Agrippa and the Roman legate, Cestius Gallus—to Jerusalem to speak with the Judean leadership."

"Oh," the man shook his head and smiled, "Agrippa is not my king, and your legate has no power over me." He flicked the hand at his side as if waving off the Roman's words.

Phebus came forward as Borceus stood frozen. He opened his mouth to speak—to tell the man they meant him no harm—and the first arrow, from behind the rough man before them, entered his mouth and protruded from the back of his neck. Phebus choked on his own blood and on its feathers. A second and third arrow skewered the sergeant, and Tertius went down with shafts in chest and neck.

Borceus still had not moved. A chorus of bowstrings and of whistling swishes through the air—and he knew the soldiers with him were down, wounded, or dead. He brought up his staff. "The legate wishes a truce—to talk—and promises amnesty if you throw down your weapons. He offers his surety, Roman surety... forgiveness, and wishes peace-"

The arrow that cut off his statement missed its mark and struck Borceus high on the chest, above his heart. A second pierced the flesh above his left hip and spun him around. He staggered through a gap in the bushes along the road and fell where the land sloped toward a ravine that paralleled the road, a deep crevice.

Simon bar Giora followed to where the slope sheared off to a steep drop. Looking down, he knew the man must be dead. He returned to the road and called out to his men. Unseen in the bushes and thick scrub, they lined up and filled the folds and creases of the hills, the just-brightening day began to reveal them. "On to Jerusalem!" he called as he strode up the road.

LXXXI

NEAR JERUSALEM

It had taken three—nearly four—days to complete what should have been a one- or two-day march, even with a force as unwieldy and large as this. Nicanor shook his head at the road climbing ahead of him. Mount Scopus loomed two hundred feet over the almost three-thousand-foot-high plateau that Jerusalem sat upon a mile southwest of them. When Nicanor had visited Jerusalem at Passover, which now seemed a lifetime ago, he had thought how difficult an assault on the city would be. The city's two long hills lay side by side, and at their lower end, the three flanking deep ravines joined to form a single, broad valley. Jerusalem was secure behind three tall, strongly built walls of square-cut stone masterfully fit together, dotted with towers and ramparts that encircled the city and protected different parts of it. It was also supplied by an aqueduct and had many cisterns and a perennial spring. A difficult siege would ensue if the city and its defenders were well prepared and undivided.

Nicanor never thought he would become part of an attacking force that had to breach those walls. He wondered if Agrippa's ambassadors were within them now and if they had accomplished anything. The Judeans had proved a point with their successful raids on the Twelfth Legion and its allied forces. They had to be taken seriously, but he had heard of all the dissension among them. What single voice of reason would stand forth from them? Agrippa thought it worth trying to find one. Nicanor leaned forward in his saddle and patted at Abigieus's neck. The horse blew through his lips; he did not like the slow pace, and the braying of whipped mules grated on him, making his ears twitch.

The sun was low, and three-quarters set on Mount Scopus as the snaking column wound around its east flank to where the advance units had determined the best location for their encampment. On its southern side, angled slightly west, they would look down on nearby Jerusalem. He patted Abigieus again and straightened, rubbing the small of his back that now pained him when he spent too long on horseback. After the next bend, he saw the sprawl of the city—its three walls casting growing shadows beyond it. He could just make out the Fortress Antonia, which from their vantage point obscured the view of the Temple.

Nicanor thought of Yosef. When they had been afloat on the sea and awaiting death, they had had no reason to hope for rescue, Yosef had told him of his home—and of this summit, the mount of watchmen, the sentinel watching over Jerusalem. Now, it would become the perch from which angry Roman eyes stared down upon the rebels of the city. Was Yosef down there in the city, or was he somewhere else in this land? Nicanor scanned the horizon. He did not know which would be better for his friend and hoped that he would not see him again until peace had returned to Judea. He shifted in the saddle to look at the mass of men behind him—on foot and mounted—and then back to a similar sight ahead of him. The prospects for peace seemed little more than the dirt under thousands of tramping feet.

* * *

"On advice and because of a request, I have waited with hope to hear from the emissaries," Cestius Gallus told the assemblage of the legion and allied officers and nodded at Agrippa, who bowed his head, an acknowledgment of approval and thanks.

Nicanor understood Agrippa's desire to talk to the Judeans, to bring them back from the brink of a war they could never survive. Militarily he might concede the Judeans the two tiny victories in the harassment of the Roman force. That was just the yapping of a small dog at a sleeping lion. Awake and unleashed, the lion would rip the dog to shreds. Still, he wished for peace and did not want to kill more Judeans nor destroy their city. And he did not need a soothsayer to tell him that was what would happen if the emissaries failed. Agrippa wanted to avoid that. But why did Tyrannius Priseus have a smile on his face at another delay in pressing the attack against the seat of Judean leadership? On the march from Gibeon, he had repeatedly advocated immediate action. Something was calculating in the man's words about dealing with the Judeans that conflicted with his efforts. And that no doubt had affected Gallus's thoughts and decisions. Nicanor turned to the legate, who had picked up a map from the work table behind him.

"Lord, has any word been received from them, from Phebus and Borceus?"

"No, Centurion." Cestius Gallus shook his head.

"What of the contubernia, the men escorting them?"

The legate shook his head again and motioned to Galerius Senna. "Tribune, send out units—infantry supported by cavalry—into the neighboring areas and small villages"—he tapped the map. "Seize their grain and other foodstuffs. Take most of it but not all... leave some for the people."

JERUSALEM

For three days they had awaited a sign that Agrippa's envoys had succeeded and would bring the Judeans out to talk or send word for a Roman representative to come forth to discuss a path to a resolution. Nothing and no one. Nicanor had grown tired of waiting. Tired with leading daily patrols to swat away the Judean skirmishers nipping at the edges of the force. They made foraging for supplies a risk to men, equipment, and horses. Finally, the legate, too, had had enough, and the evening of the third day ordered half of the force into action the following morning. The attack point was the northernmost part of Jerusalem—the New City, known as Bezetha. It was more sparsely populated, and despite the city's third and latest outer wall surrounding it, it was not well manned or as fortified as the two inner walls. Four legion cohorts had breached one of the gates, and the auxiliary forces assigned for the assault had poured through. Much of the wall itself, they had discovered, was thicker and stronger than the others, thanks to the work of King Agrippa's father. Rome ordered a halt to those improvements in suspicion that such walls around the entire city might have made the city completely impregnable.

Nicanor reined Abigieus to one side. His galea was heavy and hot despite the chill of a fall morning. The heat came mainly from the burning timber market whose flames had spread and were now a conflagration devouring Bezetha—they must now push around and farther from it as it burned out behind them. He pulled off the helmet, hinging the side cheek-guards back so he could quickly get it back on if needed. The heavy smoke would throw off precise aim—and they had yet to encounter archers—but he had learned to always be ready. The helmet's crest of black horsehair like Abigieus's mane and tail had been singed as they skirted the flames, the air full of embers and hot ash. Palm-wiping his eyes a last time with one hand, he settled the helmet back on his head and flipped the bronze guards down. Abigieus was foot-stamping, eager to move away from the heat and stench. Something other than wood now burned. He caught the sound of a horn's echo and turned toward it. An alae draped in chain mail rode toward him. The buccina now hanging from a lanyard around his neck, he gripped a long spatha sword in his right hand and held a clipeus, the round shield usually carried by auxiliaries, in his left. He guided his mount with knees and heels.

"Centurion, the Tribune has ordered all units to converge where the city's second wall joins the old one on the west side, north of Herod's palace."

Nicanor nodded. He had memorized a map of the city and its layout. "I know the place. There should be open ground there, for a local cemetery and crucifixion hill has made it unclean, keeping locals from building in the vicinity. And it has a good view of the entire city."

With a salute of the sword, the man left him and went in search of other unit commanders to ensure that all received the orders.

The wind had shifted, and the smoke cleared. Nicanor hand-signaled his senior optio to form up their men. He watched as the lieutenant used the same gesture to the junior lieutenants and sergeants. As the first of the men formed ranks, he signaled them again to follow him. Within an hour, his men trailing behind him, they came upon rows of hundreds of tribulus... murex ferrus. Large and small, the jagged iron devices formed the perimeter of the Roman strike forces' newly set camp within the city. The sharp pointed spikes slowed enemy infantry and horses. Nicanor and his men passed through a gap. That single opening, the entry to a camp being hastily set up, was secured by a dozen heavy infantry in full-body scale armor, short swords at the hip, carrying short stabbing spears and scuta, the legionaries' large, rectangular shields.

Nicanor spotted the senior military tribune leading the force. Cestius Gallus and the camp-prefect had remained at the base camp on Mount Scopus. "Tribune," he asked, "are we to hold here overnight?" Nicanor eyed the wall that separated them from the Upper City and Temple enclosure. With what siege machinery they had remaining and the even smaller number brought with the strike force, it would be difficult to keep that wall free of rebels firing down on them. He saw units of infantry clambering up those walls towing armor and arms behind them, but still the wall would be difficult to secure without pushing beyond to defend the far side.

"Yes, Centurion. The rebels seemed to have left, pulling back as we advanced. The legate will join us in the morning once we've secured this area."

"That's too soon to be sure we hold it safely; why is the legate coming here?" Nicanor did not understand the legate putting himself at risk by entering the city. The tribune studied Nicanor for so long he became uncomfortable.

"He has something—I don't know what—he wishes done here immediately on his personal command," Galerius Senna shook his head, "and wants to talk to you in person before he issues that order."

LXXXII

CAESAREA

Gessius Florus kept track of his wife's affairs through his majordomus, and Glaucio was a diligent watcher. Each morning and evening he reported the lady's day, and those reports had led Florus to remove his household centurion Jucundus. The senior military tribune in Alexandria still felt the widespread influence of Florus's family and was happy to arrange army assignments beneficially—to Gessius Florus. Jucundus—who was too loyal to Octavia—would soon be on his way to Alexandria to assume some trivial post—far from Caesarea and any helpfulness he might be to Lady Cleo. Jucundus's absence had elicited no questions from Cleo, but her anxiety for news from Antioch was apparent even in her silence. Her interest in the messages brought by the routine couriers had been at first a pleasure to see, but to his irritation, he could not draw her out so he could deliver the sting of denial.

"Still no word from Antioch?" he asked. "Nothing from Lady Octavia about you visiting her, or about your Syrian friend?" His tone lacked any concern, for he would no longer pretend. The latest message from Tigellinus had shown Nero's favorable reception to his proposal, and that signaled a significant change was coming soon. His suggestion to the emperor addressed the two things that pressed hardest. First—the demand for Nero to replace him. He had learned that replacement—Marcus Antonius Julianus—had already left Ostia and was en route on the last ship south to Alexandria, Egypt for the season. And second—a solution to the emperor's need for more revenue. Getting hands on the Jewish treasure, though delayed from the original expectation, was still the driving factor in Nero's decision making.

"No," Lady Cleo said as she wrapped the heavy robe tighter around her shoulders. "No word."

Florus had to admit but not admire that Cleo had transformed from the noblewoman he had wed in Rome. Her words no longer held the manner of a wife who loved her husband. But that hardly mattered now that she had fulfilled her purpose. So what if things were not going according to the original plan? Still, he had hoped to orchestrate a chaotic war with the Jews, and that was underway. And

357

he had a grasp on the strings required to provide him with the wealth he had dreamed about—the Jewish treasure. He watched Cleo—such classic, beautiful features—as she looked at the sea. The evening breeze was strengthening. It lifted locks of hair from her face, and the tendrils swirled around her. The weather would soon shift as fall turned into winter. Rain would sweep from land toward the sea this time of year, and its scent was thick in the air.

"Do you wish to go inside?" Florus asked as he stood, knowing she would not join him, but his role as a husband could not be wholly abandoned just yet. That role would continue until she was no longer needed. To cut her off completely, for something to happen to her now, would be problematic. He needed everything to stay as usual until the time was right.

"No, I'll sit here a while longer." Cleo didn't turn from her view of an empty sea.

Florus walked away without replying, nor worrying what she contemplated as she stared at nothing. He gathered his robe closer to him and thought about the message Capito had brought him earlier in the day from Geganius Murena. It was another loose end to tie up when the timing suited him. The Roman agent in Jerusalem had excellent news from the mole in the new Judean government, but he had also made a minor but bothersome admission: he had not found and executed the man killing his spies in the city.

Florus pushed that aside. Jerusalem's destruction was coming just as surely as winter was upon them. He dwelled in a pleasurable daydream that warmed him despite the wind's chill—soon he would return to Clazomenae with his wealth. His family and connections there would shield him from prying eyes should any have interest in his disappearance from Judea. Shrewd financial strategists and practitioners, they could multiply the treasure he brought with him to the point that he would wield real power and need never serve others again.

JERUSALEM

Yosef watched the ebb and flow of conversation in the chamber. Excited voices discuss their progress in gathering gold and silver for the new coins. Having their own coins and identifiable currency was meaningful for many Jews, and their enthusiasm had yielded a flood of precious metal. The treasury coffers had swollen, and the smelting and reminting was proving to please everyone—well, almost everyone. He still agreed with what Miriam had said, albeit disrespectfully: more important things than minting coins should have been decided first. His comment to that effect prompted a question from the small group of men gathered around him. "Yes, I've seen more of the Romans and their army than any here. But I don't know why they would attack, penetrate so deeply into the city and then stop and hold outside the second wall."

"They surely won't hesitate long. We should counterattack. Shouldn't we? What do you think, Yosef?"

"That is not my decision," Yosef said, turning to Yehudah ish Krioth, who had just proudly reported how well things were going with the reminting he had volunteered to lead. "Yehudah, they have at least ten thousand men inside the city now... and another twenty thousand only a mile or two away that can descend like locusts from Mount Scopus. We should use their hesitation, as we have so far, to strengthen defenses as we wait for more troops of our own to be consolidated. Simon bar Giora, we've been told, is moving the bulk of his men from Gibeon to the outskirts of Jerusalem. But we still need Yohanan ben Levi of Gischala. In Galilee, he controls many more thousands of men we desperately need—but he has not committed them, according to Yohanan ben Zaccai." Yosef turned to his father, who stood between Shimon ben Gamliel and Eleasar ben Ananias. "There is one Roman strategy they never fail to use, and it has secured them countless victories—it built their empire and still sustains it."

"But they did not win at Beth Horon," Eleasar interjected. "They lost hundreds of men, not to mention much of their supplies and most of their draft animals."

"Yes, it was a small but important success for us, Eleasar," Yosef agreed. "But we also lost leaders like Kennedeus and Monobazus of Adibene, a powerful ally. We need them now and will even more in the future, but they are gone from us."

"Son," Mathias said as he touched Yosef's shoulder, "what were you about to say... the strategy Romans use so well?"

"Purpose, discipline, planning, and execution to bring to bear their insurmountable manpower and military might. This force now camped across the wall from Herod's palace is but the tip of the Roman wedge. The balance of the Twelfth Legion is the mallet that will descend and strike it to split the city... and us."

"What can we do," asked Shimon ben Gamliel, "other than gather more men?"

"We must focus on a concerted effort. We must have unity and no divisiveness among us at all"—Yosef shook his head, scanned the room and thought of the two headstrong men he had just mentioned they hoped to count on—"and pray the Roman arm does not swing too soon. We need time." *And ten times the number of men we have now,* Yosef thought, *and for God to look down and truly favor us.*

* * *

Geganius Murena felt it in the air, a dense miasma carried on a current that twisted and wound through the city, touching everyone. He had experienced it in cities and towns across the empire, and often he had been one of its primary's instigators or the catalyst that brought it upon the citizens. Fear and uncertainty were the two things that set most people, their households, and their nations on edge. Those two emotions were also what kept him busy—seeding and cultivating the teetering—at the orders of men who benefited most. He had sown fear multiple times in many places and hunted and killed countless men. But he had never had to stalk and kill another hunter. That changed the dynamic he was accustomed to, and this man—the killer Romans had started calling "the Hand"—was an enigma. The negligible trail, vague at its best, had faded entirely, and recurring tangible evidence had ceased. There had been no appearance nor attack since the spate of Roman deaths attributed to him. Only a bloodied handprint here or there on the wall and door of residences or businesses... these signs believed to be mere warnings against any thought of Roman collaboration. But soon he would find this Hand and deliver his head to Gessius Florus. The procurator had discovered what motivated him after his twenty years of service to Rome that had rewarded him with little. Lord Florus had promised Murena his weight in silver coins, and for that, he would kill many men.

LXXXIII

Though he had not been re-shackled, Sayid knew to remain close to the far wall when one of his guards came into the room they held him in, empty but for his rough bedding. He tried to gauge the time from the light coming through the high window. *Midmorning*, he thought and wondered at the change in the routine since he had spoken with the Judean rebel leader days before.

The large man with a high-pitched voice gestured to him and said, "Come with me."

Despite his dwindling fear of being killed, Sayid still worried about the passing of time. It had been so many days now, and he had no idea whether he could reach the legate Cestius Gallus in time to stop an attack on Jerusalem. The guard took him to the chamber where he had met the rebel leader previously, opened the door, and led him inside.

Yohanan ben Levi—that was a name Sayid had learned—sat at a square table with a map spread on top. Another man leaned over it and spoke as his fingers traced something upon it. "At Beth Horon, Simon and his men—positioned on the ridges and ledges above the pass—attacked the flanks of the Roman baggage train. They killed several hundred Romans and separated many of the supply carts, capturing them." The man paused as Yohanan ben Levi looked up at Sayid, then continued when Yohanan lowered his eyes to the map. "The Roman legate and Twelfth Legion pushed on to Gibeon, where they camped for several days."

"Why?" Yohanan interrupted. "It makes no sense for them to halt a force that size for several days until they had it where it was to be used."

"I don't know, but Simon and his men struck again the night before they marched on, taking more of their supplies and draft animals, killing even more of them they couldn't get away with."

"And where is the legion now?"

Sayid could not catch the man's words as he bent lower but saw the rebel leader's head nod as he then straightened.

"We'll talk later"—Yohanan rolled the map and handed it to the man, who left the room, then motioned for the guard to bring Sayid closer. "It seems things as they are... do not go well for your Romans, so what good would it do us to be concerned with what's in the letters you carry? How do they help my people?"

"Mistakes can be made by even the mightiest," Sayid said, "but it's not wise to count on them for success, sir. Even young as I am, I've learned that in the Roman army. I'm sure you have seen far more than I have—and know that to be true." He took a step closer and felt the big man's grip tighten on his upper arm. "You've read enough in the letters to realize that they have nothing to harm you or hurt your cause."

"Whoever this person is—the one you and those letters claim has instigated this war and has a hand in its course—that person is helping my people and me. Why alert the Roman legate about him and spoil that benefit?"

Sayid shrugged, trying to loosen the guard's grip. "My mother told me when I was young—I think trying to teach me about greed— that bait tastes sweet until the trap is sprung." The Galilean leader's eyes narrowed, and his head nodded slightly. "Roman losses now—I overheard what was just said—will only fuel their anger and their desire to punish all rebels and your country harshly. Roman losses will not dissuade the legate or the Twelfth Legion—they will inflame the Romans." The Galilean's expression shifted, and Sayid knew this was his last and only chance to sway him. "If Lord Gallus—the Roman legate—sees those letters and what's in them and that helps explain some of what's gone wrong for him, he may halt or pull back to find out who works against him from within. That might perhaps even set the stage for a talk about a peaceful resolution. At the very least, doesn't that help you gain more time to prepare?"

"If I let you go, you'll have to find your way to the Roman legate. I will not escort or protect you so you can reach him," Yohanan said. "And any Judean rebel or bandit you come across will kill you without question. It's likely you will die. Are the letters, is your loyalty to those who wrote them, that important?"

JERUSALEM

Nicanor stood next to Galerius Senna and watched as a half-cohort of heavy infantry and armored cavalry approached. The leading element parted, and the legate and his personal guard continued into the secure area of the forward assault camp.

"Lord Gallus," said the senior military tribune as he stepped forward to hold the legate's mount as the legate dismounted, "I have the First Centurion here, as you requested."

Cestius Gallus nodded at Galerius Senna. He looked more haggard than when he had last seen him, Nicanor thought as he saluted. "At your command, Lord Gallus."

The legate nodded his acknowledgment and gestured to his aide, who turned to the men of the personal guard and motioned them to form a line facing the wall separating the Romans from the Upper City of Jerusalem.

"Why do they carry bows?" Nicanor asked as he leaned toward the tribune, who did not answer. But the legate spoke:

"Centurion, I recall some of your story—the shipwreck, and that you saved the Lady Cleo... and I remember your... Judean acquaintance." Nicanor noted the pause and choice of words as the legate continued: "Is he not a young Jew, a member of a prominent Judean family, one who evidently has a voice in... at least in this city's"—he waved a hand at the wall—"leadership?" He stopped and looked at Nicanor expectantly.

"Yes, Legate... you speak of Yosef ben Mathias. He—" Nicanor stopped. Cestius Gallus had turned to his aide and whispered instructions. The aide went to a camp clerk holding a dozen sheets of parchment with something already written on them. The clerk took the square of wood hanging from a lanyard around his neck and pivoted it up to grip in one hand. The other hand placed the sheets on the wood, then with a charcoal stick added a name to the top of each page.

"Continue, Centurion," the legate said.

"Yosef and I got to know each other on the *Salacia* and afterward. Then in Rome even more."

"And you would call him a friend?"

Nicanor ignored the snort from the tribune and answered readily: "Yes, Legate. I do."

"And he—this Yosef—would call you a friend?"

"Yes, Lord Gallus. I believe so."

"You escorted Lady Cleo to his family's home for their Passover, right? Met his father and others?"

"Yes, lord."

"Good." Cestius Gallus looked at his aide, who nodded at the clerk who took the dozen sheets of parchment to each of the legate's personal guards. They had pulled out thick white-painted arrows—blunt, squared tips. Each archer took a sheet of parchment, wrapped

363

it around the shaft, and secured it with two leather straps tied to firmly hold the parchment. "Send them." The bows bent, and arrows flew, not one losing its attached message as they arced over the wall at different angles. "We will wait a day to see if they reply." The legate nodded at the tribune and Nicanor.

"Wait for what, Lord Gallus?" What he had just watched puzzled Nicanor.

"In the messages, I've asked the Judeans to have this Yosef ben Mathias come talk to you. You will be my spokesperson on behalf of Rome—our one last attempt to reason with the rebel leaders."

LXXXIV

Eleasar ben Ananias paced at the front of the chamber. He gripped a white-shafted arrow in one hand and a piece of parchment—its corners and ends curled—in the other. "Eleven arrows came over the second wall with messages from the Roman legate"—he waved the parchment and turned toward the men seated in front of him. "Cestius Gallus wishes to meet to talk before we shed more blood."

"Then we should," Mathias replied. "I know you disagree, but as a new government hoping to have our voice heard, we should use the Romans' willingness as a chance to speak with them and resolve our issues."

"We should ignore them to show we truly choose independence," replied an unfamiliar voice raised in that chamber, "and not compromise our authority to bow to theirs."

Yosef had been watching his father's features, noting how gray, tired, and careworn he had become. He had expected the Temple guard captain to say something like that or one of the other Zealots to do the same. Instead, the declaration had come from a surprising source, and he shifted in his seat to look.

"If we comply, doesn't that send a message to the Romans?" Yehudah ish Krioth asked, stroking his silky beard, "a message that we are not prepared to fight them for our sovereignty?"

Mathias raised his heavy eyebrows. "You think we are adequately prepared to do so, Yehudah?" He turned back to the Temple guard captain. "Eleasar, do you think we're ready to face the Romans now that they're here, in force within our walls... before our homes and all we hold dear?"

"Simon bar Giora is now encamped just outside the city, adding to our defense. Our army grows every day." Eleasar walked toward Mathias, tossing the arrow aside and unfurling the parchment as if to reread and disregard the request it contained. "The Romans are up to something. I do not trust this"—he waved the message again.

"Then doesn't talking with them give us more time?" Mathias asked. "Time for more men to be gathered and to improve our defenses? Should we instead rush to battle and have our people die?"

"So, Mathias, you say we should trust them. We should meet and talk with them, and we should not worry they'll kill or harm those who will speak for us." Eleasar shook his head and studied the older man.

"I'm not afraid to meet with them, Eleasar."

"But they don't want to speak with you, Mathias—or any *official*." That word twisted into a different meaning as Eleasar held the sheet out. "They do not want a representative from our government." He looked past Mathias to Yosef. "Would you worry about your son? Because it is Yosef, the Romans wish to meet and speak with."

* * *

"I still don't understand, Yosef," Matthew said. "You say you know this Nicanor, and you trust him—I know I met him at Passover. But what is a centurion doing speaking for the Roman legate?"

"I don't know." Yosef shook his head wearily. He had spent most of the night replying to variations of that question from several men and then his mother once he got home. Now the sun had risen, and the Temple guards around him doused their torches as they approached the meeting place proposed in the Roman message and at the time indicated. Several carts piled high with heavy loads of stone still blocked the gate. Matthew waved forward the drovers with their strings of donkeys and oxen, and they watched as the animals were hitched to the carts.

"Be ready to back them up and secure the gate again," Matthew ordered, but he doubted it could be done quickly enough if this was nothing but a ploy and the Romans were poised to charge through. Despite Yosef's assertion that if the Romans wanted to breach the wall, they would have done so by now and would not have stopped the effort to talk.

The teams of draft animals strained, and wood and wheels groaned as the carts moved slowly away from the opening, Yosef did not see charging legionaries, only a centurion in full armor. Behind him, a dense forest of locked shields, burnished cuirasses, breastplates, and helmets. The mass of armed might and manpower bristled with spears—all pointed at him. The opening was now wide enough for a man to pass through, and the carts creaked to a stop.

"Are you sure, Brother?" Matthew gripped Yosef's shoulder.

The centurion slowly raised both hands, lifted the helmet from his head, and tucked it under one thick arm, and Yosef saw the coarse, grizzled face of his friend and a ragged, still-raw scar that slanted from brow to jaw. "Yes, Matthew," Yosef answered. He stepped forward with his brother close at his back.

The centurion met them in the portal, stone arched above them and on either side. There was a host of Romans to the north and a much smaller number of haphazardly armored and equipped Judeans to the south of the gate.

"I suspect you've never had a vision of this meeting, have you, Yosef?" Nicanor's gruff voice was followed by his bark of laughter.

"No, my friend," Yosef replied with a shake of his head, "but so far most of my visions have not boded well, so perhaps that's best for us."

*   *   *

There were many men on the turreted walls of the Hasmonean palace, and all watched as the Temple guards, supplemented by two hundred militia, moved toward the Gennath gate. Miriam was thankful for the crowd. Zechariah had warned her to not trust her men's garb and fat man's padding to fool anyone for long in the bright daylight. But after what she had heard her father tell her mother about Yosef and Matthew and what they were doing right now before her eyes, she knew she must see for herself. A hurrying man pushed by and jostled her. She half-turned toward him. He did not stop until he had reached the handful of men standing with her father. He tapped the arm of a man in fine robes, and his combed and oiled beard caught a sunbeam as he turned to the shorter rough-looking man. Something in the flash of emotion on that carefully groomed face at seeing the burly man at his side drew her attention. Despite her father being nearby, she moved closer.

The well-dressed man she now knew was Yehuda ish Krioth, one of the men Yosef had helped free in Rome, and a colleague of her father's. She had seen him in the Lower City talking with another coarse man who had proved to be a Roman mercenary. A onetime meeting with such a man could be an accident or a casual business acquaintance—her father had told her Yehudah's family were traders. But a second meeting with a man of similar type raised questions in her mind. She got within two arms' length of them and shifted as if looking away, but her head cocked toward them as she listened.

"Yes, yes..." Yehudah told the man as if answering him. Something in his whispered voice nagged at her as he continued: "Simon's men are in the city and will position along the second wall." She closed her eyes and heard that hushed voice in the dark—it was the voice of the Jewish man who'd been with the Romans in the tunnel before she had been... before she... Miriam turned to face Yehudah, not caring that he saw her. Her hands instinctively slipped inside opposing sleeves to touch the hafts of her knives. A flutter went through the cluster of people around her as she drew in a deep breath.

"Look!" the man next to her cried out and pointed.

Miriam turned in that direction. The blockade at the gate had parted, and she saw two men pass through—her brothers. Above them scurried dozens of men—there must be one hundred or more—bent low behind parapets as they ran and aligned themselves atop the wall. Behind them, as if chasing or trying to stop them, was a man in the robes of the Sanhedrin.

LXXXV

Sayid had followed the lead of others when he had headed north to Antioch through Damascus. Coming south before his capture he had been guided by the legionary sergeant Arruns Vulso. Now the only direction to head was south, toward Jerusalem, where the Twelfth Legion must be by now. That morning he had awoken to find neatly stacked next to his pallet a clean set of Judean clothing, a goatskin of water... and the pouch of letters—all intact. The door was wide open, and no guards were around. Stepping from the room, he found his way outside, where a dozen men moved about, but other than giving him some sharp looks, they left him to go.

Not far away he had found a path that kept the rising sun mostly on his left shoulder. He still limped; the wound in his thigh radiated an ache that spread the length of his leg and up into his hip. By the time the sun was directly overhead, the pain had deepened to more than a throbbing hindrance, but he had covered a few miles. A man trundling a cartload of wood was wary of him at first but had given him directions to an easily followed southerly route, the fisherman's road that ran directly to the vast Lake Gennesaret of Galilee. Sayid knew that from there he could skirt the lake's western bank to where it continued into the River Jordan, the Yarden, as the man called it. He knew that major river ran due south into the other large lake in Judea—the Asphaltitis—that he had heard nothing could live in or around. That northernmost point of the lake was directly east of Jerusalem. The Romans must be encamped along that way, the only approach for a force the size of a legion.

He would find them if he did not get killed first. The fisherman's road had been heavily trafficked, and he hoped that once he was off the road and following the natural shore of the lake and then the west bank of the river, he would be alone or least draw no attention.

* * *

Sayid was thankful. Despite the close call with the bandits or rebel patrol that forced him to run, then stumble into a thicket of reeds along the river, where he remained to hide, he had come upon a thatched fish trap some fisherman had surely cursed at losing. It was

369

caught in the tangle of growth at the riverside, and he had gratefully eaten raw the two fish still trapped within it, his first food since his rations the last day of his imprisonment. The thought of freedom had sustained him since he awakened to discover he had somehow persuaded Yohanan ben Levi to let him go.

Then the band of men had seen him within the reeds and flushed him inland. He had angled as best he could to the west and south toward an area just north of Jerusalem, sure the men he'd overheard talk of Jericho had continued to follow him. As soon as the twists and turns took him out of sight, he clambered down the path that ran atop a ridge and into its parallel ravine that took him west.

He was starving and felt weak but lurched steadily on. The first three nights had been spent shivering more than sleeping in a semi-dream of his mother. He'd basked in the warmth of her arms and how she always had enough food for him, though he suspected sometimes she went without so he would have enough. Then last night or early that morning, the dream suspended as his urgent task overwhelmed him. He must get to the legate in time, before an all-out attack on Jerusalem. In his new dream, he had seen that Lady Cleo had feelings for Yosef and that he would meet him again. But that could never be, not now. He prayed to the gods that his friend would not die—had not already died—at the hands of a Rome he once admired. If he could reach the legate in time, maybe that outcome could be averted.

NEAR JERUSALEM

Sayid heard something that was not the now-familiar moaning of wind twisting and passing through the crevices of the ravines that scarred the landscape he had traveled—headed west—since reaching the northern shore of Lake Asphaltitis—the day before. Though he had still been afraid of climbing up to travel an easier path on the road or one of the rutted trails, he had drawn close enough to see that men—Judeans—were also moving west in large groups.

Hunkered down and hidden on a natural stone shelf beneath the ledge running parallel to the ridge, he heard one group talking as they camped astride the road. Thousands of men willing to fight the Romans were converging on Jerusalem. And the word was that the Romans were encamped on Mount Scopus and that the Twelfth Legion already had a foothold in the city. Sayid almost cried out then, thinking he was too late. But the men discussed the plan that they would reach Jerusalem in time, the very next day. *Maybe*, Sayid thought, *if I can get to the legate in time*—or even reach Nicanor—the messages he carried could still make a difference.

The keening of a hurt animal came from below him. The movement of men had made game scarce—Sayid had seen none since leaving the river. The sound grew stronger as he got closer to the bottom of the gorge, where it broadened and flattened out. It was a clear night, and his eyes had grown sharp in the dim light. He spotted the large gray figure half crawling, half pushing its way along, using a long stick and dragging one leg.

"Who is it?" the man called out as Sayid got near enough to see he was wearing a bloodied white robe. The light-colored staff he gripped as he rolled onto his back was also smeared in swaths of dark that must be blood. "Don't kill me!" the man moaned.

He was Roman! "I won't. I'm a friend," Sayid replied in Latin and then repeated in Greek. He kneeled beside the man. "Who are you?"

"Borceus," the man croaked, "an emissary from Lord Cestius Gallus, the Roman legate who now leads the Twelfth Legion." The man sank back and fell silent.

Sayid leaned over him, placed a hand on his chest, and bent down to listen. He felt the man's heart still beating and heard the shallow breathing that passed through his lips. The man lived but had fainted away. He should help him, but to bring him along would slow him even further. Sayid straightened and took several steps in the direction he must go, and quickly. He closed his eyes and at that moment saw Arruns Vulso come back for him... a middle-aged Roman legionary saving a young foreign auxiliary. Could he—would he—not save a Roman?

Sayid shook his head, turned, and went back. The man's leg was broken, and he would need to straighten it and push the broken bone back beneath the skin, then bind the leg to hold long enough to get him to a Roman medic. He picked up the man's white staff, an emissary's sign of unarmed peaceful intent. Sticking one end under a large rock and levering it over another, with an effort—he had grown so weak—he snapped it in half. Setting the two pieces beside the leg, he placed the heel of his right foot in the man's left armpit, grabbed the broken leg by the foot and pulled to extend it. Holding that, he used his other hand to push the ends of the splintered bone until they slid beneath the flesh. Careful to not dislodge the bones, Sayid firmly straddled the leg with the two halves of the staff and, using the white sash from the man's robe, tightly wound and bound the rough splint into place.

Pain shooting through his own leg, Sayid gasped with exhaustion and sat back to wait for the dawn. At sunrise he would begin the final part of this journey—a long haul—to find Cestius Gallus. He must warn him of what Gessius Florus had done to start the war, and was still doing to keep its flames fanned and growing. He prayed again that he could reach the Roman commander in time.

LXXXVI

Nicanor's eyes looked beyond Yosef to Matthew, who was equally armored, helmeted, and equipped with a sword. "My brother Matthew," Yosef said. "You met at Passover."

"I recall," Nicanor said with a nod but did not come closer. "Is he your bodyguard, my friend?"

"No, I trust you, Nicanor." But Yosef could see the wariness in the centurion's eyes and understood it. He hoped that Nicanor was as understanding of his own hesitancy. "I'm not a soldier, which you know well, having proved it while trying to teach me some of what you know." He smiled a little. "My brother refused to let me come to this talk alone."

The centurion nodded again and shifted his helmet to the other arm. "So, how have things come to this?" He panned his gaze around as if taking in the city as well as the world beyond the stone portal.

"I wish I could say that I don't know," Yosef said sadly, "but I do."

"The malcontents have brought this on us all?" Nicanor asked, and his free hand went up to rub the new scar that still itched.

"Is that from the recent fighting?" Yosef pointed at the wound. "I'm sorry for that."

"I doubt you were the bowman, Yosef," Nicanor chuckled, but without humor. "Still, so many have been wounded and killed... Romans and Judeans. Can this—the destruction and killing—be stopped?" he paused and studied the two men. "My legate, Cestius Gallus, may not be a professional soldier," Nicanor continued, "but he is a thinking man and a good administrator, Yosef. He knows few good things come from war... especially not from one started by a rebellion such as this."

Yosef felt Matthew stiffen and shift his stance and that Nicanor had noticed, too, and moved his helmet to free his sword arm. "Easy, Matthew," Yosef reminded him. "We are friends."

"Strong feelings and emotions have played a part on both sides," Nicanor said, his eyes locked on Matthew. "But Rome cannot let a revolt occur... and the rebels responsible stand unpunished."

"Then why has Cestius Gallus hesitated to press his assault on the city?"

"There are those who wish him to do so," replied Nicanor, "to first clench the Roman fist before crushing the rebellious."

"Those who would benefit—" Yosef began.

"I know who you speak of, Yosef—the procurator. But I think both sides have men with agendas who benefit from conflict. You've told me during our time together of how some in your country chafe at Roman rule and will do anything to break free. There is no way to resolve that because Rome will not relinquish a conquered province. And your own history you've shared with me tells of how your past rulers invited Roman rule to consolidate their power and defeat enemies within their own country. Again, those with an agenda serving their own needs. We meet because the legate feels this the last chance to talk—facilitated by our personal connection—to stop an all-out war before we reach a point of no return."

"Will you... will the Romans cease the attacks on my people?" Yosef asked.

"We have." Nicanor lifted a hand to his ear, inviting Yosef to note that the morning was still and silent around them.

"But you have a massive force inside our walls and an even larger one nearby," Yosef said.

"I know—Cestius Gallus knows—that Gessius Florus instigated this conflict, and thus his replacement will soon arrive. Florus will no longer have a say or a hand in Roman actions against your country. But your people, the rebels, have provoked this escalation by slaughtering our garrison here in this city and at Masada."

"We have," Yosef acknowledged, "but what does the legate propose?"

"If the rebels cease hostilities and end their reprisals against Romans and Roman rule, and lay down their arms, the legate will pull back the force inside Jerusalem."

"And what of the larger force on Mount Scopus, the force that threatens the city?"

"The Twelfth Legion would remain, though some allied forces may be removed, encamped away from the city if a truce holds and stable peace is maintained. Reparations must be worked out."

"You mean we must pay Rome to stop you from killing us," Matthew said tensely and took a half-step toward Nicanor. Yosef grabbed Matthew's arm.

Nicanor did not move, but his hand rested on his hip next to the hilt of his gladius. The sword would come out as fast as an adder's strike. "Better that than blood," he replied, and then said to Yosef, "will you present the legate's offer to your new government?"

"Yes, we'll—"

A scream cut through the morning stillness. Yosef saw a body fall from the parapet above them and strike the ground behind Nicanor, on the Roman side.

"What in Tartarus?" Nicanor spun around to approach the body. Just as he cleared the portal, a melon-sized rock came down, grazing his head, and struck his shoulder. He staggered as an avalanche of them followed, many falling at the closest edge of the mass of Romans.

"Nicanor!" Yosef ran to his friend, helping him stand. A gash above his right ear flowed red down the side of his face and neck.

"Get back!" Nicanor shoved Yosef away from him and back within the portal's protection as the rain of stones from the Jews was replaced by a shower of arrows.

The Romans arrayed outside the gate formed a testudo, with its protective of interlocking shields. Nicanor pulled his helmet on, drew his sword, and paused long enough to glance back at Yosef and shake his bloodied head. He then ducked and ran to an opening in the testudo, which closed around him.

"Yosef!" Matthew screamed and dragged his brother backward. Behind them, the heavy cart's wheels were already turning and slowly moving back to seal the Judean side of the gate. They barely got through.

* * *

"Ananus ben Yohanan's death is my fault." Shimon ben Gamliel rubbed his face with both hands. "I sent him up on the wall to stop Simon bar Giora's men."

"Why would Simon order that attack?" Yosef was still shaken, haunted by the expression on Nicanor's face. Had his look been condemnation? Did he think Yosef had known of the attack and played a part in it?

"Simon does not believe we should attempt anything but violent revolt against Roman rule, and there are those"—Mathias looked at his sons, considering how close they had come to being left to the Romans—"there are those among us who have fueled his flame."

"Who?" Matthew demanded and scanned the faces of the handful of men in the room. Only his father and brother did not shift their eyes away from him.

"That is a rumor without a claim of ownership." Matthias shook his head. "And now the Romans are like a hornet's nest, stirred up. From atop the Hasmonean palace, I watched as their heavy infantry formed eight sections of their tortoise formation to protect their engineers as they erected beams and lattice above the workers undermining the wall."

"The second wall is quite thick. Can they break through it?"

"If they work at it long enough," Yosef said, raising his head to reply to Shimon ben Gamliel. "But they'll also look for weaker spots."

"Like farther east toward the Temple," Yehudah ish Krioth said as he smoothed his beard.

LXXXVII

Miriam had lost sight of Yehudah ish Krioth in the turmoil caused by the surprise attack on the Romans. Forgetting him for the moment, she had rushed to get an unobstructed view, worried about Yosef and Matthew. Seeing them slip through as they resealed the Gennath gate lifted her heart. When she turned back to Yehudah, he had disappeared, and there was no hope of finding him in the chaotic mass of men rushing toward the gate and to ascend the walls and deploy along the parapets. Roman bugles echoed from the high ground. Yosef had told her their strident, piercing calls had particular messages for Roman legionaries. She hurried down the steps of the Hasmonean palace to cross the Tyropoeon valley and enter the Lower City. She had to speak with Zechariah.

* * *

"You really believe this Yehudah ish Krioth is a Roman collaborator? Of the worst kind?" Zechariah's milky eyes studied her.

"I know it was his voice I heard in the tunnel that day. And I've seen him—twice now—talking with men that don't look like Judeans."

"There are many nationalities of merchants and traders in Jerusalem, Miriam."

"Not with the bearing of these men. They weren't sloppy or fat, but hardened, and moved as if they were marching with a purpose. They did not stroll along or walk as most men do. The one I killed proved to be such a man, a Thracian mercenary who served the Romans."

"And you heard them—Yehudah and this man—talk as if they knew of Simon bar Giora's attack before it occurred?"

"Yes."

"Miriam, are you so certain... that you're willing to kill one of our countrymen... a Jewish man?"

The silent moment that question evoked turned into minutes. Miriam thought of where she had paused on her way to Zechariah's when she had passed the Tyropoeon escarpment and entered the Lower City just south of the Temple enclosure's royal portico. Few now loitered at the building that had been the palace of Helena. Years ago, on one of their many days exploring the city, Yosef had told her of the queen of Adiabene and Edessa, and how she had chosen Judaism over her birth religion, Zoroastrianism. She had also chosen Jerusalem as her home and had died here ten years ago and was now entombed just north of the city. Noted for her generosity to those of her adoptive faith, during a famine in Jerusalem twenty years ago she had sent to Alexandria for grain and to Cyprus for dried figs to help the people suffering from starvation. She had also given presents to the Temple: a golden candlestick installed over the door so that the rays of sunrise reflected on it and signaled the time for reading the Shema, the morning prayer service. She also gave a golden plate on which was written the passage of the Torah that a priest read when a wife suspected of infidelity was brought before him.

Helena's palace remained a monumental building at the southern foot of the Temple enclosure. Miriam as a child had seen its elaborate frescos and basement-level mikveh, the ritual bath. She wondered if anyone had been there since Helena's death, and she felt the spirit of a woman so moved by devotion to an adopted faith that she had made dramatic changes in her life. Could Miriam kill someone of the belief that inspired such a woman? Kill a man of the faith of her father, mother, and ancestors? And what of her own beliefs?

Miriam knew adherence to religious rules was not surety of righteousness. Men and women, no matter their faith or how pious their behavior, could fall and had fallen prey to avarice. She had killed Romans, but that had nothing to do with their belief—it had everything to do with how they had harmed and killed her people. And Romans had hurt her in a way that would never heal.

She raised her head and met Zechariah's blind yet penetrating gaze. "Yes. If I learn he is working with or for the Romans against Jews or Judea, then I'll kill him."

"And he a member of the Sanhedrin and a colleague of your father's?"

"Would that stop you... if you were sure that he had done things to hurt our people? That he had worked with Romans to do so?"

Zechariah had picked his staff up as she talked. She watched as his thick, corded hands gripped it, and the muscles of his forearms knotted. He shook his head, and she nodded, knowing he could sense it. "I'll find and follow him, and if I see he is as I think, then I'll kill him, Zechariah."

* * *

Headed home, Miriam had just left the steps that had taken her from the Lower City to where they climbed into the southernmost section of the Upper City. She was almost even with the House of Caiaphas when she saw her father and Matthew and Yosef. The relief she felt seeing her family so close was eclipsed by the sight of who was with them—Yehudah. Still disguised, she had slowed her pace so as not to get too close and be recognized. Now she sped up to make sure not to lose Yehudah again. As they entered the upper agora, she watched as Yehudah said his goodbyes and took the steps to the viaduct bridge that crossed to the Temple enclosure. With a backward glance at her father and brothers, who appeared to be going home, she hurried after Yehudah.

At the western retaining wall of the Temple, Yehudah descended past the broad steps that led up to the royal portico and crossed down into the Lower City. At the base of the steps, he turned onto the street that wound eastward, then bent southerly to the place she had followed him to before—the merchant's stall that served wine and beer. There, waiting for him, was the man who had spoken to him that morning at the Hasmonean palace.

Miriam quickly moved against a building out of sight of the men who now bent over their cups and talked. Her heart beat so loudly she thought anyone on the street could hear it. Not looking as if she had been watching them, she stepped away from the wall and walked to the stall to sit at a small table near theirs. With what she hoped was a manlike grunt, the drop of a coin and a gesture, she ordered from the merchant a small cup of wine. She sipped it and studied the two men without seeming to.

Yehudah, lean and well-kept, sitting tall, bowed toward the shorter, simply dressed man, who seemed rough cut from a block of gray stone. The stranger was speaking Aramaic with the hint of an accent.

"Why did you insist we meet," she heard him say, "if you don't have any new information of value?" He glared at Yehudah. "You've been paid for contacting the rebel leader and coaxing him into that attack today, so unless you have other news..." The man waited for a second and then rose from the table.

"Murena, wait, please," Yehudah pled. "Geganius, I need you to help me get out of the city."

"Why?" The man settled back in his chair. His eyes had narrowed to slits as he stared at Yehudah, who shifted closer to him.

"You know the Romans will not hesitate any longer, not after what happened today," Yehuda whispered. "And I do not want to be here—in the city—when their wrath falls upon it."

"He wants you here—to help further things, as you've agreed." Murena shook his head.

"I have already helped Lord Florus—"

Murena's hand shot out to grip Yehudah's hand. Hard. He cut off what Yehudah had been about to say, as he winced in pain. "Do not speak his name," Murena threatened, and he did not let Yehudah go as he scanned around them. His eyes paused on her. She hoped her disguise still worked.

"In Rome, he promised me—"

Miriam heard the crack of bone as Murena bore down and squeezed Yehudah's hand. "I will only warn you once. Shut your mouth and do what you have been paid to do." Murena straightened and spun so quickly Miriam was still unconsciously leaning toward them and flinched as he stomped by her table.

Yehuda, cradling his hand, waited for a minute before he rose and left. Miriam followed. He went back up toward the western side of the Temple. Dusk had deepened; it was that time of day when the setting sun cast long shadows onto the streets. This time he turned right and passed through the gate that led into the Akra, the Outer Courtyard of the Temple. She hid behind one of the pillars as he emerged from the cloister's colonnade into the open area the courtyard, then followed him along the southern wall. The courtyard was nearly empty now of its daytime inhabitants. She caught up to him just as he entered the gate heading into the outer sanctuary.

"Traitor!" Miriam hissed as she closed on him. As he turned toward her, her blade shot up under his chin. The blood bubbling from his lips poured onto his silky groomed beard. His hand came up to grab her, and she slapped it away. Though smaller and lighter, she drove him back against the wall next to the gate and held him there as he died. Letting Yehudah slide to the ground, panting, she lifted his hand. She straightened the fingers that Murena had broken and flattened the palm against the blood-soaked beard, then pressed it against the wall beside the body, holding for a second and then letting it fall to leave behind a dripping handprint.

"So, my suspicions have proved correct. My setup worked, and I have found the one I seek!"

Miriam whirled around. Geganius Murena faced her, a Roman pugio in each hand, the daggers gleaming in the last rays of sunlight winking from behind him.

He charged at her, the knives slashing in arcs that pulled back and retraced their pattern in front of him. Their first pass missed her as she twisted aside. The next—a double thrust, a one-two—sliced across and cut through the wrap that pinioned her breasts and tore open the wad of padding underneath and over her stomach. Seeing the bare mounds of flesh, Murena paused. Miriam scrambled away, stumbling over Yehudah's body. Sprawling, she saw the mercenary recover from the realization he faced a woman as he brought both blades down to drive into her chest.

A dark shape shot between them, and she heard a gasp as one of Murena's blades, rather than reach Miriam, ripped through the side of her savior's own throat, and the second pugio was driven through his back to protrude through his chest. The man who had intervened for her, his head turned to one side, had cloudy eyes. Just before they dimmed forever, she looked into Zechariah's face. "I followed..." he said, "had to protect you... you always made me think of my daughter." Then he died.

With a scream, she surged up, grabbing Zechariah's staff from beside his body as she did. Its iron ferrule, that Zechariah sharpened every day, speared through Murena's right eye before he could regroup. Her other hand pulled a knife from her forearm sheath, and with that, she took his other eye. As he shrieked, she cut his throat.

Breathing heavily, her heart in her throat again, Miriam heard the shouts before the footsteps echoed on the portico's stone floor, rushing toward her from within the sanctuary. She kneeled quickly and closed Zechariah's sightless eyes, then ran quickly into the shadows.

LXXXVIII

Yosef scanned the chamber before sitting in the front row. He had agreed with Mathias that there should be no further separatist meetings, whether in the House of Caiaphas or elsewhere—no Zealot or rebel leaders should appropriate the Hasmonean or Herod's palace. They must all stand together, and Judean leadership both political and religious would meet here and decide things jointly. Though Simon bar Giora had elected to remain with his men outside the city as they harassed the Romans, Yosef knew some would report on them to the rebel, and Simon would quickly learn anything said or done within the walls of the meeting room.

"You can smell the fear in the city," Matthew whispered to Yosef. "Do you think anything father says will settle down those who wish to flee?" Mathias who stood before the full Sanhedrin, which included members of the new Judean government.

"I don't know," Yosef said, shaking his head. "Do you remember father telling us how Herod Agrippa—two decades ago—started the construction to thicken the third outer wall? The Romans ordered him to stop. I wish we had twice as many walls, twice as thick and twice as high. After what happened at the Gennath gate, what we have now will not keep the Romans from us much longer. They've breached the second wall and now have access to the entire Northern City."

"Eleasar told me earlier today that the Roman engineers are protected by a cohort of heavy infantry forming a shield barrier, and they have now moved to focus on the northern end of the west wall of the Temple sanctuary." Matthew rubbed his eyes. There had been no sleep for him or Yosef since the night before the meeting with Nicanor at the gate. "I was with the men observing the Roman position from Antonia until just before dawn. We had beaten off three sorties of Romans with arrows and stones from cloister walkway. Eleasar relieved me then, but just after sunrise the Romans attacked in waves and now have a foothold at the base of the wall; it seems they will inevitably breach it. I ordered a team of men to break slabs of stone from the Outer Courtyard and to manhandle the chunks atop the wall there to cast them down upon the Romans. We are short of arrows until more are brought from Masada or can be manufactured. Many of the rebels who joined us late are now fleeing the battle and the city altogether. We may not last another two days."

A Levite guardsman rushed in and caught Eleasar's attention to whisper in his ear. The Temple guard captain's face stiffened, and he nodded to the guardsman, who spun on his heel and hurried out. Eleasar went to Mathias, spoke with him a moment, and then he, too, turned and left.

"Where is Eleasar going?" Matthew mused aloud. "I know he had much he wanted to say about rallying all Judeans to unite against the Romans. This meeting is important."

"He's right to want us united," Yosef replied. "While your night was spent on the walls repelling Romans, Father and I talked. I've struggled for months to find a resolution, some way to prevent war with Rome. But the events, the signs—everything seems to work against that wish. So, now I must do what I can—take what I've learned from the Romans—to help defend our city and our Temple. I will go with you to the Temple to see if we can't rally the rebels that remain into making a final stand, even if it's inside the sanctuary."

The brothers saw their father—who had stood with bowed head since Eleasar's brief words in his ear moments before—straighten and turn to the assembled men. He raised his arms and lowered them, hands palm down, waving them to stop their conversations and sit. Their muttering and chatter stilled to silence.

"We are perched at a perilous moment and faced with a terrible threat attempting to break through our walls," he began. "I ask you all to help steady the men of Jerusalem because that sets an example for everyone throughout Judea." Mathias's stern face, already creased with fatigue, now showed pain as well. "What I've just been told, that I'll now tell you, and it will add to our worry. But that cannot be helped."

Mathias took in a deep breath and let it out. "One of our own—a member of this body, the Sanhedrin—has been killed at the gate of the Temple sanctuary we hold so dear and are trying to protect. Yehudah ish Krioth was killed last evening." Cries of shock swirled among them and then grew louder, sharper. "Quiet, please. I know, I know—it's upsetting and unsettling."

"Who killed him?" Shimon ben Gamliel demanded, suddenly on his feet. Yehudah had been his assistant and friend for many years.

"We do not know. Yehudah was found with two other dead men. One was a potter and lamp maker in the Lower City, and"—Mathias hesitated—"based on his tattoo, he seems to have been a Roman auxiliary or possibly—likely—a mercenary."

Now more than a worried babble broke out. That one of the Sanhedrin could be killed within the Temple enclosure elevated fear of what was outside their walls to a near panic—now no one was safe within those walls. Roman retaliation might target any leader in Jerusalem.

Yosef and Matthew went to their father, who stood there allowing the outcry to run its course. "Is that what Eleasar is doing?" Yosef asked. "He's looking into this?"

Mathias nodded. "Yes."

"What else is there, Father?" Yosef could tell there was something withheld. His father was a straightforward man; he carried with discomfort the words yet unsaid that needed to be said, like stones in his mouth.

"Come with me"—Mathias drew his sons to one side, away from the clusters of men braying their consternation and distress. "The potter was a blind man known to many. It was his staff that took out the mercenary's eyes, but a Sicarii dagger—found beside the bodies—was used to cut his throat." Mathias paused, and it seemed he might stop there, but he then continued: "The mercenary's Roman dagger was still in the potter's throat."

"So, they killed each other." But Yosef saw the stones still there, his father's jaw clenching at them, and prodded him: "Or—what else, Father?"

"It would seem that the Sicarii dagger was also used to kill Yehudah."

"Do you think a Jewish Sicarii killed Yehudah?"

"I don't know, Yosef." Mathias closed his eyes, "But the mark of the Hand was there on the wall next to him. We may be in danger from our own as well as from the Romans."

LXXXIX

Outside Jerusalem

Borceus was taller than Sayid, which had made the journey difficult—agonizing for both. Both had pain in their legs that had expanded into a strained full-body ache that overrode even their hunger pangs. Thankfully, Sayid had found a plentiful supply of water that morning.

"Do you know where you are going, boy?" Borceus gasped. "Wait—please stop for a while. Let me rest here on the ground."

Sayid lowered the Roman and carefully arranged his broken leg and tightened the binding of the splint. "The legion will camp to the north of the city."

"North of the city covers a lot of territory," Borceus groaned.

When the ravines no longer ran to the west, Sayid had climbed—half-carrying Borceus—to a ridge that ran to keep the rising sun behind them. His mother had always bragged, "How strong my son is!" And his father, able to visit once or twice, had said in a moment of playful wrestling that the young boy had strength. It must have been so, because, despite the pain and his burden as he climbed the ridge, he had kept a good pace, and they now neared Jerusalem. To the south, a mountain rose above the plain that their ridge had merged into. Ahead he thought he caught the shimmer of sunlight glancing off what could be the Temple buildings in Jerusalem. To the north was a taller mountain, and below its peak, a group of mounted men broke into a canter toward them. The shafts of a slanting sun caught the metal of armor and what Sayid knew must be the small round bucklers heavy cavalry carried--iron-framed shields, layered hides with a bronze boss at each shield's center.

The leading cavalrymen, the largest on the biggest mounts, wielded kontos, and as the patrol neared, they lowered the heavy lances to point at him as they closed to within feet of the travelers and came to a stop.

Sayid knew better than to run—as if he could—and to not try to craft some made-up story to explain who he was. He would tell them the truth. He stepped forward before the patrol could overrun them both. These soldiers, called clibanari—or oven men, because of the armor that tortured them during warmer months, were known throughout the Roman army as notoriously ill-tempered. And there he stood dressed as a Judean, their current enemy. "Noble Centurion," Sayid said as he saluted the cavalry officer leading the patrol, "we are glad to see you." The officer's nudged his mount closer until the lance tip was inches from Sayid's chest. "We're searching for the Twelfth Legion"—his teeth clicked as his mouth shut at the touch of the lance to his flesh.

"You found them, though I doubt you are glad of it." The officer barked a laugh. "We've killed a dozen like you already this day, though most had more meat on their bones and carried weapons."

The Roman behind him brought his horse alongside but withdrew his lance and rested it in mounts on his saddle, so it rode smoothly along his thigh. "Quintus," he called to one of his men, "that man"—he pointed at Borceus, who was struggling painfully to undo his splint—"looks Roman." He heeled his mount closer and leaned down toward Borceus, "You there, what are you doing?"

Tears in his eyes at the red and inflamed flesh now exposed, showing the ends of splintered bone that formed an ugly mound rising from the split in the skin, Borceus held up the pieces of his staff. "I'm an emissary from King Agrippa and the Roman legate, Cestius Gallus." He dropped the pieces of wood with their markings of office and gripped his thigh above the broken bone. "This boy—this man— is a Roman auxiliary who saved me, and he has important messages for the legate. You must take him to Cestius Gallus immediately."

XC

NOVEMBER 66 CE

MOUNT SCOPUS

"You wanted to see me, Lord Gallus?" Nicanor asked, worried that what he had feared had now come—as a result of his failed effort at diplomacy. He stepped into the legate's command tent and stopped just inside.

"Sit." Cestius Gallus motioned for him to join the two others seated at the wide table he rested his elbows on.

With a nod to Galerius Senna, the legion's senior military tribune, and a stiff, curt one to the camp-prefect, Tyrannius Priseus, Nicanor sat on a camp stool. The legate studied the three men silently for long enough that Nicanor wondered what he had been summoned for.

Gallus picked up a worn hide pouch from the table—it looked bloodstained to Nicanor—and untied the leather cords securing its flap. He took out several squares of folded parchment and vellum. Unfolding each, he flattened them on the table. But he did not look at them as he spoke. "These are letters that contain troubling information. They suggest not just corruption, but that Romans in positions of authority and responsibility have done things for purposes other than the good of the empire." Gallus paused and picked up one letter, refolding it and then rotating the square with his fingers. "And those things they have done have played a considerable role in bringing about war and the deaths of thousands of Romans and Roman subjects and the destruction of Roman property."

"Lord"—Tyrannius Priseus leaned forward—"anyone can write letters and make claims."

"This one"—Gallus held up the square he had toyed with—"is from my wife, in her handwriting, whom I have complete faith in." He stared at the camp-prefect until the man sat back. "In this letter, she states that she believes that these," his palm flattened atop the other messages in front of him, "are credible and to be taken seriously. These happen to be from someone I know and feel is trustworthy." Cestius Gallus swept the letters back in the pouch and re-tied the flap.

"Who are the letters from, Lord Gallus, and what do they say?" asked Galerius Senna with a sideways glance at the camp-prefect.

387

The legate ignored the question and turned to a clerk standing in the corner shadows behind him. "Bring them in," he said.

The clerk stepped through the back of the tent partition into the legate's private quarters. He returned with a big man in full armor with his helmet under his arm, and when Nicanor saw who was with him, he blinked. *Sayid!* The boy looked older than the passing of time would merit, and Nicanor noted his limp, how he favored one leg.

"Decurion, do you attest that this auxiliary was found escorting a wounded Roman emissary—one of two that have been missing, the other dead? And he told you that this boy"—Gallus waved a hand at Sayid—"had important letters for me and that they were in this pouch?"

"Yes, lord, I checked what was in there"—he pointed at the pouch—"but did not read the contents. I wanted to be sure there was nothing else—a weapon or valuables."

"And on the emissary's word you brought him directly to me?" After days among his legionaries and their officers, noting the nature of some of them, Gallus was sure the search was as much—likely more—for valuables.

"Yes, Lord Gallus. He hasn't left my side."

The legate nodded. "You may go, Decurion, and take the boy—this soldier—and see that he is tended to and has quarters. Remain with him until I relieve you or send someone for him."

"Yes, lord." The cavalry office saluted and took Sayid by the arm. As Sayid passed Nicanor, they exchanged nods.

Cestius Gallus noticed. "So, you know this auxiliary, Centurion?"

"I know him well, sir... Lord."

"I'm sorry, Lord Gallus," Tyrannius Priseus sneered, "but you trust that this scruffy Syrian boy has brought you legitimate information?"

"What he brought me comes from those I trust." Gallus turned to Nicanor—"and trust means everything. The boy—Sayid—says he knows you well, too, Nicanor, from on board the *Salacia* and afterward. Do you trust him?"

Nicanor shifted on his stool and straightened, meeting the legate's stern look. "With my life, Lord Gallus. He's a stout soldier I have counted on before."

"A half-Greek vouching for a Syrian peasant... really, Lord Gal—"

Nicanor's left hand came down on the camp-prefect's forearm and squeezed as his right automatically went to the haft of the pugio at his belt. "Watch your words, Camp-Prefect... watch"—Nicanor released his grip—"what you say. For nearly thirty years my battles have been fought with blades... not words. So my reply to you won't be with words."

"Both of you stop. There's been enough talk from Romans"—Gallus glared at Tyrannius Priseus—"that has led to many problems and to what we face now." He turned to the military tribune. "Galerius, send messengers to our officers in the city. They are to cease their attack, secure their positions, and hold in place until they receive further orders from me."

"But Legate, we are nearly through the wall and close to their Temple. We breach that, and the Judeans will capitulate. Revolt or not, they won't risk the destruction of their Temple."

"Order the cease and desist, Tribune Senna. Now." Cestius Gallus stood. "All of you... leave me. Nicanor, I want to see you and the Syrian auxiliary first thing in the morning."

"I shall join you, with the Tribune, Legate," the camp-prefect said.

"No," Gallus replied, "you will not." He put the pouch with the letters under his arm and disappeared into his private quarters.

With a poisonous glance at Nicanor, Tyrannius Priseus and Galerius Senna left. Nicanor released the breath he seemed to have held since that tense moment with the camp-prefect and wondered if he would have done to Priseus what he had said. It had been decades since he had been riled at anyone slighting his birth blood, but Priseus had found that still-raw nerve and pressed it. Exiting the tent, Nicanor went in search of the decurion to join him in keeping watch over Sayid. Remembering the fate of his friend who had been the previous camp-prefect, he did not trust Tyrannius Priseus.

* * *

Nicanor watched as Cestius Gallus's clerk refilled the legate's clepsydra, the twelve-hour water-clock that accompanied him in the field, and noted that the vigilia quarta—the last watch of the night—had just ended, at dawn. He caught the end of the legate's question for Sayid and answered for him:

"Simon bar Giora is the rebel leader who has been the largest thorn in our heel, Lord Gallus. Unlike this Yohanan ben Levi of Gischala, Giora is aligned with the leadership in Jerusalem and appears to be their most capable military field commander, though I don't know if that's an official rank or one he has taken upon himself. Reports have Giora all over the country, but it seems his main camp is at Masada. He leads many men—possibly two or three thousand, mostly peasant militia—who believe an end to Roman rule will improve their lives." Nicanor shook his head at how leaders of many nations used that promise as a lure for men to fight for them.

The legate's attention went back to Sayid. "And what of this man in Galilee that captured and then freed you?"

"Lord Gallus, Yohanan ben Levi seemed to care only for Galilee, for his part of the Judean Provinces. He seemed to have little respect for Jerusalem and none for the new Judean government. He told me he preferred dealing with the Sanhedrin."

"Would he negotiate a surrender of Galilee to Rome?"

"I don't know, lord," replied Sayid with a glance at Nicanor, distinctly uncomfortable at answering questions directly from the Roman legate.

"Lord..." Nicanor paused. Cestius Gallus had half-turned from them as if counting the drops of the water-clock... measuring the passing of time. "Legate," Nicanor said again, and with the capture of the man's attention continued with a nod at the device, at the time they did not have. "Legate, what is your decision about the attack on the city?"

"Winter is soon upon us, and our raids still do not replace lost supplies," Gallus said as he straightened and rubbed the gray bristles on his chin. "We—I—have made poor decisions. But I think now I based them on some questionable advice." He nudged Sayid's pouch of letters with the back of his right hand. "These Judeans have proved most surprising, more adept at fighting and bolder in their attacks than I had ever considered possible." He looked up. "Centurion, do you believe I've been a poor commander, and that what's in these letters"—he paused as if to change what he was about to say. "The boy has told you what's in them, hasn't he?" He waved away Sayid's frightened expression with a hand. "It's okay, boy. You shared it with someone you trust, someone I feel I can trust, too. Well, Centurion?"

Nicanor nodded at Sayid, who still stood rigid and worried; he understood Gallus's unasked question and his point. "Yes, Legate. You followed what you thought was worthwhile advice. But now it seems that at worst it came from corrupt officers, and at best... from the negligent. Either way, their counsel has hurt us badly and cost many lives. I think what brought this all about was someone's self-interest. I know the lady who wrote the letters—and the man she married, and I trust what she said that moved your wife to write to you, and to send Sayid at risk of his life. I think both women write the truth."

Cestius Gallus's chest expanded and contracted as he sat silent for several minutes. The last breath was exhaled loudly.

"Centurion"—he glanced at Sayid and then back at Nicanor—"this auxiliary is now assigned to you. Though he proved a bearer of bad news, what he carried confirms something I should have heeded at the first foretelling of what was to come, and he will not return to Caesarea. That would prove dangerous to him as soon as what I must do is known. See to his equipment and assignment—he returns to serve the Twelfth Legion."

Sensing that was their dismissal, Nicanor said, "Yes, Lord Gallus," saluted and turned to leave. Sayid turned a half-second behind him.

The legate's next words stopped him.

"And, Centurion, send me Galerius Senna. I'm ordering our men out of Jerusalem, and once they're reformed here, we will march to Antipatris and camp there. Then I will inform the emperor of what's happened... and of this"—he picked up the pouch.

"Shall I send the camp-prefect to you, too my lord?"

"No. Tyrannius Priseus can receive his orders from the military tribune. I'll let Galerius Senna deal with him from now on."

XCI

BETH HORON

"Futuo!" Nicanor cursed. Pausing two days at Gibeon had been a mistake. He swore again and wiped sweat and blood from his eyes with the back of his hand. Instead of continuing what could only be called a retreat from Jerusalem, the legion now stood down—making it appear they were pacifying the rebels. The rebel army led by Simon bar Giora had torn at their flanks, chewed through the hindquarters of the legion, and they had had to abandon the remaining supplies and equipment. Pushing through the passes at Beth Horon, they learned the rebels had used their delay in Gibeon to take up blocking positions. Large numbers of the rebels moved down from the heights to seal off the valley and trap them while the rest picked them apart from above.

As a fresh torrent of arrows fell, one grazed his neck and then struck and deflected off the shoulder cap of his scale armor. Two hit his saddle and remained there, vibrating like feather-ended pennants. He snapped them off and wheeled Abigieus around, searching for Sayid. The chaos had separated them. All around were bodies of dead legionaries and their mounts. The floor of the narrow pass had become a killing field. A horse's scream turned him in the right direction, and he found Sayid down, his mount pierced by several arrows, the boy pinned beneath the dying horse.

Nicanor vaulted from his saddle, grabbed Sayid by the shoulders, and heaved backward, dragging him from under the twitching horse. More shafts dropped from above, through the chilling fog that had crept into the pass. A thick, heavy bolt struck Abigieus, angling down to pierce deep into the animal's upper chest. The horse screamed and his front legs buckled. Nicanor got to him with Sayid under one arm. Laying the unconscious youth aside, he lifted the horse's head.

"Come on boy." Nicanor rested his head against Abigieus's, feeling the animal's painful shudder. "You can get up. You must stand. We will not die this day, not here." Another arrow slashed down and scored a deep furrow across the horse's neck. More blood spilled down Abigieus's chest, and the smell of it was as thick as the growing mist. Nicanor crouched and got his arms under and around

Abigieus's neck and with all his strength helped the horse rise. "That's it, boy. I knew you could."

The horse lifted his head, nickered, and rubbed his nose along Nicanor's cheek. Head higher now, ears up and canted forward, Abigieus roared to match the piercing quality of any Roman bugler. His cry echoed off rocks and stones around them, his tail whipped, and his ears laid back as he tossed his head. Nicanor lifted Sayid and draped him over the saddle. Taking the reins, he whispered into the horse's ear, "Let's get out of here, boy." They walked toward where he had last seen the legion standard-bearer, who would be close to the legate and the command staff. They must figure out how to escape this valley of death.

* * *

Aulus looked at Nicanor and said, "I'm a medic... but for soldiers, for men. I've never attended to wounded animals. And it's well buried"—he studied the arrow still embedded in the animal's chest—"I pull that out through thick muscle, or cut, more likely, and he'll bleed to death."

"Abigieus is a soldier, a legionary, Aulus—get that arrow out and treat him. Save him as you would any of our men." Nicanor kneeled next to Sayid, who sat beside a small fire. His head was freshly bandaged, but a blotch of blood now seeped through from the gash across his crown. "Good thing it was one of the smaller rocks that hit you, right, Sayid?"

With a weak nod, the boy smiled.

"See that Aulus tends to my horse's wounds," Nicanor said as he stood.

"Where do you go?" Sayid asked as he looked up.

"To the command tent to meet with the legate and tribune and see if we can figure a way out of this predicament." Nicanor reached down and patted Sayid's shoulder. "I'll be back as soon as I can."

* * *

The moon was a pale blob that shed little light through the fog and clouds had blanketed the pass from the ground to the rocky peaks above. Darkness had stopped the rain of arrows, and the Romans knew the rebels were repositioning for a final massacre in the morning. As Nicanor approached where he had left Sayid and Abigieus, he heard a soft nicker. The horse stood beside Sayid's bedroll outside their field tent, and the beast was strapped and wrapped with bandages like almost every man Nicanor had seen on his way to Cestius Gallus. The field staff meeting was one he had never expected to be invited to, especially since his participation in the last briefing had not gone well. "How are you, boy?" He bent to run a gentle hand along the chest bandages that wound around the horse's torso and neck. Fresh blood showed on them in large spots.

"Nicanor?" Sayid sat up and then shakily got his legs under him and stood.

"Get your weapons, boy... a blanket and your canteen and nothing else, while I saddle Abigieus."

"What's going on? What are we doing?"

Nicanor grunted as he lifted; his neck wound shot darts of pain as he gently settled the saddle in place, and he felt a trickle of new blood beneath his own bandage. Abigieus snorted and blew through his lips. "It's okay, boy"—he patted the horse's shoulder and stroked his neck above the bandage. "I hate to ask this of you, but I promise you'll be rewarded when it's done."

"When what's done, Nicanor?" Sayid was beside him now, a blanket folded and hung over his shoulder.

"You will ride Abigieus and join the men forming toward the westerly opening of the pass—but quietly as you can. Leave that tent up and the fire burning here."

"What are we doing?"

"Escaping. The legate and tribute are leading most of the legion and the allied forces out of here tonight." He looked up into the night sky and swiveled his head, seeing nothing but pitch black beyond the edge of fog that encircled them. "But the rebels must think we are still here."

"But they'll know we're gone."

"Some will remain—as decoys—to make them believe we're all still here."

"How many?"

"Four hundred and the legion standard-bearer—to make the rebels believe Gallus is here with us." Nicanor shook his head at that decision and tightened the saddle's cinch. "Desperate times, Sayid"—he waved him over—"up you go."

"Us? Wait, what about you?"

"Someone's got to command those who stay, someone who knows enough to make it seem a whole legion is stuck here in this valley fighting our way out. I'll have my own buglers, boy." Nicanor's grin slipped and ended lopsided. "You must go, mount Abigieus and get moving."

"I'm not leaving you, Nicanor."

"You have to, Sayid." He patted Abigieus's neck. "Someone has to save my horse."

As Sayid settled in the saddle, Abigieus twisted his head back to nicker at Nicanor, who wondered if he would ever see him again.

XCII

Beth Horon

Nicanor stood by the large fire, hoping its glow was easily seen by the rebels. He rolled his head side to side, front to back, and shrugged his shoulders; the tug and a stab of pain meant he had pulled the neck wound open again. But he needed to loosen up for a full range of motion. He had few to count on to watch his back in the coming battle. He scanned the camp, dotted with several equally large fires and many smaller ones—they were now burning every stick of wood they could gather. There were only a few hundred men to fill a space occupied by thousands just hours before. The fog was thinning, and dawn's gray light touched the peaks above. Two hours earlier, he had confirmed the legion had entirely cleared the valley pass into the open, well on to where they could maneuver and fight on a straight road to Antipatris. Thinking the Romans camped and resolved to fight as a force from within the pass, the rebels had only a nominal force guarding the exit. These guards were stealthily killed, and Nicanor had not seen or heard any alarm or alert that the insurgents had discovered the legion's escape yet, but they soon would.

Nicanor turned to the five men with him. "Position your buglers on any rise close to your position—stack dead horses for them to stand on if you must—but get them up where they can see," he ordered the sergeants. All the other officers had left the legion—left Nicanor in high command. "When they see the aquila dip three times"—Nicanor motioned to the legion standard-bearer, who pumped the eagle up and down as an example—"then the buglers must blow formation call. The rebels will, I hope, continue thinking the entire force is here. Then after giving time to seem as if we are forming up, I'll have the standard dipped three more times, and then the buglers must blow advance. Got it?" Each nodded. "Join your men"—he eyed the brightening sky—"it won't be long now. And remember, if the rebels commit to a ground attack, try to pull together and form on me in the center of the field."

* * *

The rain of arrows had been as thick as before. They must've emptied the armory at Masada, Nicanor thought, *but struck fewer men*. Four hundred Romans spread across the valley floor made for fewer casualties than when they were a packed mass of thousands. Nicanor had agreed that the legion needed all the remaining horses to carry as many men as could escape. So, he and the bait were on foot, trying to hold the rebels in the pass. As the arrows ceased falling in sheets like a storm burst, the rebels surged from both ends of the valley. Hundreds were mounted and carrying cavalry lances or heavy spears, but awkwardly. Behind them came their foot soldiers, most in Roman armor. He hoped his sergeants would act as ordered, gather their men, and get to the center of the field to form up and fight as a unit. Maybe they could punch through the rebels ahead of them as testudos and break free. As he eyed the horde of rebels bearing down on them, he doubted it.

* * *

An hour later, the doubt proved true. His sergeants had almost made it. The mounted rebels rode at a headlong gallop, heedless of strategy... or injury... and slammed into the leading edge of his forward unit. The hastily formed turtles buckled and gave way in front of Nicanor as the men were pushed back and piled onto the legionaries behind them. It all came apart then; there was no hope to arrange a defensive formation, much less an offense. With a dozen men around him, they clawed and cleaved through live rebels and over dead Romans to reach a cluster of rocks that offered partial protection. Atop one of these, Nicanor scanned the field. It was a massacre. He saw the standard-bearer go down, his severed arm and hand still gripping the aquila. A rebel with blood streaming down his face and white teeth flashing in triumph tore away the dead man's hand and raised the Roman eagle high. Nicanor had never seen a legion's standard in enemy hands. Something struck him, and he spun to the ground, the gold eagle against the bluing sky the last thing he saw.

NEAR ANTIPATRIS

Cestius Gallus took the corner of his once-bright scarlet paludamentum and tried to find a clean spot on which to wipe his face. He sighed; the soiled cloak would only add more grime, and he dropped it to drape across his thighs. His elaborate helmet and armor were creased and scored by a dozen arrow strikes, but other than nicks and cuts on his forearms and along one leg, he was unhurt. The crimson cincticulus around his waist, hung along his saddle and its ends stuck to the lathered side of his mount. He had just seen the Syrian boy, Sayid, reel by on a large, staggering horse with strips of bloodied bandages hanging from its neck. Exhausted, he sat higher in the saddle and looked around at the moving mass of men. Most of them were wounded, and the men and animals were exhausted. He felt beaten. Galerius Senna, as stained and worn out as he, reined in beside him.

"Report, Tribune," Gallus ordered with a nod to him.

"More than five thousand infantrymen and a full cohort of cavalry are dead, all lost back at Beth Horon before we escaped, Lord Gallus."

"Any sign of the decoy force?" As he asked, Gallus knew there wouldn't—couldn't be. The legion had taken all the horses that were left. The mounted rearguard pushed the infantry to a man-killing pace but also watched for any trailing behind them, to see if any of those left behind had broken free and tried to catch up. They had reported nothing but the rebel attacks snapping at their heels.

"No, Lord Gallus. But the rebels have stopped their strikes at our rear and flanks."

Cestius Gallus nodded. "Get the men into Antipatris. Use its existing walls and any fortifications and secure the perimeter of the encampment. As soon as my tent is set up, I must draft my report to the emperor."

XCIII

The morning brings much news, thought Gessius Florus as he studied the messages on his desk. According to one message, the last vessel to sail from Ostia before the winter storms set in had arrived in Alexandria, and the courier on board had immediately pushed overland with the diplomatic and administrative messages. The ship had delivered to Alexandria Florus's replacement, Marcus Antonius Julianus, who, after a suitable delay in Alexandria, would then travel to Caesarea to relieve Florus of his Judean procurator duties.

He laughed. That bothered him not a bit, and he picked up the most decorative scroll of parchment with the emperor's sigil. He had read it once and enjoyed seeing it—a guarantee of his imperial protection and new authority—in writing. The guarantee could just as easily be rescinded, and that gave him a pause of concern, but such action would take time. Time enough for him to—

"Why do you smile so, Gessius?" Cleo asked from the entry to his office.

"News from the emperor. I am to become an equites—equestrian fiscal procuratores—an imperial collector of revenues and tribute. I will serve the emperor's interests in the whole region, not just in Judea." He waved the formal declaration sent with Nero's seal by Tigellinus, the emperor's praetorian prefect. "The emperor is concerned that corruption has led to the recent unfortunate events that impact the imperial revenue"—he looked up at Cleo, and then continued—"and I am empowered to see it doesn't continue."

Cleo forced her expression to remain unchanged at his words, but she knew better than to believe mandated legalities set in place by paper—all of it supported personal agendas and not morals and fairness. Poppaea's suspicions continued to prove true. "I heard about Cestius Gallus's decision to halt the attack on Jerusalem," she said.

The rumors had poured into Caesarea, though Florus wondered if perhaps his wife was too willing to hear more than she should. "And that will prove to be his downfall," Florus nodded, and his grin widened.

"I applaud it," Cleo couldn't help the scorn in her tone, "too many lives have been lost that should not have been."

Florus did not usually listen to such softhearted compassion or naïveté and ignored her. He set the emperor's proclamation down and picked up the coin. Tossing it in the air, he caught it and read its inscription aloud: "Freedom of Zion," he sneered. "The rebels must be taught a lesson, but that falls to the new procurator and whoever the emperor sends to replace Cestius Gallus."

"Will he—Lord Gallus—be replaced?" Cleo asked, alarmed. Nero's form of replacing an official was often not pleasant and usually accompanied by a man's immediate family suffering a similar fate.

"Of course. He's failed. A Roman legion he led was defeated by rabble, its aquila taken... imagine a Roman legion's standard in the hands of such. There will be consequences." As Florus said it, some of his good feeling faded. Galerius Senna, through a private courier, had informed Florus how he and Tyrannius Priseus had been unable to get the legate to change his mind and to continue an all-out assault to subjugate the rebels and take Jerusalem. They were thus unable to manipulate the situation. They had tried to convince Gallus that a plan should be made to move the Jewish treasure to a secure Roman camp for its safekeeping until things were resolved with the new Judean government. They'd explained that there would be such damage to the Temple—damage they would ensure—that the treasure must be secured as soon as possible.

Florus had readied the centurion Capito—stretching even that man's servile patience—and a force of men disguised as Judean rebels. The plan had been to steal it back for the Jews. Senna would report that "theft" of the treasure to Gallus, who would be forced to report it to Nero. Thus, Gallus would be blamed for losing the treasure, which would by then be in Florus's hands and well hidden. He would then prepare its movement to Rome for Nero, with a large portion kept for himself. It was a perfect plan that would have worked if only that idiot Gallus had done as any competent Roman leader should do. It seemed that something had changed Gallus's mind at the last minute. Or someone—someone working against his plans, had changed Gallus's mind. He would have to find and eliminate the culprit. After such a defeat, an advisor like that could surely be branded a traitor.

"You no longer smile, my husband."

Florus's head snapped up toward Cleo, expecting a mocking look, but she showed no sign of sarcasm. "When this new procurator—Marcus Antonius Julianus—arrives from Alexandria," he said, "we will move to Ptolemais where I'll assume my new duties for the emperor. You must ready our household; see to it with Glaucio."

Florus dismissed her and sat at his desk. With Galerius Senna's help, he would cast doubts on anything Gallus reported to the emperor, ensuring that any fault for the failure of the attack rested at the legate's feet. Then Nero would surely appoint someone experienced to take command and crush the Jewish revolt. He needed someone more corruptible to play a role—paid for by Nero— to help steal the Jewish treasure or to look the other way as it was stolen. Florus was the only Roman—thanks to Yehudah, the slain Jewish mole—who knew how vast that treasure had grown. He could take half for himself, and Nero, unknowingly, would still be pleased with what was left. But regardless of the new military commander, he had other men in Jerusalem and would send more mercenaries to find and kill this Jew they called "the Hand." Florus picked up the new Judean coin and tossed it again. *There are always men*—Florus smiled at the thought that history had proven—*you can buy with the promise of silver.*

* * *

Cleo had not gone in search of Florus's majordomo because she was sure Glaucio was skulking nearby and would appear. Intercepting the courier when he had been announced that morning had been a risk that had not yielded her any news—no letter from Octavia in Antioch and still nothing from her brother, Marcus Otho. And what of Sayid? Had he reached Cestius Gallus, and was that why the legate had stopped the attack on Jerusalem? She had heard the rumors and what she could overhear from the report given to Florus—that the rebels had killed thousands of soldiers as the Twelfth Legion retreated. Was Nicanor one of the dead or wounded? She thought of Yosef and his family. Had they fled, or were they still in Jerusalem? Those she could trust were no longer anywhere near her.

"My lady..."

The sharp echo of the false ingratiating and irritating tones made her jump.

"What is it, Glaucio?" Cleo straightened and stepped into the atrium.

The man met her there with his honeyed voice and cold stare. "My lady, there is a messenger here asking for you... from Lord Gallus."

XCIV

NOVEMBER 66 CE

It was dark, cold, and dank—not just a feeling that knifed through the skin into bone making him shiver... but a smell. And the stench of fear from the bodies. Whose? The odor seemed to come from above, like the voices that filtered through the stone and soil he knew must be between him and the sound of others. He rose from the damp stone floor, stiffened from sitting so long in the chill. He half-stumbled in the pitch dark toward the place at the wall where the voice seemed strongest. It was a man's voice he recognized but couldn't quite place that called to him:

"Yosef... you must surrender... come out... you must... you will be safe—"

Awake, Yosef sat up. The knocking on his door was accompanied by his mother's voice. "Yossi, Matthew is here now, and your father wants to speak with you both before Shabbat dinner."

Yosef blinked away shreds of the dream. So, he wasn't trapped in one of the tunnels beneath Jerusalem as he had feared. He glanced at the window. The late afternoon sun spilled in around the wooden shutters. Tired from meeting and talking with members of the new Judean government through most of the previous night and into early morning, he had lain down for a nap. He went to the small table by the window, poured water in a bowl, then splashed his face, wiping it with his hands. "I'll be right down, Mother."

* * *

"Simon bar Giora's men returned with a large amount of Roman equipment, Yosef." Matthew reached for more fruit. "It is a gift from God. We can use it to improve our defenses."

Yosef nodded. "Father, I've heard some prominent families now plan to flee to King Agrippa—thinking their safety lies in his province—and abandon the city—"

"And their country," snapped Miriam, who had been quiet since being made to join them. "They should be made to stay."

"Do you blame any who don't want to suffer what's coming?" Yosef asked his sister. She glared at him without speaking.

Their father spoke from the end of the table: "Many now feel all those that were labeled false prophets have now been proven right. To force the Romans to retreat shows the hand of heaven must be on our side."

"We were surely beaten," Mathias said. "God must have put fear into their hearts to turn tail and run like that for no apparent reason. But that does not make some any braver or more willing to persevere. Agrippa will accept those who scuttle from Jerusalem. We must build our own defenses with those who will stay and fight."

"Yosef, I've met with many of the fighters," Matthew said with excitement. "They say it must've been just the same when Judah Maccabee's army defeated the Greek Syrians at Beth Horon over two hundred years ago. A miraculous deliverance! And we've proven we can beat the Romans."

"Brother, we've proven we can kill Romans," Yosef replied. "But beating them? I don't believe we've done that. It is beyond my understanding, but yes, the Roman legate broke off the attack. Why did Gallus do that?" Yosef shook his head. "His decision had nothing to do with anything we did." The tendrils from his dream came back, closing his eyes. He was—Jerusalem was—in that dark space with voices speaking that he could not understand—determined voices trying to tell him something.

Yosef blinked and shook his head, but that dire dread remained. The familiar Kiddush, his father, recited over the wine after his mother lit the two Shabbat candles had not comforted him as it usually did. He looked over the flames at Miriam. The crescent-shaped smudges under her eyes, badges of sleeplessness, were as dark as the shadows that flickered in her gaze at him. The light that he thought had shone again in her eyes was now muted. He felt the room, the city and the world around them grow even darker—the weight of a massive black curtain had dropped.

Yet he hoped it would rise with tomorrow's dawn. So much was taking place among the Romans right now. Were Nicanor and Sayid alive and did Nicanor—if he lived—hate him for what had happened at the Gennath gate? And Cleo, would she leave Judea with Gessius Florus? Just thinking of her stirred up feelings he could not suppress.

Uncomfortable with Miriam's steady scrutiny, he moved in his chair, eyes passing over his brother, father, and mother, each reflecting on their inner thoughts. He came back to Miriam's flat look, lightless, as she continued to study him.

"Yossi"—her eyes dropped to his hand—"is that what I think it is?"

Yosef realized he had pulled Leah's kinyan from beneath his tunic. Its cord was wrapped around his fingers, and he twirled it in the opposite direction until it unwound and hung straight down. The coin twinkled in the lamplight. He knew his love for Leah was still more than a poignant memory or a bittersweet part of youth. Oh, that life could have turned out simpler—just the two of them—no war with Rome. It made his heart ache. But what should he do about Rachel? She was so attentive each time she saw him... was it wrong to let her feel as she did?

Miriam's eyes went again to his face, which he knew was full of many doubts and the questions they all faced as they awaited Rome's inevitable response.

# # #

IF YOU ENJOYED THIS BOOK, PLEASE CONSIDER LEAVING A REVIEW ON AMAZON. IT IS THE PRIMARY WAY INDEPENDENT AUTHORS GET THEIR WORK NOTICED.

THE STORY CONTINUES IN BOOK TWO.

For updates please visit the author's website at:

WWW.CRYFORJERUSALEM.COM

Made in United States
North Haven, CT
31 October 2022

26138950R10230